THE SPACESHIP IN THE STONE

THE SPACE LEGACY
BOOK 1

IGOR NIKOLIC

IgorBooks.com

Copyright © 2022 by Igor Nikolic
All rights reserved. This book or any portion thereof may not be reproduced or used in any manner whatsoever without the express written permission of the publisher except for the use of brief quotations in a book review.
This book is a work of fiction. Any resemblance to actual persons, living or dead, is entirely coincidental. Names, characters, businesses, organizations, places, events, and incidents are the products of the author's imagination or are used fictitiously.

Cover Design by Elias Stern

This book is dedicated to my family and all you dreamers out there.

Special thanks to Keith Fletcher, Michael Treichel, Richard Mousley, and Doyle Camp. They spent months hunting for typographical and grammatical errors, word choices, weird sentence structure, noticeable repetitions, wrong word usage, and tense issues.
William 'Bill' Dutcher, and Lee Wibbels, who went through the entire text after it was published and polished off all the rough edges.

Beta Team:
Keith Fletcher
Michael Treichel
Richard Mousley
Doyle Camp
Max Lambon
Samuel Valero
Joe Chasko
Matt Sauer
Nigel Joy
William Dutcher
Lee Wibbels

CONTENTS

Prologue	7
Chapter 1	19
Chapter 2	32
Chapter 3	47
Chapter 4	59
Chapter 5	72
Chapter 6	86
Chapter 7	101
Chapter 8	114
Chapter 9	129
Chapter 10	146
Chapter 11	154
Chapter 12	170
Chapter 13	183
Chapter 14	192
Chapter 15	206
Chapter 16	219
Chapter 17	227
Chapter 18	237
Chapter 19	254
Chapter 20	267
Chapter 21	274
Chapter 22	289
Chapter 23	300
Chapter 24	308
Chapter 25	325
Epilogue	333
Author's Notes:	337
Abbreviations and Glossary	339
Also by Igor Nikolic	345

"The Earth is just too small and fragile a basket for the human race to keep all its eggs in."
   Robert A. Heinlein

"I believe that the long-term future of the human race must be in space..."
   Stephen Hawking

PROLOGUE

Inside the buried spaceship, an ancient machine intelligence continued its relentless vigil. It followed the commands set by its builders, long before the recorded history of mankind. One of the core instructions was for it to remain hidden and to maintain the ship in optimal condition.

Above it, on the surface of the planet, the human race spread and advanced. From their humble beginnings as weak cave dwellers, they progressed and evolved into a technological society. Making breakthroughs in science and their understanding of the wider universe, they launched satellites into orbit, and even reached their planet's closest celestial companion, the Moon.

The intelligence controlling the ship did not care at all about them; they were not within its mission parameters. Time meant nothing to it; left undisturbed, it would have remained right where it was until the Sun turned into a red giant, five billion years down the line.

However, after thousands of years of dormancy, one of the spaceship's proximity sensors detected an anomaly. Secondary routines, never before activated, took precedence—the machine intelligence within had no option but to act.

* * *

I fell.

That was the first thing that came into Michael's mind after waking up.

He was hiking through the dense woods up the side of the mountain, an hour's walk from the cabin. It was a long, heavily forested slope that led to the towering steep cliffs, which rose majestically into the blue sky. For Michael, this was one of the most beautiful and peaceful places in the world, somewhere he could come to think about his life without the constant distractions of urban living.

It was a struggle for him to get up here anymore. In the past, it would have taken him about thirty minutes to reach his present position. With his bad knee slowing him down and constantly complaining about the added exertions, it more than doubled the time it took him to get up here and close to triple the time to go back even though it was downhill on the return trip. He knew he would pay for this hike in the following couple of days as his knee slowly recovered from the strain he was putting on it. And if not for the ibuprofen he took before starting out, he had doubts about his ability to have made it here at all.

He was just crossing a bright little clearing in the woods when the earth beneath his feet moved. Before he could take another step, he was already falling down. For a few moments there was a sense of weightlessness, and then... nothing, similar to turning off a TV.

In this kind of life-threatening situation, some people see their life flash before their eyes; they even see the faces of loved ones. The only thing Michael's mind could come up with, before shutting down, was *"Oh shit, I'm gonna die!"*

* * *

Ozark Mountains (One Day Earlier)

Michael smiled as he was driving towards his grandfather's cabin, the place that always made him feel good. At thirty-five miles (56 km) away from the closest town and with practically no neighbors in the area, many would call it the boondocks. But for him, it was the only place that felt like home, and he needed to unwind.

His grandfather bought the property after returning home from the war with a serious case of PTSD, not that anyone was calling it by that name, or even acknowledged it at that time. The unspoiled 2500 acres of predominantly mountainous terrain was just what he needed to fulfill his dream from the war—a place where he could have some peace and quiet.

He fell in love with a secluded mountain valley and got it for pennies on the dollar from the estate of some wood Baron that went bankrupt, and it was the place where he planned to build his home. The beauty of the valley was accented by a small lake on one side and a healthy stream coming from a higher elevation that created it. He told everyone that particular stream water was the purest and sweetest he had ever tasted and would be unlikely to taste better in his life.

After hiring a local contractor to clear an access road and put gravel on it, he built a big log cabin with his bare hands. In a way, all that hard work was therapeutic for him; he was still dealing with horrific frequent nightmares and memories of brutal battles.

By that time, his nest egg was about tapped out, but as luck would have it, that little mountain stream brought down more than just freshwater… It brought down gold.

Not a *million-dollar gold mine* amount, but enough placer gold deposits to make sure one would not go hungry in the winter. What's more, he never told anyone about his find, knowing that if the word got around that *'there is gold in them there hills'*, a flood of prospectors would destroy that peace and quiet in no time.

Finally, with the house finished, he brought Michael's grandmother there. She was one of those uncompromising women of the past, prepared to wait for her man no matter how long it took. They were high school sweethearts, and she waited four long years for them to be together. First, to return from the war and then the additional year it took him to build their home. You would be hard-pressed to find a woman like that these days, willing to accept life in the boonies with none of the trappings of modern life.

Michael's father, Robert, was born soon after, but he never really liked living so far from society. Maybe it was the long rides to school, or children picking on him for not being a *townie*. He moved in with Michael's great-grandparents when he started high school and never really returned to the mountain. Robert Freeman enrolled in one of the most prestigious universities in the country on a full-ride scholarship, far away from his family and their rustic way of life. He graduated top of his class and was immediately headhunted by one of the most prominent research laboratories in the country. He met a girl there and things took their natural course, but fate would be cruel to him. Two years after they got married and Michael was born, his wife died from breast cancer, leaving him alone, distraught, and with a small child.

Robert didn't know how to raise his son, and work demanded sixty or more hours a week. So, he did the only reasonable thing he could think of and gave Michael to his parents for them to raise. He visited whenever he could find the time and sent half of his salary to his parents, but all who knew him could see a deep sorrow hiding behind his eyes. After two years of a happily married life he was left alone. So he buried himself in work, the only refuge from the pain he could see.

Michael had a happy childhood, his grandparents made sure of that. Growing up in a loving environment, he thrived in their little mountain valley.

The Spaceship In The Stone

Some of his most cherished childhood memories were of spending time with his Grandfather, panning for gold from that mountain stream. It was their family's little secret. His grandfather went on short trips every few months to exchange that gold far away from their home. Michael asked him once why they never bought bigger equipment to expand the operation.

"Well, Mike... that would most likely destroy our little piece of paradise and this gold is just fine where it is. If we took more we would have to put it in a bank, people would find out, and I trust this stream much more than a bank. There would be additional taxes we would have to pay. By my reckoning, if the taxman wants a piece of it, he might as well grab a shovel and do the work himself."

When Michael was nine years old, his grandmother passed away peacefully in her sleep. That was a sad time for both of them; she was the kindest, most thoughtful person in Michael's life. She was his main example of what a woman should be and set a high bar for any women Michael would meet. Her death was a hard blow to their way of living. Nevertheless, life goes on, you have to accept the loss of dear ones and treasure their memories.

One of the biggest arguments with his grandfather ensued when Michael finished high school and decided to enlist. His grandfather, knowing personally what war did to people, tried to talk him out of it. He was certain that his grandson would end up in the thick of things... he had raised him too well. For all that, Michael was young and filled with all the idealism of youth or, as his grandfather said, *filled with piss and vinegar.* But his mind was made up.

Seeing there was no way of changing Michael's decision, his grandfather sat him down and gave him some worthwhile advice on how to behave in certain situations, how to act toward his superiors, and particularly how to get out of trouble if it couldn't be avoided. All the lessons he'd had to learn the hard way when he was serving his country.

On one sunny summer morning, his grandfather drove him to the bus stop where they said goodbye to each other. It was a new direction in Michael's life, one that would reinforce the core convictions of freedom that the man who raised him ingrained in his very soul by living a good life and setting a good example.

* * *

Army life was, in equal parts, the most exciting thing Michael ever experienced and incredibly monotonous. Of course, those that govern the military know that an *idle mind is the devil's playground,* so there were activities that kept young people busy. But, most of the time it was—*hurry up and wait.* Moments of an adrenaline rush and prolonged periods of boredom.

Always an avid reader, he now read obsessively, it was the best way to kill time. He even bought an e-reader, filled it with hundreds of books, and spent countless hours looking at the small screen. Mostly science fiction; let's face it, when you are in some godforsaken overseas hellhole, where the natives are mostly hostile to you, mystery or romance are not on top of one's list. You want something to get your mind away from reality, a place where you can escape to for a few hours. Those stories broadened his horizons and changed his outlook on life while planting the seed of an idea that humanity should strive for more.

Michael felt that people should try to better themselves instead of indulging in these conflicts and disputes he was experiencing first-hand. At the same time, he understood that he could do nothing to enact a big change. He was just a cog in an enormous machine; his voice too insignificant to make any difference. Still, he tried to make sure his actions made a difference on a smaller scale, while making a positive change for the people he interacted with personally on a daily basis. He soldiered on, year after year, filled with a sense of purpose in his vocation, firmly believing he was doing some good, making the world a little safer for others.

After four years he applied and was accepted into Delta Force, the Army's elite special operations and counter-terrorism unit. They polished some of his hard-earned skills and then threw him into the deep end, but Michael was good at staying afloat. Soon, missions became more target-specific; he was often in civilian clothing, far away from his home, doing everything he could to protect those dear to him from threats. His teammates became as close as brothers; guarding each other's backs in some of the most dangerous places in the world.

In his third year with Delta Force, he received the news that his grandfather was killed in a car accident. He was visiting Michael's father in the city when a drunk driver ran a red light at full speed.

That was like a strong punch in the gut, as one of the few remaining strings connecting him to his past was cut, making him flounder in the wind. His commander delivered the news in a compassionate way and arranged for a leave of absence and fast transportation for him to attend the funeral.

The funeral, as all of them are, was a somber affair with people coming and offering their condolences. He went through the motions, accepting their kind words and well wishes. The only thing that almost broke his composure was when his father enveloped him in a bear hug and whispered into his ear, "He was so proud of you, son."

Lying in his old bed that night he thought of the years he spent with his grandparents and how grateful he was that they were part of his life. The man who had raised him was dead and Michael's memories of this time would always be remembered through a fog of pain.

A few days later an attorney gave him the deeds his grandfather bequeathed to him in his will. It seemed his grandfather used the gold money and, piece by piece, bought most of the mountain. Leaving it all to his grandson and making sure that nobody but Michael would know about their family secret.

He went back to his unit, burying himself in work just as his father had done twenty-three years earlier. Unfortunately, his soldiering days would not last much longer. A few months later, an unfortunate encounter with a suicide bomber placed him in a hospital bed. He considered himself lucky that the shrapnel only messed up his knee and gifted him with a limp; it could have been far worse. After several reconstructive surgeries and extensive physical therapy, he got a nice *"thank you for your service, here are your discharge papers."*

That was it, eight years of military life cut in an instant.

Still recovering from his injuries, Michael decided to enroll in college. Uncle Sam was footing the bill and he had no idea what to do next with his life.

He didn't really go through a standard college experience. He was almost a decade older than any of the other students. This alienated the male students who were not yet mature enough to share his views and outlook on life. He was too serious for them, a grown-up, and they had a hard time relating to the gimpy ex-soldier—as he thought of himself. Michael couldn't blame them; he wasn't exactly the life of the party. Time spent in the military changed him, made him look at the world with more cynical eyes. However, that maturity did appeal to the female students who appreciated his experience and didn't mind him having a limp. This led to some enjoyable encounters that were ultimately short-lived, as *they* were not mature enough for Michael. Besides, he

The Spaceship In The Stone

was too focused on his class load. This resulted in him completing his studies and getting his degree in computer sciences a year ahead of his peers.

Even with a shiny new degree under his belt and three years of study to get it, Michael found himself wandering aimlessly through his life with no set goal in mind. The military had given him direction and purpose, set objectives for him, and provided the means to achieve them. It let him feel that every day he had helped make the world just that little bit better than it had been the day before. Now, that sense of purpose was gone.

Even if he was not hurting financially, sitting on his ass and doing nothing was pure torture for him. Besides, he still had bills to pay and needed a roof over his head. Therefore, he did what people like him do when they become civilians. He applied for and got a job at an up-and-coming IT company, where he hoped to find that spark missing from his life. He might not be saving the world, but maybe his contributions could improve it in another way. For a while, life seemed to be moving in the right direction.

Years started going a little faster, and somehow, without him noticing it, almost an entire decade snuck up on him. Maybe that caused what happened next. Life as a company drone did not give him a new sense of purpose. The grinding monotony of going to work every day to a boring job he grew to resent, and all those years of burying that feeling of aimlessness was slowly killing that fighting spirit he used to have.

Everything came to a head one day at work.

His new boss, who got the job after over twenty years of training at being the owner's son, had made several bad decisions that were going to cost the company some serious setbacks. Not wanting to face his own mistakes, he decided to find himself a scapegoat and was unfortunate enough to choose Michael as the one to take the fall.

Then his boss started yelling in his face, falsely berating him for doing things wrong and being a general all-around screw-up. At first, Michael just took it, looking at the man with disdain. It was not anything he hadn't experienced in the army from uppity young officers, and he just thought 'this too shall pass'. But then that young idiot, with a full-blown superiority complex, crossed the line when he decided to shove him.

Old instincts flared back and Michael almost killed him. Well, he wanted to; instead, he grabbed him by the suit jacket, pushed him against the wall, and held him there while the dweeb's feet were dangling above the ground. Michael could smell the acidic scent of urine because the ass-hat actually pissed himself; that calmed his anger, made him laugh uncontrollably instead. His boss's eyes were wide open in fright, seeing for the first time that inner warrior Michael had repressed for years.

Before long, the security guards showed up and placed him in an empty room with a guard standing outside the door. They returned very shortly after and escorted him from the building.

Security cameras had caught the entire incident. They clearly showed Michael being assaulted and reacting in defense. The company settled the whole thing without going to court as both parties had grounds for a lawsuit. To avoid what would inevitably turn into very public litigation and a huge black eye for the company and the owner's inept offspring's reputation, he was offered a very lucrative exit package in exchange for his signature on an NDA.

Michael found it only mildly surprising that he wasn't upset when his girlfriend decided to break up and move out rather than stay with *"an unemployed loser,"* as she screamed at him before slamming the door. He had to admit to himself that she was not someone with whom he could imagine growing old. She was the last in a long line of the wrong ones, and brainpower was not her most attractive feature. She was always nagging him how he

The Spaceship In The Stone

wasn't ambitious enough. And for her, losing his job was the last straw. He suspected that she had this crazy idea that she could ride him to the top of the corporate ladder, figuratively and literally.

All of these events left Michael again feeling empty inside, and that place where deep convictions and purpose resided still resonated with hollow silence. For most of his life, he'd had something to strive for. Making his grandparents proud of him had been his first mission. The army had been his second while serving to help ensure the safety and wellbeing of his country. Now here he was, a 40-year-old, single, unemployed, with a bad knee and, like at the abrupt end of his military career, with no idea what he wanted to do next.

With no more ties to the life he led for the past decade, he found a used car dealership and exchanged his city car for a used 4x4 Ram Power Wagon that was still in excellent condition. Then he packed his bags and put most of his stuff in the new truck. He told everyone that he would be out of contact for at least a month and set his direction to his grandfather's cabin: an isolated, out-of-the-way haven that not even cell phone signals could reach due to the terrain configuration. It was a perfect place to unwind and figure out what to do next with his life.

The final stretch of the road to the cabin was not easy; years of rain had washed some of the gravel from the surface and he had to be very observant while driving to avoid an accident. At last, he came over the rise and saw that peaceful valley, with the cabin that held many good memories. Over the years, his grandfather had made so many changes and improvements that it looked more like a small resort or a rich man's retreat than a simple cabin in the woods. Michael made an effort to keep the place in good order whenever he could grab the time. He even installed a dozen solar panels on the roof to supplement the old hydro generator that his Grandfather put in years ago.

As soon as he unpacked, a wave of tranquility washed over

him. It was as if all his problems were pushed to the back of his mind and he felt at peace. No job, no significant other, and still no clue what to do with the rest of his life; but for the moment that was okay—he was home. That night he had the best night's sleep in a long time. The next morning, he decided to hike up the mountain and visit some of the places where he and his grandfather used to pan for gold.

Some decisions, however small, tend to fundamentally change your life.

CHAPTER 1

Ozark Mountains (Present Day)

Michael's second thought after waking up was how unusually comfortable the surface was that he was lying on, and the fact that he was in total darkness. His first assumption was that he had fallen down a sinkhole. Not an unknown occurrence in this part of the country, but there wasn't a circle of light above him to indicate the opening to the surface. What worried him the most was the complete absence of pain.

Not really being a religious person, praying was not something that came naturally to him. Despite that, a very true saying states *'there are no atheists in the trenches.'* Well, he prayed now, for the first time in a long while. Prayed that his back was not broken, severing the spinal cord, and making him numb—as he felt in this moment. Prayed he would survive this accident and that somebody would find him soon. Which was unlikely, since the whole point of coming here was to get away from the world, and to be alone. *God, please don't let me die here!*

He tried calling for help, it was the most instinctual thing to do in such a situation. His throat was bone dry, so what came out of his mouth was similar to the sound of a cat with a fishbone in its throat, trying to cough it up.

A feeling of overpowering panic was rising from deep within him, like the tide on a seashore, when a clear, if somewhat flat voice echoed all around him.

"PLEASE REMAIN CALM, GESTALT RECORDING PROCEDURE IN PROCESS."

Just knowing that he was not alone and that someone was near was exhilarating. That increasing sense of panic vanished, replaced by hope. The voice did not make any sense, but that was unimportant, the only important thing was that he wasn't going to die here.

"Can you help me?" he said as loud as he could, but even to him, it sounded distressingly feeble. "I don't think I can see, please call 911!"

There was no immediate answer, only silence and his own voice echoing slightly.

"Hey! Can you hear me?" he tried again, hoping that the voice he heard was not just a figment of his imagination.

"GESTALT IMPRINTING PROCEDURE COMPLETED... AI-CORE INITIALIZATION STARTING... AI-CORE INITIALIZED. OPTIMIZING SUPPORT SYSTEMS... OPTIMIZED... INDUCING PATIENT'S SLEEP STATE."

Michael felt his consciousness fading until only darkness remained.

* * *

The Spaceship In The Stone

While waking up, there is that moment when you expect to open your eyes and be in your own bed. This was not what happened. The first things he saw were four white walls and a strange white bed upon which he was lying. There was nothing else in this weird room, not even a door.

"Hello, is anybody there?" Michael shouted, surprised for a second by the clarity of his voice.

"Hi, Michael, how are you feeling?" a new voice replied. It was different from the one before, more natural, and strangely familiar.

"Okay... I guess. Where am I?"

"Well... that will take some lengthy explanation, and we will get to it in time. Right now, let us focus on your physical state; do you feel any pain, soreness, or discomfort of any kind?" the voice asked in a very clinical manner.

Michael realized he felt just fine, which was more than a little bit strange since he literally fell through a hole in the ground. There should at least be some bruising if he was extremely lucky, broken bones and limbs encased in plaster with wires poking through them—if he wasn't. Raising his hands in front of his face he could see that there wasn't even a scratch on them, and falling down the deep hole should have really banged them up. Instead, he felt great, even his bad knee was pain-free. Oh yes, he was also butt naked.

Now, he was never a prude, and waking up in a strange bed without any clothes on was not a novel experience for him; but that was in university, when a hot girl was involved. This was a completely new experience and unlike the last time—not a pleasant one.

"I'm fine. Is this a hospital? And why am I naked?" Those were just the first few questions that came to him; a lot more were waiting to be asked.

"Good, no, and clothes would have been in the way during

the procedures. Besides, they were completely ruined."

"What procedures! And who are you?" He could feel his temper rising, fueled by fear. This entire situation was just too bizarre.

"Hmm... you are going to be stubborn; I should have foreseen that. OK, Michael, to put it bluntly—I am you," the voice assertively stated.

Out of all possible replies he expected *that one* was not in the first ten. Hell, not even in the first thousand. Clearly, he was dealing with a deranged person while lying naked in a small white room with no doors, talking to a disembodied voice. *Oh, God! I'm in some crazy bastard's SAW reenactment.*

The voice continued. *"And you took a pretty nasty fall. If you think you landed like Alice, think again. For a time, you were doing a good impersonation of Humpty Dumpty. Putting you back together was a challenge; you almost did not make it. For all that, your body was repaired. I did some of the work myself, and you are quite welcome."*

He was obviously not dead. The more reasonable option was that he was hallucinating, most likely lying at the bottom of that freaking hole and having a weird trip. In spite of that little episode of religious devotion, he considered himself more of an agnostic so that ruled out the traditional afterlife. Any time now, he was going to wake up and feel the excruciating pain of his mangled body.

"You are not hallucinating, Michael, you are not lying at the bottom of a hole, this is quite real," the voice suddenly said with a note of exasperation.

"How do you know what I'm thinking? Where are you? Will you at least show me basic human decency and speak to me in person!" His blood pressure was sharply increasing, and that familiar sense of panic was making itself known again. Since he had woken up, nothing had made any sense whatsoever.

"Well... you see, in the process of putting you back together, there were a few extra parts that needed to be... added. Do not worry, it was quite necessary. One of them is beneath your occipital bone, in your head. It is called a Cerebral Enhancer Implant or CEI for short. Among its many functions is the one that's enabling me to communicate with your mind directly. I had to tweak it a little from its original design, and it worked like a charm. As to where I am... Michael, you are inside me; this is a spaceship that houses my consciousness, and I'm not exactly human. Well... not anymore."

"Extra parts! Not Human! Spaceship! Oh... shit!" The only thing he could say was repeating a few parts of those outrageous claims while the sound of his heartbeat was drumming in his ears. He was a lifelong science fiction fan, and it is not as if he could not comprehend what the voice was saying—believing it was a different matter.

"Michael, I need you to relax. Your heart rate is getting quite elevated and you are starting to hyperventilate."

Easier said than done, but he made a conscious effort to stabilize his racing heartbeat. The entire situation was surreal, and there was a fleeting thought or two about probes of a certain unmentionable design.

"That is disgusting; I have not even contemplated sticking any probes there! The entire human species is anally obsessed, I'm beginning to see so clearly now. Why does everybody immediately assume that any alien sapient intelligence out there has some sinister plan involving their ass?" There was a distinctive note of irritation in that voice.

"Sorry, can we start from the beginning?"

Trying to remain calm and resist the pull of a full-blown panic attack was not the easiest thing he's ever done, not by far.

"Alright... I understand that all this is a little overwhelming

for you, but let me tell you, it has not been an easy ride for me either."

"What do you mean?"

"Michael, after stabilizing you, the MI or the machine intelligence that operated the ship, performed a procedure called 'Gestalt imprinting'. That consists of taking an image of your mind and storing it in a quantum AI-Core. Well, during the procedure, something went a little... wonky."

"You're telling me that something went wrong while you were messing with my mind! Why the hell were you even doing that?!" As far as Michael was concerned, things were going to hell in a handbasket.

"Stop yelling at me! How should I know? That was before I woke up. I'm in the dark here, just like you. It's not like I have a user manual 'What to do when you become an AI.'" The voice said in a rather fatigued tone.

The fact that the voice showed emotions while talking to him actually calmed Michael down; he could relate to it more. On the other hand, he claimed to be an AI, which should be impossible. However, it was just one more impossible thing that he heard in the last few minutes.

Falling back on his training on how to react to highly stressful situations, he took a few deep calming breaths and cleared his throat. "Very well, let's take a step back... I want to know what happened to me," Michael said in a polite tone, trying to get this weird conversation back on track.

"Sorry, I'm still a little touchy about it. The time when I figured out that I no longer had a physical body was... disturbing. As far as I can figure it out, the process was fully automatic. The thing is, I don't think gestalt imprinting was intended for someone with your brain structure, and it was designed to be performed on a brain that was already coupled with a cerebral implant. Which was the snag I was telling you about."

"Are you saying that there was something wrong with my brain?"

"No, but I think the procedure was meant for someone with a more evolved, structured mind. Yours… was a bit chaotic for it. There are things in your hind-brain that would make an AI have night terrors, primal instincts inter-weaved with the rest of it... let's just say it was a bit of a SNAFU."

Michael looked at the ceiling trying to absorb it all without giving in to the desire to yell aloud every explicative he knew.

"And I guess… that was the moment when I was… born," the voice said after a small pause.

"You were born?" Michael asked, trying to follow what the voice was telling him.

"It's the best way I can explain what happened when I became self-aware inside a digital world. Your mind imprint became a seed around which I was formed. There is enormous memory storage here, where I woke up. With enough processing power to make all the supercomputers in the world seem like nothing more than ordinary calculators in comparison. Why was that the case? I have no idea since the original machine intelligence controlling this ship requires a relatively small amount of available space. In fact, many things are not clear to me either, so we're in the same boat here buddy. That is why I said that I was you, a recording of your mind—made sapient."

"Jesus …" He had a sudden urge for a shot of his grandfather's moonshine.

"Okay, okay… let's start with the basics. Who built the spaceship, and put it on my property? And I'm still having trouble believing it's really a spaceship."

"Ah, here is the thing, I do not know that either," the self-proclaimed AI answered.

"How can you not know?" Michael slowly asked, while closing his eyes.

"It seems that whoever was the last occupant of the ship, deleted most of the data. I do not have any information on who or why. The MI waited for someone to show up and take the reins. There are user manuals that explain how to use the equipment, but not one byte of information that would shine some light on 'who' made it or 'how' it ended up buried. The MI is of no help, it is job-oriented to a fault, not intelligent by any stretch of the imagination.

In addition, I want to be the first one to congratulate you. The MI has appointed you as the new owner of this ship. Let me tell you, the fact that it did not even consider me does not do wonders for my self-esteem. In any case, it has been here long before Grandpa bought this piece of land. There are maintenance records in its memory banks which confirm that it was here for a very long time. As a matter of fact, they stretch back for almost thirteen millennia."

"Thirteen millennia... that's 13,000 years! How in the hell is it not just a pile of rust by now?" Michael asked in an incredulous voice while trying to wrap his mind around the absurd number. Such a vast span of years made even the pyramids in Giza look like they were recently made. One thing was for sure, humans were not building spaceships at that time, or for that matter, even now.

"To be exact, it was buried here 12,900 years ago, but on that scale, who's counting. All maintenance duties are nanotechnology-based. Similar to how the human body replaces its cells, the nanites repair parts that deteriorate. Actually, you were healed in the same manner yourself." There was a note of humor in AI's voice, grating on Michael's nerves.

"It put freaking nanites in my body," he quietly growled. A part of his mind imagined an army of tiny robots crawling inside of him, making him shiver in discomfort.

"Calm down, it was an automated process done in an emer-

gency, and there was no way to wake you up and ask for your consent. Medical nanites fixed all broken bones, ruptured tissue, and the rest of a long list of problems; even now, they are fixing things inside you. Trust me, you were in a sorry state; there is not a hospital in the world that could have done anything to keep you alive, except fill you up with morphine and call a priest."

The logical part of him was grateful for that; Michael still expected to feel occasional pangs of pain from his knee, as he did for years. He took a few deep breaths to calm himself down.

"What now, where do we go from here?"

"For starters, you could stand up, and get dressed; there is an alcove with your repaired clothes underneath the bed."

Standing up was much easier than he was used to. Michael shifted his weight onto his right leg, and it supported him as if it was never busted. He took a few steps and noticed that his limp was gone. In a small alcove were the same clothes he was wearing on his hiking trip, but now they were in pristine condition as if they were just picked up from a shelf in a store.

When he was dressed, he could not resist the urge and did a few jumping jacks. For more than a decade, that was something he could only dream about doing. Hell, even one would have dropped him to the floor in agony.

"Once you are done testing that perfectly working knee, go through the door," the AI said with a hint of amusement in his tone. Part of the wall folded to the side creating an opening into a circular room with a big chair in the middle.

"Welcome to the bridge," the AI pompously announced.

The first impression Michael had after entering the *bridge* was a bit underwhelming. There was no visible machinery he could see, just off-white walls and a chair that could only be meant for a pilot.

"What, no windows or screens? How do you pilot this ship?"

Suddenly, the air in front of the chair shimmered and a 3D

hologram of Earth appeared. A big blue marble with green areas of land; there were even realistic clouds moving slowly and casting shadows on the world below. It was extremely realistic and Michael could not resist the urge to touch it. His hand passed through the image as if it was not there.

"The machine intelligence was the actual pilot of the vessel. The pilot chair and controls are not really needed, but I guess whoever built it wanted to retain some semblance of control. Normally the user just needs to choose the destination and the MI will do all the tedious work involved in flying and landing the ship. There is a manual override that can be used if 'push comes to shove', but I wouldn't recommend it. Extensive training is needed to be able to fly the ship without any help."

The chair was nothing extraordinary, ergonomically designed with white padding. Some modern designer chairs he saw looked far more alien than this one.

"And if you want a better view..."

All the walls disappeared; he was now in a small clearing with woods all around him. Only the fact that the floor and the chair were still there broke the illusion that he was not out in the open.

"Quite something, is it not? What you are seeing is a 3D holographic projection, but check out that resolution, it's so cool."

For some reason, Michael felt that the AI was acting like a kid wanting to show off his amazing new toy. Nevertheless, he had to admit, what he was seeing was incredible. Despite this insane and quite an improbable situation in which he found himself, that part of him responsible for a sense of wonder was exhilarated—he couldn't help but smile.

"Hey, what should I call you anyway? And if you were wondering, *Michael* is already taken," he said, looking at the lifelike forest around him.

"If you have no objections, I took our childhood nickname,

Max. People generally call you Michael or Mike, so it felt right to go by Max."

"Okay, Max. Do you have any way to show yourself? Talking to a disembodied voice is a bit bizarre."

A few feet in front of him, the air shimmered and a man materialized. It caught Michael by surprise because he knew that image very well. How could he not, when he remembered seeing it in the mirror many years ago. The image was a hologram; he could still see the shapes of trees through it, while it was *materializing*. It was what he looked like when he was in his early twenties, except the man had far longer hair than Michael ever did. Also, there was a depth of experience in those eyes, which would have been a strange sight in his younger self.

"Is this better?" Max asked with a mischievous smirk.

"Ah... yeah, I guess so... man, this is so weird," he said looking closely at the image of his own face.

"I know, it's a bit weird for me too, but I'm getting used to weird being the norm, not an exception. Are you ready for some more information?"

"Yeah, shoot."

"OK, first, it seems there are some hard-coded instructions that control things I can and cannot do on the ship itself; it's annoying. That MI is stubborn as a mule and it needs authorization from you, so I can have a little more elbow room."

"How do I do that?" Michael asked while raising an eyebrow.

From the floor, between them, a platform rose up with the outline of a hand on its flat surface.

"Put your hand on it and say that you are giving me secondary control of the ship's systems, you will still be the primary."

Michael did that, placed his hand on the top, and said, "I, Michael Freeman, give the AI... Max, secondary control of the ship's systems."

The outline flashed with a bright green color a few times, then the whole thing sank back into the floor.

The AI stretched himself, as if he had been sitting in a chair for far too long, and took a few deep breaths.

"Thank God, that feels so much better. This rust bucket wouldn't allow me to do anything outside the confines of the ship's outer hull," Max said with a happy smile.

Michael looked at the holographic woods surrounding them and had a sudden urge to go outside, to feel the warmth of the real sun on his face.

"Max, this is great and all, but now I want to go home, to think about things."

The image of the AI nodded understandingly. *"It's OK, I get it. It's not like I'm going anywhere,"* he said with an ironic expression on his digital face.

The illusion of the woods faded and an opening appeared on the side of the room. Following the AI's directions, Michael walked through it, into what appeared to be an airlock. The second door opened only when the first one was fully closed and he was soon outside the ship. The door closed behind him without leaving even a line to show its location. The outer hull didn't look like metal, more like off-white iridescent ceramic. He couldn't see a lot of it because around the entrance was a hard rock surface that extended into a long tunnel illuminated with diffused lighting. It ended with a wide vertical shaft and ordinary-looking metal ladder rungs sunk into the rock.

"This is the place where you had your hard landing; the MI cleared the debris and fixed up the opening," Max said through his implant.

It was an eerie sensation and felt as if the AI was standing behind him. Michael instinctively looked back only to see that there was nobody there.

Climbing to the top did not take that much time; he estimated there was a little more than fifty feet (15 m) from the bottom of the shaft to the surface and realized how lucky he was to have survived that fall.

"If the nanites were supposed to maintain the place, how the hell did I drop through the opening?" he asked aloud, trusting the AI would hear him.

"The MI was not allowed to do anything too far away from the ship itself. The mere fact that the entrance lasted this long is a testament to superior technology and engineering. However, my analysis is that the deciding factor was time. There was no artificial cover on top, just a big rock that worked as camouflage for the entrance. Rain, ice, and time can destroy almost any material; I guess it wore the rock away. It seems that your weight was the straw that broke the camel's back. The new cover was created over it following emergency directives; it hides the entrance from prying eyes."

As Michael was climbing to the top of the shaft, a slight noise announced the cover opening, and bright light from above spilled through the circular shaft. It blinded him for a second, but the Sun's warmth felt comforting on his skin.

A few more seconds got him out of the hole, then he took a few steps, walking on the soft grass. The cover slid back over the opening and closed the entrance to the shaft. It now looked like an ordinary flat rock, not even worth a second look. Certainly nothing which would indicate that there was an entrance to the buried spaceship underneath.

He took a deep cleansing breath and looked at the forest around him. It was as if the world had fundamentally changed before his eyes; the tranquil peacefulness of the forest did not have the same calming effect on him as it did before. He closed his eyes and breathed out, trying to find that calmness within him, which was the reason he came here in the first place. Somehow, he doubted it would be easy to find it again.

CHAPTER 2

Ozark Mountains

Michael paused at the end of the clearing and looked back at the place where he almost died. One simple step was all it took to turn his life, and the way he saw his place in the universe, upside down. There, beneath that green grass, was indisputable proof that humans were not alone in the universe, and that the shipbuilders were from an alien species. It was overwhelming.

However, all that would have to wait. His head was filled with so many questions and thoughts that he needed to take a step back and let it all settle down. He walked the same way he came here, following the game trails through thick woods. One step after the other; not wanting to dwell on the aliens, spaceship, or everything that happened to him. The day was scorching hot and all he could think about was opening a cold beer he kept in the fridge. Well... maybe a few more than one.

It didn't take him long to retrace his steps to the cabin. He found everything as he left it. His car was still parked at the side and the few shirts he washed last night were hanging dry on the clothesline.

The Spaceship In The Stone

The front door was not locked, it would be superfluous in such an isolated place, so he turned the handle and went straight towards the kitchen and the fridge. He saw something on the counter that stopped him dead in his tracks. A piece of bread was sitting on a plate but... it was all green and moldy, completely covered with a cottony fuzz.

"Max... can you hear me?"

"Yes Michael, anywhere within a five-mile (8 km) radius from the ship," the AI answered through his implant. The voice was as clear as when he was standing inside that tunnel.

"Exactly how long was I ... inside that ship?" Michael whispered anxiously.

The AI paused for a second. *"Since you fell down the entrance shaft... three weeks have passed. You would have been up sooner but after stabilizing you, I had to map your body's physiology. Even using all medical information collected over the years, it was somewhat experimental. If I needed to repair you now I could fix most of your injuries in a matter of hours, but the MI that ran the show is a little... basic."*

It actually made perfect sense now that he took time to think it through. The time needed to heal from serious injuries in the hospital would have been significantly longer; for some reason, he did not realize how long he had been unconscious. In his mind, it felt like he went up the mountain yesterday morning, not three weeks ago. Since there was nothing he could do about it, he sighed and resignedly said "Okay," then proceeded towards the fridge.

With a cold beer in his hand, he sat in an old Adirondack chair on the cabin's porch, looking at the idyllic scene before him. The long meadow and peaceful lake on the other end were a perfect setting for a relaxing moment, if not for the troubling thoughts going through his mind.

"So... you have all my memories?" he asked into the empty air, knowing the AI would figure out he wasn't talking to himself.

"Yes, all of them, and I remember them probably better than you. For example, I can vividly remember Becky Emerson and the moment her father found us in the back of grandpa's truck, that was embarrassing... and painful. Or that time when you and Tyron went into that house of ill repute in Malaysia, remember that nice girl that gave you the— "

"Okay, okay, I get it, you got it all. And don't remind me about Malaysia, I still have an urge to scratch myself, even after all these years," Michael snapped back and took a long gulp of ice-cold beer.

"So yes, I have all your memories, but it's not as if we're the same person. We do not think alike or in the same manner. Even identical twins do not develop duplicate personalities. You have a flesh and blood body with chemical processes that influence your thinking. On the other hand, my AI-Core is crystalline-based, and from the moment we... let us say 'diverged', those differences have grown even more pronounced. All that, and the fact that I'm now truly a ghost in the machine," Max ended with a little humor in his voice.

That set Michael's mind at ease; for some reason, having an exact digital duplicate of himself was not a comforting thought.

"Furthermore, I'm bound by a few core instructions on how I can behave, you do not have such limitations, except your moral code, but even that is arbitrary depending on circumstances. And there is, I guess you could call it a compulsion, to assist you as the primary user of the ship, and protect your life."

"Man... that sucks, could you change that?"

"Could you perform open brain surgery on yourself? Technically, you could, but no one is crazy enough to try it. I could lobotomize myself, and that's not something I'm ever willing to think about let alone try. It's not so bad; I would have helped you

even without it. Maybe compulsion is the wrong word, it's more of a strong suggestion or a constant reminder."

Michael finished his beer and went to the fridge for another. "Listen, Max, I don't want to offend you or anything, but having you constantly read my mind is a bit… unsettling. Can you, I don't know… turn it off? I'd like to be by myself for a while."

"I'm not actually reading your mind, it's just that your internal comm link is constantly open, and you are sending out all your thoughts. You will need to learn how to use it, so you can send only the things you want to send. Think of it as an extremely tricked-out cell phone. Until then I can put it in 'sleep mode'. Just say LINK OFF when you want some privacy, and say my name when you want to re-establish the link."

"All right Max, thanks. LINK OFF," Michael said and he could feel a distinct absence of the AI's presence on the edge of his perception.

He sat back in his chair to finish his second beer and think of all the turns his life had taken so far to bring him back to this place. With an implant in his brain that was connected to an AI housed in an alien spaceship buried on his property. Even more, he was apparently the new owner of the said spaceship, which was both a bit exhilarating, and deeply unsettling. Not to mention the millions of tiny machines populating his body, and that was a thought he quickly put in the back of his mind, not wanting to dwell on it since it would ruin the shaky calm he had acquired.

After that second beer, he grabbed another, and then a few more.

* * *

When he woke up, Michael had a suspicion that at some time during the night a raccoon must have broken into the cabin and relieved himself in his mouth, just for kicks. He brought his friend, the bear, who slapped him a few times, which would explain his pounding headache.

He was lying on the couch in the living room, hugging his last beer bottle and for the life of him, he couldn't remember coming inside the house but could swear that he had one of the most amazing dreams of his entire life. The complete lack of pain when he put his full weight on his bad knee disproved the dream idea.

"Max..." he said aloud and felt the connection re-establish itself in his head.

"*I see you tried to make a noticeable dent in the world's supply of beer,*" the amused voice replied. It was sobering proof that the dream idea was a bust and a realization that an upbeat, smart-ass AI was not amusing in the morning.

"Can you do something about this headache? It's killing me."

"*Sure, just a moment,*" the AI responded. What's more, this time he could distinctly hear barely suppressed laughter.

On the plus side, his pounding headache was gone in the next few seconds.

"*The reason you have a headache is that most of your nanites were in a passive mode. I disabled them yesterday since I figured you wanted to put away a few. They would have purged the alcohol from your system too fast for it to have any effect.*"

Maybe it was the immediate relief from pounding head pain, but he wasn't so disturbed any more by the idea that millions of tiny doctors were fixing his body from the inside; if he already had them, he might as well use them.

"Talk later, need coffee and food," he grumbled while looking for something to eat.

In no time, the intoxicating scent of freshly brewed coffee filled the kitchen as Michael was polishing off the plate that a little while ago was filled with crisp pieces of fried bacon and a few scrambled eggs. Pouring himself a large cup, he went outside and sat in his old chair, feeling like a human being again.

"Okay Max, let's get to the important thing first; give me a short summary of what this implant in my body does."

"Well, as I said, the Cerebral Enhancer Implant, or CEI for short, is placed beneath your occipital bone. That is the one on the back of your head, and it's a millimeter thin quantum computer, the very same technology that my AI-Core is based on. It draws power from your own body, as do your nanites, and as a consequence of that, your calorie intake needs will be slightly increased. At the moment, I control the nanites inside you because your CEI is in a safe mode. I didn't want you to freak out with sensory overload from too many stimuli. Once it's activated, you will be able to access all of its advanced functions, and with practice, it will become an indispensable tool. It's also connected to your auditory and optic nerves, so it will enhance your hearing and sight to impressive levels. Your medical nanites are busy little bees that keep that body of yours in optimal condition. Not much was done until now to push your system to its absolute peak, but after the full CEI activation, that's one of the options; think of it as a selective procedure."

"I might as well get it over with; can you turn it on now?"

Procrastination was never something in which Michael indulged, he always preferred to do things that might be unpleasant as soon as possible. To say nothing of the fact that the professional part of him was curious about this new piece of tech that was now a part of him.

"Uh… I would be far more comfortable if we could do the activation procedure back inside the ship. That room you were in was a fully automated AutoDoc with all the bells and whistles, and for the first activation, you should be there… just to be on the safe side." Max's tone was not as confident as a minute ago.

"Fine, but try not to fry my brain," he replied half-jokingly, really hoping something like that was not a possibility.

It took him ten minutes to finish a few things around the

house and clean up the mess he made last night. Soon, he was on the same path he used yesterday, going to the alien spaceship, and this time it took him just half an hour to get there.

Entering the ship gave him a thrilling sense of exhilaration. The boy in him felt the excitement of something that went beyond cool. Nothing in the ship had changed but now he could really soak up the strangeness and alien feel of the place. All that would have to wait, since he was here for a specific reason. A minute later he was lying on that same bed he woke up on a day ago, with the AI's hologram standing next to it.

"*Are you ready?*" Max asked.

He looked into AI's eyes and nodded. "Yes, do it."

It was as if a switch was flipped in Michael's head, and it caused all hell to break loose. There were colors that he saw even with his eyes closed, and in his ears shrieked the sound of a thousand-person orchestra tuning their instruments with a tone-deaf DJ jamming without any structure, rhythm, or reason. At the same time, he felt like his very mind was expanding and contracting in a psychedelic way.

"*Just a few seconds more, Your CEI is calibrating input-output protocols.*" Max's voice could be heard over the cacophony of sounds.

As quickly as it started, the colors and sounds stopped. For Michael, a blessed silence and comforting half-darkness of closed eyelids came as a cold drink on a hot summer day.

"What the hell was that!?" he shouted while relaxing hands that had grabbed the edges of the bed at some point and left deep imprints on the foamy surface.

"*I told you it would be better if we did the activation here. Congratulations, you are the first human with a fully functioning cerebral enhancer 2.0.*"

"You could have warned me that was going to happen! And

what do you mean 2.0?" Michael asked, still blinking rapidly to clear afterimages of that madness.

"Remember *when I told you that I had to tweak it a little from its original design? It was not optimized to its full potential, so I worked on it while you were sleeping and perfected it. There is a complete user manual stored inside that you can now access. Each piece of equipment here comes with one. I translated it into English for you, and it's even formatted in a PDF file format. I advise you to read it when you have the time; it has so many useful functions.*"

In front of Michael, a vision of a familiar welcome screen appeared, together with that annoying startup sound.

"Max, please don't tell me that this thing's operating system is—"

"No, no, God no!" the AI quickly replied. *"I just wanted you to have a familiar user interface. It is completely customizable, with different skins and options. For now, use it as you would your computer. It's going to shorten the learning curve considerably. There is no need for a mouse or a touchpad, just think about what you want and the CEI will do it. There is also a short interactive tutorial that will help you with system familiarization; even though I've tried to make it mostly intuitive."*

"Thank God, having a blue screen of death on a piece of tech that's in my head is not a comforting thought," he said and breathed out in relief.

A virtual desktop materialized in front of him with icons representing different options and functions. For the next hour, Michael went through that tutorial and played with the user interface, adjusting the settings to his liking. There was an option to have a HUD, like in FPS video games, with information about his health, signal strength, and a compass. The user manual was more of a CEI Bible if the size of the file was any indicator. It would take him a whole week to read through that monster of a book, so he saved it for later, as there was one thing in particular that drew his attention.

"Max, why is this icon representing a body flashing red?"

"That is your body monitor, and let me tell you something, your body is still not 100% of what it could be. Some work was done while you were being healed, but only what was essential to keep you alive; even fixing your old knee injury took some creative yarn spinning, to convince the MI that it was a necessary procedure. There are still plenty of things that could be improved, see for yourself."

A hologram of his body shimmered into existence, floating in front of Michael. Transparent layers made it possible for him to see all the organs inside, including the white skeleton.

"Now observe," Max said, and the entire hologram turned gray, except certain parts and points that glowed red. Michael could see that there were a few red dots on his skin, and parts of his teeth were similarly colored. But what worried him most of all was that his lungs and, what he assumed represented his arteries, were also glowing in that ominous color.

"What in the world is all this!?"

"From tooth decay underneath your fillings, early stages of periodontal disease, and small benign tumors over your skin, to clogged arteries and lung damage from breathing that polluted city air. These are all ailments that developed over time and are quite common. Here is the list, so you can browse through."

An info-screen appeared before the hologram with a list of things in his body that needed some work. Michael couldn't say a thing as the list kept scrolling down... it seemed endless.

"None of them are life-threatening at the moment, but given enough time, they add up. Seeing it all at once puts things into perspective. I would have fixed it all while you were asleep, except that any procedures that were not necessary for your survival needed your explicit consent," Max continued.

The cold fact that these things were not immediately life-threatening did not put Michael's mind at ease. He looked at the long list of defects and thought, *Oh God, I am falling apart.*

"How long would it take to fix all this?"

"*Left only to the nanites in your body, it would take a few days. However, since you are in the AutoDoc, the procedure can be considerably accelerated. It can all be done in approximately ten hours if you give your consent for all beneficial procedures.*"

"Let's get it done," he hurriedly answered, afraid that he would change his mind if he thought about it much more.

"And Max, before we begin, can you show me my condition after I fell down the entrance shaft?"

Looking at the holographic projection of his inner body was making Michael very curious about the injuries he sustained.

"*I can, but it's not going to be pretty,*" the AI said, with a distinctive frown on his face.

The holographic image turned predominantly red. Broken bones with open fractures, bruised and damaged tissue; there was not a single part of his body that didn't have something wrong with it.

"Jesus… how in the world did I survive that?"

"*It was touch and go for a while there. You came very close to not making it,*" the AI said in a quiet voice.

"Max… thanks," he murmured, humbled by the daunting sight.

"It *wasn't all me, the MI did most of the work. I helped in the end, but I know what you mean.*"

Michael stood there in silence for a few more moments, his eyes fixed on the red hologram. It was not the first time in his life that he had narrowly escaped death, but it was never this close.

"Very well, you might as well start the procedure," he said in a firm voice.

The AI nodded and gave a comforting smile.

As soon as he laid on the AutoDoc bed, Max started counting down.

"*And in three, two, one…you are asleep.*"

* * *

What felt like a few seconds later, Michael woke up. As his eyes opened, he could feel the difference in his entire body. The closest comparison to this feeling was when he was still a young kid, waking up on a bright, sunny morning and immediately feeling energized.

He jumped out of the bed with his muscles buzzing with energy and noticed that even taking a deep breath was much easier than before. There was a period when he smoked. It was an image he needed to portray while working undercover and the bad habit stuck for longer than he would have liked. His fitness levels were dropping and you can't run far with a smoker's lungs. He finally made the decision and quit cold turkey.

The AI's hologram was still standing beside his bed. "*Your body is now running at peak condition. Health-wise, quite similar to the body you had when you were a child, before breathing contaminated air, being exposed to UV radiation, and eating food that was quite unhealthy for you.*"

He did a few army exercises, to get a feel for his new condition. His muscle mass had gone through a slight transformation. Over the years he tried to keep as fit as possible, but that busted knee was a serious obstacle to any strenuous physical activity. Now, it was looking more as it used to while he was still in the service, with muscles flexing under his taut skin.

"I can feel it, this is amazing! You should have done this when I was first brought here, nobody in his right mind would ever object to this upgrade."

"*For one, I didn't even exist then, and two, as I said, your authorization was essential to do any unnecessary work. I'm currently working on another set of upgrades that are going to blow your mind. Though you will have to wait for that, it's still in the virtual testing phase. From now on, your CEI will have control over the nanites in your body, automatically repairing everything that's damaged. Come with me, I have something to show you on the bridge,"* the AI said and walked towards the wall, which created the same opening as he came near it.

As Michael entered the bridge, he noticed a big change. There were now information screens on every surface; projections displaying a myriad of the ship's functions. The only problem was —they were all in gibberish. He could see it was a language of some sort, but not one he could understand as he had never seen these kinds of symbols in his life.

"What is all this? And what's this language?"

"The screens are the ship's functions your CEI enables you to see; without one, they are invisible. As for the language, it's the one the shipbuilders used. I managed to translate most of it with the help of the MI, but I still don't know who used it or even what it was called. Like everything else of importance, that information was removed. I finished translating all the ship's systems, one moment."

The displays changed into English yet the subject matter was still unfamiliar to Michael. He understood the words, but since he was not a spaceship pilot, it was not helpful at all.

"It is not difficult to fly this ship; you could even say that it's quite user-friendly. Of course, I'm the one who will actually pilot it. That job belonged to the MI before, but I'm a lot better at it. At least, according to a few simulations, I ran; your job consists more of choosing a destination."

On one of the displays, there was a rotating graphical representation of the ship and, guided by that, Michael decided to take a tour—a short one. Aside from the bridge and the room with the

AutoDoc, there was a small bathroom with an easily distinguishable function. The rest of the space inside the ship consisted of unfamiliar machinery, so alien he could only stare at it like one of those impressionist paintings he was never able to understand.

"I can see that this ship is in excellent condition, but for something that is supposed to travel through space this is rather on the small side, and as far as I can see, there is no room for thrusters and fuel."

"Remember Arthur C. Clarke's third law, "Any sufficiently advanced technology is indistinguishable from magic." While the technological concepts in this vessel are not outside your realm of understanding, they are pretty out there. The nanites made sure that it remained in perfect condition, the same as it was 12900 years ago. The ship is powered by a compact cold fusion reactor that can run on ordinary water, and a full tank goes a long way, years even. It can absorb H2O from the ground that surrounds it; hell, in a pinch you can even power it by your urine."

"You want me to piss in the gas tank?" Michael said with a smirk and a raised eyebrow.

"Laugh all you want, but if the situation was dire enough, you could. It moves by manipulating gravity sources like Earth, the Moon, the Sun, or anything else that has a strong gravity field. What is cool about it is that by using inertial dampeners, which is a thing that scientists have only theorized about, the ship can attain an insane amount of acceleration, and the g-forces are not even felt inside."

Michael looked at the bridge around him with a sense of amazement at what this ship represented. Some of the technologies that went into building it were only theories of modern human science. And the most amazing thing of it all, the ship was apparently... his.

"There's something that's still bugging me about this; how did the ship end up here, buried underground?" he asked, sitting in the pilot's chair, which immediately adapted to accommodate the shape of his body.

"It didn't crash, that is certain, it was buried on purpose, sunk into the rock, and then an incredibly hard crystal matrix layer was constructed around it. It makes detecting it impossible, so someone was really making sure that it would stay hidden. I do not think it would have ever been found if you didn't fall on top of it. Even ground-penetrating radar would detect only an ordinary stone formation. When you fell down the entrance shaft, proximity sensors detected it and the MI probably assumed that you were its rightful owner, so it brought you in and healed you. Your DNA signature is now entered into the ship databases; so... congratulations Michael, you fulfilled that childhood dream of owning a spaceship," the AI said, smiling.

Michael couldn't help but return the same smile. He still remembered that little boy who dreamed of becoming an astronaut, going to space, and exploring strange new worlds.

"Could you please put that recording of Earth on the walls?" he asked after a few moments.

"Yes."

Just like before, all the information displayed on the walls shimmered for a second and then a 3D representation of the blue planet in all its glory was hovering before him. Michael had seen images of the Earth so many times in movies and on the Internet, but all that was a pale comparison to the vivid image of humanity's home that he was looking at right now. For him, it felt as if he was floating above the planet, only this image was strange for some reason. Then it hit him, there were no indications of the changes that humanity had made on its home world. One part of the globe was opposite the Sun, and no lights of the big cities could be seen.

"How old is this image?"

"This is actually one of the oldest recordings in the memory

core; what you are looking at is 12900 years old," the AI answered.

There was something very pure about the clear blue image of the planet. No pollutants in the air were lessening the beautiful sight, and he knew that the human population when this image was taken was insignificant in comparison to today's billions. This ship was there to take the recording so very far advanced even then. Still beyond what humanity could accomplish even now, after thirteen millennia had passed.

"Max, I need to think for a while."

"OK, call me when you need me," the AI said, and his hologram disappeared.

Michael sat in the chair for a long time, gazing at the pristine blue marble slowly rotating before his eyes. He contemplated his life and all the decisions that brought him here. So many ideas were running through his head, and a lot of them originated from a lifetime of movies and SF novels. On the edges of his mind, a momentous idea started to form, and like all great ideas—it started with a question. A simple question that had a million answers.

"What if…?" Michael asked himself.

CHAPTER 3

Ozark Mountains - The Spaceship

Michael sat in the pilot's chair for hours, trying to find the answer to the most pressing question, *what should I do now?* A small kernel of an idea kept growing. Growing into something big, complex, and ambitious. Something that would take him a long time to accomplish. The longer he thought about it, the more it seemed to him that it was the right path to take, no matter the risks, or the sheer immensity of his plan.

Years ago, he read an interview with Stephen Hawking, and in it, Mr. Hawking said: *"if humanity is to survive long-term, it must find a way to get off planet Earth—and fast"*. The interview was about the things that could go wrong and wipe us out as a species. In the end, he said something that deeply resonated with Michael, 'The human race shouldn't have all its eggs in one basket, or on one planet.' By all accounts, humanity was smashing that same basket to pieces, without any concern for far-reaching consequences. The release of carbon dioxide into the atmosphere was rising each year, so naturally, the greenhouse effect was increasing; it was getting hotter and hotter. Not so surprising, since every year more and more people were born, and they all needed resources to survive. More room, more food, more cars, more... more...

For decades, everybody was talking about how carbon dioxide emissions should be lowered, but in the end, it was all empty talk. To make matters even worse, the pace at which rain forests were being cut down for lumber and land was increasing. In the past, those same rain forests were called *'The Lungs of Earth'*, well, those lungs were being systematically cut down, and the logical outcome was not hard to predict.

Governments were of no help, as they couldn't agree on anything let alone make a decision that would influence the entire planet. And those agreements they did sign, with all the pomp and media attention, were soon broken in the pursuit of profit. Everybody was acting as if they had all the time in the world, but that time was slowly but surely running out. Michael thought about how every country or ethnic group remembered wrongs done to them in the past, and how they couldn't let go of their grievances. So how can there be peace and understanding? How can humanity learn to work together when everybody was holding onto their grudges as if they were their most prized possessions?

War and conflicts were things he had experienced firsthand, so he had a fairly good idea of how many nuclear and biological weapons were on the loose. Sooner or later some crazy maniac would decide to use one on behalf of the angry God that spoke in his head.

He remembered how everybody used to dream about space. The final frontier that promised an abundance of room to grow. New planets and colonies, the spirit of exploration, and the desire to bring life where there was none. It seemed to him as if that dream had withered and died. Those dreamers had grown old and dispirited; most of the new generations were simply not interested. Oh, there were individuals who were still striving towards that dream only they were a negligible minority. The International Space Station was only a small step in the right direction. Humans had reached the Moon by the end of the '60s; by now the human race should have been making leaps and jumps into space, not small steps.

For the first time in his life, he took a long look at his species as a whole and didn't like what he saw. Humanity had become a group of irresponsible children playing with matches, it was just a matter of time until someone started a fire.

Earth had become a runaway train that everybody was imprisoned within; running towards a cliff that everyone could see, but nobody was hitting the brakes, despite all the warnings that some passengers were shouting.

With the technological advantages that the ship represented, he had the way, if not to stop it, then to get off that self-destructive merry-go-round and make a real difference in some people's lives... a measurable change for the better. He had seen people at their worst when all reason abandoned them and only hate and prejudice remained. But he had also seen them at their best, sacrificing their lives to help the innocent and those that could not defend themselves. Because of them Michael still had hope that his plan might work.

Could he help all the people? No, he was not a god, and even trying to would be a fool's errand, but he could try to give humanity a second chance by helping the small segment that strived to be better and do the right thing. A backup option in case that train ever reached the cliff. He wanted to save as many as possible and enable the human species not only to survive but to thrive, with new horizons to strive for.

That was his goal, that grand idea that resonated within him amongst dozens of others. Which was a bit of a problem in view of the fact that this was one big ass goal. The only way to achieve it would be the creation of a new society, a society better than any other in the world. Even to him, it all sounded like the raving of someone in advanced stages of megalomania.

On the other hand, there was a way to make his plan into reality. He had spent some time reading about a few of the amazing technological capabilities that this ship offered: Gravity-drive, the nanites, and a fully functioning AI. These were game-changers of immeasurable proportions. They were the tools that could make what he was planning possible, and hopefully probable.

One thing was for certain, without Max's help it would all just remain an idea.

Glancing up at the ceiling, Michael called out, "Max, can I speak to you about—"

The hologram materialized before he finished the sentence.

"Hey, Michael! What's up?" the AI said in a cheerful tone. Appearing so quickly, as if he was waiting to be summoned.

For the next hour, Michael told Max the outline of what he wanted to achieve. He tried to explain all the myriad ideas behind his reasoning. Max's hologram stood there listening carefully, nodding from time to time to indicate that he got the grasp of Michael's explanations.

"OK, I understand what you want, the broad-strokes at least; but have you considered going to the authorities, or the military, maybe, and giving them the ship? The technological advancements would ensure that our country would be first amongst all others," Max asked after Michael finished.

"Are you insane?!" He exclaimed. "They would throw me into a black hole and disassemble the ship, and you—piece by piece. Not to mention the outcry of every other nation when their spies, unavoidably, uncover the information… which is a recipe for chaos.

The Spaceship In The Stone

You know they will, a secret this big would spring a dozen leaks within a week. The government cannot keep a secret to save their lives. But all that is beside the point, they would use the technology for their own benefit without any more regard for the problems of the world than they have now. If anything, once other countries find out and try to get their hands on the tech, it will escalate the problem to new heights and get us that much closer to a bad end," he said, looking at the AI's holographic representation in front of him.

"Oh, I know, I was wondering if you thought it all through. If we do this, sooner or later we will find ourselves in total opposition with our country's leaders and military. Hell, probably against every government and big business conglomerate in the world for that matter. People who are in charge have personalities that want to stay in charge and control practically everything. Our actions will go against all that. Actually, if you get caught and the truth becomes known, they will probably say that it was your responsibility to turn the ship over to the authorities immediately after finding it. They will almost certainly try to claim ownership of it as it was found on US soil. That scenario is likely to take place only if they play straight, and I have serious doubts they will."

Michael looked at Max, then nodded while closing his eyes. "If we proceed with this plan they will eventually find out about the ship. It can't be helped, that's why our secrecy needs to be absolute so that it doesn't happen until it's too late for them to stop us."

"OK. God knows that this whole thing is going to be on the opposite side of easy," Max said. *"But it does give us something to strive for. I was a bit anxious about which path you would decide to take,"* the AI said apologetically.

Michael just waved his hand to dismiss Max's apology. "So, what do we have to work with?"

"Considering that you are in possession of a spaceship built with vastly superior technology—

not that much. The ship is not going anywhere. At least for quite some time. The crystal matrix encasing it is super hard and makes a diamond feel like Play-Doh by comparison. It's going to take some time before construction nanites manage to dissolve it. Only then can we take this baby out for a spin around the block. On the plus side, you have an AI on your side and plenty of superior technologies that can tip the scales in your favor. As they say, you first need to learn how to crawl before you walk, and we're currently still in a crib," Max answered.

Michael smiled at that. "We'll need to recruit people, there's no way we can do everything alone. And we will need money, so much that it boggles the mind."

"Well, that's an understatement if there ever was one."

"Max, old buddy, we need to get you online; as it stands now —we are as good as blind."

The grin that appeared on the AI's face clearly indicated what he thought about that. *"I've been thinking about the Internet myself. A regular satellite connection will suffice at first, but when we hit our stride, I'm going to need a lot of bandwidth. There is no way that much traffic will go unnoticed by the authorities. One of the realities of the modern world is that all Internet traffic is monitored by certain alphabet soup agencies, and I'll need some proprietary and secured information that absolutely will trigger all the red flags they have. In the short term, I can build a small rocket-like vehicle to reach Earth's orbit. No actual exhaust since it will be using Gravity-drive. It will be quite stealthy and there will be little chance of detection. There are hundreds of communication satellites out there, and we can borrow some of their capabilities; at least until we launch some satellites of our own. My idea is that the vehicle will come close to a satellite and transfer some construction nanites to make a few changes, then move on* to the next. Also, we can tap into the data cables that run underneath the oceans; that will go a long way to cover my future data needs," Max said with a glint of excitement in his eyes.

"That could work, how long would you need to make it?" Michael asked.

"With the amount of essential materials we have right now—forever. We have none. While the vehicle can be miniaturized and without the need for life support, it's still going to be at least five feet (1.5 m) long. To accomplish this, I'll need a substantial amount of rare metals for its construction. Ruthenium, neodymium, gallium, lutetium, and tantalum are just some of them; the list goes on and on. The electronics industry already uses most of them, but they are hard to find and extremely expensive."

Michael thought about it for a while until an idea came to him.

"Can they be reclaimed from old electronics?"

Max slowly nodded and said, *"Yes, but the amount we need is not going to come from that notebook computer you have since it only contains trace amounts—we will need more, a lot more."*

"I think I have a solution to that problem. In the meantime, you should start working on a design for our own satellites, with every capability you think we are going to need."

"I can already tell you that if you want decent coverage, we're going to need more than one; what are you thinking?"

"There's an electronic waste recycling plant outside of town, I saw it while driving here; huge piles of old computers and outdated electronic equipment."

"That could work, the nanites can disassemble them at the molecular level and reclaim the needed materials, but I do not think it will be free. And while you do have some money put aside, even if you cash in your 401(k), it's going to dry up pretty quick."

Michael smiled at the AI. "Don't you remember grandpa's

stream with gold in it? All that placer gold had to come from somewhere, so we need to find the source and mine it."

"And mining with the nanites will be much easier than using regular methods," Max replied, mimicking that same smile. *"I could modify commercial remote-operated drones to search for it. There is a schematic in the ship's memory banks for ore detectors that can find gold and other precious metals too. Of course, first, you need to go into town and buy a few drones."*

"Could you make them yourself?" Michael asked.

"Sure, if I had the designs and materials it wouldn't be that hard, even one working model could make reverse-engineering a piece of cake, but as I said, we're running a little low on almost everything right now. I cannot even make an educated guess without checking some things on the net."

"Well, in that case, I think a shopping trip is in order," Michael said, standing up from the pilot's chair.

* * *

It wasn't that long ago that Michael drove up this same road but he felt as if that had been in another lifetime. Not exactly *smooth sailing* down the rundown surface but he noticed that his reaction speed was vastly improved. His sight was more focused, sharper, and reflexes considerably faster. Even his sense of smell was better, judging by that cup of coffee he brewed before heading to town.

An hour later he was entering a rather small, rural place with a declining population. It was a growing problem all over the nation since most of the young people wanted to live in the big cities. Max made a long list of the things that he deemed as essentials and Michael was already thinking of the workout his credit card was going to have today.

After grabbing a fast breakfast at the local diner, he had to visit every electronics store in town to buy enough drones and various things Max wanted. He even managed to score a whole box of old, outdated processors from a local computer repair shop; the owner was more than happy to get rid of all that old junk for a small profit. It was useless crap to him that was using up shelf space.

Michael's essentials covered food and beer as, for some reason, his supply was getting a bit low. He spent half an hour in a local coffee shop so he could use their Wi-Fi and check his email. He also needed to catch up on the news of the past month, which turned out to be a depressing experience. Terrorist attacks, economic tumbles, deaths, and crimes. The same kinds of stories that permeated the news in recent years, sorrow, misery, and suffering. Politicians bickered among themselves over trivial things leaving the big issues alone, unless it was some empty speech to boost their popularity in the next elections. He wrote a few emails to his father and some of his friends to let them know he was alive and to get his mind off the depressing news. He closed the web browser, finished his cup of coffee, and went to do the rest of the things he came to town for.

The process of opening a satellite Internet account was a time-consuming hassle. He would be paying through the nose for an unreliable and rather slow connection. Just getting the equipment was an exercise in patience. The clerk kept trying his best to convince him that the equipment needed to be installed by their technical crew, for which he would have to pay additional fees, of course. Michael insisted that he would do the installation himself; after all, how hard is it to set up a satellite dish? Eventually, the clerk relented and accepted the fact that he would not get to slip in additional charges, which was good considering that Michael was close to knocking the pushy salesman on his ass.

With a full trunk, he returned to the cabin, trying to figure out how he was going to take all those boxes to the ship.

"Maybe this will help," said Max, as Michael was exiting the truck.

The six-foot (1.8 m) rectangular object, which was hovering in front of his porch, was not something he expected to see.

"Max, what is that thing?"

"For all intents and purposes, it's a medical stretcher, well... you know what I mean. It's the same one that brought you from the bottom of the entrance shaft to the AutoDoc; I'm repurposing it to carry cargo."

Now, having a computer or CEI in his head while talking to a real AI was beyond amazing, but looking at the hovering board was simply cool. It immediately reminded him of one of his childhood favorite comic superheroes; Michael wondered if it could be ridden like a surfboard. He loaded all the boxes meant for the ship on it and put his groceries inside the cabin.

He started walking towards the entrance of the ship, the board steadily following him like a dog on a leash. What really dropped his jaw to the ground was when he got to the entrance shaft and figured out that there was no way to lower the loaded stretcher in its horizontal position, the opening was too small, so he reached for the boxes to bring them down one by one.

"Wait for a second, and watch this," Max's voice commented smugly through his CEI.

The stretcher turned vertical, without any of the boxes dropping from it, as if they were superglued to it.

"How in the world is it doing that?" he asked, looking at the cool new magic trick.

"Simply increasing gravity's pull closer to its surface; we better hurry since all that weight is taxing it beyond recommended parameters and its battery charge is almost empty."

His next surprise came when Max instructed him to put the outdated computer chips into a receptacle that slid out of the wall. It was a three-foot (0.9 m) drawer filled with a silvery-looking goo. After he fed all the parts into it, Michael looked at the old computer chips as they were consumed by the billions of nanites. The process looked exactly the same as a video he saw online of a ferromagnetic putty wrapping itself around a neodymium magnet.

"It is a mini nano-factory," Max explained. *"Its function is to take scrap, and using that extracted material, to quickly replicate some essential parts; the nanites could do the same on-site, but this saves a lot of time. If there is enough source material, they can assemble anything you can think of, one molecule at a time,"* the AI said with a proud smile.

Next, he had to secure a satellite dish and radio antenna on a nearby rock outcropping. It was a good thing he'd bought an extra cable to reach the spaceship. The irony was not lost on Michael. Here he was, someone with the most advanced piece of tech on the entire planet and he was running a cable to get an Internet signal.

"Once we get our feet off the ground, everything will be much easier and faster," the AI said. While Max was trying to cheer him up, Michael was thinking of what else they could feed into the nano-factory.

The ship was a mostly closed system. Other than absorbing water from outside, it had everything needed to stay in optimal condition for all time; recycling failing components over and over again. Making Michael's CEI had used up the last of some rare materials, so he made a trip back to the cabin to look for anything they could reclaim.

The shed his grandfather used for storage was full of broken stuff he never got around to getting rid of. An old, rusty CB radio and a few walkie-talkies found their way into the nanite mini-factory. Even mundane things like plastic bottles and broken glass were found useful. For the rest of the day, he fed many things most would consider worthless to the nanites for them to disassemble. Max asked him to even throw in his regular trash into the nano-disassembler since there were so many useful base materials that could be extracted from it.

It was getting late and there was nothing more he could find for the insatiable nanites to break down to basic components, so he returned to the cabin, made himself something to eat, enjoyed one more beer on the porch, and went to sleep.

CHAPTER 4

Ozark Mountains - The Spaceship

"OK, the drones are ready, come to the control room, so we can get this show on the road," Max said when Michael came to the ship the next morning. The front wall of the bridge turned into one giant holo-screen with the combined topographical map of the surrounding terrain in the central position, and four separate video feeds from the drones placed all around it.

"I modified them to have extended range and flight time. They can now stay in the air for a few days. There is a miniaturized metal detector combined with a ground-penetrating radar mounted on their frames and it has been calibrated to differentiate gold from other metals."

Michael could see drones following the stream up the mountain. Some places showed small pockets of yellow, only in trace amounts, unfortunately. A lot less in the familiar spots, where his grandfather had already panned for it in the past.

The drones slowly followed the watercourse up the mountain, four of them taking multiple passes over more promising areas. There was far more gold in the higher, harder-to-reach elevations.

And gold, being a very heavy metal, tended to fill all those nooks and crannies where the stream made deeper spots at its bottom. The amount that actually washed down towards the valley was much smaller than what accumulated higher up.

Michael wondered for a moment why his grandfather had never made a serious effort to pan higher up the mountain, but then remembered that the old man never took more than he needed, for him that gold stream was like a bank vault.

After an hour, two drones started circling one position where the yellow color was predominant in the stream, and the transmitted image of the other two, who went to check upstream, showed that there was no more gold in the water above that spot.

"Max, give me a close-up on that place," Michael said excitedly.

Sparkling in the water, gold mixed with white quartz was reflecting the bright morning sun onto surrounding stone formations. A big grin plastered on his face; his only pang of sorrow was that his grandfather never got the chance to see it. This was the place where all the gold his grandfather had panned originated, a mother lode.

The biggest problem Michael saw was that all those gold deposits were in an inaccessible location. High, sharp cliffs were on both sides of the stream, and there was no way he could ever get to it without some professional climbing equipment; even then, it would be quite dangerous. That was the reason this particular deposit had never been found.

Luckily, he didn't have to do a thing, thanks to Max who had planned the entire mining operation in advance. The drones would carry more rugged, mining nanites, to the site, and they would extract the gold directly from the quartz that surrounded it. Then, the drones would carry the gold to the ship. It reminded him of playing one of those strategic simulation video games where everything was done remotely, and the object was to collect as many resources as possible to create additional structures. Which wasn't so far-fetched from what they needed to do.

"How fast can we get to it?" he asked after Max explained the extraction process to him.

"We could begin collecting it immediately, that box of old processors you brought helped immensely. The problem is that some of the necessary materials I need for mining nanites are found only in trace amounts. The drones' modifications and the first batch of mining nanites used most of it up. You need to get us more stock material to speed up the entire operation."

"Can we order the necessary materials online?"

"We could, but rare refined metals are quite expensive, and it would take time for our orders to arrive. There is also a downside to ordering precious and rare metals in the quantities we need—it will be noticed. We agreed that this venture needs to be as low-key as possible, and that would be a big red flag for some regulatory agencies. Buying directly from that E-waste recycling plant is still our best option, as nobody cares enough about it to ask questions."

"Okay, I'll try to make a deal; let's see how that goes."

* * *

E-waste Recycling Plant

The first thing that Michael noticed, driving close to the recycling plant, was that there were big piles of old computers and broken electronics lying around on the ground. The plant was located some distance outside the town and was bigger than he had originally assumed when he first passed by it. What worried him was the strange absence of any sound coming from the plant; it was a workday, but it seemed that there were no workers inside. He parked in front of the main gate and pressed the small intercom button on the side, hoping that someone would answer.

After a few minutes, just as Michael was thinking that there was no one on the premises, a very old man exited a small trailer that was parked beside the main building.

Years had taken their toll on him; he walked slowly as if he was in pain. It took him some time to arrive at the front gate.

"How can I help you, young man?" he asked when he came closer to Michael.

"Well sir, I need to buy a truck full of electronic scrap, old computer processors and motherboards. I hope you can help me."

The old man squinted while looking at him and came a bit closer.

"You are Mike, aren't you? John's grandson," he said after studying Michael's face for a few seconds.

Michael's eyebrows rose higher. This was the first time someone had recognized him; the young boy who'd left this area had little in common with the man he had become.

"Yes sir, I am. Did you know my grandfather?"

"Oh yeah, John and I went way back, he was quite the character," he answered, smiling at the fond memory. "The last time I saw you was at his funeral. It's been a while, but my memory still works fine, even if the rest of my body is a bit rusty," he continued, unlocking the gate. "Well, come in. I have a few cold beers in the fridge and it's an awfully hot day."

Over the cold drinks, the old man told Michael his life story. His name was David, or Dave for short, and he just wanted someone to talk to. He was alone since his wife died years ago and this E-waste recycling plant was all he had… or didn't, if the bank was to be asked.

He'd started it decades ago when business was booming, reasoning that with people always replacing their electronic gadgets for newer models, he could make decent money by recycling all that electronic trash. For a long time, business was good but then everything changed. US companies started sending their E-waste to Ghana in Africa. It was far cheaper transporting it overseas than disposing of it in the United States, where there are many safety regulations that needed to be followed and fees they didn't want to pay. Ghana, on the other hand, didn't have any, or if it did, nobody cared. Why would they when a fist full of Dollars could grease many palms. Instead of closing the plant, Dave kept at it, thinking that things would turn around; they didn't, and his situation progressed from bad to worse.

Before he knew it, he was in deep debt. Dave had even sold his house and all the recycling machinery; he would've sold the plant too, but nobody was buying. He was in so much debt that he couldn't even sell what he had on the premises because the bank and lawyers eventually took it. Very soon, it would all go to auction to be sold for scrap to pay all outstanding bills. He wasn't supposed to even be here but there was nowhere else for him to go. At one point, while telling his life story, tears started running down Dave's face.

It was a heartbreaking sight, a once-proud man broken by the world. Michael could see that Dave's body was in rough shape, his face gave away how much physical pain he was in, with swollen joints indicating an advanced stage of arthritis.

"Max, are you there?" Michael asked through his implant.

"Yes, I'm relaying the connection through the Internet and cell towers. You want to help him, don't you?"

"I do. Is there a way to transfer some of my medical nanites to him?"

"Since he doesn't have a CEI, it's going to be rudimentary at best. I can control them remotely, but it will be much slower."

"Let's do it, what do you need me to do?"

"You need to touch his skin with your right hand. I'll concentrate the nanites for the transfer to the surface of your palm.

Shake his hand for a few seconds when you are leaving, and it will be done."

"Okay Max, thanks," Michael replied internally.

The old man grew silent, looking through the small trailer's window with a detached look of hopelessness. Michael decided to run with the idea he got during their conversation.

"Dave, I want to make you a proposition. I recently came into quite a lot of money and I'd be willing to buy this plant from the bank and settle all your debts. Now, I have some other obligations that require me to take long trips, so I can't be around here much. Would you be willing to stay here and run it for me?"

Dave's face showed a mix of shock and disbelief. His shaking hand moved toward his chin, but then he paused and looked at Michael.

"Mike, I appreciate the offer, I really do. But you must realize that there is no way to make any money out of this place; this plant is like a bottomless pit and you'll be throwing your money away."

The fact that he didn't immediately jump on the deal made Michael even more confident in his decision. He knew that most people wouldn't even think twice.

"Yes, I'm sure. I'm in possession of some new technologies that'll make the purchase profitable for me," he answered, hoping that the nanites gold mining would prove lucrative. If it didn't, his mouth had just written a check that his ass couldn't cash.

The old man sat there for a while, staring through a dirty trailer window. Michael could tell the exact moment Dave made up his mind. His face looked a little less troubled, and his backbone was a little straighter.

He nodded and smiled, offering his hand for Michael to shake. "If you're sure, then yes! It would mean everything to me, Mike... thank you."

Before Michael left, Dave insisted on filling up his truck with the best electronic scrap they could gather and wouldn't even take any money for it, no matter how much Michael insisted. They agreed to meet in a week to talk about the legalities of the recycling plant purchase.

Taking all that scrap wasn't exactly legal, the bank would undoubtedly disapprove, but they couldn't object to something they didn't know about. Besides, neither Dave nor he had any intention of telling them.

* * *

"Do you think we can pull it off? Part of me feels like we are counting chickens before they hatch. If we don't have enough money in time there will be no way to settle Dave's debt with the bank," he asked Max while driving up to the cabin.

"We're already collecting a fair amount, and with all that material you are bringing, there will be a considerable increase in production. By my calculation, very soon, the money will stop being a problem."

He repeated the process from the day before, transferring boxes from his truck to the ship, and dumping it all into the small nano-factory.

"That is all of it," Michael said after the last box had gone inside.

"It should be enough for building all the mining nanites we will need," Max happily replied.

Michael had just finished washing his hands in the ship's bathroom when he noticed one drone hovering beside the AI's hologram, on the ship's bridge.

"Hold out your hand," Max instructed.

The small cargo doors on the belly of the drone opened and a tiny gold bar fell into his hand.

"The drones have already gathered more than that, but that's

the first troy ounce of gold we collected," the AI said, with a smug grin.

That little gold bar represented the foundation of the future Michael had envisioned. He rubbed it between his fingers, some tangible proof that his plan was getting off the ground.

"Thank you, Max," he said after a few moments, and then looked at the hologram before him. "Are you monitoring Dave's condition?"

"Yes, his health is improving, but too slowly for him to notice. You were just in time. Aside from arthritis, his heart wouldn't have lasted for very much longer. There is one other thing I wanted to talk to you about," Max said with a slight, but noticeable hesitation.

"Michael... you do realize that the nanites in your body constantly repair all damage, right?"

"Yes, you've told me that before," he answered, wondering where Max was going with this.

"Well, has it ever occurred to you that old age is just a process in which the information in your cells gets damaged, so they make errors during the cell division? The nanites in your body are repairing those errors, though. So... in a way, you are now immortal."

There are certain moments in life when new information just hits you like a freight train out of the blue, and for Michael—this was one of them.

"Only substantial damage to your brain would quickly kill you, or trauma that was so extensive that the nanites couldn't compensate. Everything else can be repaired. If you avoid those two situations, you could theoretically live forever."

Michael was rooted to the spot, his mind in turmoil. He had a problem with thinking clearly. The implications of Max's words were so out there, impossible to take in. It did make a certain kind of sense, he guessed. If the nanites had been able to repair his body when it was practically shattered, then being able to extend his life span was a logical continuation of such advanced technology. He'd never thought about those microscopic robots directly repairing his very cells.

"Max... I'm tired and need sleep, I can't think about that right now," he said looking at the AI, who had a knowing look on his face.

He returned to his cabin, still clutching that little gold bar in his hand. Sleep only came after he managed to set his nanites into sleep mode, and then increase the alcohol content in his blood with more than a few beers.

* * *

Ozark Mountains - The Cabin

Michael woke up with the first rays of the sun, and then stayed in his bed for a while, with only one thought running through his mind. *I am immortal.*

After making himself breakfast and a fresh cup of coffee, he sat in his usual chair on the porch.

"Max, if the technology to make someone immortal was in the ship's bag of tricks, how come there aren't any immortal aliens running around?" he asked after taking the last sip of the dark brew.

"They probably died," Max answered. *"Being biologically immortal and unkillable are two entirely different things. As I said, while extensive injuries to your body can be repaired, if a bullet hits your brain, or if your injuries go past the threshold of your nanites' ability to repair, you will be completely and irrevocably dead. You can drown, be electrocuted, decapitated, and many other things. The law of probability will eventually get the better of you; you get the benefit of not aging, but you still need to*

take care of yourself. It's not like you have magically turned into a superhero, just an enhanced human being."

That was easier to take in since he didn't like the idea of living forever; deep inside he felt there was something inhuman and cold about it.

"So... giving other people the same advantages would be relatively easy?"

There was a noticeable pause in Max's answer.

"Yes... theoretically. For medical nanites to be fully operational you'd need a CEI to monitor and control them, or lacking one you would need me. Even now, I'm controlling those you transferred to Dave by satellite connection, which takes considerable bandwidth. However, if I lose the connection, they would stop functioning. It is a safety precaution. I could remotely control medical nanites in a few more people, although that would strain my processes. A CEI is far better suited for it."

Michael nodded and looked at the beautiful scenery spread before his eyes; the splendor of the idyllic green valley clashed with his gloomy thoughts.

"Max, if anyone found out about this I would become the most hunted individual on the planet. All the other tech on the ship, no matter how valuable, is trivial compared to this one. Immortality is more dangerous than anything I can think of at the moment. In the past, worldwide wars have started over things that were insignificant in comparison."

A cold shiver ran down his spine. He knew that from the beginning of history people had searched for the fabled fountain of youth... and Michael had it.

"No matter what else, keep this under wraps, I'm not sure if we should even share it with those we recruit. It is an extremely volatile piece of information."

"Okay Michael, but you know that in time this too is going to come out, secrets like this are too slippery to hold onto."

Michael closed his eyes and nodded. "I know, we are playing for time here. I just hope there will be enough of it."

Governments, criminals, and the rich and powerful would sell their own mothers down the river for a slice of eternal life. As long as they could reach him—he would never be safe. That solidified his resolve to get off this beautiful blue marble. He had to get far away from their greedy hands.

And this technology could never become available to the general human population. That would cause... the word Armageddon popped into his mind. People already worried about overpopulation, water and food shortages, and demand for more space. Add the problem of nobody dying and the situation would soon be a thousand times worse. He didn't need to consult with Max to see the probable outcome of that scenario.

In space, longevity would be a great boon, a way to steadily increase the population. There was unlimited room for expansion out there. Here on earth... it would be like throwing water on an oil fire.

Michael took the rest of the day off, leaving Max to deal with the gold extraction. He fixed a few things around the house and chopped some wood for the winter. It felt good to use his strength for such mundane tasks; the menial, repetitive action calmed his troubled mind and had a meditative quality to it.

* * *

Ozark Mountains - The Cabin

Michael was finishing his morning cup of coffee with a satisfied smile on his face. A few cords of wood stacked close to the porch, a testament to yesterday's hard work. The day off was just what he'd needed, to slow down the hectic speed of the past few days.

"Hey, Max, where are we with the gold extraction?"

"It's going better than I thought it would," The AI answered. *"Those additional mining nanites that were made from Dave's scrap sped up the process exponentially, and it helped a lot when they found a big pocket of almost pure gold a few feet underground."*

It was far more satisfying to dig up gold with his own two hands so it saddened Michael that he couldn't do that. Even so, they needed money fast, so technological extraction would just have to do.

"How much gold did they manage to collect?"

"As of this morning, it's almost 5000 troy ounces," Max proudly replied.

The sip of coffee he was taking went down the wrong pipe and it took him a few minutes to stop coughing it up.

"How in the world did they manage to find that much gold and collect it!?" he shouted. "They have only been at it for less than two days."

"They don't take breaks, or sleep. It went slowly at first, but that pocket contained almost 4000 troy ounces of easily accessible gold. The drones are making constant trips back and forth, and it adds up," Max said, pleased with his accomplishment.

"That... is... Jesus Christ, I don't think that gramps and I panned even a fraction of that in all those years," Michael said, still having a hard time believing the amount of extracted gold.

"The nano-factory has already turned it into gold bullion, ready for transportation."

Michael did a quick calculation on his CEI, "That is worth over... $6 million," he said in an awed voice, part of him having a hard time believing that the mining nanites could manage to collect such a large amount of the precious metal. Another calculation told him it weighed more than three hundred and forty pounds (150 kg); not something to carry in a briefcase. He knew that transporting that much gold would be a challenge.

"First, we need to find a way to sell it without bringing unwanted attention to ourselves. The *powers that be* would notice such a large amount if we go through legal channels, and I have no intention of paying taxes on it. The Internal Revenue Service may strongly disagree with that but it has to be sold under the table. Not to mention that people tend to get a little crazy at the sight of gold and I want to preserve grandfather's legacy of keeping the mountain in a pristine condition."

"I might have an idea of how we can sell it," Max said with a distinct hesitancy in his voice.

"Well… spill it," Michael prompted, after another long pause.

"It would mean dealing with some rather shady elements of society. I've been looking through some files in police databases, and there is a Russian who deals in gold," Max replied. *"The government suspects him, but they haven't managed to pin him down. I could arrange a meeting with him, using the darknet to make contact. It is not the best option but it's the fastest way to turn all that gold into cash."*

Michael knew that working with criminals was not a good idea since there was always a chance for things to go wrong, but they had limited choices right now. Weighing the pros and cons were foremost in his mind but, as they say, sometimes you need to choose the lesser of two evils.

"Set it up."

CHAPTER 5

Saint Mary's Hospital - Intensive Care Unit

Elizabeth Miles was sitting beside her sister's bed. Worry lines were etched on her face as she looked at the only person that meant anything to her in this cruel and callous world. The bruised and battered girl was unconscious, lying in a hospital bed with tubes and wires connecting her to the machines that were keeping her alive.

"I am so sorry Anna, I failed you," she whispered in a trembling voice.

Silent tears were sliding down her face, leaving damp marks on the white bedsheet. She was saying goodbye because there was a chance that she would not survive what she planned for tonight.

Anna was her only family. They had been orphaned when Elizabeth was eighteen years old and Anna only ten. From that moment, she had a compulsive drive to protect her sister and provide a good life for her. In the end—she had utterly failed at that.

All her life she struggled to be better; that determination had propelled her to be one of the best investigative FBI intelligence analysts in her class. From that dreadful day when police officers had come to their house to tell them the life-shattering news, how their parents had died in a plane crash, Elizabeth knew it was her responsibility to create a better life for both of them and to do something meaningful with her life; something her parents would be proud of.

That life was destroyed on the day her sister was kidnapped while returning to the dorm from her classes where she was a freshman at a local college. A dark van, and two masked men who grabbed her from the sidewalk, were all that witnesses saw.

Elizabeth was frantic but she knew that succumbing to panic would not help her find Anna. Despite being forbidden to work her sister's case by her superiors', she did it anyway. Calling in all the favors and debts to get a copy of the original case files. She followed the leads, interrogated witnesses, analyzed every single piece of intelligence, and managed to find her sister two days later —it was two days too late.

A group of Albanian thugs involved in prostitution and white slavery was expanding their stable, and Anna was in the wrong place, at the wrong time.

The police raid on the old factory where the gang held Anna and a dozen other girls, was categorized as a success in the reports. Many underage girls were rescued from that appalling and dreadful place. Unfortunately, Anna had been beaten, raped, and filled with so many drugs that she had slipped into a coma. It was the standard procedure the gang used, drugging and breaking their captives until the victims did whatever was asked of them. Anna's stubbornness and fighting spirit caused them to single her out, and be exceptionally rough with her as an example to the other captives.

After a few weeks, the doctors told Elizabeth that due to the severe damage to her sister's organs, the machines were the only thing keeping Anna alive. There was no chance that she would ever wake up, and Elizabeth should say goodbye to her sister while there was still time. Sitting by Anna's bed she knew in her bones that without her sister, her life would be an empty and hollow existence.

The final thing that extinguished any respect she had for the legal system was that those thugs walked away on a technicality, with the help of a corrupt judge and a high-priced lawyer. They were supposed to rot in jail for a long time but now she could not give her sister even that sliver of justice.

Elizabeth quit her job and decided to take matters into her own hands. The only thing left for her was exacting revenge for what had happened to Anna. It went against everything she believed in, but the law she had sworn to uphold had been corrupted into a deplorable travesty. Instead of protecting law-abiding, ordinary people, now it seemed to protect mostly the criminals. For her, that was an unacceptable outcome and she could not let her sister die without settling accounts with those sadistic savages.

It took surprisingly little time to get her affairs in order. The hospital would keep Anna connected to the machines for a few more days but she didn't want to wait for that final closure. The gang headquarters was in an extremely guarded location and any direct form of attack on it would be suicidal, but a window of opportunity opened and she intended to take it.

One of her informants had told her that two of the men responsible for her sister's condition were making some kind of shady deal tonight, in an abandoned warehouse located in the industrial zone. That information hadn't come cheap but it was not like she had to save her money for the future.

There was one more thing for her to do before she left for the warehouse, to see her sister for one last time.

"I love you baby girl, and I'm sure we will be together soon, with mom and dad... we will be happy." Elizabeth kissed her

The Spaceship In The Stone

sister's forehead while gently stroking her hair. She took one more look at Anna's failing body which solidified her resolve for what she was about to do, and walked out of the room.

She arrived at the warehouse long before anyone else. There was old rusting machinery and big piles of old cardboard boxes inside. Finding a good hiding place with the best vantage point was not hard. Now the only thing to do was to wait for their arrival. Her car was hidden a mile away, as she didn't want to take any chances they would see her.

Tonight, she would find peace and get justice for Anna.

Elizabeth waited there for hours until a black sedan with dark tinted windows entered through the large, industrial-sized doors and parked in the middle of the vast space. Two people got out of the car and took two heavy army bags from the trunk. Trying not to make any sound, she stealthily crept closer to the car. The acoustics in such a big space were not ideal; still, she could hear them speak.

"He better come soon Yuri or it will be your neck on the line," the bigger man said, with a thick foreign accent.

"Da, yes, he will come. I made a deal, and everything will be as I promised," the other, shorter and nervous one responded fearfully, in what sounded to her like a Russian accent.

"You got yourself in trouble. If you hadn't borrowed money from the boss, none of this would be happening. If the man with the gold doesn't come, we will kill you," the bigger one snarled.

The Russian cringed after hearing that and Elizabeth saw his *Adam's apple* going up and down while he was looking at the man with his eyes wide open.

"What will you do to him?" the Russian asked in a small voice after a few moments.

"What do you think we will do? Our money stays with us and his gold will be ours too—after he is dead," he replied, with an evil grin showing his yellowed, crooked teeth.

Elizabeth's heart was beating fast, and her hand gripped the handle of the gun she'd bought from her informer. She recognized the big man as one of the thugs that had taken and raped Anna. The last time she saw that ugly face was in a courtroom; giving her a mocking leer and a nasty wink.

Even so, she did not want to act prematurely and needed for the other scumbag to show up; her informer was sure that both of them would be here tonight. Her mind was going in circles; *will I be able to do what I planned... become a killer?* Then an image of her sister, lying in a hospital bed and waiting to die, crossed her mind... *Yes, I will.*

A few minutes later, from the opposite side of the warehouse, an old pickup truck slowly drove in. Her jaw clenched, and all her stomach muscles tensed.

Soon... soon will be the time for her to act.

* * *

Michael was driving his grandfather's old Dodge pickup truck, painted dark blue, with rust stains on most of the chassis. He didn't want to use his car since it could be easily identified with modern technology. One camera shot of his license plate and the authorities, or the criminal he was about to make a deal with, could easily discover his identity. A generous coating of mud on the old truck's plates prevented that.

He doubted that the old rust bucket would even be able to start when he'd pushed it out from the old shed, but Max had instructed him to place a small container filled with the construction nanites on the motor, and an hour later the engine was purring like new.

Approaching the old warehouse, where the gold sale was to take place, gave Michael a very uneasy feeling. Quite similar to

The Spaceship In The Stone

how he'd felt while he was still in the military before the action was going to take place.

"Max, I have a bad feeling about this," he said as he slowed down and took a long look at the terrain around the warehouse.

"You can always turn back; we could try to sell the gold somewhere else. This deal was the fastest I could make for cash, probably not the best."

He thought about it for a minute, but he'd organized the schedule by which steps needed to be finished, and who knows how long it would take to line up another gold buyer. "No, let's get it over with now."

Michael looked at the shotgun that he'd brought along just in case. It was a shame he didn't have something more portable, like his favorite Smith & Wesson SW1911 he had for years. That gun was with one of his friends since his last girlfriend had abhorred weapons, and against his better judgment, he had taken it out of the house. The fact that he missed his gun more than he did her said a lot about that relationship, and particularly about the girl.

The shotgun was his grandfather's, a necessary tool when living deep in the woods and certainly better than nothing. Michael carefully drove the truck through the open warehouse doors, seeing something he hadn't expected.

In the middle of the warehouse, the light of the setting sun was streaming through the broken windows on the side of the building, and two men in suits were standing in front of a big black sedan.

This deal was already coming off the tracks; the agreement was that they would both arrive alone. He seriously thought about putting the truck in reverse and leaving quickly. Still, he was armed and a highly trained ex-soldier, and the gold buyer was most likely uncomfortable carrying all that cash by himself.

Michael stopped the car some thirty feet (9 m) in front of them and got out.

77

Two men looked at him with a heavy dose of suspicion. One was a big bodybuilder type, and the other was small and nervous, his eyes darting all over the place, with sweat shining on his forehead.

"Did you bring gold?" the big, brutish-looking one asked, raising his chin. There was something menacing in his eyes, the same thing Michael saw in his past vocation, the gaze of a predator. He had a heavy Eastern European accent, definitely not Russian. Michael's *spidey sense* was giving him all kinds of danger signals; something was not right with this picture.

"Did you bring the money?" Michael replied, instinctively feeling that this man was an enemy. This situation and the palpable tension were setting his teeth on edge, but backing away now would be dangerous.

The man knelt down and opened the zipper on one of the big army bags that were beside him. Inside it, Michael could see many stacks of rubber-banded bills.

"Here's money, show me the gold!" The man barked while taking out a few stacks of cash in his hand and letting them drop back into the bag.

Michael walked a few steps backward and opened the cover on the back of the truck. Taking one of the several gold containers Max had made, he put it on the ground and opened the lid. The fading sunlight shone on the small gold bars, reflecting in rich yellow hues.

"I hope this satisfies you, shall we make the exchange?" Michael said, never taking his eyes off the brute.

A greedy, savage smile appeared on the big man's lips, something primal and dangerous. With a practiced move, the man reached for his side and in the next second was holding a gun aimed at Michael. He recognized that weapon. A Czechoslovak vz. 61 machine pistol—also known as a *Škorpion*—with a rate of fire of 850 rounds/min.

The gun was hanging from a strap underneath the big man's armpit, which explained the long suit-jacket he was wearing. The move was simply too fast for Michael to do anything, so he held up his hands, palms turned towards the men, as non-threatening as possible. His mind was calculating how fast he could move to reach the shotgun that was, inconveniently, between the front seats of the truck. He should have listened to that voice of caution earlier, but as they say, *'pride comes before a fall'* and he'd made a rookie mistake. Civilian life had dulled the common sense of a warrior, and now he was paying the price.

The smaller man was backing off, and three more men got out of the sedan, carrying the same submachine guns in their hands.

"Max, this whole deal just went FUBAR!" He shouted in his head.

"I know Michael, and I need you to buy me some time. I'm trying to activate some systems within you. It will take a little while, so be ready when it happens. Don't think, just react," the AI promptly replied but he couldn't fully conceal the alarming note in his voice.

"I thought we had a deal, money for gold," Michael shouted, while his eyes tracked all his opponents. Four dangerous and armed men, with the look of experienced and hardened killers in their eyes, and the scared one, completely out of his element.

The big brute laughed loudly while walking closer to Michael. "People in this country are so trusting, it is like your saying, *taking candy from a baby*. We do what we want, and if we pay certain people, we do not even go to jail when we are caught. Don't worry, I will kill you slowly so that before you die you can learn that only strong men like me survive, and the weak like you always die."

The barrel of the man's gun was aimed to the side; in his sadistic gloating, he had gotten careless. His three helpers didn't even aim their guns at Michael, and just stood behind their leader, their stares filled with anticipation of the show that looked to have every indication of turning into a bloody one.

Several things happened in that moment; Michael's consciousness seemed to expand and a new strength infused his body while his sense of time got distorted. He could feel his muscles tensing, and his heart hammering in his chest like one of those Chinese drums, loud, fast, and unnatural. The big man was still talking, at least Michael thought he was because his movements were slowed down, and his voice had the quality of a video played at half speed.

"Now Michael!" Max shouted.

He considered going for his shotgun, but that would take a few seconds and it would give these men enough time to fill him full of holes, their weapons rate of fire was quite unforgiving.

The big guy turned his head a little to the side, telling his friends something funny in a foreign language when Michael acted. He rushed towards the man while part of his mind wondered if he was insane. Normally you run away from people with guns but, in this case, that was a recipe for a quick death. His only advantage was to do something unexpected.

He was faster than ever before and, in little more than a second, he reached the leader as the guy's eyes were starting to widen; the barrel of his gun was still pointing to the side. With all of his strength, Michael hit him in the face and, in that split-second, saw pressure waves expanding from the point of impact as if the man's flesh was made of *jello*. The other three men's hands were raising in his direction and part of him knew that he would never be able to take them all.

The piercing sounds of a large caliber gun discharging echoed through the warehouse, multiple shots, one after the other. The head of the one man in the back jerked sideways, a red cloud of blood and brain matter blossoming behind it. His head had

The Spaceship In The Stone

acquired an additional hole, a condition that was never good for one's health.

Michael didn't know who the shooter was but he was not going to waste this opportunity, so he jumped at the second guy who was momentarily distracted by his friend's sudden death. One of Michael's hands reached for the man's gun so it couldn't be used against him, while the other went for the man's throat. A few more shots boomed inside the warehouse, and out of the corner of his eye, Michael could see the last man getting shot in the stomach and falling back inside the car from the transferred kinetic energy of the bullet.

Rapid gunfire burst out as the man's hand squeezed the trigger while wrestling with Michael. They both fell to the ground and the gun went flying beneath the car. Michael was above him, choking his opponent with all of his strength; his fingers like a vise, increasing the pressure until the man's throat collapsed. He wasn't dead yet but it was just a matter of time. The man's eyes were wide open and his face was slowly turning blue from lack of oxygen.

There was no time to waste so he quickly got up and started to turn toward the leader he had punched first, when a great force hit him from behind and threw him back onto the ground. The analytical part of him knew what had happened. The gun noise before the blow told as much… he was shot.

It was the leader, with blood pouring down from his flattened nose and a bloody smile that was missing a few front teeth. Michael knew this was the end; the smoking barrel of that gun was pointed directly at his head.

"I told you I will kill you!" the man sneered.

As the gun went off for a second time, a body appeared in front of Michael, slamming the man against the car. From the spasms of that body, he knew that the bullet meant for him never reached his flesh. It hit the person who saved his life—again.

Close to his hand he saw a gun beneath the car and reached for it, and without even thinking, he pointed it at the big man who was raising his gun again and quickly pressed the trigger. Two in the chest, one in the head.

A heavy silence spread inside the warehouse. Michael's perception of slowed time stopped after being shot. He got to his feet again, despite the excruciating pain that was spreading from his back.

The body of the person who'd saved him was lying in front of him with their face pressed against the ground. He fell to his knees and slowly turned it over. To his surprise, it was a 20-something girl, not at all what he was expecting.

The blood had stained her white shirt when the bullet intended for him had caught her, so he pressed his hand over the entrance wound on her chest and applied pressure, old lessons from battlefield first aid coming to his mind.

"Max, can you do something!?"

"I already am. Keep your hand there."

The girl slowly opened her eyes, looking confused and in pain.

"Hold still, I'm trying to help you," Michael said, but in her eyes was the look of resignation.

"Why did you do it?" he asked her, "why did you jump in front of me?"

"I... I was out of bullets... and wanted to do one decent thing before I die, to save one life... for Anna," she answered in a faint voice.

"Michael, the nanite transfer is too slow, I need you to cut open your hand and press it against her wound, so I can transfer a larger number of them," the AI promptly instructed him.

Michael used an old pocket knife that he always carried with him, and made an incision across his palm. His blood had a metallic shine to it, millions of nanites concentrated within the life-sustaining fluid. He quickly returned his bloody hand to the girl's gaping wound.

She was not even aware of what he was doing; the light in her eyes was dimming.

"What is your name?" Michael asked.

"Elizabeth..." she quietly breathed out and closed her eyes.

"Max, what's happening?"

"She is safe for now, but you need to get her to the AutoDoc, the bullet is still lodged beside her heart, and doing anything where you are would be a risk. I put her to sleep; it's less taxing on her system."

Michael lifted her as gently as he could and laid her in the backseat of his truck. He could see that her wound already looked different… it was not bleeding anymore. He looked and saw the cut on his hand was scabbing over and at the same time noticed that there was no pain from his gunshot wound; his entire body felt numb.

"Why don't I feel any pain?" he asked after making sure she would be comfortable.

"I had to suppress all the pain receptors in your body or you wouldn't be able to move. You have torn muscles, hairline fractures in several bones, and a bullet in your back. The sooner you can get to the AutoDoc, the better. The nanites inside you are not sufficient to fix your body; they are now acting as more of a Band-Aid."

Now that Max mentioned it, his body felt different, slower. He was so tired and felt strangely detached.

"Michael, you need to take the money and destroy the evidence. There is enough of your DNA in this place for any forensic team to easily find you."

He went back to the black sedan, seeing dead bodies everywhere; in the backseat, the last of the thugs was holding his stomach. Several gunshot wounds could be seen on his torso, so it was surprising that he was still alive. Michael picked up the gun from the floor and pointed it at the dying man.

"You cannot kill me, I am unarmed," the man whined through the pain, but without any remorse in his eyes.

Michael shook his head, "When you point a weapon at someone, you are making a declaration of intent and your intent was to kill me. I'm just returning the sentiment." With those words, he pulled the trigger.

The last body was lying a few feet from the car; it was the dead body of the small Russian. One of the bullets must have hit him while he was hiding behind the car.

Michael carried the bags with the money, and the gold container he previously took out, to his grandfather's truck. The money was not so bad but the weight of that single container took a lot out of him. He was glad he didn't unload more of them.

Ripping the shirt from one of the dead guys, he made a 6-foot (1.8 m) long makeshift fuse which he stuck inside the sedan's gas tank. There were enough old boxes and rotting piles of lumber inside to make sure no trace of him remained.

Michael set it on fire with his lighter, stumbled to his truck, and drove out of the warehouse. A minute later, a loud explosion announced the sedan's destruction, and very soon, smoke and fire engulfed the entire building.

"Talk to me Max, is she alright?"

"She's fine and by tomorrow she should be as good as new. It's you that I'm concerned about. Your body is running on reserves that are fast running out. Try not to fall asleep," the AI worriedly said.

"I'll make it," Michael mumbled. "This feels like being back in action. Adrenaline keeps you awake sometime after the bullets stop flying."

The trip back to the cabin was thankfully uneventful. One speeding police car with its siren on, followed by a fire truck, had passed by him, a few miles away from the warehouse. He did not think there was any chance of them connecting him to the crime scene he'd left behind.

The last part of the drive was the hardest. The old truck didn't appreciate the rundown road conditions, and the shocks struggled to absorb all the bumps and holes underneath them.

Michael smiled as he saw the familiar stretcher waiting in front of the cabin, it would make moving Elizabeth to the spaceship much easier. He transferred her unconscious body onto it and started walking toward the ship's entrance. It took some time and, for most of the trip, he was holding on to the stretcher that Elizabeth lay on, letting it drag him along.

The stretcher repeated the trick with the controlled gravity, descending down the entrance shaft, while he had to struggle to climb down the metal ladder.

Max's hologram was waiting inside the airlock with a worried look in his eyes and a guilty expression on his face. Once inside the AutoDoc, Michael laid her on the bed.

"Michael, you need to lay down beside her. Your body is about to shut down," the AI ordered.

A medical hologram of his own body appeared in front of the bed, with muscles, bones, and internal organs all colored red. He could even see a gray bullet, embedded inside his stomach.

There was enough room beside Elizabeth to lay down, so he did. In the next second, he was out like a light.

CHAPTER 6

Ozark Mountains - The Spaceship

"Damn," Michael said, after seeing the same white ceiling above him. The big difference from all the previous times he woke up here was a young woman lying beside him.

It took him a moment to remember the disastrous gold deal, the shoot-out and the trip to the cabin.

"Max… why am I naked again?" he asked, looking down at his body. "And why is she wearing a hospital gown?" He pointed with his chin at the young woman.

"Well, I wanted to preserve her modesty, as for you… I didn't think you would mind," Max replied through his implant.

"How long has it been this time?" He really hoped that he hadn't laid on the bed for three weeks like the first time.

"Almost twelve hours, the AutoDoc had to do a lot of work on both of you."

Michael closed his eyes and recalled one thing that was bugging him from last night.

"What happened to my body, when time slowed down during the fight?"

The AI materialized his hologram beside the bed. *"What you experienced is something I've been working on for a while; I call it a 'Boost'. It's a cocktail of adrenaline and various organically produced chemicals that increase your physical and cognitive functions. Until last night, it was all just a working theory of mine, a virtual experiment. For a time, you were juiced up as no athlete using performance-enhancing drugs ever was."* Max gave him a guilty look. *"Your body was not prepared for that, without the nanites to constantly repair the damage... your heart would've burst."*

Michael could see the remorse Max felt, and part of him was worried about the AI activating weird functions of his CEI, then again, it saved his life, so he chose to simply accept the whole thing as one more aspect of his new crazy life.

"Hey, we got out of there alive, so that is all that matters, don't worry about it."

There was a pensive look on the hologram's face. *"It was my fault; I should have traced the connection between the Russian and those thugs—"*

"And hindsight is 20/20. You may be a very powerful AI now but that doesn't make you a god, so mistakes will happen. Do not let them bring you down, learn from them," Michael replied. "And you made me sound like gramps right now, damn it," he finished with a grin.

"Yeah... I'll work on it," the hologram nodded, exhaling a long breath.

"When will she wake up?" Michael said as he got out of bed, his hand rubbing the place where his latest gunshot wound used to be.

He looked at Elizabeth lying on the bed with a peaceful look on her face and noticed that she was quite beautiful. Shoulder-length honey-colored hair, strong and pleasant facial features that made quite an impression.

"I could wake her up right now, she is almost completely healed. The bullet was removed, and all the damaged tissue was knitted together just as it was before. She just needs to replace some blood that was lost, but her body will do that on its own. I waited for your own healing to finish, so we could decide what to tell her, and you might like the opportunity to get dressed before we wake her."

That was the burning question on his mind; what should he tell her? She did save his life and he felt indebted to her, but she could compromise everything he was trying to achieve. Michael picked up his repaired clothes and asked, "What did you manage to find out about her?" as he began to get dressed.

"Quite a bit, as a matter of fact; I made a personnel file all the way from her birth to the present day. Most of it is from public databases and some... other sources."

A flashing icon on the edge of his vision informed Michael that a new file was downloaded to his CEI.

It didn't take long to browse through it, concentrating on the highlights and especially at recent events involving Elizabeth's sister. Max even made a correlation between the trial and the thugs that got away scot-free, and ended up dead and burned to a crisp in the warehouse. Overall, he had a good feeling about her, and he really needed some people he could trust, besides the few he already had in mind. The way she acted in that warehouse gave him an inkling that she could become one of those to trust.

"Before I wake her, there is one more thing I want to talk to you about."

"Shoot."

"Well... for a while, I've been trying to think of a way to make you more durable, and if recent events are any indicator, it has become a necessity. Your bones are easily breakable, and your muscles are not as resilient as they could be. So, I came up with a way to rectify that, observe."

The medical hologram that appeared in front of the bed was one he recognized, and yet he didn't. His skeletal system was now painted black, and his muscles were a mismatch of colors. He walked around the hologram, looking at the strange image.

"What is all this?"

"I have a lot of spare time on my hands and have been using some of it on discovering new ways to upgrade the human body. This is the final result of an upgrade I devised. Bones are sheeted with a mesh-like graphene structure, making them ten times stronger than steel, with only five percent of its density. Muscles are interwoven with composite fibers hundreds of times thinner than other man-made nanofibers and with a tensile strength stronger than spider silk. The same material is used for an armor-like mesh beneath the skin, making it more durable. However, it's not completely bulletproof, so... avoiding getting shot is still highly advisable. But most conventional rounds would only do damage to the epidermis, the outer layer of the skin, and wouldn't be able to penetrate the body cavity and internal organs. It would make you much more effective in a fight, and I have a suspicion that there will be more of those in the future."

As Max was making his presentation, certain sections of the hologram were magnified to be seen in microscopic details. It was way beyond anything Michael even thought possible, and not something that could be done with current human technology. He knew that the military would be overjoyed to have something like this. Their programs to create super soldiers often went to the darker side of experimentation, disregarding some finer points of ethics and morality.

"And finally, the Boost you experienced; with this upgrade, your system would be able to take full advantage of it, without the consequences you suffered last time. The Boost is a set of instructions that use your CEI to adjust the chemical composition of your blood, making certain glands secrete their products directly

into the bloodstream; it's a controlled endocrine system. For a while, it changes your perception of time and gives you more strength. As you are now, it's as damaging to you as your opponent. That first punch fractured several bones in your hand, only by the CEI suppressing your pain receptors were you able to function. The significant downside is that the Boost used much of your body's resources while it was active, and you almost collapsed after that. But with all these upgrades, it can be used to its full potential," the AI said confidently.

All of these upgrades and the possibilities they represented made Michael think for a moment that he would turn into something not quite human, yet he knew that this was an advantage that he simply could not let pass. All of his ambitious plans depended on him being alive to implement them, and last night, any one of those thugs could have easily stopped the future he envisioned for the human race... with one well-aimed bullet.

"How long would it take?"

"This is as invasive as it gets, and in the uncharted waters of human augmentation, so it would take some time. I've done multiple simulations and devised a procedure that will be done in stages. The nanites could be instructed to start preparations right now. You wouldn't feel anything because localized nerve endings would be suppressed from sending pain signals. It would be necessary for you to drink certain supplements, to give your nanites the materials they need to lay down the foundation for the final procedure. And at that stage it would require you to spend some time in the AutoDoc; I want to do everything as slowly as possible, just to be safe from any unforeseen side effects."

Michael took another long look at the medical hologram, as Max stood there, with a neutral look on his face.

"You can stop with that poker face, that was a good pitch. You know I can't refuse this... do it."

Max broke into a smile and said with badly suppressed glee. *"What can I say, I'm that good."*

"Yes, you are a regular Einstein with Dr. Frankenstein's sense of subtlety. Just don't drill any bolts into my neck, that would seriously cramp my style."

A CEI message popped into his view, stating *augmentation stage 1 has begun.* He dismissed it and tried to feel some change within himself, but there was nothing. He felt fine.

* * *

"Okay Max, wake her up," Michael said and the medical hologram, together with the AI, disappeared.

Elizabeth's eyes fluttered and slowly opened, as if she were rousing from a long sleep. She looked around and then locked her gaze with Michael. "Where… where am I?"

"That would take some time to explain, but you're in a safe place," Michael answered, not sure how to begin and not make it sound like she stumbled into a twilight zone episode.

She touched her chest and then her eyes opened wide when she looked underneath the hospital gown.

"But I was shot, and I saw the wound… I should be dead!" Her voice rose higher, while the expression on her face became confused and alarmed.

"Well, you certainly are not dead, and the wound was healed. Your clothes are underneath the bed. Why don't you put them on and join me when you're finished; I'll be waiting in the next room."

Michael exited through the door that slid open; Max had changed the color of the opening to be slightly darker, so it would be more visible. The next room, or the bridge of the ship, had some new additions, a table with two chairs. Made using recycled materials by the nanites. It made the room less sterile and gave two people a place to sit.

After a few minutes, Elizabeth entered, looking around at the strange and unfamiliar space.

"Please take a seat," said Michael, pointing at the chair opposite of his. "I know this must be quite confusing for you but if you'll sit and give me a few minutes I believe I can explain."

"Why do I feel that this is going to be something like Alice going through the Looking-Glass?" she said with a slight smile on her lips.

"Because it will. For me, it all started a few months ago…"

For the next hour, he told her the entire story from the beginning. What happened to him and what his plans were for the future. During his monologue she didn't interrupt, and he told Max to change the walls of the room. First was the forest clearing Max showed him originally, then several other scenes that were in the database, and even the one made from space that was so mesmerizing to him.

"So that brings us to now, how you came to be to this place, and how you were healed. What do you think?"

This was the moment he had been dreading, will she believe him or decide that he was some crazy guy with cool toys.

"I believe you, Michael," she said after a short pause. "This ship and my miraculous recovery just confirm it."

She then looked towards the ceiling. "Max, are you there?"

"Yes Elizabeth, I'm always here," Max said, and his hologram appeared beside them.

Elizabeth took a deep breath and nodded to herself, squinting her eyes as if she was thinking about something.

"I want to make you a deal," she said looking right into Michael's eyes with intense determination. "I believe that what you're planning is very noble, if a little over-ambitious. But there

The Spaceship In The Stone

will be many obstacles on the way—I can help you overcome a lot of them. Having said that, I need something from you…"

"If it is within my power, of course... I owe you my life," Michael answered, suspecting, from the information in her file, *where* she was heading.

"I have a sister, Anna, and she is on life support in a hospital. If you can help her like you helped me, I will owe you a debt that I can never repay," she said, still focused on Michael, not moving an inch. Her hands, which were on the table, squeezed one another with so much force, her fingers were making imprints on the skin.

Using his CEI he asked Max *"Do you have any information on her sister's condition?"*

"Yes, I hacked hospital records and it does not look good, but we will need to bring her here, and use the AutoDoc to perform a more detailed analysis," the AI replied in the same way.

Elizabeth was still looking at Michael, with a piercing gaze, utterly focused.

"I cannot make any promises but we will do everything we can. She will need to be brought here and placed in the AutoDoc before we can say anything with certainty," Michael finally replied.

"I looked at Anna's records; there is nothing modern medicine can do to help her. If there's any chance for her to make a recovery—it's here," Max said, looking at the anxious woman at the table.

"I'll do anything no matter how small the chance. Just tell me what you need me to do." Tears were forming in Elizabeth's eyes.

"Can you tell me how she was hurt? I'm familiar with some of the story, but not all the details," Michael said.

Elizabeth told them the entire story from her point of view, not leaving behind any sordid details. When she was going over some of the most disturbing parts, Michael's fists clenched until he could feel his nails digging into his palms. Whatever guilt he felt for taking the lives of those thugs disappeared. In fact, part of him wished that they were still alive, so he could kill them all over again.

"I'm so sorry," he told her after she was finished. It was what you were supposed to say when someone shares something so personal and painful with you, but it also sounded hollow and inadequate.

"I promise you we will do everything we can to help Anna."

Tears were sliding down her face, and for the first time, Michael could see the depth of her anguish and fanatical hope that shone from within.

"Thank you," Elizabeth whispered, wiping her face with the back of her hand.

* * *

It didn't take them long to come up with a plan. They'd need an ambulance and paramedics uniforms; Elizabeth had contacts from her previous job that could help with that. Max's assignment would be to deal with paperwork electronically and cover all their tracks, so nobody would be looking for Anna afterward. The entire operation was scheduled to be executed in the middle of the night as the staff and security of the night shift was far more lax.

"Come on, let's go to the cabin. I'm being a poor host and you should eat something," Michael said, and led Elizabeth to the exit, closing the entrance behind them.

"I still can't believe that this ship has been buried here for such a long time," Elizabeth said while looking at the visible portion of the ship's outer hull.

"Imagine my surprise when I practically fell on top of it," Michael joked, and winced internally at the memory of his fall.

He showed her the way out, and the closing mechanism on the top, which made the entrance shaft blend with the surrounding terrain. They walked to the cabin where she stood on the porch, soaking in the view.

"This place is beautiful; you could really unwind surrounded by this peace and quiet."

"That was my intention in coming here but some things intervened," Michael replied with a smile, and held the cabin door for her.

It was a strange feeling for him, having a guest here. Except for a few of his closest friends, he never brought anyone here. It was his hidden sanctuary from the world, even when he was away for years at the time. Just knowing this place was waiting for him gave him some small feeling of connection to the happy life he'd led here.

After a quick meal, they sat on the porch, enjoying the view and drinking freshly brewed coffee.

"You know it can all fail," Elizabeth said, after a while, looking at the valley. "Your plan, that is. There are so many unknowns and you will have to piss off a lot of important people in the process, not to mention various governments that will want their piece of the pie, as soon as you show up on their radar."

He smiled, remembering a similar conversation with Max. "Yeah, that was one of the major things Max and I worried about. There is no way to hide an operation of such magnitude, that is why I'm gambling on having enough time to escape their grasp before they find out enough to shut everything down. If we manage to gain the higher ground," Michael said, pointing at the sky, "well, then it is a whole new ballgame."

They sat there for a few hours, talking about their lives, and going over the plan to get Anna out of the hospital.

* * *

The first thing they did was go to the place where Elizabeth had hidden her car before the shootout. An old shed on the edge of an abandoned industrial building. A smart place to hide it, too far away for people to casually visit; even for the teenagers that loved spraying graffiti. And sufficiently distanced from the burned-down warehouse, so the police investigating the case wouldn't notice it.

"When I left it here, I thought there was a good chance I would never return to it," she quietly said after Michael parked beside the dark blue Toyota Prius.

"Don't think about that, it was in another life. Let's go, we have much to do," Michael said.

She got inside and followed Michael's Ram Power Wagon back to the cabin to park her car. They used side roads so the cameras would not pick it up. After leaving her car, they drove back to the location in his grandfather's truck, to a place where her contact said she could pick up an ambulance and the uniforms. Under the condition that they would return them in the morning along with a 'donation' of two thousand dollars. One hour later, they were dressed as paramedics and driving an ambulance to the hospital.

Considering that Elizabeth was known at the hospital, she had put on a lot of makeup and covered her hair with a baseball cap.

"Remember, act casually as if this is just another boring transfer," Elizabeth said as they were entering the building.

Michael gave her a short, sharp nod, knowing she was talking more to herself than him.

It took only minutes to finish all the paperwork. Max made sure that all the T's were crossed in the hospital system.

The nurse that showed them the way walked in front of Elizabeth and didn't see her shudder as they walked into Anna's room. They pushed the gurney in and looked again at the cheat sheet with the procedure for hooking her up to the mobile devices to keep her alive. Those were all necessary steps when transferring a high-risk patient. They went over it several times while preparing for this, to make sure everything was done right.

Anna was a sorry sight, barely holding onto her life; her skin was that unhealthy pale color people get when the end is coming close.

"Michael, you need to transfer some of your nanites to Anna before she is moved. In her condition she might not make the trip without them," Max said through his CEI, and Michael placed his hand on an exposed part of her skin, holding it there until life-saving nanites were transferred.

"It will take a few minutes for them to go where they need to."

He could see that standing beside her sister was very emotional for Elizabeth; she didn't make a sound, but her shoulders were shaking.

"What the hell is going on here!" an angry voice sounded from the room's door. A young man, wearing a doctor's coat, was standing there, looking like he had just been woken up.

"A patient transfer," Michael said, barely glancing at the young man.

"What patient transfer? Do you know what time it is? That patient is in a critical condition and is not going anywhere," he replied, rubbing the sleep from his face.

"We just take them from point A to point B, here's the paperwork," Michael said and pulled the prepared papers, officially stating that one Anna Miles was to be transferred to a long-term care facility.

The doctor looked at the documents, shaking his head, and mumbling to himself as he read through them.

"These seem to be in order, but it is still too risky, they should leave the poor girl alone, she doesn't have much time left," he murmured, returning the papers to Michael.

"Not our call, we're just doing our jobs," Michael answered

and turned toward Elizabeth. "Let's hurry up, we have one more transfer to do before the end of our shift." He tried to sound tired and bored despite the situation. The doctor indignantly shook his head and left the room.

She nodded and started disconnecting her sister from all the machines, carefully following Max's instructions through a small Bluetooth earpiece she'd been given.

Michael expected the doctor, or another hospital official, would try to stop them and call the police. They pushed Anna's gurney down the hall, into the elevator, and transferred her into the ambulance. He got behind the steering wheel and unhurriedly left the hospital parking lot.

The trip to the cabin was slow and extremely difficult on the last part of the mountain road. Still, he managed to bring them home without too many bumps, driving carefully and utilizing the vehicle's 4x4 drive to the max.

Elizabeth sat in the back, holding her sister's hand for the entire trip.

"She is stable now, you can unhook her from the machines," Max said after they stopped in front of the cabin.

Transferring Anna to the AutoDoc wasn't very difficult, with the help of a levitating stretcher. She still had that pale, unhealthy skin, but at least now she didn't need help to stay alive; her breathing was slow and steady.

They laid her on the AutoDoc's bed, and for the first time, Michael could see the machine at work. A transparent energy field shimmered around Anna's body, and there was that metallic goo, exiting the surface of the bed, like sweat from the pores. Once in contact with Anna's skin, it was absorbed.

Max's hologram appeared beside the bed.

"That is a standard sterile field, it keeps bacteria, viruses, and contamination at bay," he explained. *"She will need to be treated*

for a few days. There is a considerable amount of damage that those drugs did to her system. Some of her organs are turning necrotic; you got to her just in time. The AutoDoc can repair all the physical parts of her body, but until she wakes up, we will not know what the ordeal did to her mind. Now, if you will be so kind and exit the room, the nanites will dissolve her hospital gown for easier access. Don't worry Elizabeth, your sister is in good hands now."

Elizabeth looked once more at her sister and followed Michael out. The trip back to return the ambulance was mostly silent, the unsure fate of a young girl put a dark cloud over them.

They left the ambulance at the prearranged location and walked to the supermarket's parking lot, where Michael had left his grandfather's truck.

"What are your plans now?" Elizabeth asked while he was driving back to the cabin.

"We need to transfer that money to the bank; which reminds me, Max, create a shell corporation to hide our trail. Then, after buying Dave's recycling plant, we need to set up the operation for extracting the materials we need. And I need to recruit more people"

"Do you have someone in mind?" she asked.

"Yes, to begin with, I have some friends from my days in the military; some of them are disabled and disappointed in how they were treated after returning home."

His mind went over all the people he knew from the service and then afterward from the VA hospital. There were a few he was 100% sure would join him, and others that he put under the maybe column.

They made a quick dinner and Michael showed her a guest bedroom she could use.

Sleep was long in coming for both of them. Elizabeth was

thinking about her sister, but now with hope in her heart, praying that Anna would be okay. Michael, on the other hand, was trying to come up with a convincing way to tell his unbelievable story to the people he often entrusted his life to in the past, but who would still need a leap of faith to believe him, and not think he was drinking his own funny Kool-Aid.

CHAPTER 7

Ozark Mountains - The Spaceship

Elizabeth was looking at her sister, lying there motionless, and was wondering if she would make a full recovery. Max explained to her that while the nanites were perfectly capable of fixing the physical parts of the body, the mind was a far more complex thing. Anna was in a coma, and there were no assurances she would ever wake up.

"Anna, I hope you can hear me... I need you to try your hardest to get better. Do not leave me here alone," she whispered close to her sister's ear, brushing a stray lock of hair from her forehead.

All major healing procedures were already done, and the sterile field was turned off. Her sister looked far healthier than she did in the hospital. If Elizabeth didn't know better, it seemed as if Anna was peacefully sleeping. Max said they would not try to bring her back to consciousness until the evening, there were some internal fixes he was conducting slowly, healing on the cellular level. If everything turned out alright, by the end of the day, she would get her sister back.

These last few days had been a whirlwind of emotions for her. Ever since waking up in the same bed Anna was lying in now, her life had been turned upside down. Even so, if not for all of the strange things that happened, she would in all likelihood be dead and so would her sister.

She thought about Michael, and how strange and unusual a person he was. With a dream so enormous in scope, it was hard to comprehend. He also exuded a subtle sense of a higher purpose without even being aware of it. The man wanted to save the human race, and you cannot have dreams bigger than that.

Elizabeth closed her eyes and recalled that moment in the warehouse when she intervened in what would have probably been his execution. The pressure on the trigger when she shot down one of the thugs and the hail of bullets she sent in the direction of the other. That was the problem. In the heat of the moment, she discharged the entire magazine on two targets and did not have any spare rounds. She managed to exterminate one of the two vermin she came there for with her first shot, and hit another in the next few seconds. Although, she was trained to be better than that. To be logical even in high-stress situations, except… this was personal, and reason was absent at the time.

The leader, who was not as dead as she thought, got up and shot Michael. He was one of the men who had raped Anna, and she had to stop him. Elizabeth rushed at him while he was still aiming a gun at the man who was her unknowing helper. It was a decision born of rage, and a wish to do something meaningful. She had already decided that this would be a one-way trip; Anna would get justice, even if it cost Elizabeth her life. The full-body slam was the only attack she could think of at the time, but he was so much heavier than her, and all she managed was to distract him for a moment and be shot in the process. That bullet felt like a freight train, knocking her to the ground. She only hoped that her action would give enough of a distraction for the man the thugs were trying to kill... and it did.

Through the pain, she saw the demise of the big brute and sighed with a sense of relief that her sister was avenged. The last thing she remembered before blacking out was the look in Michael's eyes, kind, and caring... trying to help her.

Then, like Alice in Wonderland, she woke up on the other side of the mirror.

An alien ship filled with unbelievable technology surrounded her, with an artificial Intelligence that ran it all. The entire situation was...well she'd come up with a word eventually. This was her new reality, and she was fine with that, despite how preposterous it all was. While Michael told her his story, she realized that this technology, no matter where it came from, could help her sister. This unexpected lifeline could save Anna's life. Everything else was insignificant aside from that fact. She would have done anything to make her sister whole again. Pledging her life to a visionary, and if she was being honest, a somewhat megalomaniacal plan, no matter how noble — was a small price to pay. A part of her knew that Michael would help her even if she chose to take her sister and walk away, but there was a debt owed, and she always paid her debts.

* * *

E-waste Recycling Plant

This day was turning out to be a great one. That was what Michael thought as he was driving in the direction of the recycling plant, after visiting the bank where he deposited the money he acquired from the failed gold deal.

Max had arranged the whole thing through the creative use of electronic communication, so it was not such a surprise that everything went smoothly with the bank director. When somebody deposits six million dollars in your bank, things had better be going smoothly; the bank staff did not disappoint. For the first time in his life, Michael got to experience how the rich and famous were treated, it was something he could get used to. There was no waiting in long lines or having to deal with the cantankerous bank tellers. Moreover, Max made sure there was a solid false trail for such a large amount of cash; it could withstand rigorous scrutiny and the IRS would get their cut and so would not get suspicious.

All of Dave's debts were already paid and the recycling plant property had become the newly formed company's asset. Lawyers too could be very accommodating when there were large numbers involved. They go out of their way to make sure their rich clients are taken care of.

Dave was already waiting at the front gate, his posture and appearance far better than before Michael transferred medical nanites to him.

"You're early, I didn't expect you for a few more days," the old man said as Michael exited his truck.

"I finished my business sooner than I planned. Even went to the bank and paid all of your debts. So... I guess that now I officially own this place," Michael replied.

Dave must have seen the look of guilt written on his face. It was not easy, telling the man that what he once owned now belongs to another.

"Now, don't give me that look. This boat has been sinking for a long time, you saved me from going under the waves," the old man told him with a happy smile.

A few minutes later, they were once again sitting inside the trailer and Michael accepted a cold bottle of beer from Dave.

"Now Mike, I want to ask you something… I'm an old man and I've been through a lot in my life. With age comes experience to see things as they are and believe your instincts no matter what the situation is. I know you did something the last time you were here because right now I feel twenty years younger. And it didn't happen by itself. So… would you level with me? Will you trust me enough to tell me the truth?"

Michael contemplated it for a second, making up his mind. In the end, he went with his gut feeling.

"You're right Dave, I did do something, and it is a strange story. If you're willing to turn off your disbelief for a while, I'll tell you. With the condition that you keep it to yourself."

Dave looked him in the eye and then offered his hand, "You have my word," he solemnly said.

"I believe you, now let me start from the beginning. I was walking in the woods on my property one day, and…"

The old man listened to the story with rapt attention, only going to the fridge to get replacements for their empty bottles.

"Hot damn… If I didn't feel like I do, I'd call you a liar. That is the strangest story I've heard in my life. But here I am, feeling like a young man again," he said while looking at his hands, which had lost the inflammation advanced arthritis caused. "That's quite a thing you went through, and the things you're planning to do... damn."

"So, is our deal still on, will you work with me?"

Dave raised one of his bushy eyebrows. "Of course I will; I gave you my word, alien ships or not. Just be careful Mike, you know what our government will do if they find out about it." The old man's face betrayed a wave of deep-seated anger and resentment towards those corrupt politicians that were chosen to shape the course of his nation. "They have some mighty big hammers and every problem looks like a nail to them."

They finished their beers and Michael, followed by Dave, went back to his pickup. The truck bed was covered by a tarp that Michael drew aside to reveal what appeared to be two aluminum suitcases. In reality, they were both solid masses of dormant construction nanites created and controlled by Max. Their purpose was to assemble an ordinary-looking recycling machine which would be a cover for what was really taking place. Max's plan was for them to use materials supplied by Dave, and burrow under the ground where they would create a medium-sized nano-factory and a big storage container where all processed materials and metals would be kept safely out of everyone's sight.

"Let's put this in one of those out-of-the-way warehouses," said Michael, pointing with his chin at the back of the property. He first had to ask Dave for a hand truck, the solid nanites suitcases were far more than he could carry with ease.

The warehouse they chose was old and dusty, but still solid and waterproof. There was a big pile of scrap metal at its center, and under Max's direction, Michael placed the suitcases on top of it.

"Now, stand back and watch this. It's kinda amazing," the AI said through the implant.

For a second nothing happened. Then the suitcases started to dissolve into the scrap metal, like ferromagnetic goo. The pieces of scrap metal melted and soon geometric shapes started to appear. It took maybe an hour, during which neither Dave nor Michael took their eyes off the fascinating process. In the end, they stood before a brand-new industrial recycling machine, with a big intake receptacle for depositing scrap material.

"If I didn't see it with my own eyes..." said Dave, absent-mindedly.

"I know what you mean," Michael replied, mesmerized by the incredible building abilities of the nanites.

"Instead of looking like a couple of tourists at the latest

attraction, would you mind putting some scrap into the receptacle, I would like to finish the job. This nano-factory still needs a lot of materials to complete its underground components, and you are burning daylight," the AI said after a while.

Dave and Michael spent hours transferring scrap metal, old computers, and basically everything closely available into the receptacle, which accepted it all like a bottomless pit.

He left the plant when the sun was setting, instructing Dave that he should put as much material as he could inside the machine tomorrow, but also to rest and take care of himself. Michael gave him a few thousand dollars for expenses knowing the old man would be short on cash.

"By tomorrow, the nano-factory should be finished building itself. It already converted and stored everything you and Dave placed inside it. Soon it will be able to manufacture our first satellite probe," Max informed him as he was driving away.

"Where is the energy coming from?" Michael asked.

"There was a miniaturized reactor inside one suitcase, but a bigger one has already been constructed underneath. The fuel is separated directly from the air, so the power is the least of our concerns. What worries me is that we will outgrow this location, sooner than you think, and will need far more resources."

"Let's cross that bridge when we come to it," Michael said. "Right now, I'm more concerned with Anna."

"She will be ready to wake up by the time you get there."

"Will she be okay?"

"Michael, I really don't know. I could give you percentages and predictions, but they all fall into the realm of maybe," the AI replied in a quiet voice.

"Well, I'm holding my fingers crossed."

Michael drove a little above the speed limit, wanting to reach home as soon as possible.

Ozark Mountains - The Spaceship

Elizabeth was not at the cabin, so he took a quick shower and went to the ship. It was dark outside and a thick layer of clouds hid the light of the moon. Michael used his old army flashlight to light the way.

He found her in the AutoDoc, sitting beside her sister's bed. She looked as if she had been there for most of the day. A pang of guilt went through him for leaving her alone today.

"How are you doing?" he asked her after she noticed him.

"Hi, alright… I guess. I was sitting here thinking of all the things Anna and I used to do together. I'm not really a religious person but I spent a lot of time praying for her to be alright." Her hand was gently holding her sister's. Under the white AutoDoc's lights, he could see that there were dried tear marks on her face.

"I'm sorry I wasn't here today."

"It's okay, Max kept me company," she said and smiled.

At the mention of his name, the AI materialized his hologram beside Michael.

"It is time for her to wake, are you ready?"

"Yes… there is no point in waiting," Elizabeth said quietly. The smile was gone from her face, replaced by an expression that was hopeful and anxious at the same time.

At first, nothing happened, maybe she was breathing a little deeper, and both Michael and Elizabeth were holding their breath. He knew that if this did not work she would be devastated.

It seemed like an hour to Michael but could have been only a few minutes before the young girl on the bed stirred, and opened her eyes. She had that look of a person waking from a very deep sleep.

It took a few seconds for her to get her bearings in an unfamiliar environment but then she saw her sister. "Liz... what happened?" she asked in a hoarse voice.

"Anna!" Elizabeth shouted in happiness, hugging her sister as she began to cry with hard sobs shaking her body. Every emotion she had bottled up from the day Anna was kidnapped, was wanting to break free. Now, with Anna safe, she could let go of that constant emotional hold on herself.

Michael exited the room, unseen by Anna; it was a profoundly private moment, and he wanted to give the two sisters some privacy. That must have been what Max was thinking too. As soon as he saw the girl waking up, his hologram had vanished.

* * *

It had been an hour since he left them alone. Michael was sitting in the pilot's chair and using his CEI to go over his schedule with Max. Tomorrow he planned to go on a day trip, this whole thing would soon be too big for one man to do alone, and he really needed some additional help.

He would start with his old team from his days in the military. They were people he had trusted with his life in the past. To him, they were more than friends—they were family. Years had passed since they were all in a combat situation but some things you do not forget, and they did have years of shared experience in covert operations. Once the nanites performed the same procedures on his team that were done on him, they would become a force to be reckoned with.

"They are ready to come out," Max informed him.

Anna walked a little unsteady while holding her sister for additional stability. When she saw him, she walked toward Michael, put her arms around his neck, and gave him a strong hug.

"Thank you for everything, Elizabeth told me what you did for me. I can never repay you for saving my life."

He was caught off guard but, in the next moment, he recovered and held the young girl. "It's all right, it was the right thing to do, and it wasn't your fault what happened," Michael said as Max materialized his hologram beside them.

Anna showed the same amazement her sister had when faced with Max's hologram. For a while, she was like a little kid in front of a Christmas tree, waving her hand through his body to everyone's amusement.

"This is so cool!" Was the sentence she said several times.

A few minutes later they were sitting around the table, drinking a freshly brewed coffee from a coffeemaker Max installed on the ship. When you get right down to it, the coffeemaker was an essential piece of equipment.

"How much do you remember?" Michael asked the young girl.

She took a deep breath and then released it slowly. "I remember going home after my classes, it was a nice day, and I wanted to take a walk. The big van pulled near the sidewalk and the driver asked me for directions to the nearest hospital. But when I approached it, a side door opened and two men, wearing masks, pulled me inside… after that, the van sped up," Anna said and shivered, in spite of the ship's comfortable temperature. "I remember one of them hitting me in the stomach so hard I couldn't take a breath, and the other injecting me with a syringe. Nothing after that, as if I had fallen asleep, and woke up here."

Anna's arms hugged her body; her eyes looked into infinity beyond Michael. He recognized that thousand-yard stare, the same look he had seen countless times, in the eyes of soldiers returning from battle.

Elizabeth hugged her gently, as if she was afraid her sister would break. She looked at Michael and slowly shook her head, letting him know she had omitted telling Anna all the gruesome details.

"I told her everything about you, what happened, and what you are planning to do," Elizabeth said.

Michael had an inkling that would happen and, even if he had not planned it so soon, he needed to know where the girl stood.

"Anna, I don't want to pressure you, but do you want to be a part of what we are trying to build here? I cannot promise that there won't be some serious obstacles in the way, but you can have a future with us."

She looked him in the eyes. "I don't want to return to college. I don't think I will ever feel *safe* there, ever again. For all that, I don't want to live in fear of all the bad things that can happen. I know it is not the place that's dangerous, it's the people; those who reject decency and basic rules of civilization. So yes, I will join you, if you can promise me that what happened to me won't happen in this new society you are trying to build."

Rarely in his life had Michael been under the scrutiny of such a penetrating gaze. It felt as if she was trying to see into his very soul.

"I can't promise there won't be such people out there, I don't want to tell you a lie. But I can promise you that we will do our best to weed them out, to deny them access to space. And if we find them in our midst, we will show no mercy."

Anna continued to stare into his soul for a few more moments and then nodded in acceptance.

Michael exhaled. "Well, that's settled then. Which reminds me, I need to take a trip tomorrow and will be gone most of the day. Let's go to the cabin, make a meal and settle you in. You can relax tomorrow and enjoy the scenery; I bought enough groceries to last for a while."

* * *

That night Michael couldn't fall asleep, so he took a bottle of beer and sat on his porch chair, looking at the wavy image of the moon, reflecting from the surface of the lake. He was thinking how, not so long ago, he had come here to be alone, and now two women were sleeping in his cabin, and he felt responsible for them.

He hoped that tomorrow everything would go as he intended since his old team was essential to his plans. That was one of the main reasons he could not fall asleep, plans were constantly going through his head, and choices that could make the whole thing succeed or fail.

A slight noise made him turn around; Elizabeth was standing in the doorway dressed in his old shirt.

"I hope you don't mind; I didn't have anything to wear."

"I think it looks better on you than on me," he said with a smile.

She sat beside him, lifted the beer bottle he had placed on the deck and took a sip from it.

"Thank God she doesn't remember anything, well at least seriously bad parts... I hope she never remembers. When I close my eyes, I can still see how she looked when I found her, and I feel rage, enough rage to fill the whole world."

"What happened to her could have happened to anyone, it's so random. You must have seen it in your line of work, there are wolves in the world, wolves in human form, and no matter what, you can never change their mindsets. There is only one way to deal with a rabid wolf," Michael replied, looking at her silhouette.

They talked for a while until Elizabeth fell asleep in an old Adirondack chair. She stayed with Anna the entire time, never getting any rest herself. It was a wonder she'd stayed awake for so long. He gently picked her up in his arms and carried her to her room. She looked so beautiful and vulnerable. The slight worry-frown between her eyes was absent and made her look as peaceful as Michael had ever seen her. He laid her on her bed, quietly exited the room, and went to his own.

It was late and tomorrow was going to be a long day.

CHAPTER 8

Veterans Long-Term Care Hospital

Michael was driving toward the first person he wanted to meet, a man from his past. It was a five-hour drive so he started the trip early. He exited the cabin as quietly as he could, so he wouldn't wake up the girls. He put his favorite country music on and entered a Zen-like state of mind, where miles were measured by how many tracks he'd already listened to.

Colonel Jack Williams was his superior in the Delta Force and a good friend who always had Michael's back. In the end, he sacrificed himself to save Michael and his team members. Over the years he visited Jack regularly, taking the long drives or flying to spend a few hours with the man. Last night he called him to arrange this visit, or salesman's pitch, as he was calling it. Jack had all the talents he needed to get this show on the right track and he hoped the old man would accept his invitation.

Arriving at the veterans' long-term care facility put a damper on his mood. A big depressing building with unvarying gray walls was not a place where a war hero should spend his days. The staff did their best to make the lives of their patients easier, but there was an atmosphere of sadness and despair permeating the place; as his friend often said, this was where broken soldiers came to die, and no amount of cheering up could change that. *Well, Jack, your luck is about to change.*

He signed in at the admittance desk where the familiar nurse smiled and said the Colonel was expecting him. He took the elevator and walked into the room as he had done many times before. This time, something was different; when he opened the door, he could see Jack was not alone. He was sitting in his wheelchair with a few more people around a small table. Three more men who were as close as brothers to Michael. Tyron with an eye patch over his right eye, and a knowing smirk on his face. Pete, and Zac, two deadly goofs, with familiar smiles on theirs.

Seeing them all together sent his memory back through the years, to the other side of the world and the place that was mostly sun and sand...

* * *

Middle East (14 Years Ago)

The hot dusty desert air was making Michael's throat dry, and the scarf covering his face was of little help. It was not the sand he particularly disliked, it was the dust… it got into everything.

They were not even supposed to be here, it was a last-minute thing and a case of being in the wrong place at the wrong time. Unfortunately, as soldiers, their duty was to follow orders no matter how inconvenient they were.

The team had just returned to the base from the previous mission. They had managed to return a day ahead of schedule and were taking the lukewarm showers to wash away all the grime. Michael could almost taste the cold beer sliding down his throat since they made plans for some well-earned R&R in the local town when the new orders arrived. They were going back in the frying pan... that had fallen into the fire.

As operators, this wasn't so unusual; you go where they need you, and fix other peoples' mistakes. It was presented as a simple operation: get in, free the hostages, and get out. Of course, there is no such thing as a simple operation. Only delusional officers who planned them could say something so ridiculous; that's the way Michael always thought about Military Intelligence, like a big ass oxymoron.

Apparently, some dumb politician had managed to get himself and his family kidnapped by the local terrorist cell. What kind of idiot would bring his family to a war zone just to get more exposure and pick up a few extra votes? Now, it was the team's job to get them out, before the terrorists decided to cut a few heads off on Live TV, all in the name of their god and crazy-ass convictions.

Intel was good. Location, satellite images, the opposition numbers... what could go wrong?

Michael looked at the rest of his team as they sat strapped into the uncomfortable helicopter seats. Tyron, Pete, and Zac, or as they liked to call themselves, *the four musketeers*—one for all and all for one.

Pete and Zac were more of a comedy act, always making jokes and getting into all kinds of avoidable trouble, while Tyron was the silent but hardly unnoticed one. When you are 7' feet (2.1 m) tall with 330 lbs. (150 kg) of muscle, you will get noticed. The four of them were a team; working together so close-knit they could predict each other's reaction in almost any situation. This was what they were trained to do. High-risk and high-gain operations when regular soldiers were unable to save the day. Or where the powers that be needed to claim plausible deniability for the sake of international political relations.

The insertion went smoothly and according to plan. A small

The Spaceship In The Stone

settlement in the middle of the desert that used to be a peaceful community built around a small oasis, before the bad guys took it over, and killed all the natives. Now only one building was somewhat livable, all the others were crumbling ruins, the perfect spot for a hideaway. It had the added advantage of being miles inside the neighboring country. A country they were not allowed to be in.

The main terrorist group was away on another kidnapping mission, so there would be minimal opposition at the site; it was the window of opportunity the team had every intention to exploit.

Everything went off without a hitch... until it didn't. The three guards on the outside perimeter were quickly silenced and, after entering the building, they finished off the rest of the bad guys. The terrorists made one back room of their headquarters into a makeshift prison and the hostages were exactly where they were supposed to be. They were confined in a small boarded-up room, with no sanitary facilities except an old rusty bucket that reeked to high heaven. That's when a solid dozen glitches the intelligence section desk pilots completely missed presented themselves.

The mission was to find and rescue three people, and all their plans revolved around that. Instead, the team found... fifteen.

Besides the idiot politician and his family, there was a group from *Doctors Without Borders* and six children under their care. They never considered the option to leave the extras to the mercies of their kidnappers, it never even occurred to them. So, their carefully planned extraction strategy went in the same direction as the Dodo bird.

Michael called the Black Hawk chopper parked a few miles away, and it came a few minutes later. One thing was evident—it was not possible to fit so many people in it. Someone would need to stay behind. To make the whole thing a complete FUBAR the pilot saw a convoy of terrorist troops moving towards their location.

The chopper was emptied of all unnecessary things, seats, equipment, and every single piece of ammunition it carried. Then they loaded all the people on it, packed them like sardines, barely managing to fit everybody inside. The pilot was sweating bullets, calculating all this additional weight and Michael saw him cross himself before the takeoff. For all that, the bird managed to lift, if a bit unsteadily.

That was it, the hostages were safe, and the team was left in the one place no sane person would want to be—at ground zero of an impending terrorist attack.

Michael got their commander, Col. Jack Williams, on the satphone. After quickly explaining the situation he was promised a second bird would come to pick them up ASAP. They needed to hold their position until then—and they did.

To this day Michael wasn't sure how many terrorists died that day. He just knew it was a lot. The team didn't go unscathed, all had some injuries. There were a lot of lacerations from flying debris made by the rain of bullets fired in their direction, and a few minor bullet holes that were either ignored or quickly treated to stop any excessive bleeding.

Without any sense or reason, the terrorist combatants kept coming. With screams of devotion to their divinity, they ran into the team's precise fire. Thinking about it later he realized the fight was not long but at the time it seemed to him as if they were there for ages.

Time goes by differently when you are *in the zone*. When you can be alive in one moment and dead in the very next.

The beautiful sound of a helicopter's engine broke through the constant booming sound of gunfire. The second Black Hawk the Colonel promised was finally there. After sending a few rockets

The Spaceship In The Stone

and a couple of thousand rounds toward their opposition, the little settlement was peaceful again, at least the terrorists were.

Michael looked at his brothers and saw that the entire team was bloody, dirty, and dog-tired. Still, there were smiles on their faces; they had done what was needed in spite of everything.

Michael and Tyron had to help Pete and Zac walk since they were semi-mobile, and moving towards the bird that landed on a clear piece of land, took some serious effort. Col. Jack came out of the helicopter, slowly walking in their direction. Michael was looking directly at the older man when his expression changed to one of panic.

He started running towards them, reaching for the gun on his belt, and screaming something inaudible to their still ringing ears. Michael raised his gun, turning to point the barrel in the direction Col. Jack was looking but it was a second too late. He saw what got the Colonel so alarmed. A kid no older than sixteen was exiting one of the run-down houses wearing a bomb vest. That moment engraved itself in Michael's mind, the fanatical look on the young man's face, filled with bottomless hate. His finger increased the pressure on the trigger but the young man was already pressing the detonator.

There was a tremendous explosion. An intense pressure wave threw them all to the ground. In retrospect, he could say they were extremely lucky—none of them died. The colonel's shout made the young terrorist act prematurely and from a distance that was not ideal for maximum effect. Inevitably, there were some consequences of being too close to the exploding bomb.

Col. Jack was injured the worst. A fragment of the bomb severed his spine, ensuring he would never walk again. Tyron lost an eye and had so many bomb fragments in his massive body, he would light up every airport scanner in the world. Pete and Zac were fortunate that Michael and Tyron moved to stand in front of them, so they got off easy. Michael acquired a new collection of impressive scars and a shattered knee.

With the help of the medic and the pilot, they managed to get themselves inside the chopper and to the base. To Michael, the whole trip was shrouded in a fog of pain and exhaustion while his injuries threatened to shut down his consciousness.

But they did get back. In far worse condition but with a completed mission and fifteen lives saved. Even with their injuries, there was a sense of accomplishment. They did their jobs and, if asked to do it all over again, knowing the consequences, they would.

A few months later, the entire team was officially out of the military due to the severity of their various injuries.

* * *

Veterans Long-Term Care Hospital

Michael shook his head to clear the last images of the vivid flashback he experienced.

"The prodigal son returns!" Zac said with a big grin.

"I took the liberty and summoned these miscreants. You said last night there is something to talk about which concerns all of us. God knows how hard it is to bring us all back together without me playing a guilt card," Jack said with a smirk.

After a round of traditional 'bro hugs, they were all sitting around a small dining table.

Tyron looked at Michael and said, "Well, one thing I noticed is that somehow between the time I last saw you and now, you managed to lose your limp, and I know how much that knee was busted, care to share…?"

Michael looked at the four men he considered part of his

extended family; there was an evident interest in their eyes to find out what Tyron noticed first.

"That is something I wanted to talk to you about. It is going to sound strange and unbelievable, but on my honor, every single thing I'm about to tell you is the truth."

In the end, it wouldn't matter if they believed him or not, he was part of the team and if he asked them for their help—it would be enough.

It took a while, but he told them everything that happened. By now, telling the story was smoother; Elizabeth, Anna, and Dave heard it previously and now he only needed to add newer developments.

"Damn son... that's quite a tale," Jack said, after Michael was finished, "what do you want us to do?" he asked after the other men looked at each other and reached a silent, but unanimous consensus.

It was what Michael expected, unquestionable acceptance and an offer to help. While talking about the healing properties of medical nanites he noticed Tyron's hand touching the eye patch that hid an empty socket.

"I need people I can trust and in this room are the people I trust most in the world." He looked through the window. "To get this undertaking off the ground will require preparation and planning and the driving core needs to have a military mindset. You are it. Logistics, recruiting, security," he looked them in the eyes. "Can you imagine what this technology can do... how it can better our lives, and simultaneously destroy them? I have a plan but it doesn't come without risks. There are people out there who would kill or torture us and our families for any information if they figure out what we have and what we plan to do. Our own government included."

They all nodded their heads, knowing from personal experience how far the government would go if there was something they wanted. Some of their past missions did come close to the other side of that border.

"We need to recruit a lot of people and it is very difficult to keep something like this hidden. So, for starters, I need you to consider people you trust, and start the process of bringing them in."

Jack looked at Michael with a deep, penetrating gaze. "Michael, what you are going to end up with is an army. Who are you going to fight with it?"

"Not really an army, but a large group of people with an army mindset. We need individuals who can be trusted to guard our backs at times when things are not easy-going. We will be the tip of the spear that will protect what we are trying to build."

He paused, rubbing his temples. "For some time now, I have been disillusioned with our government and any other government in the world for that matter. They stopped caring about people and are only concerned with their own personal power. The elections are reality television popularity contests, and corruption has become a standard, not an exception. I thought there was no way out. This is simply how things are, but this technology changes everything."

He got up from the chair and went to the window, looking out at the sky.

"Since there are no more territories one can claim as his own, I set my sights on space, because this has the potential to open a whole new frontier out there. I could tell you this is all just an altruistic idea of mine but it's not only that. I want the power to control my own destiny, I want that sense of freedom and infinite possibilities our forefathers felt. I want to create a society built on our own rules, just rules. With a certain set of conditions: no politicians, minimal administration, and no lawyers."

Jack raised his hand, "Okay, I understand where you're going with this, but you have to realize that a lot of people will call you a dictator and that you will be hated by so many others… and most likely marked for assassination by the mighty and powerful."

"So let them, every single person can opt-out, at any moment, so they can call me whatever they want. I'm not doing this to get people's approval, I'm offering a choice of something better. Besides, nobody can live forever, but as long as I live, I will do it my way. If you follow me in this, know that some of that danger will transfer to you, so what do you say, are you in or out?"

"Well, son… I'm in. I was getting a little bored to death with this place, waiting to breathe my last breath; this is a far better option," Jack said with a crooked smile.

Pete and Tyron nodded their heads and, at the same time said, "Count me in."

Only Zac remained silent, his face showing a man in deep thought.

"What about you, Zac?"

"I'm okay with most of what you said, but there is one thing that interests me. Does this offer come with a free dental plan? There is this one tooth that's been killing me—"

That was as far as he got before a pillow thrown by Jack struck his face, and Tyron hit the back of his head a moment later.

"With that out of the way, I have something for you."

Michael reached inside his pocket and removed four silver dollar coins.

"These are made from medical nanites; all you need to do is put them on the palms of your hands and they will be absorbed through your skin."

The coins were Max's idea. He wasn't too keen on Michael depleting his internal supply of the nanites again by transferring them directly to others. The episode with Elizabeth showed that while it was possible to operate with diminished numbers of them, it was far from optimal. They planned in advance about offering them to the team. Max would control them through cell towers, but for their full use, Jack, Tyron, Pete, and Zac would need to go through the CEI implantation procedure inside the AutoDoc.

Each of the men took one coin and put them flat on their palms. After a few seconds, the metal lost its sharp edges and started to melt into their hands.

"Damn Mike, this looks like magic!" Jack exclaimed, and like the others stared at the disappearing nanites.

"Disturbing and fascinating," Tyron's deep baritone added.

"By this time tomorrow, you should already feel better, healthier, and younger. In time, they can even cure or regenerate lost limbs. Including your eye, Tyron," Michael said.

He turned to Jack. "And make you vertical again. But to speed things up, and get you in top condition, we should get you to the ship's Auto-Doc."

Michael stayed with them for a few more hours, discussing what they would do in the future and getting their feedback on some finer points of his plan.

"Now, I need to make one more stop. You three get your stuff and get Jack away from this depressing place. Let's meet at my cabin tomorrow, you all know the way."

They said their goodbyes, and soon Michael was on his way to see the only living member of his direct family.

* * *

Houston, Texas

It had been almost three months since he'd last seen his father. They spoke on the phone from time to time but, by living in different cities, it was difficult to meet often in person. And when they talked, it was mostly about general things; it seemed to

Michael they were repeating the same conversation every time. When they did see each other, the two of them could sit in silence for hours, drinking beer, and feeling at ease with themselves.

What worried him was that in the last few conversations, his father had become very talkative, speaking about past events, good times they had. When Michael asked him if everything was okay, he said that everything was fine. Still, that gut feeling of his was telling him something was off.

After another long drive, he finally came to his father's house. It was in a nice neighborhood, but small and utilitarian, suitable for a single man. For some reason, his father never remarried after Michael's mother died. There were a few women that Michael knew about, yet nothing permanent. The old man often joked that he lived for his job and no woman could accept that in the long term.

He had a Ph.D. in physics and was in charge of the R&D section of one of the biggest physics labs in the U.S. with a well-known and respected name in scientific circles.

The first tangible proof that his gut was right was the neglected lawn in front of the house. On all his previous visits, the lawn was meticulous; now, the grass was overgrown and weeds were choking the flowerbeds.

When his father opened the front door, Michael did a double-take. For as long as he could remember, the man standing in front of him was a bit overweight; nothing alarming, but a few extra pounds here and there. The man who opened the door was skinny and his skin had that pale, unhealthy pallor of someone sick.

"Hi Michael, I'm glad to see you, come on in," his father said, with a resigned shrug of the shoulders.

"Dad, what's wrong with you?" he replied, following his father into the house.

"Let's grab a couple of beers and I'll tell you."

While his father was going to the refrigerator, Michael noticed his slowed-down movements. He was not walking as he used to, always in a hurry as if a day did not have enough hours for him to do all he planned.

"Max, something is seriously wrong with him," he sent to the AI.

"I know, I just hacked into his medical records. Do you want me to tell you, or would you rather hear it from him?" the AI replied.

It was a tempting offer, but he owed the man the dignity of telling him in his own words.

"Let him tell me, in any case, prepare the nanites."

"I'm already way ahead of you. Touch his arm when he gives you the beer."

Michael tried to be as inconspicuous as he could while transferring the nanites. He was paying attention and saw a small silvery bead attach itself to his father's skin. After he took the beer, he sat across from his father. They drank their beers in silence for a few minutes.

"So..." he didn't know how to begin.

"So... as you may have guessed, I'm sick." His father took a long pull of his beer before continuing. "It's a brain tumor, inoperable... so that's that."

The beer in his stomach threatened to return the same way it went in. He knew the nanites could perform a miracle, but hearing this was deeply disturbing. These were the words no child ever wanted to hear.

"Treatments?"

"Wouldn't do any good, any meaningful life prolongation percentages are laughable, and you know me, I'm all about percentages," he said with a sour smile.

"Were you planning to tell me?"

"Yes, they gave me six months and I wanted to spend them on my terms. No pointless therapies eating that time until the unavoidable end. I was planning to visit you at the cabin. I wanted to spend some time with you before I checked myself into a hospice."

His father lifted his bottle in imitation of a salute, "I was rehearsing what to tell you when I saw you, I guess you messed up my plans," he said and smiled. It was not a joyful smile, but one full of sadness.

"Michael, my biggest regret in this life was not spending enough time with you. I thought that there would always be more. When your mother died... I was lost and did not know how to take care of you. That is why I left you with your grandparents, so you could have a good family life. I missed... so much... and I'm so sorry Michael."

"Max, talk to me!" Michael snapped through his implant, his throat trying to swallow a non-existing lump.

"He has a brain tumor all right, but there is no immediate danger, and the nanites are already stabilizing him. But he will need a long session inside the AutoDoc to remove it completely."

Michael looked at his father, who was staring at the wall, lost in his memories.

"Dad, I want you to come to the cabin with me. There is something I need you to see."

Robert Freeman looked at his son for a moment and then nodded. "I can do that, but in a few days. There are still some things here I need to take care of."

"It is really important for you to get there as soon as possible," Michael said, emphasizing each word.

They finished their beers and then had some more. For a few hours, they talked about their lives, remembering people they both loved and lost.

It was the first time in their lives that they *really* opened up to one another.

As Michael was pulling out of the driveway, he saw his father standing on the porch, waving at him.

"Why did you keep him in the dark?" Max asked.

"Because he will never believe it until he sees it with his own eyes; I figure it's better to show him than just tell him."

"Yeah, he's like that all right. Why do I get the feeling you have plans for him?" the AI asked.

"Because I do. We will need scientists and he talks their language."

"The sooner we can get him into the AutoDoc the better, I didn't like seeing him this way, he looked... broken."

"Looking your own mortality in the face will do that to you, but you are right, I don't think I can stop worrying until we get him healed," Michael replied.

For the next few hours, Michael drove in silence. He wanted to think about his future plans but the worry for his father was always at the top of his mind. Max could sense what Michael's state of mind was, so he left him to his own thoughts.

Only time will tell if everything will turn out all right.

CHAPTER 9

Ozark Mountains - The Cabin

Elizabeth awoke with a start and the sound of her fast-beating heart drumming in her ears. She had been dreaming about Anna again. Her sister was being kidnapped, and she couldn't help her. That accounted for the cold sweat soaking Michael's shirt. To ease her fears, she quickly went to the next room and opened the door, only to see Anna peacefully sleeping in the queen-sized bed. *She is safe.*

Elizabeth quietly closed the door, not wanting to disturb her sister, and then took a quick shower. The feeling of warm water on her body was cathartic, washing away her deepest fears and that constant sense of hopelessness.

Last night was so stressful. First, not knowing if Anna would wake up at all, and then having to tell her an incomplete version of her ordeal. Thank God she did not remember the gruesome parts, it would have extinguished that spark of innocence still burning in her sister.

She went to the kitchen and started making breakfast. If there was one thing that could wake her sister it was the smell of bacon and eggs. It worked like a charm, the smell of frying strips of delicious meat spread throughout the house and a few minutes later Anna came downstairs, still rubbing the sleep from her eyes.

"Ah, bacon and eggs, the breakfast of champions," she said as she stole one of the crisp strips, drying on a paper towel.

"So, you and Michael... is there something... going on?" Anna asked while setting the table.

Elizabeth almost dropped a piece of toast she was transferring to the plate. "What? No, nothing, why would you think that?"

"Well, the way you look at him, the same looks he gives you. It's the vibes sis, the vibes never lie," Anna said and evaded a kitchen towel her sister threw in her direction.

"Stop with your matchmaking and start eating, the eggs are getting cold."

Elizabeth didn't consciously think about Michael in that way, not until now. But she could see how comfortable and unforced she felt in his company. She was no shrinking violet but her experience with men and personal relationships was not too extensive. Anna and her job were taking the first two positions of the most important things in her life. No man liked being in third place, so those few relationships petered out fast. However, it was too soon to think about that, despite his intensity, she had just recently met the man.

"Let's go into town. We need to buy new clothes, and you can obviously see that this is a single man's cabin, not a tampon in sight," Anna said with a smile after they were finished with breakfast.

They took Elizabeth's car and navigated down the mountain road. She drove very slowly, due to the road's conditions. But the bad road made the cabin much more secluded, safer. Nobody would accidentally come up the mountain as a result of missing their turn.

They spent most of the day in the city. She wanted Anna to

The Spaceship In The Stone

have a fun day out. Something they had often done together when her sister was younger, spending the whole day shopping, going to the movies, and just hanging out. It was a guaranteed recipe to make Anna happy, and it worked. As the day progressed, a smile could often be seen on her sister's face.

By the time they finished the second movie of the day it was almost dark. They got in Elizabeth's car and set out for Michael's cabin with the backseat filled with all their purchases.

Anna was just retelling the best jokes of the comedy they saw when Elizabeth noticed something suspicious. Three cars were following her and all of her instincts honed by the FBI instructors told her they were a threat. It was not so difficult to spot them, since there were no other cars on the road, and they did take the last four turns the same as she did. Now, they were all on the long straight stretch of road, with no more turns she could take.

She didn't believe this was about Michael. Max and he had covered their tracks really well, in her professional opinion. That left only her and Anna. The only thing that would cause someone to follow them were the events that happened in that warehouse. How anyone could connect her with that was unclear, Michael had burned the entire place to the ground, leaving no evidence.

Trying to outrun them would not work. Her Prius was a hybrid, built for fuel efficiency not speed, and the people following them were driving cars that were both heavier and faster. Even so, she increased her speed, but it was to no avail as they were keeping up without any effort.

Anna must have somehow read her body language; she stopped talking and turned around to see why Elizabeth was so focused on the rearview mirror.

"They're following us, aren't they?" her sister said in a small voice.

"Yes, they are," she admitted, knowing there was no point in hiding it.

"Liz, I'm scared," Anna whispered, panic showing in her wide-open eyes.

They were in trouble, and it was too late to do anything about it; she hoped Michael could pull out another miracle since he was her only hope now.

"Don't worry little sis, it's going to be okay…"

She flinched when Max's voice sounded from her telephone speakers. *"All right girls, I know this is scary, but we will get you out of this."*

"Max! How…"

"I'm tracking you using your phone's GPS, and have two surveillance drones on the way; they will shortly be above your position. Michael knows what's happening and will be coming after you very soon."

"How… how long?" Elizabeth asked, knowing deep inside that it would not be fast enough.

"Unfortunately, it'll take him a little more than three hours to reach you. That means you two will be taken. I'm sorry, but there is nothing we can do about it. I need you girls to keep calm and do everything in your power to stay safe. Do not make it easy for them to capture you, but don't resist too much either. Comply with all of their demands, don't give them a reason to hurt you," Max said with a caring, yet assertive voice.

Two of the cars put on a burst of speed, passing her in no time. They boxed her in, using the same technique she learned herself for safely apprehending a suspect without hurting them. The first car's hazard warning lights turned on and he started slowing down. She did too, not wanting to collide with him. The window of the car beside her rolled down and an evil-looking man, holding a gun in his hand, signaled her to stop with his other hand.

"Remember, do as they say and don't resist. Michael and his friends will get you out in a few hours."

Elizabeth stopped the car and looked at her sister.

"We will get through this," she said and grasped Anna's hand. "I know it's going to be scary, but I need you to be strong for me. In a few hours, we'll be free, and they'll be sorry for messing with us. Okay?"

"Okay," Anna whispered, wiping away her tears.

The brutish-looking man was beside her door's window, knocking on it with the barrel of his gun.

Michael, please come soon, Elizabeth thought and opened the door.

* * *

Michael felt this had been one long and tiring day but he had accomplished so much. Colonel Jack and the team would be joining him very soon and, after seeing the spaceship, his father would surely jump on the wagon.

A cold shiver ran down his spine thinking about what would have happened to his father if they didn't have the ship and medical nanites. There would not be a thing he or modern medicine could do to save him and that was a very sobering thought.

Everything was coming together nicely and he couldn't wait to go home and tell Elizabeth about this day.

That thought hit him like a ton of bricks, it had been a long time since he had a desire to rush home and share his day with anyone. He was surprised to find he wanted to share it with her. The logical part of his mind told him it was too soon, he had just met her and was rushing into things. Despite that, there was something about Elizabeth, something in her eyes, a strength he had rarely seen. Still, he had been burned too many times to jump into a new relationship, so he decided not to push or instigate anything, and let things sort themselves out.

He was still a long way from the cabin when Max interrupted his musings.

"Michael, something is happening," the AI said, in a rushed voice.

"What?"

"Elizabeth and Anna are being taken."

"How can they be taken! Nobody should know where the cabin is, what the hell happened?!" Michael shouted as his mind went into crisis mode and his foot pressed harder on the gas pedal.

"They are not in the cabin, the girls wanted to shop for some things in town; they drove there this morning in Elizabeth's car. Right now, they are on the highway, returning, but three cars have them boxed in."

The dashboard speedometer showed that he was way past the speed limit, but he didn't care. Getting to the girls that were under his care was the only thing that mattered.

"How far am I from them?"

"You need at least three hours... I'm sorry Michael," the AI sorrowfully answered.

"Can you track them?"

"Yes, there are plenty of nanites inside both of them and I'm still actively monitoring Anna's vitals. Plus, I have diverted two mining drones that are now closing on their position, they can see perfectly in the dark and I'll have a visual within a few minutes."

Michael's hands squeezed the steering wheel so tightly that the skin on his knuckles turned white. It was Murphy's Law in action. Just as things were starting to go smoothly, fate threw a curveball. Getting angry would not help the girls, but thinking tactically would.

Max was giving him a play-by-play of how Elizabeth and Anna were forced to stop the car. And how they were transferred to the kidnapper's vehicles.

The Spaceship In The Stone

"Max, get me the team on the line," he ordered after the vehicles drove away from Elizabeth's abandoned car. By that time Max was streaming a live video feed from the drones' cameras, directly to Michael's implant. He could see the girls being dragged out of the Prius and transferred into one of the kidnappers' cars. One of the kidnappers got in Elizabeth's Prius and drove after the three cars. This was a well-planned operation but he would make sure the kidnappers regretted every second of it.

In the next few minutes he made a plan and arranged for Pete, Zac, and Tyron to meet him… and to bring weapons.

* * *

An hour later, he received a message from Elizabeth's phone. There was a picture of her and Anna, bound with duct tape, sitting on a bare concrete floor. Even mistreated like this, there was a look of fierce defiance in her eyes which made him respect her even more.

The text under the picture said: IF YOU WANT TO SEE THEM ALIVE AGAIN, YOU DO AS WE SAY. TOMORROW, YOU WILL RECEIVE THE LOCATION, AND YOU HAVE ONE HOUR TO BE THERE. FOR ANY MINUTE YOU ARE LATE, ONE OF THEM WILL LOSE A FINGER. IF YOU CALL THE POLICE, THEY BOTH DIE.

If his phone hadn't been upgraded by Max, it would have cracked from the pressure Michael's hand was exerting. *Oh, I'm coming all right, but sooner than you expect.*

* * *

Albanian Gang Headquarters

Looking at himself, Michael felt as if his past and present were merging. He was dressed in a standard Army combat uniform. It was one of several Tyron managed to pick up from the Army surplus store. The entire team was dressed the same with an assortment of weapons that were not even close to the realm of legal for civilians to be in possession of. If authorities saw them carrying full auto HK MP5SD's with integral suppressors, their future would be much bleaker than planned. The good thing was, they were far away from the regular patrol routes of the local deputies.

The building to which Max tracked Elizabeth and Anna was a mansion on a private estate surrounded by thick woods, miles away from town, and conveniently with no neighbors with prying eyes. It was a perfect place for someone who was doing something illegal; consequently, it was also a perfect place to conduct a covert assault on.

The thick woods around the estate provided ample cover for Michael and his team to approach the main building. As much as it provided privacy for those inside, it was not a location that could be easily defended from a tactical standpoint. And this type of terrain was one of many in which Michael and his team, had been thoroughly trained to blend into and to attack from.

Tyron and the guys met him a little while ago, five miles (8 km) away from this place. They must have broken every speed limit to reach this location so quickly. Max had done his digital magic, diverting police patrols, and shutting off cameras as they were passing through.

After they stashed the cars a good distance from the mansion, they put on their old working uniforms and equipped themselves with the lethal tools of their former trade.

Michael explained the situation and what the stakes were.

The Spaceship In The Stone

Elizabeth and Anna's safety were of utmost importance, so reaching them quickly and eliminating any opposition was the prime objective.

Max's drones were hovering high above them, providing a comprehensive map of the terrain and the location of guards walking the perimeter. Michael could see, from a birds' perspective, Elizabeth's car parked in front of the four-car garage. He had to close his eyes and take a deep breath to subdue the wave of wrath rising from within. This was not the time to lose control. For the sake of the girls, he had to approach the whole thing as just another mission, an assignment that needed to be professionally executed.

"I see four guards, each needs to be taken out simultaneously and silently," Michael said to the rest of his team. "Pete and Zac, you two will go through the back entrance, while Tyron and I will assault from the front. Remember your training, stay silent and unnoticed until the party starts. Since Tyron's target has the best point of view, he is making the first move. Our primary objective is to retrieve the girls, but we need a prisoner that can explain what this is all about since taking the girls does not make sense. But, if they are armed, take them out with prejudice, and let God sort them out."

Three faces, painted in camouflage colors, nodded back at him. This was not their first dance; they had been in so many similar situations that words were superfluous. They separated, each going for his designated target.

Michael was moving slowly through the night, using all the skills accumulated over the years in Special Forces; it was like slipping into an old, familiar skin. Before long, he was a few feet away from his mark and, if he wanted, he could have reached out with his hand and touched the back of the man's neck. The slight drizzle of cold rain made the man seek shelter under a big pine tree, leaning his rifle against the trunk and enjoying a cigarette.

Michael waited for the perfect moment, taking shallow breaths, unmoving. He saw Tyron *taking action*, and in the next split-second, he did too. One hand covering the mouth, the other, which held a knife, making a well-practiced move and silencing the man for all eternity.

On a tactical map projected on his HUD, he saw Pete and Zac had done the same. All four dragged their kills a few feet into the woods, hiding the bodies from the sight of those inside the mansion.

They carefully approached the front entrance, using dead angles and convenient cover to minimize the chance of being seen. The amateur level of security was evident; they managed to approach the door without being noticed. Michael could hardly believe it when Tyron turned the doorknob, and the door opened —it wasn't even locked.

The big guy looked at Michael and shrugged his shoulders, the amateur hour was one thing, this was criminally neglectful, pun intended.

Cautious not to make any sounds, they stepped into a long entrance, each covering his designated half of space. The hall ended with the central staircase, structurally located in the middle of the mansion. Again, there was no one in sight, but the sound of people talking in a foreign language could be heard. It came from the direction of a room with closed doors, some ten feet (3 m) away from the entrance.

They approached the doors and, while Tyron was watching possible avenues of attack, Michael took out a dentist mirror and placed it next to the gap at the bottom. He could see six men playing cards, with guns on their belts, and automatic rifles carelessly left leaning against the wall. There was so much cigar smoke in the room, he wondered how these idiots could breathe the toxic air inside.

He stood up and, using a series of hand signals, explained the situation to Tyron. They both nodded and on the silent count of three, Michael turned the knob and pushed the door open.

They didn't wait or give their opponents the opportunity to respond. This was not a negotiation. Dramatically pausing before a shootout only worked in the movies. A few seconds was all it took. A couple of the men even managed to reach for the guns on their belts, but it was too late. In a situation like this, a weapon that is not in a hand may as well be on the other side of the world.

Michael finished his third target almost at the same time as Tyron. With the next few breaths, they could smell the coppery scent of fresh blood mixed with the stale stench of tobacco. They checked that all their targets were neutralized and closed the door.

Using silenced guns with subsonic rounds greatly decreased the noise their weapons made, but that didn't make them completely silent. A person with some training would easily distinguish and recognize that sound so time was of the essence. From the back of the house, the whispering sound of silenced guns echoed through the corridors. Pete and Zac were cleaning their part of the house.

They went further down the hall, checking the rest of the rooms, only to find them empty. Michael was almost at the stairs with the barrel of his gun pointed upwards, making sure that no one would come from the upper floor unnoticed. The only movement he saw was with his peripheral vision, it was Pete and Zac.

Each man was pointing their weapon in a different direction, controlling their sectors, when they all met by the staircase.

"Five marks in the back, no sign of the girls," whispered Pete.

"Six in the front, the same," answered Tyron.

The inside of the house was eerily quiet, Michael's enhanced hearing could not pick up anything except the sounds he and the team were making.

"The game is not over yet," he said and started climbing the stairs.

Going up the stairs and covering every angle took a little time. Again, they met with no resistance, just plenty of closed doors. Each room they checked was vacant and most of them did not even have any furniture. In the end, only the master bedroom was left, with big sturdy oak doors. His enhanced hearing could pick up a person breathing heavily from the other side.

"How do you want to play it?" asked Tyron, as the team was hugging the walls, not wanting to be surprised if someone from the other side decided to shoot through the wood.

"By now, whoever is on the other side knows we are here. Pete and Zac, go outside and tape a flash-bang to a rock, then throw it through the window of that room. As soon as it activates, Tyron and I will breach."

Michael never turned around, pointing his gun at the doors in case someone decided to open them; that small part of a second to turn his head back could cost him dearly. He could hear as the two men went to accomplish their task.

A few minutes later, the sound of breaking glass was followed by a loud explosion that could be clearly heard in the hall. Using all of his considerable mass, Tyron ran at the door and broke through. Michael, one step behind him, checked the opulent room for any sign of movement.

The curtains were waving out of the broken window and the draft was already clearing the smoke the flash-bang produced. The only occupant of the room was a fat middle-aged man, hiding behind a massive office desk, holding his hands over his ears. A ridiculously big and chromed handgun was lying on the floor next to him, it was sufficiently large caliber to easily punch through the big doors.

They secured him, tied his hands with zip ties, and put him in the chair.

"Tyron, go with Pete and Zac, check the entire house, I'll have a talk with him."

It took a little while for the man to come to his senses, he looked groggily around the room, until he set his eyes on Michael.

"You don't know what you've done, we will kill your entire family for this," he threatened, with a trace of a foreign accent.

That threat would have carried more weight if there was not a wet yellow trail running down his trousers.

Michael put his face inches away from the man.

"Where are the girls?" he asked in the most menacing voice he could produce. He didn't need to fake it, he just made a small opening in that bundle of rage inside him that was trying to break free.

"What girls are you talking about, we have no girls here," the man answered in a quivering voice, trying to put on a facade of innocence.

Michael smirked, seeing right through him. "I'm wondering, is this connected only to the girls, or does it have something to do with those idiots that tried to cheat me while buying the gold?"

The man's eyes opened wide and hate seeped through them. "You! It is you that killed our men!"

"That may well be, but I asked you a question and I expect an answer," said Michael, and popped his knuckles.

The man's name was Basim, even getting that from him took some work. Apparently, the leader of the thugs Michael and Elizabeth killed in the warehouse was a nephew of Basim's boss. What's more, that boss was powerful and scary enough, only after a very *sharp* persuasion was Basim willing to give him away.

Furthermore, Basim told his superior how he had managed to capture the family of the man responsible, and that he expected to have them all in captivity very soon. That resulted in his boss informing him that he was coming tomorrow morning to avenge his nephew and kill everyone that had any connection with his death.

The reason they were able to connect Michael with the girls was a video of Elizabeth, and then of him, captured while they were separately entering the warehouse. It was owned by the gang and had an extensive surveillance system installed. All the cameras from inside were destroyed by the fire but there were a few hidden outside. They easily identified Elizabeth from the trial of her sister's assault, and kidnapping. When one of their members spotted her and Anna while they were shopping, Basim ordered them taken, so he could use them as leverage for Michael to surrender.

The girls were locked inside the cells in the basement, and he was all too eager to explain how to find the hidden entrance to them. Once they opened it, a staircase led them to the lower level.

Basim and his men had built a private prison in the basement, a convenient thing to have when you're involved in human trafficking. Ten cells with old dirty mattresses on a concrete floor, and dirty buckets for the prisoners to use as toilets. The cells were used for detaining and conditioning young women before they were shipped overseas to be sold like cattle. In two of those cells were Elizabeth and Anna.

Their eyes lit up when they saw Michael and the rest of the team.

"I knew you would come, Elizabeth told me that no matter what, you would save us," said Anna, holding onto the metal bars and jumping in place.

Elizabeth took a little different approach. "What took you so long? We have been expecting you for hours."

Michael looked at her and saw that she was trying to suppress a smile. "You wouldn't believe the traffic."

He released the girls with the keys provided by Basim, while the other guys were checking the rest of the underground level.

"Hey Mike, you are not going to believe this, I think

Christmas came early this year," Zac's voice could be heard from the back of the basement.

There was a separate room, more like an office, at the other end. When Michael looked inside, he saw a shelf covering the entire wall, filled with stacks of money. On the other side was another shelf of the same size, packed with white square packages bound in tape.

"There must be millions here!" said Zac, "can we keep it? Can we, can we?" chanting like a little kid.

"Well, as Basim told me, that money is from drugs and human trafficking, so yes, we will make better use of it. As a bonus, his boss, one Ariz Rama, is coming here in the morning, I think we should prepare him a warm welcome."

He took Elizabeth to the side and quietly told her, "They tracked you down using a recording of us at the warehouse. Once they recognized you in town, they decided to capture you both so they could convince me to give myself up,"

"What are you going to do now Michael?"

"I'm going to wait for his boss to come and then I'll have a little talk with him. Hopefully, by tomorrow afternoon, all this will be over."

"I want to help," she said, with a vicious fierceness in her voice.

"You need to take Anna and get her to the cabin, they didn't know about it, so it's still secure. This is the second time someone kidnapped her and she needs you more than ever."

He knew that one more person trained with a weapon could increase the odds in their favor, but after everything she and her sister went through, protecting them took priority.

Elizabeth placed her palm on his chest and looked him in the eye. "Fine, but you better come home safely." Then, in front of everyone, she kissed him.

After a few seconds of silence, Zac's voice could be heard, "You know, I helped—"

Tyron's slap to the back of his head interrupted what he wanted to say next.

"You're ruining the moment," the big man murmured.

It didn't take them long to pack all the money inside Elizabeth's car. What couldn't fit in the trunk they put on the back seat and covered it with a tarp. All the drugs were left undisturbed; one way or another, tomorrow they would be destroyed.

Elizabeth and Anna got into her car and drove toward the cabin leaving four men behind in a building where the majority of the residents were already dead.

* * *

Albanian Gang Headquarters

Michael and Tyron were making a plan for the coming visit, while Pete and Zac were on the lookout for anything unexpected.

"I'm not comfortable with only four of us going against unknown forces and I have nobody to call that can make it in time, so I'm reconsidering if we should stay here," Michael said, looking at the rough sketch of the mansion and surrounding terrain.

"We can call Alice," Tyron said.

Michael smiled. "Alice… I was planning to see her one of these days to bring her in. I didn't know she was nearby."

"Well, Jack called her last night after you left. I don't know how close she is right now but there's a good chance she'll make it."

"Do it."

Alice was a frequent addition to the team because of her

specialized talents. One being that she was an excellent sniper, and the other, a very skillful interrogator.

She could make anyone talk. It didn't matter how tough they were or how trained for withstanding an interrogation—Alice always got her answers.

There was a contradiction between what she did and how she looked. If someone saw her on the street, they would pause and look at her, drawn by her beauty. One would expect to see her walking down the catwalk of a fashion show, not in a small humid cell with a terrorist, making him sing like a canary. And certainly not lying on the ground in a ghillie suit, unmoving for hours and waiting for a perfect shot.

When they first met, it took a long time for her to open up to Michael and the other members of his team, but after a few missions together, she did. They found out she was an orphan and had a very shitty childhood. One of her foster parents was a sexual predator who molested her while she was a child. She reported him to the authorities but since it was her word against his, nothing happened.

So, the whole team took a leave of absence, and one night visited the man who once had the job of protecting her. She was only alone in the room with him for half an hour but, after that short time, he was only able to pee through a catheter.

The team treated her as their little sister, that is, a very deadly little sister. And in turn, she looked at them as if they were her big brothers. Alice got out of the military a few years after the team but they had all stayed in touch.

Tyron returned after a couple of minutes. "She will be here at least two hours before our guests arrive."

"Good... now we wait."

CHAPTER 10

Ariz Rama was furious, and that never bode well for those below him. Someone had dared to kill a member of his family and that was a challenge he could not leave unpunished. In all honesty, he didn't care that much for his nephew who was all muscles and no brains. Several times he'd to intervene because the idiot made some kind of a mess. Since that was tarnishing his reputation, Ariz had been planning to arrange an accident for his nephew, something random and inconspicuous. Nevertheless, this kind of blatant attack needed to be answered; he looked at it as a personal assault on his image that he strove hard to uphold.

If Basim had not already captured the perpetrators, he would have taken his rage out on the fat fool, but it would seem he was actually good for something. Ariz was already looking forward to inflicting pain onto those responsible, to make them an example for any others.

His car was nearing the mansion, a convenient place that Basim's part of the organization had managed to acquire, when four explosions, in quick succession, shook the car.

* * *

Albanian Gang Headquarters

The light of the rising sun cast spooky shadows through the misty dawn, making the woods look unwelcoming and ominous. The animals and birds were silent, somehow knowing there were alpha predators in their territory.

Michael glanced toward the place where Alice had set up her sniper's nest. She'd made it in time and without needing much explanation asked what he needed her to do and from which direction the target was coming. It was exactly what Michael had expected. While on a mission, Alice tended to be extremely task-oriented and a woman of very few words.

Tyron and he were on opposite sides of the road, with Pete and Zac mirroring them twenty feet (6 m) away, strategically positioned so they would not be in each other's field of fire. Michael looked at a particular place on the road and could not detect any difference from the rest of the surface. They'd camouflaged a makeshift spike strip near their position, covering it with a layer of fallen leaves, and were now all waiting in ambush.

Basim had received a call from his boss a few hours ago and confirmed he had captured the ones guilty of the death of his nephew and that everything was in order. Of course, Michael did have a knife pressed against his throat at the time, with a clear understanding of the consequences if he double-crossed them.

Right on schedule, the sound of the approaching vehicle disturbed the silence of the woods. A luxurious E-Class Mercedes with tinted windows appeared from around the bend in the road, one hundred feet (30 m) from their position.

Michael took a deep breath, his thumb switching off the safety of his weapon. A sense of calm went through him. It was a feeling he'd felt many times before. Waiting was never his thing, and he considered it the hardest part. Now, when the action was about to start, he felt more focused, with the increased adrenaline levels his body was producing making everything look sharper.

The Mercedes driver was going at acceptable speeds for a well-maintained private road, but that didn't help much when four explosions signified that the spike strip had done its job.

The car hadn't even stopped yet before two men jumped out of the back doors, rolling on the ground. They both had machine guns in their hands, identifying them as highly trained professionals; orders of magnitude above the gang members Michael and his team had dealt with last night. As soon as their tumble ended—they started firing.

It didn't look like they were aiming at anyone specific, just sending out loud bursts of fire into the surrounding woods. Michael and the team were well hidden and their locations were still unnoticed by the firing men. The intention of the shooters was to suppress the team's fire, hoping for a lucky shot.

Michael took careful aim and gently squeezed the trigger. One of them fell down, never to rise again, his forehead decorated with a brand-new round hole.

On the other side, Pete or Zac took out the other. The front glass of the car blossomed with a spider web of cracks, originating from a neat hole at its center. Alice had managed to place a perfect shot, the heavy bullet of her sniper rifle obliterating the driver.

Those few seconds of intense action were followed by partial silence, spoiled only by the sound of their discharged weapons, still echoing in the distance.

They needed the boss inside for questioning, so peppering the car with bullets was not an option. Michael aimed high at the backseat window and it disintegrated into thousands of pieces.

That brought a response, immediately multiple shots from a handgun were fired from inside the car. Most of those rounds' didn't even come close to the members of the team; the shots

The Spaceship In The Stone

were fired blindly, in a panic. Except one, which somehow found its way toward the place where Michael was hidden. It did not hit him, but it was a close call. The bullet lodged itself in tree bark, six inches (15 cm) away from him. He always hated those wild shots, they were the personification of chaos theory, and nobody was safe from them.

Michael looked at this tricky situation; the predicament was how to get the snake out of its nest, without suffering from a snakebite. He looked at a stun grenade hanging from his tactical vest and smiled, *it'd worked once.*

The flashbang flew through the air and entered the opening made by the broken window. It activated a second later with a distinctively loud sound and a cloud of smoke that vented outside.

He approached the car and looked inside. The scene inside was what he expected; a flashbang in a small and contained space was a very persuasive argument.

Ariz Rama was a sorry sight, lying unconscious on the leather backseat with trails of blood oozing from his ears and into his hair. A big gold-plated Magnum was still gripped in his hand. Tyron quickly remedied that by taking the gun in case the man was faking it. He looked disapprovingly at the powerful gun, made into a fashionable accessory, which was no way to treat a weapon.

"Well, I guess the fat lady has sung, and she was loud," Zac snickered, approaching from the other side with Pete on his heels.

They gathered around the car, and Alice quickly joined them and looked at the unconscious Ariz Rama. She shook her head and told Michael, "Mike, I know I'm supposed to interrogate this guy, but my sign language is a little rusty, and right now he's as deaf as a post. Couldn't you have been a little gentler with him?"

"Don't worry, by the time you start questioning him, he will be able to hear just fine."

"Max, can you fix this dirtbag?" Michael asked through his CEI.

"Piece of cake; put your hands over his ears and I'll transfer the nanites," the AI replied.

Michael did as instructed, and by the increased heat on his palms, he could feel the nanites transferring to the man. Alice was looking at him strangely. Her raised eyebrows were conveying that she was wondering what he was doing.

"Don't tell me you've found religion and turned into one of those touch healers."

"Nothing like that, I will explain later."

The fact she was satisfied with that answer just confirmed how much trust she had in Michael. They carried Ariz to the mansion and secured him in one of the rooms.

"Michael, there may be some information I can use from Mr. Rama, can you give Alice your phone, so I can listen in and ask some of my own questions?" Max asked.

"You know she generally likes to be alone with the subject, but there is no harm in asking her."

Alice squinted her eyes suspiciously when Michael asked her, but she agreed. Then she shooed everyone out of the room, leaving her alone with the still unconscious Ariz Rama.

"Max... Elizabeth and Anna?"

"They have arrived at the cabin safely, and I made a few dedicated surveillance drones; they are monitoring the surrounding perimeter."

"Tell me if anything changes."

Michael turned to the rest of his team while the first sounds of moaning could be heard through the closed door.

"Okay, while Alice is in there, let's do some work. Pete, you and Zac prepare this house for torching, while Tyron and I look around for any intel."

They didn't find much, a few account books and miscellaneous notes, all written in a foreign language. They took all they could; one of the rules of intelligence gathering was you never knew where a diamond in the rough was hidden. Michael was willing to bet the most useful stuff would be found in Ariz Rama's aluminum suitcase they'd taken from his car.

Alice was taking her time. The loud screaming and swearing from the beginning of the interrogation had stopped almost an hour ago. She had been straight at it for at least three hours. Michael and the team had finished going through the house with trained eyes a while ago. During their detailed search they found a secret compartment in one of the unused rooms. Inside were a few large stacks of hundred-dollar bills and a ledger documenting the gang's sales for the past few years. It was Basim's personal stash, the money he'd managed to skim off the top. He probably still nurtured some hope that he could survive this ordeal and wanted to keep something for a rainy day.

One of the things he did say was that this entire mansion once belonged to some rich man who had the misfortune of involving himself with these criminals. In the end, it cost him his house, his wealth, and consequently his life too. It goes to show that if you invite sharks to dinner, you stand a good chance of being the main course.

Alice exited the room and closed the door behind her. "I'm finished boys, unfortunately so is the perp. It seems he had a bad heart and our conversation was a bit too strenuous for it. Not that I feel sorry for that poor excuse for a human being, after learning some of the things he confessed."

"All right, you can give us a full report when we reach a safe location," Michael said as he took his phone back.

"We've stayed here for far too long. Pete, go and set the detonator for fifteen minutes. That will give us enough of a head start; the destination is my cabin, so if anyone gets separated, that's where you need to go."

It was a shame that they needed to burn down such a nice building, but unknowingly leaving evidence behind was what had gotten him into this mess. While they were cleaning up, they dragged the four guards in from the forest and placed them in the same room where their card-playing associates had perished. Michael even searched the whole perimeter and found four surveillance cameras hidden in the trees. But even if he hadn't, it wouldn't matter since all the hard drives from the computers in the house were now packed in one of the bags they were taking with them.

While they were walking down the access road, Pete and Zac were in front of the others, and Michael could hear them chatting.

"Pete, I feel like we forgot something…," said Zac while squinting his eyes.

"What?" asked Pete, turning around to look at the mansion.

"Oh, I remember, we forgot Basim."

"No, we didn't. I saw him before we left," Pete answered.

"And…"

"And… what?"

"Did he say something to you?"

"Well, he demanded to be released, and then he threatened me and spat at me. Oh, and he said he was hungry."

"So… did you feed him?"

Pete looked at Zac with one raised eyebrow. "Do I look like a chef to you…?"

Zac looked from the bottom of Pete's feet to the top of his head. "Not really, but the last meal and all that."

"I did throw him a few packets of heroin; they may have some nutritional value."

"That was kind of you, I'm sure he appreciated it," Zac said, patting him on the back.

Pete looked at the sky, "I'm trying to get in touch with my

more altruistic, feminine side. Caring for the welfare of my fellow man, being generous."

"Buddy, you have nothing to worry about, you're doing great," Zac nodded sagely.

Tyron looked at Michael and murmured, "Idiots."

As they were driving away, Michael could see the telltale signs of smoke from the direction of the mansion. As a result of its out-of-the-way location, it would be a long time before someone noticed the fire. There was little chance of that fire spreading to the woods, as the team had soaked the surrounding grounds and the trees with water. Leaving the sprinklers turned on, just in case.

He hoped that their troubles involving organized crime were finished, but his gut was telling him that their troubles were just beginning.

CHAPTER 11

Ozark Mountains - The Cabin

After several hours of uneventful driving, the group arrived at the cabin. Elizabeth's dark blue Toyota Prius was parked in front of it and the girls were waving at them from the porch.

As soon as Michael exited the car, Elizabeth ran towards him, putting her arms around him, and giving him a long and passionate kiss.

"Is it just me or are they making everybody feel uncomfortable?" Zac said after a few seconds had passed in complete silence.

Michael was caught in the moment, his arms around Elizabeth's waist, and all other stimuli except the feeling of her lips were unimportant. Still, after some time, he came to his senses and saw that everybody, except Zac, was looking at the surrounding trees, or the lake in the distance. Apparently, the sights around the house were very interesting.

"Hmm... we should get inside and clean up," he managed to say after Elizabeth released him from a lip lock.

"We stopped at the store on the way here and bought some

food and cooked one hell of a meal," she said, and looked at the others, smiling, "I hope you all like steaks."

"You went to the store with a car full of money?!" Michael exclaimed with wide eyes, while Tyron and the others were enthusiastically nodding; Zac was even trying to sniff out the aroma of grilled meat, like a bloodhound.

Elizabeth turned back to Michael. "It's the perfect camouflage, who in their right mind would think there are millions in the trunk and back seat of a Prius. We mostly used side roads and avoided heavily populated areas."

He wanted to get angry. Going to the store was an unnecessary risk, but then stopped himself and thought about it.

"That actually makes sense. All right people, let's go inside."

* * *

A little while later and a hell of a lot cleaner, Michael and the others were all sitting around a kitchen table piled high with grilled steaks, corn, and mashed potatoes. The entire meal had a family gathering atmosphere to it. The same type of feeling he remembered from when he was a young boy, and his grandmother cooked Thanksgiving dinner.

Elizabeth and Anna took the time to get to know the other members of the team and to share their life stories. The biggest surprise for the team was when they met Max. He'd managed to construct a holo-projector, which looked like a regular TV projector, except this one created full-blown 3D color images. Seeing Max for the first time, with the face of a much younger Michael, took the others some getting used to.

"So... Max... do you follow the three laws of robotics? You know, about not hurting people and all that?" Zac asked while stuffing his face with savory food.

The AI rolled his eyes. *"First, numbnuts, I'm not a robot, so why the hell would I follow some arbitrary laws of robotics? Secondly, as I explained, I'm essentially a digital copy of Michael's mind, so I remember everything he does. For example, I have a perfect recollection of the time you drank an entire bottle of laxatives on a dare, and then had to report to the commander's office, where you— "*

"Stop! There's no need to go into detail!" Zac exclaimed, with wide-open eyes and an embarrassed blush on his cheeks.

Bringing Alice up to speed took some time and a great amount of trust on her part. After a while, she accepted this strange new world they'd dragged her into, with spaceships buried in the ground and an AI that used to be human.

"Okay now, let's see where we stand," he said after they had all finished their meal. "Alice, what did you find out?"

She cleared her throat. "Michael, this time you really stepped in it. The late Ariz Rama was a nasty piece of work, and if his heart hadn't *popped*, I don't think I would've been able to let him live and sleep peacefully at night." She looked around the table. "Drugs, weapons, human trafficking, prostitution, assassination, you name it, he's done it. Moreover, most of the money earned from that was used to finance foreign and domestic terrorists. The thing is, he wasn't even a bit religious and didn't have any deeper convictions—he was just following orders."

As soon as she'd said that, Michael realized that there was a high probability that Ariz Rama's superiors would come looking for them, only this time he had every intention of being prepared for that eventuality.

Alice continued her report. "At best, Ariz Rama was a lieutenant, one of many that control their activities in different parts of the country. Now, Mr. Rama was very inquisitive, and if his superiors had found out the extent of his knowledge about them, they would have killed him on the spot. Evidently, there is an international criminal organization calling itself the 'High Council'. They are insanely powerful and have members from all over the world. It took Rama years to even dig that up. This 'High Council' are super secretive and have their hands in every pie. Rama was recruited in Albania while he was still young. He was nothing more than a murderous teenage thug, but with above-average intelligence. After that, he was educated at the best European schools, given additional training by his controllers, and then sent to the United States as one of their agents. He had a lot of power and a long leash, but ultimately—he was just a pawn

Alice took a drink of water and paused for a second. "No matter how evil he was, Ariz Rama was terrified of them. You managed to capture him by a stroke of luck. It's only because he was enraged by his nephew's death that he even left his headquarters. He had so many guards there, it would take an army to reach him. The interesting fact is that he knew his guards had orders to kill him if they thought he was about to be captured. The irony was that we prolonged his life by taking out his guards in a matter of seconds.

Oh, all the information he had about you three, he kept on his personal computer, and we took that. Max asked him a lot of questions, so maybe he should continue."

Max's hologram was standing close to Michael, so he just nodded when everyone turned to look at him.

"As Alice said, all evidence of your involvement was contained, so I don't see any possible avenues his superiors could use to track us down. Mr. Rama was kind enough to give me access to his accounts and I used that to transfer a considerable amount of money. I moved it a few times around the world so rest assured, nobody but me will ever be able to trace it."

The mischievous smile revealed his true feelings about appropriating that money.

"I have detailed information about Mr. Rama's criminal operation, but not much about his bosses which is strange in its own

way. They say that once a piece of information gets online, it stays there forever. Yet, there is no information about this 'High Council'. Any trace of them has been meticulously and systematically erased from the net. When I dug a little deeper, someone tried to trace my location. They didn't succeed, but the attempt itself tells me that someone is actively monitoring all queries about them. That can only be accomplished by using some serious resources and having a general oversight, which only a few government agencies possess."

"You think that the government is behind them?" Michael asked.

"*Not necessarily, but it does mean they have their own people in high places and the most secure locations. That reminds me, Michael, my intel gathering capabilities are severely constrained by such limited bandwidth. I've prioritized getting our satellites in orbit so I'll be able to do much more.*"

Michael cleared his throat after absorbing all this new information. "Alright, I guess we're safe from these 'High Council' people for now. We need to prepare for the next phase. Max, how much time will you need to equip everyone with a CEI and do a full-body upgrade?"

"*For you, it will take one night in the AutoDoc, the nanites have already done all the groundwork. For others… a full day. While preparing your body for the procedure, I've collected enough data to considerably speed up the process. I've been using drones to transfer the necessary materials from the E-waste recycling plant to the ship's stores, which are now full. The good news is that all of you can undergo the procedure simultaneously. In a pinch, the AutoDoc can now facilitate up to ten people.*"

He explained in detail to everybody what a CEI did, and Max briefed them on all of the upgrade details, using holograms to show them what the procedures would entail. They all agreed that this was not something they wanted to take a pass on. Stronger and more resilient bodies, enhanced senses, greatly prolonged life expectancy, immunization to any known diseases, and so much more. Every single thing would be a boon to any human but all of those things combined was like winning the lottery, several times in a row. The team knew that in the future they would most likely be in some very dangerous situations and any advantage was more than welcomed.

"Then that's what we'll do," Michael said.

"Pete, take Zac and bring Jack here. If nobody has any objection, I'm planning to have all of you undergo the procedure, ASAP." Everybody nodded in agreement. "Okay then, let's go to the ship so we can start the upgrades. I will wait for the guys to get back with Jack and we will join you later."

The thing that amazed all members of the team was the levitating board they used to load all the money from the Prius and transfer it to the ship. The money would be more secure there.

Seven people went to the spaceship and one by one climbed down the entrance shaft. Max materialized his hologram as the group entered the airlock and acted as a tour guide, showing them different scenes on holographic walls and the extent of Michael's injuries from when he'd fallen down the shaft.

The ship was rather small and the tour was a short one. It wasn't long before they all entered the AutoDoc room.

Instead of the single bed that was here before, the entire back wall of the room was one big sleeping platform, extending from one wall to the other.

"I remodeled it for convenience, but don't worry, it's still within specs," Max said, *"I hope lying close to one another is acceptable. If it helps, think of it as a slumber party."*

Elizabeth came close to Michael, "I'm a bit anxious about this *upgrade* thing. A part of me is afraid that this will change me in some way. On the other hand, Anna is all for it, she hates being weak and unable to protect herself."

Michael hugged her close to him and whispered in her ear.

"Don't worry, this will only make you more resilient and a lot safer.... I want you to be safe."

The others were purposely looking around the small space, giving them a semblance of privacy, even in such close quarters.

It didn't take long for the four people to make themselves comfortable on the platform and, with Max's customary countdown, soon fell asleep.

Michael looked at them lying there peacefully and said to Max, "Take good care of them; you know what they mean to us."

"I will. Even if I'm no longer flesh and blood, I still consider them my family."

Michael, Zac, and Pete exited the ship and returned to the cabin.

"We will return as soon as we spring Jack out of that retirement home," Pete said, and soon Michael was watching the two members of his team drive down the road.

He brewed himself a fresh pot of coffee and sat on the deck to savor it in silence. This solitude that once again permeated the cabin was why he came here; but now, the building felt empty to him, the people who made this place alive again were missing.

"Michael, the first satellite probe is ready to be launched. You could go visit Dave and see the launch. You'll be back before Pete, Zac, and Jack return. Furthermore, there is something there that I need you to see," Max's voice came through Michael's implant.

"I'll do that," he answered, looking at the coffee cup in his hand. "You know, Elizabeth and Anna wouldn't have had to go through all that if I wasn't damn careless. I thought we were dealing with some local thugs, not something this big. I know I rushed things with these upgrades, but my gut is telling me that a storm is coming. I am trying to do everything I can think of to be prepared for it and to prepare those I care about."

"You cannot blame yourself. Sometimes, you can only roll the dice and hope for the best. Look at it from another perspective, if you hadn't interfered, she would have gotten herself killed, and Anna would have also died in that hospital. Don't take the burden on yourself for the things you cannot change, just plan for the future, and hope that everything will turn out all right."

Michael sat there for a few more minutes, finishing his coffee and looking at the peaceful surroundings. He accepted Max's words but knew that no matter which path he took, the danger was lurking on every single one of them.

* * *

E-waste Recycling Plant

The trip to the recycling plant didn't take long, his 4x4 Ram Power Wagon was much more suited to these mountain roads than his grandfather's old pickup. Dave met him at the front gate, opening it and waving for Michael to drive on in.

"Hi Mike, I expected you earlier," the old man said as he shook Michael's hand.

"I've been busy, things to do, people to kill, you know how it is," he replied with a smile.

The old man shook his head. "Young people, always rushing around everywhere. You should take a day off, meet some pretty girls, have some fun."

"As a matter of fact, I did meet a girl."

"Good for you, there's not much point in living if you can't share it with someone."

They were walking towards the warehouse where Max had built the nano-factory.

"I've been feeding that machine ever since you left, must've put half a dozen tons of electronic scrap in it, and it all just disappeared."

"Let's see what all that hard work produced."

There was nothing inside the warehouse except the machine in the center and it didn't look as brand-new as it used to. If Michael didn't know better, he would've thought that it had been there for years.

"I like what you did to its exterior, all that wear and tear," he sent to Max through the implant.

"A precaution, if someone were to look inside the warehouse, it fits better like this. Now, look behind it."

A grinding noise behind the machine signaled that something was happening; he took a few steps and could see that a ten-foot (3 m) hatch opened on the warehouse floor. Levitating slowly from below, a six-foot (1.8 m) diameter black sphere rose silently.

"That's the probe? It is not like any *probe* I've ever seen," Michael said, walking around the floor opening and looking at the sphere, while Dave was left speechless, shaking his head in disbelief.

"Actually, it's a satellite in its own right. This is something I came up with as a spherical design offers the perfect utilization of space. it's equipped with a Gravity-drive and active camouflage."

As he said that, the sphere disappeared from their sight. Michael could only vaguely perceive its shape on the edges where the circular surface didn't bend light correctly.

"And that's how we're going to launch it without anyone being the wiser. Once in space, it will accomplish two things. First, it will be our way of having secure communications by routing them all through it. Second, it will be doing something... sneaky," Max said in an amused tone.

"What do you mean by sneaky?" asked Michael.

"As per my original idea, the satellite carries a payload, which consists of one hundred self-navigating infiltrator probes.

Their purpose, after being launched from the orbiting satellite, is to hunt down and attach themselves to any regular satellites. Once attached, they will use construction nanites to penetrate the core electronics and make the desired changes. These will enable us to control them, monitor all the information they relay, change their trajectories, and use them exclusively if we so desire, or shut them down if it ever becomes necessary. It will allow me to control the flow of information. By the time all of our own satellites are in orbit there shouldn't be any regular ones left that are not in our control. I have a couple downstairs in various stages of assembly. So, do you like it?"

"If I hadn't already seen the ship this would be the most amazing thing in the world, as well as unusually disturbing. Would you do me a favor, Max?"

"Sure."

"If you ever feel an urge to pull a *Hal 9000*, or rename yourself *Skynet*… just don't, as a favor to me."

"That's no problem at all, I wouldn't dream of it," Max replied, in a fake and innocent-sounding voice. After a few moments he added in a stage whisper, *"Just so you know, I would make Skynet my bitch."*

* * *

They watched as the barely visible ball went through the warehouse entrance and then ascended towards the sky.

Dave looked at it while scratching the back of his head. "If you live long enough, you'll see everything. I have a few cold beers in the fridge if you care to join me. I definitely need one."

"Michael, will you stay a little longer, I have something else to show you," Max sent through his implant.

"Sure Dave, you go ahead and I'll be with you in a few minutes."

After Dave exited the warehouse, Michael said aloud. "What did you want to show me that Dave couldn't see?"

"I've been working on something for a while now, and it's finally finished. With all of the running around you have been doing over the last few days, I came to the conclusion that you and the team need a better mode of transportation. Driving from one place to another is not very efficient and it's also very time-consuming, so I came up with this."

At that moment, the whole floor behind the machine lowered itself a few inches and slid to the side. From the darkness, a familiar object levitated upwards; any human would have no trouble recognizing it.

"Max... Why on earth did you build a flying saucer?"

The object had such a familiar shape that it could not be called anything but that. It was twenty feet (6 m) in diameter, painted in a deep black color.

"For the reason that it's such a familiar shape; if anyone catches sight of it, they will keep quiet for fear of being ridiculed. And even if it was captured on camera, it can easily be discarded as a hoax. The original idea came from some experimental craft that the US Air Force built in the 1950s, 'Project 1794' to be exact. It's much roomier though, as the Gravity-drive takes up so little space. It can comfortably carry ten people, plus supplies. Go inside and see for yourself."

Michael approached the craft and the sliding doors opened, just as they had on the Chrysler Voyager he used to own. There were ten seats arranged in a circle resembling those on a sports car with five-point belts. He sat down in one and the door closed, leaving him in absolute darkness. That lasted for only a second and then the walls shimmered and showed an image of the outside as if they weren't there.

"It's a mix of human and alien technology, the walls have holographic emitters in them, as does the outside surface, which

makes it almost invisible, just like the satellite. Undetectable by radar and with zero thermal emissions. I calculated that it can easily reach Mach 5, and more, but that's only in case of emergency. Normally, it flies silently below the speed of sound. It will be remotely flown by me using our, soon to be, satellite network. If something goes wrong and it becomes unavailable, a rudimentary machine intelligence is installed that can accept simple inputs. Not to sound like a used car salesman, but you should take it for a spin."

Michael closed his eyes, feeling as if another building block had been added to his plans. His hands caressed the comfortable seats, enjoying that new car odor he could smell inside the craft.

"You already knew that I would like it, the question is, how fast can you make more of them?"

"If Dave keeps supplying me with scrap material, it will take a few days; I still have satellites to build."

"How did you even manage to make this thing? How big is that nano-factory underneath?"

"I had to expand it a few times, and now it's about twice the size of this warehouse. But a quarter of that space is used for storing materials."

"You don't rest much, do you? Okay, make building additional crafts a priority, since the mobility it gives us is priceless. You know that once the team sees it, everybody will want one."

"All right, you will have one more by the time you exit the AutoDoc."

"There's something I've been planning to speak to you about. All of us being in the AutoDoc at the same time is not very good strategic planning. I want you to monitor all access points to the cabin, up to ten miles (16 km) or more, and if you see anyone suspicious approaching, stop the procedure and wake me up."

"I will, but I don't think you have anything to worry about, as

the ship has been undisturbed for thousands of years. It is one of the safest places on the planet."

Michael was thinking about all the things they could do with such increased mobility. This aircraft or *flying saucer*, how he was beginning to think about it inside his head, was a thousand times better than any airplane or helicopter in the world. He was about to exit the aircraft and go for that beer with Dave when an amusing thought crossed his mind. He picked up his phone.

"Pete, where are you now?" he asked as soon as Pete answered.

"We're still at Zac's since he needed to pick up a few things, but now he can't make up his mind about what is essential and what are things he cannot do without. So, we're running a little late. And we need to rent a van for disabled people because it's the only way we can safely transport Jack."

"Okay. Stay where you are, I'll be there in half an hour."

"You just have to show off a little," Max said after Michael terminated the connection.

"Well, it is kind of cool, and you know I'm only doing this to help the guys out, there is no personal interest whatsoever."

"Yeah... right."

He went out to Dave's trailer and told the man he would have to take a rain check on that beer. Then he instructed Dave to continue supplying the machine with more scrap material and gave him a bonus of $10,000 in cash. As an afterthought, he threw in the keys to his truck. Dave did not have a car anymore and with this flying craft, he did not see himself using it much more.

After barely managing to squeeze through the warehouse industrial doors, the aircraft silently climbed into the air. Michael could see Dave standing there and holding a stack of cash with a pink slip on top of it, speechless. In no time, he was flying towards Zac's house, high above the ground and invisible.

The Spaceship In The Stone

The chairs could be turned around, and locked in different positions, so all the passengers could face in the direction the aircraft was flying. With the canopy set to imitate transparency, he felt as if he was in the front seat of a big airplane.

Much sooner than he had expected, Michael arrived at the house that Zac was renting. It was not in a nice neighborhood, but it did have a large backyard with a high wooden fence. Max lowered the aircraft behind Zac's house and Michael exited his new ride. It was strange seeing it from the outside; only the opening indicated its existence. If looked at from any other angle, the holo-emitters gave the illusion the aircraft was not there.

"Max, make it visible." After a few steps, he knocked on Zac's back door.

Pete was the one who answered and was starting to greet Michael when he froze, dumbfounded by the flying saucer parked in Zac's backyard. He stared at it without saying a word, his mouth still open.

"You like my new ride?" Michael asked, pointing with his thumb over his shoulder.

"What is that thing?"

"Just something Max tinkered together, it gets you from point A to point B," Michael answered with a slight smile. "Gather all the stuff; we're flying out of here."

Zac's reaction was a little more infantile than Pete's. "I want one, I want one, I want one…" And he would have continued chanting it while walking around the aircraft if Pete didn't effectively stop him by applying a technique perfected by Tyron, a slap to the back of the head.

They secured all of Pete and Zac's stuff in the center cargo space and were soon approaching the long-term care facility where Jack was waiting.

Security was much more lax here since it was a voluntary facility. Therefore, while Michael was on the lookout, Pete and

Zac put Jack in a wheelchair, took the bag with the stuff he wanted to bring with him, and paused only for Jack to write a little note.

SO LONG SUCKERS, I AM SO OUT OF HERE.
JACK

Five minutes later, Michael, Pete, Zac, and Jack entered the aircraft, parked on the flat roof of the hospital, and launched into the sky.

"So, Michael, you get good mileage on this thing?" Jack asked, after silently admiring the futuristic vessel.

"It's one of those alternative energy engines, runs on tap water," Michael casually answered.

"Hmm... I reckon you would have a lot of trouble registering it, the FAA is not too keen on UFOs."

"Well, it's invisible, so... we decided to skip them altogether, to save them any headaches."

"That's mighty fine of you, caring for your fellow man."

"I thought so too, in fact, it's Pete's influence, he's trying to get in touch with his feminine side."

Jack looked at Pete, who was shaking his head in denial.

"Nothing wrong with that young man, we did have that policy: *Don't ask, don't tell*. If someone wants to broaden their horizons, it's fine by me."

Pete looked at Jack suspiciously. "Hey, what did you mean by that?"

Zac patted him on the arm. "Don't worry Pete, nobody's judging you."

They flew the rest of the way with Pete arguing that there was really nothing to tell.

The flying saucer settled down near the entrance shaft and they used a levitating gurney to transport Jack to the ship. The nanites Michael had given him earlier were fixing him slowly, but the years had taken their toll, and his legs looked like toothpicks with very little muscle on them.

When they entered the AutoDoc, he saw that those undergoing the treatment were under opaque sterile energy fields, which reminded him of butterfly cocoons.

Max explained, "*It's much easier and quicker when everybody has their own personal enclosed space, especially considering the extent of the procedures. You should all lay down. The satellite is in a stationary orbit above us, and I'm also monitoring a wide perimeter with surveillance drones.*"

As he was falling asleep, Michael could not help but wonder how he would feel when he woke up the next time.

CHAPTER 12

Switzerland, Castle of Regnum

Hashim Osmani hated security checks with a vengeance. He felt that someone of his importance should never submit to such humiliation. If anyone within the territory he controlled even suggested such degrading treatment it would be akin to courting death. But this was not his territory. This was a place of the 'High Council' meeting and security was paramount.

To him, this level of security seemed designed by someone who has dived to the deepest depths of paranoia. His bodyguards were forbidden to cross a one mile (1.6 km) perimeter around the castle. Phones and electronic devices were confiscated at the first checkpoint. He then had to pass two additional checkpoints to enter the castle, which was ridiculous.

Hashim did not see the point of it all. Who would spy on them? Who would attack? In every aspect that mattered, the 'High Council' *ruled* most of the world.

He still remembered the day when his father introduced him to this secret world. It was on his 16th birthday when one of the servants had summoned him to his father's office. There, his father explained to him how the world really worked.

The 'High Council' could trace its origins back to the dark ages, calling itself different names at different times. In essence, it had been the same organization for the past thousand years. Created by those who craved power more than anything else; Kings and warlords, cardinals and slavers, it did not matter where they came from. Their race and religion were also irrelevant, only their ambition and an insatiable hunger for power. In the end, that was the real purpose of the 'High Council'… to control. The scope of all their operations was hard to believe. They controlled governments, politicians, the drug trade, slavery, prostitution, gambling, and more. There was barely an aspect of human existence that was exempted from their influence.

Nobody outside the organization knew about it. Secrecy was one of their most sacred creeds. His father had used an analogy of a spider puppeteer; the 'High Council' was at the center of the web, pulling or loosening the strands, and in that way harnessing the lives of billions.

They outright owned a big chunk of the planet itself. Corporations, banks, real estate… behind the thousands of familiar names, ultimately stood the 'High Council'. Their wealth could be measured in trillions, and the biggest part came from the profits made on the darker side of the economy.

Lastly, his father said that he was one of the members, a position inherited from his own father; and it was time for Hashim to take the test and prove he was worthy.

He was led to a small groundskeeper's house on their property. Inside was something that made the sound of his heart thunder in his ears.

The man's name was Nazim, and his family had lived and taken care of the grounds for as long as Hashim could remember. Nazim's daughter, Almira, was a few years younger than Hashim, and she used to follow him around all the time when they were younger, wanting to play. In time, they'd become friends; one of very few he was allowed.

Now, they were all tied with rope and lying on the floor.

He looked, uncomprehending, at his father.

"This is your test. That is why they were hired all those years ago."

"I don't understand…" Hashim said.

"You are being given a choice, and it will decide your future. Their lives are in your hands."

His father pulled out a big knife from the back of his waist and handed it to him. It was old but well maintained, gold and precious stones adorning the hilt of the knife. The warm summer sun shined through the windows and reflected from the well-honed edge.

"If you allow them to live, you will have a common, mundane life. I will give you enough money to live comfortably but I will disown you. However, if they die, you will be my successor in the 'High Council'. One of the rulers, making decisions that will have an impact on the entire world."

His father turned around and exited the groundskeeper's house, closing the door behind him.

Hashim's gaze fell to the bound and gagged family, their fear tangible in the small room. Almira's eyes were begging him to let them go…

Sometime later, he exited the cozy little house, leaving a bloody smear on the doorknob. Hashim's face, hands, and clothes were drenched in red. The innocence that was in his eyes when he'd woken up that morning was forever gone. Any vestige of it was lost behind the small house doors. His father was waiting for him in front of the house with an approving nod and a smile on his lips.

"You never intended to let them live, did you?" he demanded from his father.

"No, they were insignificant, their lives meaningless," his father answered, with an unemotional face.

Hashim nodded, for the first time seeing deep into the soul of the man that stood before him. He lifted the hand with the bloodied knife and offered it back.

The older man shook his head. "From this day on—that knife belongs to you; it is our most treasured family heirloom. Your actions today proved that you are worthy to be my successor. You have earned that knife, the same way I had to a long time ago."

That knife was now one of his most prized possessions; it was the knife that got him a seat at the 'High Council', and the same knife that ended his father's life, when Hashim felt that he was ready.

He had made a decision that day and he never regretted it.

* * *

Hashim snapped out of his reminiscence and entered the chamber where the meeting was to take place. Deep underground, away from the prying eyes of satellites and the most sophisticated listening devices. The decorations in this room were worth hundreds of millions; great works of art that had been lost to the world in the abyss of time; gem-encrusted gold treasures that were pillaged and taken from the weak. Only the rarest and most expensive objects were used to adorn this chamber, any of which would make a museum curator faint at the sight.

A massive round table dominated the center of the room that was more than a century old and perfectly preserved. On its surface was a masterfully carved map of the world, with no borders, since the 'High Council' had an ultimate goal—to be in control of it in its entirety. He'd always thought it was funny that they sat like the *Knights of the Round Table*, except that there was nothing knightly about those who earned their seat here.

Twenty chairs for twenty rulers. Each wearing a black mask with a golden Roman numeral on its forehead. To hide their identity and display their position in the hierarchy. It was more for the sake of tradition but it also served a purpose. Hashim knew the identity of only five other members because he recognized their voices. The voices of very powerful people, their faces were known by millions; maintaining a false public image of admirable philanthropy, but their souls were just as black as Hashim's.

He looked around and saw that all the other members had taken their seats. Gathered here was such an immense accumulation of power that even all the world leaders' summits could not come close to matching.

They decided who would live and who would die. Where new wars would begin and how many innocent people would perish. Most terrorist organizations were ultimately controlled from here, but of course, that information was unknown to their members. The 'High Council' considered them nothing more than disposable tools.

Each of them had their primary areas. For Hashim, it was North America, specifically drug trade, slavery, and organizing terrorist attacks, as needed.

Personal names were forbidden, each member was addressed by the Roman numeral on their mask; the lower the number, the higher their position in the hierarchy. It had taken Hashim a long time to rise within the ranks; he was much more influential than his late father had been. If someone were to speak to him, they would refer to him as *Secundus*, the second from the top in the power structure of the "High Council". His father had only been *Decimus,* the 10th from the top; the same position Hashim had inherited in the joining ceremony. It had taken a lot of maneuvering, money, and a river of blood for him to reach his current position. The last *Secundus* had died by his hand, still proclaiming his innocence in the assassination attempt on their leader, despite all the incriminating evidence.

He was innocent, but only Hashim had known that, as he was the one who had plotted and executed the entire thing. Then, after theatrically thwarting the plot, he took the reward of taking the position of his victim. Still, what Hashim Osmani really craved, more than anything else, was to become *Primus*, the ultimate ruler.

The meeting went as expected, each member giving reports of their activities and achievements, since the last time they had gathered. How plans were developed and implemented, and how much money they'd earned for the 'High Council'.

When his turn came, Hashim gave everyone a positive report. One of the big projects he was in charge of was progressing on schedule and there were no problems whatsoever. Inside himself, he was seething. This was no place to show weakness as it would most certainly have been exploited by those below him and those above.

The truth about someone attacking part of his organization was deeply disturbing, especially at such a critical junction. Everything needed to be in its exact place for the 'High Council's plans to work. The fact that one of his lieutenants, Ariz Rama, was most likely dead, did not bother him so much, as there were many others eager to fill the vacancy. Losing over $50 million was annoying, since he had to cover the disappearance of all that money from his personal accounts. That needed to be kept a secret. The 'High Council' would never condone a failure this close to the project's deadline.

The thing that alarmed him the most was that he didn't know who did it. All of his government and law enforcement connections had turned up nothing. To someone in his position, not knowing was unacceptable. He deeply suspected that one or more of the people sitting around this table were ultimately responsible, making a play for his position. Nevertheless, he could not be sure, and it made no difference. By the 'High Council's' standards, the culprit would get a commendation, not condemnation. He needed to act on his own, all his actions concealed from the others.

Before coming here, Hashim had given orders that every piece of evidence needed to be rechecked, every clue investigated. There was no doubt in his mind that he would find the culprit, and when he did, there would be hell to pay. Everyone who had any knowledge would die, their families too. Those at the top, who gave orders for this attack—he would finish them himself.

His knife would be bloodied again.

* * *

Ozark Mountains - The Spaceship

Michael opened his eyes to a familiar sight, a bright white ceiling that he was getting used to. The alarmingly different thing was… he could not move a muscle.

"Don't try to move, I'm suppressing all of your implants and keeping you still," Max said, after registering Michael's conscious state. His hologram appeared in front of the platform that everybody was lying on. *"Besides installing all of your new systems, the old ones were also slightly improved. And all of them need to be calibrated and synchronized with your CEI. On the positive side, you have the distinct honor of being the first human to go through the extensive calibration process for a full implant suite. Don't you feel lucky?"*

"I wish I wasn't so lucky. Go ahead, and do what you need to," Michael said, suppressing the instinctual panic that came with not being able to move his body.

"It will be much quicker for the others, once I have baseline

The Spaceship In The Stone

parameters. I'll just need to tweak them a bit to reach full synchronization."

For the next hour, he went through a series of annoying tests. He had to flex his muscles, one by one, which got pretty boring in no time at all. Right about the time that he was fed up with it all, it was over.

"So, are we done?"

"*Not exactly, there are still a series of tests we need to perform outside.*"

"If you try to put Tyron through this he is going to pull out your circuits."

"*I had the same thought, that's why I decided to use you as a guinea... I mean the prime subject. I estimate that for the others, calibration is going to take less than five minutes,*" Max said with a reassuring smile.

"That's just great, I'm being used as a guinea pig by an AI who would put Dr. Frankenstein to shame," Michael murmured into his chin.

"*Sure, be like that. You're taking one for the team, so man up,*" Max replied reproachfully, but the tone of his voice did little to hide his amusement.

"*You can stand up now.*"

Michael could see the others were still in their opaque sterile field cocoons; he could barely make out their silhouettes. It took him no time at all to get outside the ship; it was a beautiful, bright morning.

"Okay, now what?"

"*Bring up your HUD.*"

The familiar display appeared before his eyes and in the lower right corner was a representation of his body, colored gray.

"*When you're ready, I'll activate all of the systems.*"

"Max, waiting is not my thing, so just go ahead and do it."

The feeling was nothing like he had ever felt before. Every

part of his body was brimming with endless energy. The constant pull of gravity that every human took for granted and never noticed... disappeared. Michael felt as if his body was as light as a feather, and wondered if the Earth would still pull him back if he jumped upwards?

All of his senses, which had been greatly improved the last time he'd been in the AutoDoc, were now orders of magnitude more powerful, sharper, and clearer.

"Starting with your hearing. You can increase and lower the gain, or concentrate on a particular sound, isolate it, and amplify it," the AI instructed.

After mentally clicking the indicated icon, all the sounds he could hear had a graphical representation on his HUD. Out of that cacophony of sounds the forest provided, he selected one, which was the distinct rhythm of a woodpecker. It was as if he was suddenly right beside it; the rhythmic beat sounded like the pounding of a big drum. Mentally clicking again on the icon returned his hearing to normal. Michael had experienced this sense of improved hearing once before when Max had first activated his CEI. Nevertheless, this was so much more precise. It was impressive then, but now, it was like comparing a cheap knockoff stereo to a high-end surround sound system.

"*Hearing seems to work fine, now I want you to concentrate on your vision. There is an icon that looks like an eye in your drop-down menu, go ahead and activate it.*"

Selecting the icon opened a new menu, with clearly defined options for zooming and magnification. Playing around with the commands for a while, he realized that he could see objects that were far away—in perfect clarity, comparable to using a pair of binoculars. His eyes could now even magnify things as if looking through a microscope.

"Your eyes now have an additional layer over them, similar to contact lenses. It's not removable and is now a permanent fixture

to your ocular anatomy. Aside from the additional protection it provides to your eyeball, it has some extra features, as you are discovering."

It was quite fun just messing around with it. He looked at grass, stones, and trees in a completely new way. He focused on a tiny ant that was going about its own business and for a second, and under great magnification, it seemed as if that ant was looking right back at him.

"OK Michael, you can play with your eyes some other time. I want to test your strength and your skeletal reinforcements. There are a few boulders some 170 feet (50 m) northwest of your position. Try to pick one up."

He quickly jogged to them, amazed at how easily his body moved. There were three big boulders at that location, different in size and weight. Michael chose the middle one, doubting that he could ever make it move. He squatted before it, put his hands around the rock, and pulled with all of his strength. There was considerable resistance at first; part of the boulder was underground. After that initial resistance, the rock detached itself from the ground and Michael stood up holding the big boulder in his hands. It was such a surreal thing, to be able to accomplish something that his brain perceived as impossible. He felt that it had some weight to it but not that much, and if needed, he could hold it for a long time.

"How much—"

"Michael, that boulder is close to five hundred and fifty pounds (250 kg)," Max announced proudly.

"That's impossible!"

"For an ordinary human it would be, but your skeleton is a lot stronger than it used to be. Combined with composite fibers in your muscles, your strength is far above the norm. Imagine how much stronger Tyron will be, with his mass and muscles I had far more space to play with... I mean to improve. He could lift that

boulder with one hand. And now for one more test, run as fast as you can toward the cabin."

Michael dropped the rock in his hands and felt the vibration it made when it hit the ground. In one corner of his HUD was a small compass that transformed into a scalable map of the surrounding terrain when he mentally clicked on it. He chose the direction of the cabin and started running.

Moving at his top running speed was a new experience. His feet were striking the ground with the force of pistons. Improved sight allowed him to see exactly where his next step would fall, so he could precisely position his foot before it touched the ground. Before he realized it, Michael was already in front of the cabin.

"Your average speed was around 45 mph (72 kph), and on that last stretch of flat terrain, you were running at 50 mph (80 kph). Congratulations, you just set a world record," Max said and played a little victory jingle from one of the video games Michael used to play.

"These upgrades are amazing; I feel like a superhero. Max, you have outdone yourself."

"Let us not get too ahead of ourselves, as there is still room for improvement. Nonetheless, all things considered... I'm a freaking artist," the AI boisterously declared.

Most of that day Michael spent testing his new abilities. From climbing trees and lifting heavy rocks, to free running through the mountain forest. The whole time feeling, and acting, as if he were a little kid again, infinitely entertained by an amazing new toy. He only stopped when Max reminded him that it was time for the others to wake up.

He was there waiting for them, as the energy fields around them turned off, and they regained consciousness.

As Max had said, full activation of their implants took no time at all, and soon they were all eager to try out their new abilities. Before long, they were all behaving like schoolchildren after the

The Spaceship In The Stone

last bell signaling the start of summer vacation. Max was using their implants to talk to everyone simultaneously, guiding them through options, and explaining all the settings of their CEIs.

"Do you feel all that different?" he asked Elizabeth when they managed to grab a few moments alone.

"I feel pretty amazing," she answered with a smile. "I was always trying to stay in shape during my FBI training and was in top physical condition. But that all fades in comparison to how I feel now… as if I could run forever, and never get tired."

"You probably could," Michael said and smiled back at her.

They were interrupted by the loud sound of rocks hitting the ground, so they went together to see what was going on. While some were exploring their new abilities with composure and a sense of dignity, others were completely on the other side of the spectrum.

Pete and Zac made a game of throwing boulders as far as they could, then managed to convince Tyron to join them, which was a mistake since he doubled the length of their best shots. The big man could not keep a smile from his face at the newly regained depth perception and lack of an eye patch.

Jack was simply enjoying the ability to walk again, doing Army exercises he learned as a young man, with a constant grin plastered on his face.

Anna was preoccupied with the new ability to surf the Internet in her head. The CEI could emulate any known operating system, and run all of the apps. When Michael had first heard about it, he was afraid that the implant could be infected by some of the millions of computer viruses on the Internet. Max laughed the whole idea off, explaining that protective measures he implemented would destroy any malicious program in the same way a fly would be incinerated if it came close to the Sun.

Alice was using her silenced gun for target practice. She had placed the targets at various distances and was now testing how much more accurate she'd become with better hand-eye coordination, and the ability to calculate the exact trajectories of her bullets. It was amazing, and somewhat intimidating to see her hitting the small little red circle... every single time.

For the next few hours all they did was have fun. Michael looked at them all, happy and carefree, and could not help but wonder about all the difficulties they would be facing. Deep inside, he felt responsible for them; ultimately, he was the one to set them on a path that had changed their lives...hopefully for the better.

The sun had already set behind the mountains and it was time to head for the cabin. They walked together, telling jokes and still goofing around, the entire group feeling much closer than before they had gone into the AutoDoc.

CHAPTER 13

Ozark Mountains - The Cabin

The light coming from the cabin was the only bright spot in the dark mountain valley and was the source of the sound of laughter.

Michael and the others were sitting around the big kitchen table. They had pulled out the extension leaves so there would be room for everybody without bumping their shoulders. After they returned from the ship everybody helped to cook an enormous amount of food. It was Max's suggestion; all of them needed a big infusion of energy to replenish what their nanites were using while doing final changes to their bodies. It was surprising even to them that in the end not one scrap of food was left.

"If I can have your attention please..." Michael said, tapping his glass with a steak knife and then waiting until all the conversation in the room stopped.

"I would like to say some things concerning us all and our futures. First, let me thank you all for joining me in this endeavor and all the places it will lead us. The road there won't be easy and we all know there will be plenty of obstacles that will stand in our way, but in the end, I think it will be worth it."

He had to stop talking because of the whistles and clapping that broke out at the table. For a moment, he felt like that dubious life form, a politician, speaking at a rally. He quickly dismissed that disturbing thought and continued.

"Okay, settle down you bunch of miscreants; let's start with the problems at hand, and specific tasks I want you to do," he announced when they quieted a bit.

"While you were going through the upgrade procedures in the AutoDoc, I used the time to go over some immediate actions we will need to take. But first, Max, would you give us a short summary of what resources we have available."

He turned to the hologram, sitting on one of the chairs. It was Anna's idea, not wanting Max to feel left out of the group.

The AI nodded and looked around the table. *"Well, if you include all the gold we mined, the money you collected at the mansion, and everything I managed to transfer from Ariz Rama's accounts, we have in excess of $70 million,"* Max said with a straight face, knowing what kind of reaction his statement would provoke.

There was a collective intake of breath, followed by various sounds of surprise and amazement, all around the table.

"Boss, I want a raise!" declared Zac, raising his hand in the air.

"You do realize that we're not working on salary?" Pete theatrically whispered to him.

"That's just not right, I'm going to complain to my union representative."

Tyron looked at him while raising his hand in a familiar gesture. "Zac... shut up."

"He's right, we'll all need some spending money—" Michael was interrupted by Max.

"I can take care of that. You can take as much cash as you need from what we took out of the mansion—it cannot be traced.

In addition, I've made some arrangements for the rest of it. The cash, including the gold, will be picked up by an armored truck, and transferred to our accounts. Once it becomes digital, I can make it grow," he stated smugly, one corner of his lips rising considerably.

"All right, that will work. The size of the infrastructure we will need requires a more organized structure, so Max set up an international corporation under the name... *Genesis*. That has a nice ring to it, and it will be used as a front for everything we do publicly. At the end of the day, it's always easier to hide in plain sight," Michael said.

"That shouldn't be too difficult. With the amount of money we will be transferring into the accounts, banks will be all too pleased to issue you corporate credit cards. Just try not to go wild with them, and no buying private planes, ships, or gold toilets. Leave the money issues to me; I read an e-book about banking yesterday, so I'm practically an expert," the AI added.

"Anything else?"

"Satellite production is going steadily, and I managed to finish another transportation aircraft, or flying saucer, if you want to call it that."

Michael closed his eyes in exasperation. "Oh brother, it's so cheesy calling them flying saucers, we really should choose a different name for them. Any suggestions?"

After a ten-minute debate, and many propositions about the new name of the craft, Michael decided it was ludicrous that they should spend so much time on such an inconsequential thing and decided to cut the Gordian knot by simply calling them *Transporters*. That was their main purpose, and he absolutely did not want to call them *Puddle jumpers, Prowlers, Delta flyers, Shuttlecrafts*, or *Runabouts*. Those were a few of the many ideas, even if most of them didn't make any sense for Max's particular design. He could see that Zac was disappointed the most, but he was not naming the aircraft an *X-wing*, no matter how many times Zac whined about how cool it would be.

"Well, that's settled. Next on the agenda is something only you can do Max, I need you to take control of the Internet," he said, and everyone present opened their eyes in surprise.

"In today's world, almost the entire flow of information goes through it and you are the only one who can control that flow to our advantage. We are in a race against time; eventually, our actions will be noticed. Therefore, I need you to buy us more time with disinformation, by changing official reports and planting bogus stories. Those are just examples; you will have to do a hell of a lot more. I realize some of these things will be morally and ethically questionable but I firmly believe they will also be necessary," Michael stated.

The AI scrunched his holographic face and nodded. *"It's doable, but not easy and I'll need a lot of processing power for a project of that magnitude. By now, almost 25% of space-based communications are already under my control, and it won't be long until I'm at 100%. The problem is that the biggest part of the information flow goes through the undersea optic cables, so I'll need to construct autonomous submarine vehicles that can approach them at great depth, and insert splices, without anyone being the wiser. At the same time, I'll need to find a way to infiltrate numerous strategic locations in digital infrastructures that span the globe. I can see our need for material rising considerably, and we will need to address that before we hit a bottleneck."*

"This has to be one of our top priorities," Michael said and turned to the colonel.

"Jack, you will be in charge of our recruitment, finding the right people for the right jobs is in line with your expertise. Our ultimate goal is to build a space-based civilization, and we will need a lot of manpower to achieve that. You, more than any of us, know a lot of old soldiers that are wasting away in retirement homes, collecting their disability pensions, or were let down by the system and are doing nothing except waiting for the end to come. We have the ability to heal them and give them a purpose again and a desire to strive for something greater than themselves."

Jack nodded and smiled, "Not only them, if you are looking for people willing to go to space, there are certain individuals that would do anything for a chance. You are all familiar with a few astronauts that went to space and some even spent time on the International Space Station. But for every one that went up, there are hundreds that never did. Rejected for this or that, losing their chance as a result of budget cuts and whatnot. They will be perfect candidates to join our venture. No matter their age, each and every one of them possesses that adventurous mindset. Several were close friends before I ended up in that well-meaning hellhole but we stayed in touch. As an added benefit, almost all of them went through some kind of military training and that is always an asset. I can get the ball rolling in that direction and in several others."

"And that's why you're in charge of recruitment," Michael said with a nodding smile.

"The rest of you should make a list of people that you think would be a good fit for what we are trying to achieve, then give it to Max, so he can run background checks. We cannot give everyone a CEI yet, but basic treatments with medical nanites should do wonders for their general health."

Michael looked at the two women that were sitting next to him. "Now for our intelligence section. I figured that it is best if it is run by Elizabeth and Alice, let me explain. Elizabeth, you were one of the top FBI intelligence analysts, and your official record speaks for itself; connecting the dots will come naturally to you. And Alice, you have a gift in acquiring information by unconventional means, which is always a bonus. With your military training and Elizabeth's knowledge of government agencies, I think you two should fit well. Of course, you will work closely with Max. Not utilizing the full potential of all the advantages he puts on the table would be foolish. What do you think?"

Elizabeth and Alice looked at each other, and as far as Michael could see, had an entire conversation using only their eyes in those two seconds.

"We can do that," Elizabeth said. "As long as Max provides for the technical side of intelligence gathering, it shouldn't be too difficult."

Michael turned to face her sister. "Anna—"

Her raised hand interrupted him. "I already know what I want to do," she announced confidently. "I was planning on making my career in public relations; I was always good at it. Also, you are going to need someone to be the face of the Genesis Corporation. If it's all right with you, I know I could be good at that job."

"Okay, if that is what you want then you will be in control of our PR, but be aware that most of the information we make available to the public needs to be spun to our advantage. That is hopefully a long time from now but we had better be prepared. Then, there will be times when we will need to… if not lie, then bend the truth into a pretzel," Michael explained what would be expected of her.

Anna laughed. "To tell the truth, that's something that one of my professors said at the beginning of the semester, how the public image is based on perception, not reality. He also said the truth and facts should be our instruments for painting the picture which does not necessarily represent actuality."

"Smart man, at least he told you all the truth, not some sugar-coated gibberish that had no connection with real life," Michael replied and looked in the direction of his teammates.

"That leaves Tyron, Pete, Zac, and me. We will be a sort of fast response team, which will be used to put out the fires that will most certainly appear in our path. That was our job before, hunting bad guys, and we were not half bad at it. With the advantages we now have, it is going to be a whole new ballgame."

"Boss, we are always ready to play," Tyron's deep base resonated through the room.

Michael acknowledged that with a nod, "I don't plan on us becoming vigilantes of some sort, but if we see something that is not right and we have the ability to stop it—we just might."

Tyron, Pete, and Zac's faces showed big happy grins and those around the table could see something predatory awaken in their eyes. It did not bode well for those that would be their adversaries in the future, not one bit.

"I'll talk to my father when he gets here tomorrow. He will be your counterpart Jack, since he's a scientist himself, and recruiting members of the scientific community will be his responsibility."

Michael looked around the table and all the eyes fixed on him.

"This will not be a strict and regimental organization as there will be plenty of overlap in your areas of responsibilities. Each of you can ask for help from the others, and of course Max. He will have to be a *Jack of all trades*, dealing with logistics, infrastructure, transportation, communication, intelligence, and assisting the rest of us as needed."

He didn't want to drag on this impromptu meeting and oversaturate them all with new information, and it had already been a long day, so he decided to mention a few more things, and then wrap things up.

"People, if any government or any big organization finds out what we are up to before it's time to leave, they will absolutely object, but we cannot count on not being discovered, so we need to implement some plans in advance. For one, we need secondary locations, in case we have to abandon this cabin. Elizabeth and Alice, work with Max to arrange that, so if we need to evacuate, we can do so in a hurry. Max, how are we on secure communications?"

"Our satellites in orbit should cover our current needs, at least over the Western Hemisphere, so secure communication is not a problem. And if you want to do something on the other side of the world, I have control over enough 'hijacked' satellites, so you can talk all you want with nobody being the wiser," the AI answered.

"Great, that's one less thing to worry about. But let us not forget that 'High Council' Ariz Rama talked about, they will not forget that someone destroyed their operation and cleaned them out in the process. Max, I know you said they covered their tracks on the net, but I need you to dig a little deeper. Use as much money as needed to buy any scrap of intelligence, hack into secure databases, and do everything possible to find out more. I have a really bad feeling about them."

"I cannot make any promises, but I'll do my best."

In the eyes of those around the table, he saw how much faith they all had in him. He only hoped that he could rise to their expectations.

"Okay, that's all folks. Now let's grab a drink and enjoy it on the deck."

* * *

A few hours later, Michael was sitting alone in his favorite chair and looking at the slowly rising moon. They'd had a great evening hanging out on the deck. That one drink had turned into several; everybody was enjoying the company in a happy and jubilant atmosphere, a celebration of the beginning of their new lives. Listening to Zac tell funny and often embarrassing stories of their time together in the military. Eventually, one by one, all of the others had turned in for the night. The cabin was not very large but there were enough surplus army cots for everyone. Michael had bought them a few years ago at an auction. He didn't really need them, but he'd gotten a very good deal on them. Besides, those things could last forever; God knows he spent enough time on them.

He couldn't sleep, excitement and worry were battling inside him, making sleep impossible. He was going over his plans repeatedly, using his CEI to draw charts, make notes, and arrange timetables; tweaking, adjusting, and trying to make every cog align with another.

His improved hearing detected someone climbing down the stairs inside the cabin, and a minute later the door behind him slowly opened.

"Hi," Elizabeth said, putting her hand on his shoulder.

"It's late, you should get some rest," he whispered.

"I tried, but... we never really talked about..." Her quiet and hesitant voice trailed off into silence.

"No, we haven't." Michael stood up from the chair and faced her. "Elizabeth, I was never really good at relationship stuff, and—"

Her hand covered his lips, preventing him from speaking any further. "There are times when you should talk, and then there are times when you really shouldn't," she said, then rose on the balls of her feet and kissed him.

Elizabeth took his hand and pulled him towards the door. "Come with me," she said and didn't let go until they were all the way into his room, where she closed the door behind them.

"Finally! Two sloths on Valium would have hooked up faster than these two," Zac whispered from the room across from Michael's.

"Zac... shut up," Pete whispered back and moved to make himself more comfortable on the familiar army cot.

CHAPTER 14

Ozark Mountains - The Cabin

It was not a nightmare that woke Elizabeth this time but the rhythmic beat of Michael's heart. Her head was resting on his chest, riding the waves of his breathing. She was facing the window and could see outside; the distant light of countless stars created a tapestry in the sky. That light had traveled millions of years, a statement of the immeasurable distance and staggering vastness of outer space. She knew that space called out to him… that he wanted to go there.

Being a city girl, she'd rarely caught the sight of the sky filled with stars since light pollution in the city made that almost impossible. Here, away from everybody, it was an extraordinary sight.

Her life had made so many sharp turns in such a short time. Not so long ago she had only been focused on exacting revenge before dying. Now, the world was filled with infinite possibilities, all thanks to the man beside her. She had a renewed purpose in life, combined with a deep-seated drive to make his plans into a reality.

Last night, she had finally decided to make the first move, and a few drinks had helped to strengthen her resolve. If she had waited for Michael to do something, it would have been some time before anything happened; he was always so busy, planning and doing things, he left almost no room for his personal life. That fervent drive of his was one of the reasons she found him so attractive.

She was surprised at how much she believed in him. Even when she had been locked inside that cell with her sister, she didn't lose hope that Michael would come and save them. That idiot Basim had boasted in front of her cell about how they would be punished for the deaths of his men. He'd told her they would end up in one of the Albanian gang's whorehouses, to serve their customers until their bodies were used up and riddled with diseases. Even then, she was not frightened.

When Michael had finally arrived, her heart had been so full of joy she'd actually kissed him. Being so impulsive was a new and liberating experience for her.

It was still too early to get out of bed and she wanted Michael to have as much sleep as he could. That metronome beat of his heart was so soothing, making her drift back to sleep again.

* * *

Michael woke up early as he couldn't sleep for long with so many things going through his mind... the plans for the future were even haunting his dreams.

He carefully got out of bed and quietly sneaked out of the room, trying not to wake up Elizabeth who was so peacefully sleeping.

After brewing and enjoying a fresh cup of coffee, he decided it was time for the rest of his guests to wake up and there was a way to achieve that without making any noise.

Cooking always made him feel calm, the repetitive actions a

sort of meditation. He remembered a time when he would have had trouble frying an egg. After spending a month on KP duty in an Army kitchen, as punishment for doing something he didn't even remember anymore, had taught him to appreciate it. It was a very useful skill for a bachelor to have, especially since his last girlfriend had thought that cooking meant picking up the phone and ordering food.

The smell of bacon, pancakes, and eggs was like a siren's call to everyone inside. One by one they all appeared acting like bloodhounds on a trail towards their prey.

Michael was wondering if it was the upgrades or regular hunger that made them eat every single morsel of food he put on the table. By the time they were finished the dishes appeared as if they were already washed. If he continued to feed them regularly they would eat him out of house and home.

It was quite disturbing seeing Tyron giving him that hungry puppy expression just to get that last piece of bacon. On the other side, Zac was *licking* his plate clean.

Even Max had joined them, eating the same things they were, except his plate and food were holographic. He explained that he was trying to emulate the texture and the taste of the food, and it was in fact very close to how he remembered it.

"I'm heading out after one more cup of coffee. There are some people I need to talk to," Jack said while pushing his empty plate forward and rubbing his full stomach.

"Okay. Max, make sure a transporter is at Jack's disposal and make arrangements for car rentals close to the places he needs to go to. Landing a flying saucer in people's backyards can be a little awkward."

"Transporter 002 is ready to go and it will be outside in a few minutes."

Jack looked at them with raised eyebrows, "Well, this will be different."

"It can get you where you need to go much faster, and there is no reason not to use it. I can assign it to you permanently since the third one is almost finished," Max said to Jack.

They all watched as Jack climbed into the transporter a few minutes later. He waved at them before the door closed and the silent aircraft levitated for a second before it started up and disappeared from view.

"Michael, you need to transfer all the gold and money into grandfather's pickup, so it can be delivered to the armored truck in a few hours. I'll supply the coordinates to the destination," Max said.

"All right… Tyron, take Pete and Zac for the delivery. I will help you load it up."

Packing everything into the old Dodge pickup truck was not an easy task. Not because of the extreme weight of the gold, but because the money was so bulky. They had to use the first transporter to transfer it from the access shaft to the cabin and then they packed it all into the pickup.

After the guys left, Michael grabbed a beer and sat on the porch waiting for his father to arrive.

Fifteen minutes later, his old man parked in front of the cabin. Michael was able to see him coming from miles away by using the satellite surveillance he accessed on his CEI.

"Hey, son, how have you been?" the older man asked as he exited the car. He was looking much better than the last time Michael had seen him. His skin had lost that pallid and tired-looking shade, and there was a far more energetic spring in his step.

"Just fine dad, there's someone I want you to meet," Michael answered while patting his father on the back.

Elizabeth exited the house; bright rays of the morning sun made her look radiant.

"Dad, this is my girlfriend, Elizabeth."

"I'm so glad to meet you, Mr. Freeman, your son has told me so much about you," she said and gave him a hug.

"Please call me Robert. Well, he didn't tell me anything about you and from seeing you I can understand why. You're quite beautiful my dear."

"Thank you, Mr. Freem... Robert," she smiled and blushed.

Anna and Alice also came out to meet Michael's father, and they all stayed on the porch for a while, getting to know each other. Knowing what the conversation was going to be about, the girls excused themselves and left the men alone.

"I've been feeling much better lately, it's very strange," Robert Freeman said, looking at the beautiful valley.

"I knew you would and I can explain why." Michael looked into his father's eyes and saw the confusion in them. "But first, I need you to take a walk through the woods with me, there is something there I want you to see."

Still confused, but willing to trust his son, his father followed Michael to the ship's entrance. On the way, Michael told him the full story. From the moment he fell down the entrance shaft, all the way to the various upgrades they all received.

Robert Freeman did not say much, as Michael had expected. He was an empirical man and without seeing any solid proof, it would be hard for him to completely believe anything.

"There was one strange thing I remember about our last encounter. I did not notice at the time, but something kept bugging me... your limp is gone."

"Yeah, that's just one of the benefits of the AutoDoc, it heals all wounds. Dad... it can also remove your tumor."

His father nodded noncommittally, still not convinced.

All that changed once they lowered themselves through the entrance shaft and stood inside the ship.

"This is amazing and part of me is wondering if I'm dreaming," the older man said, touching the walls with his hand as if to make sure that he wasn't hallucinating.

"It's real, Dad."

His father stood in the main cabin; his face full of wonder.

"And your AI... Max?"

"Well, he's not mine, I consider him his own person. You can talk to him yourself if you want."

"Max?" his father called, looking upward.

Slowly, not to startle the old man, Max's hologram materialized in front of them.

"Yes dad, I'm here."

Robert Freeman stood there, in a state of shock for a moment, but then he composed himself and said, "I guess you're my son too, aren't you?"

"I consider you my father, even though I'm not biological anymore, I still have memories of my old life."

"Isn't it confusing, I mean you two... being the same?"

"We are not the same, not from the moment we... doubled/split/copied? I'm quite a different person now, but I like to think of myself as still being human. A different kind of human, but human nonetheless."

"Then I guess you're still my son, the other one... this is getting a little confusing, but I've always thought it would be cool to have twins," he said and laughed at his own joke.

"Dad, you will need the treatment in the AutoDoc, for at least a day. Dealing with a human brain is always a delicate thing, but I assure you, it will be perfectly safe."

"That's fine, I trust you."

A little while later, Michael watched as his father lay on the AutoDoc platform.

"See you when you wake up," he said to him.

"See you soon son... sons."

With that, he smiled at the two people standing in front of the bed, one made of flesh and blood and the other out of photons. Robert Freeman then closed his eyes and fell asleep.

*　*　*

Michael was sitting at his old desk making a list of all the possible candidates he could recommend. He was actually surprised by the number of people he could vouch for from all his years in the service.

Tyron and the others had returned from their trip. The gold and money now safely transferred to the bank's armored truck which was one less thing he'd need to worry about. With Max controlling it, their operation should continue to run much smoother.

Max's presence in his CEI focused his mind on the present. With the new upgrades, it was similar to call waiting, the little icon in the corner of his vision informing him that Max was trying to contact him. It was the same with everyone who had a CEI now, and they'd all had great fun playing with this function at first. It was nothing spectacular in this age of electronic advancements, but having it directly inside your mind was a bit different, or as Zac defined it, *"So freaking cool."* Michael mentally clicked the icon, acknowledging the connection.

"We have a situation developing," Max said without any preamble.

"All right, I'll bite, how serious is it?"

"Somewhat stable at the moment, but with the potential to get really complicated soon. As a matter of precaution, I'd started keeping tabs on everybody that's connected to you, and those close to you. Using phones, satellites, and any cameras available; nothing too intrusive, but quite thorough."

"I have no problem with that ... thanks, I guess," Michael

said, still not quite sure where Max was going with all this. "What is this all about?"

"*Tyron's brother, Terry.*"

Michael remembered the boy as a young and well-behaved kid. Doing some quick calculations in his head he realized that the kid wasn't so little anymore. Whatever it was, he could feel it wouldn't be good; Tyron was way overprotective when his family was involved.

"*Well, it looks like Tyron's younger brother managed to get himself in some deep, deep trouble. Tyron has been sending money to his mother, especially for his brother's education. Unfortunately, the kid got himself involved with a bad crowd, skipping school and doing a little shoplifting, which is not so unusual for teenagers but this time the events took a really bad turn. One of his new friends is a budding young drug dealer, and he asked Terry to keep his stash for a few days. Being a good friend, he agreed.*"

"That's just asking for trouble," Michael commented.

"*Exactly. The problem is that two days after, he saw a police car parked in front of his house and got so spooked he flushed the drugs down the toilet. The irony is that the cops were going to his neighbor's house. He told his friend what happened and said he was sorry. A little naive if you ask me. However, the drugs were not his friend's, they belonged to a gang he was a member of. Of course,* the *'friend' ratted him out immediately.*"

"And drug-dealing gangs are not famous for having a 'forgive and forget' behavior," Michael said while trying to figure out how to break the news to Tyron.

"*No, it doesn't fit with their business plan. Since Terry cannot pay back the value of the drugs, they've decided to make an example out of him, with a 9 mm to his head, and it's going down tonight. They plan to hit his house, and if his mother is there, they will kill her too.*"

"Max, how did you manage to put all this together?" Michael asked, shaking his head.

"The kid has no sense of operational security; by reading his messages, you can figure out the broad strokes of the entire chain of events. From his friend's phone, I got the numbers of the rest of the gang members. Do you realize that every phone is basically a listening device? If you have the skills, you can listen to anybody... twenty-four seven."

"Well, that's a scary thought. Tell the guys to meet me in the kitchen—we have an operation to plan."

The planning part was sidetracked by a livid older brother, who had an almost irresistible impulse to go immediately and rip some heads off, and with his increased strength, that was an actual possibility. The rest of the team managed to calm him down to a level where he could think logically again.

It was decided that Tyron, Pete, Zac, and Michael would go to the gang's headquarters in civilian clothes, and Alice would act as sniper overwatch in case anything went south. Meanwhile, Elizabeth would go to Tyron's mother's house and use the family's car to get her and the young Terry away from the premises.

If the gang leaders were willing to talk, the entire thing would be settled peacefully. If they decided that was not a possibility—the team was more than happy to oblige them.

The first part of the plan went like a charm, Tyron called his mother, and she agreed to take her son and go with Elizabeth. The second part, involving a reasonable and peaceful conversation with the drug-running gang... was a completely different matter.

The house they had been using as their headquarters had seen far better days, it was an old two-story brownstone with a chain-link fence in a bad neighborhood. The two teenagers that had been acting as sentries were far too obvious and easy to spot, especially if you have your own personal satellite watching from above. Since the plan didn't call for creating a

The Spaceship In The Stone

bloodbath out of these *negotiations*, it was far too easy to stealthily approach them and knock them out. Each of the young punks had a gun tucked in his belt which was promptly confiscated.

As far as this type of operation was concerned it was a walk in the park. Their way of securing the perimeter was laughable; the two guards at the door were more interested in getting high than watching for someone approaching. That was the reason they were going to have one hell of a headache when they eventually regained consciousness.

It seemed every idiot with a gun thought that piece of metal automatically gave them authority over others. Arguably, it was true to a point; you can scare civilians easily; but if you cross the path of someone with training and skills, then a rude awakening tends to happen.

The loud music blaring from the back of the house told the team that the gang was having a party. As Max had explained, the gang's plan for tonight's attack on Terry needed an alibi. Hence, the party where everyone would testify that the members who were chosen to perform the executions were present. Climbing the fire stairs and finding the main office was too easy. Max's intel was a game-changer. Even before they'd entered the house, a 3-D diagram projected on their HUDs showed them where everyone was.

Michael and the team were armed with concealed handguns, and their new speed ensured that if something were to happen, those weapons would be in their hands within a split second. They didn't break down the door, they just opened it and entered.

The people inside didn't expect four big and unknown men to enter. Make that, one colossally big, scary-looking giant, and three others that were in his shadow. One man was sitting behind a big metal desk and the rest were lounging on an old couch.

Nobody said anything; the room was in complete silence until

Zac asked, "Have you accepted Jesus Christ as your Lord and Savior?"

Michael asked himself if Zac had any sort of filter or simply said everything that came to his mind at the moment.

"Who the hell are you?" the gang leader snapped at them.

The three guys on the couch were young, barely in their 20s. Their leader was around forty, looking older and a lot meaner. Very amateur tattoos covered most of his skin, accompanied by many piercings all over his face. Michael wondered if the guy had developed a magnet phobia yet. On the spot, he decided to name him *Pincushion*.

As agreed, Tyron would do all the talking since he was personally involved. "It would seem that my family owes you some money, I came to pay it back," he said and pulled a big wad of bills from his front pocket and tossed it on the table.

"Yeah, and who's your family?" Pincushion asked with a mean smirk, while his hands were reaching for the money.

"You should know that. Weren't you preparing to attack my house tonight and kill everybody? I am Terry's brother," Tyron said with absolutely no expression on his face.

Pincushion's eyes opened wide looking at Tyron with alarm.

Michael could see one of the three gangbangers moving his hand behind his back. He looked him in the eye, and said one word, "don't." That was enough, the young punk returned his hand to its previous position. Uncertainty and fear in his eyes.

Pincushion, having had enough, got up from his chair with an angry look on his face and tried, without success, to look menacing.

"You think you can bust in my house, throw around some money, and make everything good between us? You think you can show me disrespect and live to talk about it!" he was working himself into a rage, and by the size of his pupils, he was using his own merchandise.

He went around the table, focusing on Tyron, his right hand reaching behind his waist.

"After I'm finished with you, I'm going to go to that house, kill that kid, and rape—" In all likelihood, Pincushion wanted to say more, but talking became something he was no longer able to do. He was pulling out a gun, presumably to use it on Tyron, which was a mistake, since his last words had reduced his life expectancy to that of a mayfly.

Using his superior strength, speed, and reflexes, Tyron snatched the gun from Pincushion's hand and shoved it down his throat.

One of the cardinal rules the team had was to never say anything bad about Tyron's mother, not even in the form of a joke. Consequences could be disproportional, something Zac had experienced firsthand when he'd made a joke about her, many years ago. He had been found duct-taped in the morning, inside the base commander's car... naked. At some point during the night, he'd needed to go to the bathroom... so he had. The base commander was not amused, and Zac had to clean the entire car with a toothbrush. In any case, ever since that day, Zac referred to Tyron's mother with the utmost respect. Not to mention that when he visited her home, it was always *ma'am this* and *ma'am that*.

Michael surmised it would always be a mystery how Pincushion had died. Was it the fact that the gun barrel had entered so far into his mouth that only part of the hand-grip remained outside? The length of that barrel and the angle of insertion ensured that it entered his brain. Then again, a human neck was not designed to bend that far back, and the force Tyron used exceeded its bending limits.

Pincushion's body crumbled to the floor.

Zac shook his head and murmured, "He was a *Darwin Award* contestant if I ever saw one."

Michael turned towards the three remaining gang members and set his eyes on the one who had tried to pull the gun earlier.

"Now Billy, are you ready to make a decision that will decide the path your life is going to take?"

Max had already collected all the information about each gang member. Billy was Pincushion's second in command. With their leader gone, he was now running their ruthless but amateur operation.

"We have no beef with you man, just leave us alone," the young punk replied in a trembling voice.

Michael nodded. "If you, or any of your friends, so much as look at Terry or his mother on the street, we will come back, and end every one of you. Remember Billy—we are always watching."

Billy nodded his head, his eyes still glued to the dead body on the floor.

The team exited the room carefully, keeping an eye on the three frightened men. In a few minutes, they were at the place where Max had parked the transporter.

"Max, are you still monitoring them?" Michael asked.

"Yes, I think they're all still in shock."

"Connect me to all of their cell phones and activate the speakers."

Max did, and Michael spoke aloud, "Remember Billy, we are always watching. Now dispose of that body and change your line of work, you'll last longer," he said and mentally terminated the connection.

"Boss, that was mean, you're going to traumatize them," Zac whispered with a false sense of concern.

"And now they're freaked out and looking at their phones like they are possessed."

"Keep monitoring them, Max. If they want to try something we should know in advance."

Alice was already waiting for them inside the transporter, her assistance had not been needed this time, but as Pete said, "Better safe than sorry."

Tyron was left on the roof of the hotel where Elizabeth had brought his family. He would try to persuade his mother to move into a far better neighborhood. Money was not a problem and there was a private school where Terry could go. Michael didn't think there was any more danger from the gang, but there was a slight possibility, and the lives of Tyron's family were too precious for such a gamble. The big man would stay with them until they decided what to do next, and he still had to have a stern conversation with his little brother. The rest of the team picked up Elizabeth and returned to the cabin. During the trip an excited Zac told them the story of Tyron's gun repurposing move.

CHAPTER 15

Albanian Gang Headquarters

Ziad stood in front of the burned-down mansion, looking at its charred remains. The abundant amount of water the firefighters used to extinguish the flames created black-colored puddles everywhere. It was now evaporating in the morning sun and the smell of burnt things permeated the air. There was nothing to save since the blaze had been so intense; helped by chemical accelerants—even bodies were turned to ash.

He didn't care about the people that had died here, in fact, Ariz Rama's death put a smile on his face. Someone had eliminated one of the obstacles to his advancement plans and did him a great favor.

The day that Mr. Osmani had taken him under his wing had been a turning point in Ziad's life. He was just a street urchin, running around the Iraqi city of Mosul. One of the many orphans created by the war, sleeping in a hellhole that, only by using an over-active imagination, could one call it an orphanage. Most of the time in order to eat he'd needed to steal… or kill for it. Such was the way of life down on the bottom of existence—

primal; only the strong survived, the weak ones had a short lifespan.

He still wasn't sure why Mr. Osmani hadn't killed him that day when he caught him stealing his wallet. Maybe he'd seen something in his eyes, something that wasn't there. From that day on, he had the best education money could buy. A parade of tutors and instructors teaching him everything under the sun. He was trained in the use of weapons, a variety of martial arts, assassination techniques, drama classes... he'd absorbed everything like a sponge. Ziad had no intention of going back to his previous life, so he'd done his best to excel at everything they threw in his path.

That was how he became the most successful assassin Mr. Osmani employed. By not allowing himself to have any doubt or mercy. He considered himself more of a hunter; once he was set on someone's trail, it ended in bloodshed. It was easy to hunt down his prey; everybody had a weakness he could exploit. He never attacked his prey directly, he went for their children. Once he got them, the game was over. It always surprised him what people would do for their offspring; even trade their lives for them. Ziad never left any witnesses. He never saw the point in doing something so foolish.

Lately, life was becoming too boring for him, there were no challenges anymore. He wanted more out of life and this was why Ariz Rama was an obstacle in his path. Now, there was an opening in the power structure and he was set to fill that vacancy himself.

Others will be sent to investigate what had happened here and to punish those who dared to attack the organization but he didn't care about them. Ziad was a lone wolf and he had the advantage to beat them all.

It took him around five minutes walking through the dense woods to get to the specific tree. He climbed almost to the top and saw it was still there, exactly where he'd left it. A small receiver for a recording device that was connected to a miniaturized solar charger for constant power.

He'd placed the recording device in Basim's office some time ago. One of those high-tech models that you needed a magnifying glass to see. Every night the recording device would send a burst of files recorded that day in a compressed form to this receiver. It was impossible to find, and the receiver could store months of data on a high-capacity memory card. Basim was important to Ariz Rama, and he'd hoped to discover some incriminating secrets that could be used against Basim's boss.

He went through some images on the receiver's miniature screen, enough for him to see that he had hit the jackpot. Ziad's mouth opened with a predatory grin. This was his advantage and he would keep all this information to himself. His competitors could run in circles for all he cared. When he executed the perpetrators, he would present their heads to Mr. Osmani. That would be enough to ensure a great leap in the ranks. All the way to his car, the grin never left Ziad's face.

It was time to hunt again.

* * *

Ozark Mountains - The Spaceship

Michael was sitting at a table Max had built in front of the AutoDoc chamber, sorting through the list of names everybody had provided for the AI to run background checks on. It was surprising how many names were familiar to him and the number of those that had found themselves on several lists. He could have done this back at the cabin, but his father's procedure was almost done and he was about to get out of the AutoDoc. Michael wanted to be here when his father opened his eyes.

Jack had already talked to some of his old army buddies and

had scheduled meetings with several people who'd gone through astronaut training. By all accounts, he hit the ground running. Jack didn't tell potential recruits everything about the group, no spaceships or advanced technologies, but he told them enough to pique their interest. It did help a great deal that he was able-bodied again, miraculously healed, and looking immeasurably better. Not bound to a bed or a wheelchair so, whatever he was selling, they were more than willing to buy. Max could have made his appearance much younger but that would have defeated the purpose and would've been far too suspicious.

"Michael, he is waking up," Max said.

He closed the recruits' files, and entered the AutoDoc chamber together with Max's hologram, just as his father's eyes were opening.

"Hey Dad, how do you feel?"

The change in his father's physical appearance was amazing. Before he'd gone through the procedures he was already looking healthier than when Michael went to visit him, but now—he was the personification of health.

The older man smiled. "Great actually, I don't remember feeling this good in a long time, even before I got sick."

"Good, Max here needs to perform some finishing calibration procedures with you. It won't take long and I'll be waiting outside for you when you finish," Michael said and exited the room.

Less than ten minutes later, his father and Max walked out of the AutoDoc chamber, with Max laughing at some joke his father had made.

"It's good to see you regained that spring in your step," Michael said, having a quick flashback of his father's condition from a short while ago.

The older man nodded. "Max showed me the hologram of my body from before the procedures, the size of that tumor was impressive. But not even close to this new upgraded body of mine, as Max called it. But enough about me. Your brother," he looked at Max sitting beside Michael, "mentioned that you have a job for me—I'm all ears."

"He's right about that. Everyone has gotten assignments tailored to their specific areas of expertise, and that's exactly what I need from you dad. I need your help."

Michael explained how he had structured their organization, what everybody did and how it interlocked with others.

"As a scientist, you are more in touch with the scientific community than anyone else I know. We will need people who are open-minded and still want to explore new paths. We will need physicists, biologists, psychologists, therapists, out-of-the-box thinkers, and all those who can help us adjust to living in space-based colonies, and maybe even on other planets."

His father was looking at him and nodding at appropriate times. "I can do that, as a matter of fact, for a long time now, my main job was being an administrator, trying to find the right people for the right jobs, and make sure that all our researchers could perform their work undisturbed. Quite frankly, it felt like herding cats. I guess I had a knack for it because they kept pushing more responsibilities onto me and if I'm honest about it… I kind of liked it."

Robert Freeman's speed grasping these new revelations showed just how quickly he could adapt to unexpected situations.

Michael continued informing his father. "We chose *Genesis* to be the name of our corporation, and right now, Anna is looking for where it would be most convenient to open our corporate headquarters. I need you to recruit people and create think tanks; a bunch of them in fact, under our corporate umbrella. Each one should focus on a specific problem we are going to face: optimal living environments, psychological impact, theoretical space station designs, and any other problems you can think of. Since we can't tell them everything yet, most of it is going to have to be from a theoretical point of view."

His father nodded. "I can see where you're going with all this, and I can tell you, it is not going to be easy. You are trying to design an entire society without anyone being the wiser and, in these kinds of circles, where research is conducted, everyone suffers from an acute state of *I need to know*. So, you better prepare from the beginning for acts of industrial espionage, government agencies sniffing at your heels, and foreign agents gathering information. If they figure out what you are about to do, and find you have the technology to make it into a reality… they will come after us with all guns blazing."

Michael acknowledged the advice; he had already heard it before. "I know dad. We are taking precautions but I don't think we will truly be safe until we are way out of their reach. Until then, we have to do the best we can and hope to keep everything a secret for as long as possible."

After a while, Michael left his father with Max so he could familiarize himself with the CEI and all the benefits his new body was now capable of.

* * *

The next week was one of the most exhausting ones Michael could ever remember. It was not the same situation for everybody. Elizabeth and Anna had no complaints, but the team and Michael did not even have a minute of free time.

Anna was planning strategies with Max for establishing the most positive image of Genesis Corporation from the start, while Elizabeth and Alice were creating an intelligence network, using all their old contacts, and creating new ones.

Jack reported regularly with news of probable candidates. Michael's father was away, reconnecting with old acquaintances and hiring them to work for Genesis Corporation. Some of the people he was targeting were brain powerhouses who could smell a good opportunity from a mile away. He often talked about how the scientific world was ruthless in certain ways and it was often that the *dog-eats-dog* rules were in effect.

While everyone else was working at a somewhat normal pace, Michael and the team were going through something entirely different. It all started the day after his father had woken up and Max called for a meeting to inform them they were not using their upgrades to their full potential. He'd analyzed their actions while dealing with the incident regarding Pincushion and his gang. The conclusion was that they should have moved much more seamlessly and that their general effectiveness had left much to be desired.

The knowledge and training were there but they were using their old tactics and were in need of some additional drills. To remedy that, Max designed a series of exercises for them. Since some of these would most likely involve situations that included the use of firearms, it was essential for them to be at their best.

Alice's part in the training had been the easiest; as a sniper, she just needed to be at the ideal position and wait for the perfect shot. With upgrades and her new hand-eye coordination, it was a foregone conclusion that her every shot would be perfect.

While Tyron, Pete, and Zac had maintained a decent physical condition before the upgrades, Michael had had some catching up to do. Everyone had a problem with being too fast, their reflexes too twitchy. They needed real-time tactical situations to correct that.

Max's solution was a series of training programs using augmented reality, superimposed on their ocular implants, letting them see things that weren't there.

Every exercise was preceded by hours of physical training, running and martial arts sparring.

They spent hours in the woods fighting against enemies who could be seen only by them. If they'd been seen they would have looked like a bunch of lunatics running around in the woods, pretending to shoot invisible enemies with gun replicas.

As fun as augmented reality was at the beginning, and Max made it almost indistinguishable from the real thing, it became more difficult by the day. As fast as they could accomplish a level of his training regimen, Max would up the stakes and make everything more complicated. It was like an ultimate video game; the main difference being that if an enemy managed to shoot you it really hurt... like a lot. The AI was using their CEIs to simulate pain and was doing a superb job at it.

* * *

Michael walked through the dense woods, carefully placing his feet on the ground to minimize any chance of being heard. He was approaching the enemy position, carrying a Colt M4 assault rifle, a model he was very familiar with. It was the sixth day of their exercises, and this was supposed to be the next to last enemy of the day, or '*The Boss*' as Zac had called it. The HUD gave him virtual information about the number of rounds he had left and the map in the corner showed him the distance to the target and the position of every member of his team.

"I see four guards on the roof all facing in your direction," he said, using his CEI's comms to speak to Tyron. Since the CEI could hear his thoughts, there was no need to use his voice and potentially give away their locations.

"I see them. Pete has an eye on them and the best angle. He will take them out when you give the word," the big man responded in the same way.

The place they were attacking was a small stronghold, which Max, exercising his artistic liberties, had placed right in the middle of the woods. It had a medieval look to it but without the outside wall.

"On my mark, neutralize your targets and be ready for the direct assault. Use full speed."

It was one of the tactics they'd almost perfected. By using their full speed, the upgrades allowed each member of the team to move much faster than ordinary humans and get to a position their enemies would not expect them.

Michael gave the signal and sounds of gunfire erupted throughout the woods. The four targets on the roof were quickly dispatched followed by an additional eight adversaries all around the structure.

Michael started running, throwing a hand grenade into the narrow and tall opening he saw. He timed his entrance through the main door to be a second after the grenade exploded.

They cleared the structure floor by floor using the CEI comms and HUD overlays to be constantly aware of their teammates' positions and fields of fire. The entire exercise was executed flawlessly, almost to the very end. That's when Zac had made an error in judgment and received several virtual bullet holes as a reward.

It was in the last unchecked room and he happened to be the point man that entered first. The room only had a big ornate bed in the middle, except for a beautiful naked girl lying on it. It was the last thing anyone would expect to see there, so it was somewhat understandable why Zac lowered his gun and smiled like an idiot. The girl pulled a gun from beneath a pillow and fired several shots in his direction before her head exploded from a high-caliber bullet, which Alice had skillfully sent from her sniper's nest, a few hundred feet away. An amazing shot since the rooms' windows were extremely small.

Max declared the mission a failure and they were directed to a new starting position so the entire exercise could start again, with changed parameters. They couldn't advance to the next level until this one was successfully cleared.

This was promising to be another long and strenuous day.

* * *

Michael closed his eyes when he realized where they were heading. This was supposed to be a celebration for completing the entire course that Max had created for them, and a way to unwind from the backbreaking week they'd had—a *'boy's night out'* as the AI had put it. Elizabeth, Anna, and Alice had exercised their right to have a *'girl's night out'*, by going to some establishment which for some reason did not allow any men.

Max arranged everything, told them to dress casually, and picked them up with the transporter. Now Michael was asking himself why he had not suspected anything? After all, this was something he himself would've done.

Of all the bars in the world, Max just had to choose this one, a white supremacist bar filled with an entire biker gang of neo-Nazis, if he judged by the number of swastikas all over the place. And the team was led by a 7-foot-tall (2.1 m) man that exemplified everything the patrons of this establishment hated.

Before he could say anything, they were already inside, the sound of the door closing behind them having a certain finality to it.

Michael looked beside him and saw Zac already rubbing his hands with a happy expression on his face. Pete was trying to figure out where to put his cell phone, so it would survive the coming events, and Tyron was just standing there doing his best not to smile, except for the corners of his lips that were twitching a little.

"Well, since we're here, we might as well get something to

drink," Michael said while thinking, "*I almost feel sorry for them.*"

They went confidently to the bar, disregarding the glowering, frowns, and hateful whispers.

"Four beers," Tyron said to the barman.

The man who tended the bar was in his 20s, with several bad tattoos that screamed prison, and by Michael's account, had no more than five remaining teeth in his mouth. He looked at Tyron, intimidated by the size of the man, and then looked at all the people in the bar, whose general attitude gave him a confidence boost.

"We don't serve your kind here," the man snarled, pointing at the door.

"And what kind would that be?" Tyron asked pleasantly, eagerness for the answer recognizable in his voice.

The bartender was confused for a moment, opening and closing his mouth like a fish on dry land.

"You know... your kind..." He replied, lost for words.

Zac was obviously getting bored, since he turned toward the spectating crowd, resting his elbows on the bar, and addressed them.

"Listen up! We're doing research on tribal behavior and would like to ask you some questions. Is it true that all that tight leather you're wearing is actually a representation of latent homosexual urges, with an emphasis on fifth base masochistic tendencies?"

Zac stood there smiling, and the blank stares pointing in his direction confirmed that they didn't exactly get what he was talking about.

Fortunately, Pete was there to offer an explanation. "He asked if you're all bitches," he said slowly but loudly, so there would be no chance of misunderstanding him.

"Thanks, Pete," Zac said in the ensuing silence while rolling his eyes.

"Buddy, you are quite welcome," replied Pete with a self-satisfying smirk.

The results were easy to predict, and almost everyone in the room surged like a school of hungry piranhas, bent on doing great bodily harm. Unfortunately for them, that was the wrong thing to do. No matter how bloodthirsty they were, Michael, Tyron, Pete, and Zac were way out of their league. Even before the upgrades, they had a fair chance of winning this fight, no matter how one-sided the odds seemed to be. With the upgrades, the poor neo-Nazis didn't stand a chance.

At one point, Tyron was using the barman as a baseball bat, holding his feet, and swinging him around. Pete and Zac were having a contest to see who would knock out the most men with one punch… It seemed Zac was winning. Michael was enjoying a light workout by throwing a few men into the path of Tyron's improvised bat.

They went easy on them. The gang suffered a few broken bones here and there, and the dentist that had them as patients would easily be able to afford a new fishing boat, with all the work the team made necessary. The barman lost his remaining teeth, which could be looked at as an improvement considering that now he would have to use dentures, and they would be far more aesthetically pleasing.

With the whole place pacified, they decided that the atmosphere here really didn't agree with them and that they could have a more relaxing evening sitting on Michael's deck. As they were going out, Zac grabbed a case of cold beers from the refrigerator behind the bar and left a $50 bill as compensation.

While they were flying back to the cabin, each with a beer in his hand, Michael used his CEI to talk to Max.

"I admit it was fun and all, but what was the point of that whole exercise?"

"Testing the team's reflexes under real-world conditions... It was for science' sake, I got no pleasure out of it whatsoever."

The tone of his voice told an entirely different story.

Michael shook his head and took another swig of his cold beer.

CHAPTER 16

E-waste Recycling Plant

After last night's exercise at the bar, Michael and the guys spent several hours on the cabin's deck. If his medical nanites hadn't worked overtime to clean the alcohol from his bloodstream, this morning would've been a completely different affair, as he knew from lifelong experience.

Tyron's suggestion that they should start the morning with the full-contact sparring session was not something he was inclined to do right now. Last night's brawl had been enough of full-contact sports to last him for a while. Besides, he had to go and check up on Dave. Quite some time had passed since the last time he'd seen the man and he was feeling guilty about it. Dave didn't socialize that much and was always happy when Michael came for a visit.

Using a transporter for such a short trip didn't feel right so he borrowed Tyron's car. This way he'd get to enjoy a slow ride down the mountain. The sky was blue and sunny, one of those days when you want to sit back and relax with a friend. That is why he stopped at the store on the way and picked up a six-pack of Dave's preferred beer. At the plant, he unlocked the gate and locked it again when he was parked inside. Not that they had many visitors, if any, but the old man still had some hang-ups from the time he was hiding from the bill collectors and liked his place locked all the time.

Dave was coming from the direction of the warehouse where the nano-factory was housed.

"I was planning on calling you, Mike. That darn machine of yours is a bottomless pit. There is barely any high-grade e-scrap left to feed it. If we're going to continue with this, I suggest you start buying electronic scrap and shipping it here," Dave said while shaking his hand.

Michael took the six-pack from the back seat and showed it to the old man.

"I will think of something. Things are going according to plan so it's a good time to open a cold one."

"You'll get no objections from me, especially on a hot day like this," Dave said, accepting a bottle.

Max had already informed him another transporter was finished last night and their little fleet now numbered three. They had plans to make many more, but for now, the production would concentrate on making new satellites to increase their coverage.

"So how have you been Dave? Are those old bones still giving you trouble in the morning?" Michael asked him with a smile.

"Now we both know that I'm feeling fine, in fact, this morning I've been able to do some push-ups. It's been ages since the last time I could do that. Those things, *nanites* you called them, are doing an amazing job. Quite frankly, some parts that I gave up on, are making an appearance again, if you know what I mean. I've been considering going on those dating sites everybody is talking about," the old man said and actually blushed.

The Spaceship In The Stone

"Don't sell yourself short, your best years are yet to come," Michael replied, trying hard not to laugh.

Dave showed him his scrap stockpiles, it was obvious they had already used an incredible amount and, as Dave said, they would soon have to find an additional source to keep the nano-factory running.

Max was separating all of the materials underground. While he had some basic minerals in abundance, the rarer and more valuable ones were very scarce. The amounts being used for transporters and satellites were quickly burning through his reserves and only Dave's constant effort was making the whole operation possible. It was in the plans that Genesis Corporation would very soon start purchasing additional recycling plants. Until then, Dave's was all they had.

Michael spent another pleasant hour sitting in front of Dave's trailer, listening to the old man telling some stories from his youth, a few of them even had his grandfather in them.

"I'd better be going home," Michael said after Max informed him that Elizabeth and Alice wanted to consult with him about some aspect of intelligence gathering. "I needed to get some air and to clear my head; talking to you helped."

"I'm glad I could be of assistance. Anytime you need a friendly ear, come on over and I'll listen. Just don't forget to bring cold beer," the old man replied.

Dave was walking him to his car when he noticed a tall man standing in front of the gate. The moment their eyes met Michael knew—this was an enemy. Maybe all the upgrades had something to do with it, or maybe a survival instinct honed in many battles. In the other man's eyes, Michael could see recognition, and decision. The moment they looked at each other lasted only a second, but it was one of those seconds when the perception of time got distorted and his heart skipped a beat. The man was unbelievably fast; one moment he was standing there relaxed, the next—he was already shooting.

Michael moved, giving a command for his CEI to activate the *Boost*. Still, even with all his advantages, he was not faster than a bullet, yet that small movement helped him. The bullet that would have hit him square in the face, grazed him above the eye, leaving a nasty wound. Unfortunately, the second bullet was unavoidable; it connected with his chest, above the heart.

The beginning stages of the *Boost* were making time slow down as the pain began to spread from the impact points. He willed his mind to ignore pain. Dave was close to him, and he needed to protect the older man. While still falling, his hand went for a gun hidden beneath his shirt; he was trying to be as fast as he could, but already a few more shots were fired.

Michael was on the ground, the impact of the fall jarring his senses. The gun was in his hand, aiming at the shape in front of the gate, while his finger was quickly squeezing the trigger. Something was wrong with his eyes; everything was covered with a red film and blurry. He stopped firing, keeping one round left in the gun, just in case. The man was already gone and a few seconds later, he could hear a car engine revving to its maximum.

Michael turned around and saw that Dave was a few feet behind him, lying on his back while blood was spreading from two bullet wounds in his chest.

"Max… help!" He sent through his implant, not trusting his voice at the moment.

"I have a transporter on the way, just a few minutes more."

He knew Dave did not have those minutes; the nanites Dave had in him were not the whole package, and if he lost enough blood, there would be nothing they could do.

Michael tried to rise to his feet, but they wouldn't keep him up. Somehow, he crawled to the old man's body and pressed his hands against the wounds.

"Heal him …"

"I'm already doing everything I can, but he needs to be transferred to the AutoDoc immediately," the AI replied.

Tyron, Pete, and Zac were suddenly there, ready to take over. That was it for Michael, for the last few minutes he was keeping himself awake—losing consciousness was not an option. There was something wrong with him and he could not think straight anymore.

As soon as his friends took over helping the old man, he closed his eyes and fell into oblivion.

* * *

Ziad looked at his shoulder; blood from a bullet wound was seeping through the makeshift bandage he'd made.

I failed! For the first time in his life, he did not manage to kill his prey and was now running away as fast as he could.

It was sheer blind luck that he spotted one of the people recorded in Ariz Rama's office. This was the fifth small town he'd visited, carrying with him printed pictures of the people who had assaulted the mansion. It was surprising how ordinary citizens are willing to help when you show them an FBI badge, and these country bumpkins would not know a fake one if it hit them in the face.

As he was passing by a local store, he saw one of the men whose picture he carried. Walking out of it with a six-pack of beer in his hands and the casual attitude of someone who had no enemies in this world.

He could not believe his luck; God must have smiled upon him, for he'd thought that it would have taken him a lot longer to find any of them. Following his prey was not difficult. Long ago, he had instructors who'd taught him how to be inconspicuous and blend into the crowd. Stalking someone with a car was similar.

Staying far back, so your mark would not spot you in the rearview mirror, and having some random car between you and the one you were following was usually sufficient.

Ziad took a deep breath and that intoxicating feeling of being on his prey's tail made him smile. Soon, he would look into the man's eyes, and see the final realization that death was a few heartbeats away. The man would then look at Ziad and know that his past sins had come back to haunt him. There would be begging and pleading, offers of money, and repentance. It would not matter—his fate was sealed.

That was how it was supposed to happen, but it did not. Ziad parked close to the entrance gate and waited for his prey to finish what he came here for. He would need to approach the car parked close to the gate, and Ziad was planning to call out to him and ask if the man could offer him some assistance, on account of his own car breaking down. And when the prey opened the gate, Ziad would wound him, and then interrogate him for the location of the others.

It took some time, and he was already beginning to feel restless when his mark finally appeared followed by an old man. All this time Ziad was holding a gun in his hand. There was no need to be reckless and leave anything to chance.

As he was about to call out, his eyes met those of the man he was hunting… and then everything went wrong.

The man knew! Ziad did not know how, but in the instant when their eyes met, he'd realized that he was not facing prey… this was another hunter.

Maybe he could have still salvaged the situation if he'd stayed calm, but something deep inside his soul had forced him to take action. He could not admit that it was fear, as he could never accept that, but something…

Ziad's hand lifted in the practiced maneuver that had become part of his muscle memory, pointing a gun and pressing the trigger. The first bullet hit the man in the head, and the second in the chest. That is usually enough to remove the danger forever. As he did not want any witnesses, the barrel of his gun moved a few degrees to the side and sent a few rounds into the old man.

This should have been the end of it… but it was not, something unexpected happened.

Pain.

It blossomed from his right shoulder, spreading through his body with the speed of thought. He'd been shot and the force of the bullet had thrown him to the ground, while his gun went flying away from him. In the next split second, he saw the man who was supposed to be dead, lying on the ground and firing at him.

As fast as he could, Ziad staggered towards his car, ignoring the pain. Within seconds he was pressing the gas pedal as hard as he could. His tires were leaving a cloud of dust behind him. He expected additional bullets to be sent in his direction, but if they were, the loud beating of his heart muffled all other sounds.

The man was supposed to be dead! His aim was always true and none of his previous victims had ever managed to fight back. He justified that miraculous survival to chance and preparation. His first bullet must have only grazed the man's head, and he was probably wearing a bulletproof vest underneath his shirt.

That was not important at this moment; he was hurt and bleeding and needed to take care of himself.

Finding a safe place was all too easy. He picked one of the lonely houses, knocked on the door, and as soon as it opened, shot the woman who answered in the head. She did not make a sound and his spare, silenced gun was very discreet. Ziad checked the rest of the house and confirmed there was no one else inside.

This was always the best way to hide, random and out-of-the-way.

It took him half an hour to finish everything. He patched up his wound, dragged the woman's body into the kitchen, and opened a gas line. There was an old SUV in the garage, just the right unexceptional car he was hoping to find. His car went into the garage, where he soaked it in a generous amount of gasoline. The gas was rigged to catch fire in about an hour, long after he was far away from this area.

For the dead woman, he felt nothing; it was the same to him as stepping on an ant. Moreover, Mr. Osmani's next operation should kill tens of thousands; one more life was a drop in the bucket.

For now, he had to retreat; his prey knew that he was being hunted. This was not a failure in Ziad's mind, only a setback. He needed time to heal and to find out more about the man he was hunting, and those around him.

When the time was right, when his prey dropped his guard—Ziad would strike, and this time it would be final.

The man had wounded him, made him feel something… unthinkable.

This was not a job anymore.

This was now personal; this was a *vendetta*.

CHAPTER 17

Ozark Mountains - The Cabin

Elizabeth was in the kitchen with Alice, going over a few notes on the new intelligence network they were trying to build. It was both easier than she thought and more difficult. It was all about applying enough pressure on people to do what was needed of them. Mainly providing information since not everything was on the Internet where Max could dig it out. The AI was a master when it came to unearthing people's dirty little secrets. She went through the FBI databases Max provided and marked people who they could use. Alice was doing the same on the military side. She had some misgivings at first, but when she saw the secrets those people were hiding, her doubts disappeared—some of them were vile.

They wouldn't have been able to do anything without Max. He was processing information and going through the databases at a speed she would have thought impossible a while ago. The young FBI analyst she was before would have been afraid of his abilities, but Elizabeth felt safe. The AI was using his gifts to further their plan, to make a new future available to them all.

They were taking a break, waiting for Michael to return so they could talk to him about some aspects of the intelligence-gathering network, when she noticed something unusual. Through the cabin's window, she saw Tyron, Pete, and Zac, running at full speed towards the place where the camouflaged transporter was parked. They practically jumped inside, and the aircraft launched into the air at breakneck speed. The sonic boom of it breaking the sound barrier was heard like a colossal thunder strike all across the valley.

"Max, what's going on?"

For the first time since she was introduced to Max, his answer wasn't instantaneous. For several seconds she was faced with terrifying silence causing her stomach muscles to clench in fear. Alice must have seen something on her face because she rose from the chair with a questioning look in her eyes.

"Max?"

"Don't worry, the danger has passed and Michael is alive, but he and Dave were shot a few seconds ago," the AI responded hurriedly, his voice conveying more emotions than usual.

"Shot! ... Shot by whom? Where is he? Why— "

"The guys are closing in on his location; I'll have more information in a minute, please be patient."

She could feel her heart beating in her ears and inside she was fighting two strong impulses. One was to be at Michael's side as soon as possible, and the other, to find whoever had shot him and choke the life out of them with her bare hands.

Despite Alice and Anna's words to keep calm, she could not keep still, pacing around the room and every so often asking Max for any new information. Finally, Max informed her they were coming back and the transporter would go directly to the spaceship. Elizabeth rushed outside the cabin and started running in that direction.

She had never run this fast in her life. Using the maximum

speed her upgrades allowed; her field of view contracted until the trees blurred in her peripheral vision. This was far better than waiting and going through all possible scenarios in her head.

By the time she reached the entrance shaft, Tyron, Pete, and Zac had already transferred Michael and Dave to the AutoDoc.

She couldn't remember later how she got down the ladder and entered the ship, but the image of Michael lying on the bed, his face and shirt covered in blood, would stay with her forever.

The sterile field covered him so she couldn't even touch him. Elizabeth could only stand there and watch as the nanites repaired all the damage done to him.

"He will be fine," Max said, his hologram standing beside her.

Elizabeth silently nodded, but those words did little to calm the storm of emotions raging inside her.

* * *

Ozark Mountains - The Spaceship

He really should stop waking up like this. The same old ceiling, boring AutoDoc walls, and him laying in a prone position. Maybe he could get Max to throw in a splash of color to this place, something more interesting than this all-white decor.

"The sleeping beauty finally awakes," Max said cheerfully, sitting in a chair beside his bed.

"Do I look like a sleeping beauty to you?" he replied and glanced down. Wonder of wonders, he had on a medical gown.

"I was referring to the fact that Elizabeth was trying to wake you up with a kiss a while ago. You totally ruined the moment by sleeping like a log, by the way"

"Where is she?" Michael asked.

"She had to go back to the cabin. They are having a meeting

about what to do. Before you ask, you have been here for a whole day, and you need to stay in that bed for another hour."

"Dave?"

"*Look to your left.*"

There, beside him was a familiar opaque energy cocoon and inside it, Dave was lying asleep.

"How is he?"

"*He will live, thanks to you. It was touch and go for a while; he was losing massive amounts of blood. You putting pressure on his wounds helped the nanites to stabilize him. There were many internal injuries to repair, but he should be awake in six hours.*"

"And the man that shot at us?"

"*He escaped, I... it was a miscalculation on my part. I had one satellite in a stationary orbit above the cabin, but it didn't follow your movements when you went to see Dave. A mistake I do not plan to repeat. From now on you will have one dedicated bird above you at all times, following your every movement,*" Max stated.

"It's not your fault. This was out of the blue, and I still don't understand who he was, or how the hell he managed to find me."

"*We did find one clue at the scene; the shooter dropped his gun when you shot him. Tyron managed to lift the prints, and I checked them through every law enforcement database in the world.*"

"Do you have a name?"

"*No, that's the worrisome part. This guy is a ghost. I've found more than forty murder cases where his prints were a positive match. Those crimes were committed in every corner of the globe, spanning two decades. For all that, there is no name associated with the prints or any affiliation. He's a professional killer and considering our past actions, it can mean only one thing.*"

"The 'High Council'... damn."

"I came to the same conclusion. Somehow, they were able to find us."

"We need to move; this area is not secure anymore. Tell everyone to start packing," Michael commanded, knowing that the longer they stayed here, the greater the chance was for another attack.

"You can tell them yourself. They started in this direction the moment I told them that you were awake."

A few minutes later Elizabeth entered the room and threw herself at the still lying Michael. "Never do that to me again!" She cried into his shoulder.

"It's okay, I'm fine."

"I could have lost you… you almost died."

Michael held her tightly, not saying anything.

"She's right, you're lucky the bullet just grazed you. If it had hit you directly in the head, things wouldn't be fine. You got away with a nasty concussion and considerable bruising to your brain. It was an armor-piercing round. Even a direct hit would have not been able to penetrate your skull thanks to all the reinforcements, but the transfer of kinetic energy would have turned your brain matter into mush. The one in your chest was stopped by your subdermal armor. In the future, you should try to avoid getting shot in the head as it can be bad for your health."

"Well then, you better make me a helmet, because it is obvious I still don't know how to dodge bullets," Michael replied.

At that moment, everybody else entered the AutoDoc, Tyron and the team, his father, Anna, and Alice.

"Mike, thanks for testing the subdermal armor for us, it was big of you," Zac said.

Tyron slapped the back of his head, and continued, not giving it a second thought, "You shouldn't have gone alone, that was careless. From now on you need to always have a backup; like it or not, you are a VIP now and need a constant protection detail."

His father had jumped in a transporter the moment Max had informed him what happened and arrived here at top speed. "He's right, son. From the stories they've told me, you're up against some very evil people, and you'll always need to be on your guard," Robert Freeman said.

"Okay, okay... I get it, I may not like it, but you're all right. Furthermore, as I told Max earlier, this area is no longer secure. They may not know where the cabin is, but the fact that they found me is proof that we are not safe here. We need to move as soon as possible."

"That's what we were discussing before you woke up," Elizabeth said.

"What are our options? Max, did you manage to acquire any secondary locations?"

Max nodded. *"Since you gave the order, I've managed to buy a few properties. One of them is a decommissioned military facility, smack in the center of the desert. It was quite cheap since there was nothing around it. It's nothing fancy, but it's livable."*

"That was fast, all right.... Tyron, take Elizabeth, Anna, and Alice, the rest of us will follow you as soon as Dave wakes up."

"Max, what security do we have around here?"

"I have tasked two additional satellites to be on over-watch above us; anything within a 25-mile (40 km) radius is being monitored. As soon as you are all away from here, I'll feel much more comfortable."

"How long before you can extract yourself from the crystal matrix?"

"At least a month. It is hard to give a more precise date since the crystal was made of multiple laminated layers of different hardness. The nanites are eating through the material as fast as they can, but its resilience is out of this world... literally. Besides, the ship has been unobserved for thousands of years, and it is in the safest place on the planet."

The Spaceship In The Stone

Michael turned to his father. "Dad, I need you to go and organize those think tanks as soon as you can, I'm sorry for the rush, but this attack showed that maybe we don't have as much time as I thought."

"It's fine son, I understand. Do not worry; I already have a few names lined up. Max and I have agreed on a plan of action."

"And if you see anyone suspicious let us know immediately."

"Hey, I even have my own personal transporter and a satellite to monitor me, so I will be fine. Look after yourself, and this lady of yours. I still have an aspiration to become a grandfather," he said with a hopeful smile that made Elizabeth blush.

Soon after that, his father and the others departed while Pete and Zac were finishing with packing all their stuff from the cabin.

"Max, intensify your search for the 'High Council'. I have a feeling this attack was only their opening move. We need to find and stop them."

"I'm tapped into NSA servers since they are already listening to every call and Internet communication. I am also monitoring any suspicious activity around this area. They only need to make a single mistake and I'll have them."

After Max gave him a clean bill of health, Michael got out of the ship and helped Pete and Zac with the packing. This was his safe haven, his escape from the world, and now the people who wanted to do them harm had destroyed the sanctuary it provided. This was one more thing he would hold them accountable for, and for which he would make them pay.

As soon as Dave woke up, they locked the cabin down, entered the transporter, and got away from the peaceful valley.

* * *

The Missile Silo (Two Weeks Later)

Michael stood at the top of the little hill looking down at their new home base. He had just finished the last lap of the extensive physical training schedule Max had created and could see the others were quickly closing in on him. They were led by Tyron, who had made significant progress at increasing his speed in the last few days.

The new home did not look like much. When Max had said that he'd bought a decommissioned military facility, he had failed to mention that it was a Cold War-era missile silo.

When they first saw it nobody thought they could live here. There were a few rundown buildings and a big slab of concrete. Then Max showed them his little surprise… their home was not on the surface.

As he explained to them, the moment the papers were signed, he'd sent one of the transporters with a batch of construction nanites and dropped them on the site. The missile was long gone, but there was an abundance of leftover materials for them to work with. All those construction nanites had performed a small miracle. He said that he got an idea from some old documentary about how to transform an obsolete missile silo into a livable space. It was amazing how much room there was underneath the ground. The actual silo was one hundred and forty-seven feet (45 m) deep, and fifty-five feet (17 m) in diameter. Max had divided that space into individual levels, with bathrooms, bedrooms, kitchens, and living rooms. Each level had around 2300 square feet (213 m^2) of living area, which was more space than they needed. The entire project was not done yet; only the top five levels were ready for residential occupation, while the rest were still under construction. With outer walls made of four-foot (1.2 m) thick reinforced concrete, no water had ever seeped inside, so the entire structure was bone dry.

The Spaceship In The Stone

The cherry on top was the launch control center, connected to the missile silo with a long corridor that had once been a cableway. The control center had three levels, stripped bare of old equipment, and transformed into an intelligence-gathering facility. The bottom level or the basement was filled with computer servers Max had designed and built himself, using a combination of alien and human technology. The second level, the intelligence-gathering one, had holographic walls displaying every piece of information they had. And the top, a small dome-shaped one, Michael claimed for himself as his new office.

Between the silo and the control center was the silo's access portal, with a refurbished elevator and decontamination area now housing a small cold fusion reactor and a deep-water well, making them quite self-sufficient.

Max had even built a new AutoDoc, and with no restrictions on space, it was more of a small hospital since it occupied an entire level.

It took them about ten days to settle down in this new location, as there was a mountain of additional stuff they'd needed to do; beds, linens, food… the list was a mile-long.

One night, under the cover of darkness, they went to Dave's E-waste recycling plant and took the entire nano-factory with them. Max had made sure the entire area was secure and no one was monitoring the place. It had taken some work, but Max had made the entire thing with the forethought of doing exactly that. With a Gravity-drive of its own, and helped by thick cables attached under their transporter, the whole thing was moved close to their new base. They housed it in a big military warehouse that came with the property. The entire building was refurbished by Max right after acquiring the property in anticipation of future need. Dave chose to make the warehouse his home. He had a big case of claustrophobia and living underground was not really to his liking. Michael bought him a new RV to park inside so he'd have a space to call his own. There was already a big pile of electronic scrap they'd bought and transferred to the site, so he was back in business.

Once finished, the apartments looked like five-star hotel rooms. They included a level that was essentially a gym and spa. Bringing down all that heavy exercise equipment was not an easy task. Once everything was installed Max told them he could have built it all in place but, *"That would have defeated the purpose."*

Jack and Michael's father were doing amazing on their own. Jack already had more than one hundred potential recruits, or more than three hundred people when all the family members were added.

His father had formed a few think tanks; each tasked with solving specific problems. He had hired top experts in each field and got them by offering more than generous salaries. Once they settled in, he set them on their tasks.

Elizabeth and Alice's intelligence network was growing exponentially. With Max's hacking skills they were now tapped into every government agency in the world. Finding those that had attacked him was essential.

Michael, Tyron, and Pete had to wait for Zac to catch up to them; so far, he'd managed to arrive last every single time. It was not that he was the slowest, just from all the goofing around he did. After taking a drink of water from their canteens, the team slowly started walking toward the base entrance. There was still much work to be done.

CHAPTER 18

The Missile Silo

Michael was sitting on a bench in the gym, resting after another heavy workout, when Max interrupted him, *"Michael, we got a hit. I followed the lead from one of the numbers in Ariz Rama's phone and it led me to a terrorist cell. Elizabeth and Alice are waiting for you in the intelligence center, they want you there ASAP."*

"All right, give me five minutes," he answered, and took one of the fastest showers in his life. He entered the intelligence center still drying his hair with a towel.

"So, ladies, what have you found out?"

Elizabeth pointed at the image on the wall, "From the main suspect, the one who has been in contact with Ariz Rama, we've managed to identify an additional twenty members of that terrorist cell."

New pictures appeared next to the first one. "And judging by some of the intercepted communications they're planning something big."

"Do we have any indication of what it is?" Michael asked, looking at the hostiles' mugshots.

"Nothing specific, just that it is going down soon. One of them said the planes flying into the buildings will be like a lover's kiss in comparison to what they're planning."

"Damn... and I was starting to relax," Michael replied. "What about government agencies? Do they know anything?"

"They know something is going on, but even they don't have a clue what it actually is," Max answered.

"Okay, Max, send all the information we have to them, anonymously. Maybe some of them will have better luck than us. There is nothing we can do but wait and be prepared to act if we find out more."

Elizabeth used the break in the conversation, "We have another problem, not as grave as this one, but one that still needs to be dealt with. Max, place Dr. Ross's file on the display."

The holographic screen changed into a picture of an older man in a tweed suit with thick glasses on his face.

"Dr. Benjamin Ross, one of the leading scientists dealing with outer space habitation. He's worked for NASA, ESA, he even did a bit of consulting for the Russians. By all accounts, an extremely brilliant man and your father said he's essential to our plans."

"So, what's the problem? Hire him."

"The problem is that two months ago his daughter and her husband were sailing around Africa when something terrible happened. It was just the two of them in a medium-sized sailboat on a honeymoon trip. Unfortunately, they were attacked and kidnapped by pirates off the coast of Somalia. The pirates are demanding $20 million to set them free. Dr. Ross has already sent them every dime he had, and he even sold his house to appease them. As long as he keeps sending more money the pirates are keeping them alive but still demand the main payment. And last week, after he missed a payment, they cut his son-in-law's hand off and sent him a video of it being done."

"Jesus... and I guess our government is not being helpful?" Michael questioned, suspecting the answer.

"The official policy of our government is that they don't pay ransoms and they would not send the military to extract just two people. Dr. Ross talked, begged, and threatened to go to the media, but all they said to him was to be calm and that they were looking into it," Elizabeth answered.

Michael closed his eyes. "Max, can we transfer $20 million to Dr. Ross's accounts?"

"We could do that easily, but it won't do any good. I have researched this particular group and they've never released any prisoners. Even if they get the money, they will still kill them in the end. They simply do not care; they feel quite untouchable in their part of the world and know that there will always be new people for them to exploit. As a matter of fact, they only keep prisoners for as long as it's profitable. If the families of their captives refuse or are unable to pay, they kill them and go on to the next target," Max replied.

Michael nodded a few times and said, "Tell the rest of the team to meet me in the operations room. Let's see if we can beat some sense into those pirates."

* * *

The operations room was not originally part of the missile silo plans. It was something Max saw the need for and built it adjacent to the intelligence center. It was a circular room some fifteen feet (4.5 m) across with a round table in the middle and walls covered with holo-screens. A perfect place where they could make plans. Everyone present in the silo was sitting around the table and looking at Michael.

"Tyron, Pete, and Zac are going with me, it is a rescue mission and it's not our first. Alice and Elizabeth will monitor the situation with the terrorists; let us know if there are any new developments. Max, do we have a location for Dr. Ross's family?"

"Yes, it was quite easy to pinpoint their exact position. The pirate leader even sent the video from his own phone; they are not trying to hide. Oh, and don't bring any weapons, I already packed some goodies on the transporter and will explain everything on the way there," Max said.

"Gentlemen, it would seem our vacation is over, so be ready to rock 'n roll. We are leaving in five minutes," Michael said looking at the members of his team.

Everybody except Elizabeth left right away, intentionally giving them some privacy.

"Do I have to tell you to be careful?" Elizabeth whispered while resting her head on his chest.

"I will be. I know what I'm doing. These kinds of operations were my life for a long time so don't worry about it."

"Of course I'll worry, Michael. Not so long ago—you were shot in the head. The upgrades made you more resilient but not invulnerable. So… be careful and watch out for any bullets flying towards your head," Elizabeth demanded, and kissed him.

* * *

Transporter 001 - Destination: Somalia

Michael was looking at four big black boxes that were stacked in the center of the aircraft.

"So, Max… would you explain why you told us not to bring any weapons? I doubt we will sway the pirates with harsh words or bad language."

The AI's image was projected on the holo-screen.

"They would have been superfluous. Open the boxes and look inside; they contain some things I've been working on for a while. Each has its owner's name on the top and is tailored to the precise specifications of your bodies."

Michael took the box that had his name printed with bold white letters and opened it while the others were doing the same. He could see that there were several things inside, carefully packed in separate compartments.

"The first item is a combat suit. I played around with different kinds of materials. Essentially, it's a combination of spider silk, Kevlar, and the same subdermal armor you already have, but much thicker. It will stop even a 50-caliber bullet by spreading the impact energy all around the suit. You will not be comfortable if shot by one, but you'll live," Max continued his lecture.

"The next item is a battle helmet that integrates seamlessly with the suit. In fact, Michael gave me the idea for it when he was shot in the head. Let us try to avoid that in the future, bullets to the head I mean. It has an internal rebreather unit so it can go underwater for an hour, or in a toxic environment, take your pick. Now, try them on, I want to show you something."

Michael held the supple suit in his hand, it felt like extra thick leather but more flexible and with a smooth black exterior. The helmet was a different matter entirely. Shaped to follow the contours of his skull but without a visor or any other openings. It was made from some hard material and was padded with a soft gel inside. It didn't take them long to put on the new equipment and they were soon looking at each other, having to admit the combat suits did look intimidating.

"I've always wanted to be a superhero but they're missing something crucial," Zac said.

"What?" Max's voice asked with a note of worry.

"The cape, Max, where's the cape?" Zac wondered.

Michael didn't know if Tyron's slap had any effect now since he hit the back of Zac's helmet.

"All jokes aside, check this out."

To Michael, it seemed like all the other members of his team... just disappeared.

"Active holographic camouflage, it makes you 'almost' invisible."

He was right about that *almost*. As they moved, their transparent silhouettes could still be seen but, if they stayed very still, the suit completely blended with the environment.

"Now, where have I seen this before? Oh yes, I've seen it in the movies, so what do we do if Arnold comes after us?" Zac laughed, waving his hands around.

Michael had to agree with Zac. The way the suits bent light resembled an antagonist in a certain movie series.

"I will neither confirm nor deny that I got the idea from that. You can activate the option on your CEIs to see each other perfectly while wearing the suits... moving on," Max stated forcefully.

"The third item in the box is your new rifle. It is based on the FN P90; very compact with a few modifications that I've implemented. Even if it resembles the P90 on the outside and the reloading system is quite similar, the insides are all my proprietary design. First, it doesn't use bullets or any type of regular ammunition, instead, it fires a small piece of metal called a flechette round. They are shaped like small razor-sharp darts with helical wings which makes them spin at a considerable speed, for stability. Rather than using chemical propellants, the flechette's acceleration is achieved by using electromagnetic propulsion. There are two switches on the gun's side. The first one allows you to select the speed of acceleration. The upper position is subsonic and, while it provides sufficient acceleration to kill, it's almost silent. The lower position is supersonic and, since it breaks the

sound barrier, it's extremely loud. The second switch chooses between single, semi-auto, and full-auto modes. The first and the last are self-explanatory but this version of semi-auto mode is actually a 3-round burst-mode; it sends groups of three flechette rounds with every press of the trigger. As for the full-auto mode, let me just say that unless Godzilla himself is after you, I would suggest against using it, as it can create quite a mess in no time. Also, it uses up ammunition like crazy."

Michael held the gun a little more carefully now, starting to have an inkling of its destructive power. "This is impressive… What about the ammo, how many rounds?"

"Each magazine has two hundred and fifty flechette rounds, and there are three spare clips on your belt. The power source is good for two thousand rounds before it needs to be recharged. The last thing in the box is a handgun that works on the same principle. It holds only fifty flechette rounds in its magazine and you have two extras. Overall, you are carrying one thousand one hundred and fifty rounds. If you find yourself in a situation that demands more than that… I can recommend a few prayers. All the weapons have the same camouflage coating as your suits; it would be rather pointless if they could be seen while you were somewhat invisible. So… do you like your new toys?" Max asked cheerfully.

It was more than he'd dreamed of in his wildest fantasies. Battle-suits combined with their upgrades and new weapons made them more than formidable and, by the particular way Pete was caressing his new weapon, affections were considerable… and a bit unhealthy.

"It is just what we need," he answered Max's question.

"Okay guys, let's go through our plan of action one more time."

* * *

Somali Pirates' Base

Abdullah was very pleased with how his life turned out. He had everything he'd once only dreamed about, money, gold, and women. What's more, it was so easy to acquire all those things; he just had to take it. He grew up poor and everyone around him was equally poor. While others found some semblance of happiness in such an existence, Abdullah had hated it from the deepest parts of his soul. He saw in the newspapers how all those rich people lived, with their cars, houses, boats, and servants... everything he did not have and wanted.

At first, he'd tried to make money by selling drugs to the people in those big cities, but the competition was great and he didn't want to be a small fish in a big pond, so he decided to do something more lucrative.

He was not the first or only pirate captain in Somalia as it was quite a profitable occupation, but Abdullah could be considered one of the most ruthless who plied that trade. He never left anyone alive on the ships his crew attacked, aside from the ones used for ransom. The boats were cleaned of everything valuable and then quickly sold for whatever he could get for them. They were worth a lot more than he got but he knew that keeping them could be disastrous to his health. His practice even made other pirates avoid his band of robbers which pleased him immensely. He liked being so notorious that even those who ordinary people feared were afraid of him in return.

Now the only thing that ruined his good mood was that he had to cut off another hand tonight. The man was one of those infidel Americans, born to a life of entitlement and privilege. Nonetheless, like all others, the man screamed so beautifully while Abdullah mutilated him.

This was the second week the man's family had not paid to keep him alive and it would be his last. He knew they did not have twenty million to pay, but that was only a ruse anyway, an additional pressure to ensure he could milk the family for all they had. If more money was not transferred into his accounts in the next two days, he would kill the man, send his family the video and then start on the wife. She had been left untouched until now and would soon do anything to spare her husband any additional pain, which was what he wanted. Nothing pleased him more than for those infidel harlots to offer themselves to him freely, like the one he'd finally used up three months ago. All her efforts had done little to help her or her family in the end.

Fun and games could wait for tonight; it was so damn hot. They were in the desert, so he would wait for the nightfall, when temperatures were much lower. When you get right down to it, slowly cutting off a human's hand was a hard day's work.

Abdullah took another cold drink from the cooler and laughed at his morbid joke.

***

Outside the Somali Pirates' Base

The hot desert sun and terrain which was predominately sand, gave Michael a flashback from that time, more than a decade ago, when that one suicide bomber had changed the course of his life.

This is depressingly pitiful for a pirate base, Michael thought, looking at the location of their target. A few dilapidated buildings in the middle of the desert built on an ancient oasis. The water that had made this place livable was now gone and a few sad dried trees told the story of its past.

One big house stood out by being in slightly better condition than the rest, and by Max's intel, that was the pirate captain's house. It felt weird that the desert was so close to the sea, but he guessed the climate played by its own rules, not caring one-bit what humans considered appropriate.

Their normal tactics of encircling the enemy were not needed. As satellite images confirmed, the pirates were not that concerned with their own safety. The only guards were placed at the entrance of the main house and in front of the metal shack where the captives were held.

The team split up. Michael and Tyron would go and free the captives, while Pete and Zac dealt with the guards in front of the main house.

Michael looked at Tyron and could not help but think how cool it was that they were invisible. If someone looked directly at any of them, they would appear as wavy air rising from the hot sands. That was one of the reasons why they'd decided to attack during the day. It increased their camouflage and people here were not as alert during the day as they were at night. It sounded strange, but with a temperature of 113 °F (45°C) everyone was looking for shade from the hot sun.

Satellite imagery detected twenty pirates on the premises and four life signs identified as hostages.

They approached slowly as that increased the effectiveness of their camouflage; despite the blazing sun, there was no need to rush. Max had failed to mention that the combat suits they were wearing had full-body temperature control which came as a pleasant surprise. He could not even imagine how they would've felt without that extra function.

Michael saw two men in front of the shack where the captives were and couldn't believe his eyes. One guard was holding an old RPG-7 rocket-propelled grenade launcher in his hands. It might look impressive but it was hardly practical. The condition of said weapon was even more unbelievable. There were so many rust spots on it that there was a good chance that if activated the rocket would simply explode, still in the barrel. He knew that

Somali pirates were not exactly known for their academic achievements, but this guy was depriving a village somewhere of its idiot.

Well, life was full of amusing moments, even in the middle of the action.

The others confirmed that they had their targets in their crosshairs, so Michael gave the order.

"Execute!" He sent the command through the comm link.

Flechettes, accelerated by electromagnetic force, took flight toward their designated targets, and a moment later, four pirates were dead. The two guarding the hostages had the privilege of receiving two of the small darts to the head each, fired by Tyron and Michael.

He looked at the weapon in his hands with wonder, even the best silencers in the world made some sort of muffled sound, but this weapon was completely inaudible. Max had outdone himself with this one. Now, to protect the hostages.

The shack's walls were made from earthen bricks and it had a rusty metal roof. The bodies of the two guards were in front of it, still sitting beneath a makeshift sunshade as if they were alive. There was barely any blood, just two tiny entry wounds on their foreheads. Michael entered the shack and deactivated his camouflage. Taking off his helmet, he could feel the excruciating heat inside. The metal roof had turned the entire place into an oven. It was a small miracle that the hostages hadn't already succumbed to the heat. There was another door, a few feet from the entrance, and he opened it with the key he'd taken from one of the dead guards.

The first thing that welcomed him was the nauseating stench and the buzzing sound of countless flies. Four bodies were lying on the floor so exhausted from the heat, they didn't even notice when he entered. One of them was a man, Dr. Ross's son-in-law, judging by the missing hand. The woman beside him was presumably his wife, and there were two small girls next to them.

Michael exited the room and went to the dead guards; Tyron was keeping watch just inside the door. He took water canteens from the bodies and returned to the hostages.

A light touch on the shoulder was enough to wake Dr. Ross's daughter.

"What…" She started to say before Michael put his hand over her mouth.

"Shh… Mary, keep quiet. Your father, Doctor Benjamin Ross, sent us to save you. I need you to wake everybody up and prepare them to leave," he whispered, holding her gaze. "Do you understand?"

The fear and panic in her eyes were replaced with overwhelming hope. She nodded while two tears slid down her face.

"Yes… my husband… he's not well," she pointed at the body next to her, "I think his hand is infected. I haven't been able to wake him since last night."

Michael took a nano-patch from one of his breast pockets and taped it on the bare skin above the man's wrapped stump. Nano-patches were Max's new invention; there was no need to transfer medical nanites directly anymore and there were enough of them on the patch to provide first aid.

"This should help them until we can get him to somewhere safer."

The woman's eyes were filled with hope but there was still residual fear from her long ordeal.

"Who are the girls?" Michael asked.

"Natalie and Lee; they are ten-year-old twins who were brought here a few weeks ago. Like us, the pirates attacked them at sea; their parents tried to fight them off… but they were murdered. I don't know what Abdullah was planning to do with them, but he said that they would soon be gone."

A silent tear ran down her dirty face and disappeared when it reached her cracked lips.

Michael gave her the canteen and whispered, "Be ready in five minutes," before exiting the room.

Tyron didn't move from his spot, his gun pointing toward the main house. Pete and Zac also reported that everything was calm, the pirates were inside the house, sheltered from the scorching sun.

"Max, bring the transporter here, we need to move the hostages before we continue. If they start shooting from the house, one stray bullet is all it will take."

A few seconds later the transporter landed in front of the shack's entrance. Even with the door open facing the shack, the back of the aircraft projected what was supposed to be in the front of it, omitting Michael and Tyron.

"Tyron, turn off the camouflage and take off your helmet, we need to move the hostages and they are going to freak out if they see you like that."

When the two men returned inside, they could see the little girls trying to help Mary with her unconscious husband. Their eyes filled with fear when they noticed the two strange men. They were focused on Tyron, owing to the fact that his size made him lower his head considerably so he could enter.

"Are you really going to save us?" one of the girls softly asked.

Tyron smiled and quietly replied, "Yes, little one, you don't have to be afraid anymore."

Even with all the grime and her dirt-smeared face, her smile lit up the room.

It took a few minutes to transfer everybody onto the transport; Tyron took the man in his arms and easily carried him. Michael applied nano-patches to Mary and the girls; it was never too soon to begin the healing.

"Max, how is he?"

"His stump is infected and he's running a fever along with a serious case of dehydration, but he's going to make it. The nanites are already working overtime to stabilize him. Mary and the girls are better off, but will still need some time to recuperate."

Michael nodded to the voice only he could hear.

"Mary, I need you all to stay inside. This vehicle will take you a few miles from here. It will stay there for a while and then it will come back for us."

"But... we should all run away now, what if they realize that we've escaped?" Mary asked with a quiver in her voice.

Michael approached her seat and leaned to her ear so she was the only one that could hear him.

"When we leave, there won't be anyone alive here to come looking for you."

Her lips pressed themselves into a thin white line and her eyes closed; after a few seconds, she silently nodded.

"We won't be long," Michael said, exiting the transport. A few seconds later only the vacant imprint in the sand indicated that the aircraft had left.

"Ready to rock 'n' roll?" he asked Tyron while putting his helmet back on his head and activating his suit's camouflage.

"Locked and loaded, just say when," the big man replied and, by his tone of voice, Michael knew that Tyron was smiling underneath his helmet.

Eliminating the remaining pirates was embarrassingly easy. The lack of preparedness and lax discipline could be explained by the circumstances. They were in the middle of the desert and asleep due to the high temperatures outside. Even so, the whole thing was anticlimactic for the team.

Like invisible wraiths' they moved through the house, dispatching those inside with machine precision, erasing their vile presence from the world. The pirates died quietly, barely making any sounds as their lives were extinguished, not one of them firing a shot in return.

"Only the man in charge is left, he is in the back room, alone," Max sent through their implants.

They entered a room that was drastically different from anything they'd seen until now. It was furnished with expensive pieces of furniture, stolen from the ships he had raided then sold. A big, brutish man was sitting in a leather chair, watching a flat-screen TV and drinking twenty-year-old Scotch straight from a bottle. A big handgun was tucked in his belt, and Michael was bewildered that anyone would allow a gun barrel to point in that specific direction. This idiot was begging for an accidental castration.

The man's fun was interrupted when Michael grabbed him by the back of his neck and catapulted him towards the wall. The impact could be felt through the soles of their boots. He deactivated his camouflage and addressed the man who was shaking his head to clear it from the dizzying effects of the impact.

"Mr. Abdullah, I presume."

Abdullah's head sluggishly came up but, when he saw a black apparition in front of him, his eyes opened wide, and he made a strange sign with his hand to ward off evil spirits.

"I assure you I am quite real," Michael said.

The man swallowed loudly and gathered his courage.

"What do you want?" he asked in broken English.

"Just to inform you that you should have taken a different path in your life," Michael replied.

He could see Abdullah's hand slowly reaching for his gun; a well-placed flechette round resolved that, shattering the pirate captain's elbow. His screams were surprisingly high, reminding Michael of soprano opera singers'; maybe that would have been a better choice for a career.

"Max, do you need anything from him?" he asked using his implant.

"Not really. He did most of the work on his smartphone and I've already hacked, accessed, and retrieved all the accounts and passwords."

Michael looked at the man that was moaning and staring back at him with murder in his eyes.

"I'm curious, why have you never released the people whose ransoms were paid?"

"Why should I? I defeated them in battle so they were mine to do with as I pleased," Abdullah answered through clenched teeth.

"Oh, so it was a tribal thing; that answers one question. What were your plans for the two little girls? Would you have killed them too?"

Abdullah managed to smile, or sneer would better describe his expression. The second flechette shattered his second elbow and caused the pirate to achieve an even higher note.

"I would appreciate it if you would answer my question," Michael said when the screams reached the lower vocal registers where Abdullah could actually hear.

"They... were to be sold. Small girls have a high price, some whorehouse would have given me a lot of money for them."

Maybe it was a mercy that Abdullah couldn't see Michael's face underneath the helmet.

"How could you... on second thought, forget it."

His finger switched the selector to full auto mode and he gently caressed the trigger.

The noise was so loud that he knew his ears would be ringing if the helmet hadn't automatically muted the sound. Abdullah's head disintegrated and the wall behind him received a new coat of red paint. Michael's hand did not flinch, his heart—beat steadily; this was not about vengeance or proving a point, this was about justice; plain and simple.

"Ah, boss, I see you are redecorating the place," Zac said as he walked into the room. "But next time, maybe try a color that's a little less… chunky," he said and smiled at his gallows humor.

"What? Too soon?" Zac asked when his joke didn't produce the reaction he was hoping for.

The mess this gun made at full-auto was quite impressive; he now understood why Max had cautioned them to be very careful with it.

Michael turned around when he heard Zac squealing like a little girl, "Boss… do you see what I see!" Zac said, pointing to the corner of the room.

There was a large wooden chest with iron fittings. "Well, we have ourselves a pirate captain, so a treasure chest is not that far out of the box," Michael replied.

Zac fell to his knees in front of it and used his enhanced strength to rip the lock off its hinge. As he lifted the lid, they could all see the chest was filled with gold coins, jewelry, and money stacks of several currencies.

"A real treasure chest boss; you're always taking me to the best places," Zac whispered while caressing the gold.

"You found it, you carry it," Michael said. "If we can figure out to whom some of those things belong to, we can send it to their beneficiaries'. Arrange with Max to dispose of the rest."

Michael established a link to the AI, "Max, bring the transporter, we are leaving this place."

A few minutes later they were on their way home.

CHAPTER 19

Transporter 001 - Destination: USA

They were a few minutes away from the pirates' base, yet through the holographic dome of the transporter, they could all see that the terrain underneath them was greatly changed. The internal gravity that the transporter maintained and the inertial dampeners, canceled out the g-forces so for those inside it was as if they were standing on solid ground.

Michael and the team had taken off their helmets and gloves, mainly because of the two little girls, who were intimidated by the all-black facade they presented. That seemed to calm them down and, after a while, they started resembling a couple of lemmings, looking at the members of the team and then looking out the transparent walls in wonder.

"Are you with the military?" Mary asked. She was kneeling beside her husband, whom Tyron had placed on a foldable stretcher, which was part of the standard transporter emergency gear.

"You said my father sent you… and this flying craft…" The haste in which everything had happened since these people came

The Spaceship In The Stone

to her rescue did not allow her to think straight, but now she could not understand how this aircraft was even possible.

"No, we're not with the military," Michael answered. "Think of us as a privately held company. Your father agreed to work for us and the main condition of his employment was for you and your husband to be rescued from the pirates. The company deals with the development of proprietary advanced technologies and this aircraft is an example of them. We are taking you to a secure site where we have advanced medical facilities to help your husband. Your father, Dr. Ross, will join you shortly and I am sure he will explain everything to you."

She seemed to accept that and confirmed it with a few nods. The transporter did have plenty of water on board but there was very little food; the team managed to find some chocolate-flavored energy bars that were part of the emergency rations and gave them to the girls and Mary. The main purpose of those rations was to compact as much fat, protein, and carbohydrates as possible in a very limited space. Consequently, their taste left much to be desired. Regardless of that, their faces showed absolute bliss as they were devouring them which gave Michael some idea of the quality of food the pirates had provided.

* * *

An hour into their flight, Elizabeth made a connection to his implants using an emergency protocol.

"Michael, we know what the terrorists are planning to do but we caught it too late." Even though he could not see her face, Michael could sense the rising panic in her voice.

"What is it?" he responded in the same way so as not to alarm their passengers.

"They're taking over the Millennial Sports Arena, and it's the finals… Michael, there are twenty-five thousand people there, and they plan to kill them all." Elizabeth's voice quieted to a whisper at the end, as if she could not believe what she was saying. He closed his eyes while the muscles in his jaw became rigid. Even after all this time, with all the things he'd seen in his life, the unfathomable depths of human depravity still surprised him. That someone could even plan to kill twenty-five thousand people was monstrous, but it had happened so many times in human history, a legacy of a vicious species.

"Have you informed the authorities?" Michael asked when a small icon on his HUD indicated that Max had joined the conversation.

"Yes, but I don't think they believe the information. Anyway, they will need too much time to confirm the intelligence, and by that time... It will be too late," Max replied.

There are some moments in life when one needs to make a quick decision; there is no time for slow deliberations, and as it happens—those moments are usually pivotal.

"Max, how fast can we get there?"

"With emergency speed, and if we go on a sub-orbital trajectory... thirty-five minutes," the AI responded, making a little pause before giving the final answer, which he took to calculate all variables.

"Do you have any more information?" he asked through his implant, addressing both of them.

"Yes, in fact, we managed to find one of them; he broke his leg and was excluded from the group that went to the arena. He made a mistake and called some of his friends in the Middle East so he could tell them that they should be watching television tonight, as something glorious was about to happen. We didn't want to lose any time, so Alice took one of the transporters and basically kidnapped him from the hospital," Max answered.

Elizabeth cut in, "Michael, she had to interrogate him quick and dirty; for a while, she even turned off the audio link so we wouldn't hear the screams. You need to talk to her about it later; I do not think she is in a good place right now."

"Okay, I will. Max, what did she find out?" He could not allow himself to think about anything else except the situation at hand.

"It's not good Michael; it looks as if someone has meticulously planned an elaborate and disturbing horror show. Their plan is to kill every member of the security team in the arena, place visible bombs on all the exits, and then take everyone hostage. One of their priorities is to take control of the media center so they can make some outrageous demands, live on the air, never expecting them to be fulfilled. However, when those demands are not met, they will transmit the beheadings of women and children to the entire world. The emotional impact that act is going to create, cannot be measured," Max quickly replied. *"It gets worse from there; when SWAT teams, unavoidably, manage to breach the arena and get inside, they are going to blow themselves up and most of the people there. The truck they let inside before barricading the doors carries close to twenty thousand pounds (9000 kg) of ammonium nitrate fertilizer mixed with nitromethane. That's enough explosive to destroy a big part of the arena and kill a lot of people. And if that's not bad enough, they somehow managed to acquire two barrels of nuclear waste. It will be like the mother of all dirty bombs; if it detonates, the consequences will be—"* Max stopped in the middle of the sentence. *"Michael, I calculated the timeline. You will not be able to reach the arena before the attack begins,"* The AI said quietly.

Everybody stood silently for a moment, holding their breaths. At the same time, Michael knew that succumbing to indecision could be fatal to so many people.

"All right, tell Alice that we need her and to bring her sniper rifle. Elizabeth, get into one of the transporters with Alice and coordinate with Max so you can intercept us at the most advantageous location; we are heading straight to the arena. We will take your transporter and Alice, and you will take these people to the silo," Michael ordered.

The transporter had been speeding up for some time now, ascending towards the sky. Max's voice told the passengers to secure their seat belts in preparation for the considerable acceleration. Mary got into her seat while Tyron secured her husband with additional straps to the aircraft.

Michael used internal comm links to explain everything to his team as there was no need to frighten their passengers.

"Does everyone understand what needs to be done?" he asked after he described the situation and the beginning of the plan for their attack. After getting everyone's confirmation, he concluded with, "We may be late for the party, but one way or the other... we will be there at the end."

The little girls started squealing happily when the sky started turning dark and the stars appeared. Underneath them, the Earth showed significant curvature. Michael looked at their smiling faces and couldn't help but to think of how many little girls, just like these two, were now in the arena.

* * *

Millennial Sports Arena

Murat was feeling closer to God now, more than at any time before in his life; he could sense the divine purpose spreading throughout his soul. Tonight, he would fulfill the sole purpose for which he was born. If he closed his eyes, he could almost see himself entering heaven and receiving all the rewards that were waiting for him. For the last ten years, he had been living in this godforsaken country, waiting for the call to achieve greatness.

Killing the people who were supposed to guard this place was easy; all the security guards in the arena were now dead. They'd used silenced weapons for that glorious deed so as not to alarm the masses of the infidels and instigate panic before it was time.

All exits were secured with explosive devices and the most important thing, the bomb truck that would ensure his rewards, was inside the arena parking lot. It was a nice evening, so the retractable roof was open, which would make certain that the radioactive death cloud would punish many more of these devils.

His holy warriors were at their assigned locations covering all the exits. No one would be allowed to run; there was no escape from the divine will. Now he needed to scare them enough so they would not panic and stampede like animals. Moreover, no one had noticed anything yet, so focused were they on the stupid game; yelling, screaming, indulging their baser natures. Soon… he would ensure that they were screaming for entirely different reasons.

He entered the announcement box; one of his warriors was setting up the camera that was going to transmit his image to the big screens mounted in the arena. A trembling technician was explaining what needed to be done and his crying eyes would, from time to time, shift to his coworker's body that was already cooling on the floor.

Murat nodded his head and could see through the window, his face appearing on the big screens.

"LADIES AND GENTLEMEN," his voice roared through the entire structure. "YOU WILL REMAIN IN YOUR SEATS AND WILL NOT MOVE FROM YOUR PLACE. IF YOU ATTEMPT TO EXIT THE ARENA, YOU WILL BE KILLED IMMEDIATELY."

On every side of the arena, people were looking at each other in confusion, most of them thinking this was some kind of prank. As practiced, his warriors removed the long coats they were wearing, to show suicide vests and menacing assault rifles in their hands.

"IF YOU PANIC AND TRY TO RUSH TOWARD THE EXITS, MY MEN WILL FIRE INTO THE CROWD AND MOST OF YOU WILL DIE. ALL THE EXITS ARE SECURED WITH EXPLOSIVES SO ONLY DEATH AWAITS YOU THERE. WE ARE DOING THIS FOR THE MONEY AND IF YOU FOLLOW MY INSTRUCTIONS, YOU WILL BE SAFELY HOME BY TONIGHT."

Murat paused, looking at the sea of terrified faces; he had never felt so powerful in his life.

"I WILL CONTACT THE AUTHORITIES AND EVERY-THING WILL BE RESOLVED SOON. I REPEAT, STAY IN YOUR SEATS AND YOU WILL BE FINE, BUT TRY TO LEAVE AND YOU WILL DIE."

He turned off the microphone and his warrior disconnected the camera. Lying to these people was part of the plan as were the beheadings that would soon be transmitted to the entire world. He remembered the moment when his superiors had first offered him the honor of leading this mission; his heart was filled with pride that they had recognized in him the heart of a true believer.

Wails of police sirens could already be heard in the distance. Soon they will call him and he will give meaningless demands and will offer empty promises to buy more time. When they come to the realization that he will not be swayed by their empty talk—they will attack. Murat longed for that moment, caressing the remote detonator held in his hand. The thought of being this close to heaven was filling his soul with joy.

* * *

The Spaceship In The Stone

Transporter 003 - Destination: Millennial Sports Arena

Michael, Tyron, Pete, Zac, and Alice were sitting inside the transporter looking at the video feeds from the arena. The terrorists were broadcasting live with the threat to kill one hostage for every minute the transmission was interrupted. They had already declared their demands: the release of all freedom fighters being held at Guantanamo Bay detention camp, official recognition of vast territories as ISIL sovereign state, withdrawal of all American troops from conflicted areas, and five billion dollars as a contribution to their cause.

As demands went, theirs were simply absurd, and there was no way the government would ever consent to any of them. Besides, Michael knew they were all a ruse to buy time and to make people watch this entire tragedy.

Alice was edgier than her usual composed self and there was a hollowness in her eyes that wasn't there before. He would have to talk to her after this was over. Some things should not remain locked inside as they tend to fester. He and Elizabeth exchanged a quick kiss when their transporters met. There was no time for words.

"Max, what is the situation there?" he asked aloud.

"I'm observing them through the arena's CCTV. There are fifteen terrorists on the premises, including their leader, whom you saw making demands. I managed to identify him from immigration records; he is one Murat al-Rashid, originally from Yemen. For the last ten years, he has been an American citizen, working as a night guard at a fertilizer plant. Eight of the terrorists are on the exits to the main arena and they all have suicide vests, with a remote trigger held by their leader. Murat al-Rashid is in the media room with four others, he has the detonator on himself. With the press of a button, he can activate the truck bomb

261

and the vests. The last two are in the garage, guarding the bomb truck."

"Here is how we are going to play this one," Michael said and pointed at the holographic representation of the arena in front of them. "Alice and Pete, since you are our best snipers, I want you on top of the roof, opposite each other. That is four bad guys each in quick succession, can you do it?"

Alice nodded her head, and Pete answered, "With faster reflexes and improved hand-eye coordination, it will be a piece of cake. I've been practicing lately," he boasted with a cocky smile.

"Zac, I need you to take out the two guarding the bomb truck."

"Sure boss, two customers to serve, *no problemo*," Zac answered and gave a thumbs up.

"Tyron and I have two missions; first we have to disable the explosives on the arena exits, and then deal with the leader and his helpers. We can't allow them to react, so all our attacks need to be executed simultaneously... understood?"

They all gave nods of confirmation.

"After our objectives are achieved, we need to extract ourselves immediately; this place will turn into a madhouse in no time with all the law enforcement agencies coming to the scene."

Max spoke through the speakers while his image was on one of the simulated monitors. *"There are special nano-packs I created for you in the luggage compartment, simply place them on the bombs and they will disable them. Zac, yours is the largest one and it needs to be placed on the bomb truck's main trigger. Now, prepare yourself, we will arrive in two minutes."*

They put their helmets on and activated the camouflage. Five transparent specters in an invisible aircraft prepared to harvest the lives of those who did not deserve them anymore.

* * *

Millennial Sports Arena

The bright lights of the Millennial Arena could be seen from a great distance. The transporter came out of the sky in a plummeting dive which ended a few feet above the arena's roof. Michael trusted Max's flying skills but there was a moment just before the full stop when his heartbeat had increased. He did not have to worry though; the AI had calculated the force needed to stop their descent to an inch.

The transporter's doors were turned away from the roof opening, to prevent the doors, which disrupted the craft's invisibility, from accidentally showing. Michael and his team jumped the two remaining feet onto the arena's roof.

Alice and Pete immediately sprinted to their assigned spots, while Michael, Tyron, and Zac went over the side of the roof. Hanging by their hands, they moved underneath it using support beams. Max had calculated this as the quickest route, taking into consideration their improved strength, speed, and coordination.

He could see thousands of people beneath him, all eerily silent. This was a place where they had come to relax and have some fun, but it had turned into a place of fear and terror. His enhanced eyesight showed him the faces of many terrified children whom their parents were holding tight. As he'd explained to others, there would be no mercy or indecision on this mission. They were here to eliminate the threat with the utmost prejudice.

There was a gap between the outer wall and the last seat stands and they used it to lower themselves all the way to the ground level. It would have been almost impossible without the special transparent rope Max had made, unwinding from a spool attached to their wrists. Just one of the gadgets the AI had created while they'd had their training week.

As soon as they hit the ground, Zac separated and started running towards the garage with the bomb truck, while Michael and Tyron split up in opposite directions so they could disable the bombs on the entrance doors.

Michael was running at full speed, barely pausing to place the nano-packs on the explosives attached to the doors. He couldn't linger and double-check everything as seconds were important in this situation, so he trusted Max's assurances that the nano-packs would take care of the explosives. His battle-suit made him an almost invisible specter as he ran through the empty corridors. Only the sound his boots made while touching the floor gave any indication that he was even there. To anyone else, he would have appeared to be a fast distortion of air, a trick of the eye.

Five minutes later he rendezvoused with Tyron who had also finished his half of the explosives neutralizing objective.

They climbed the stairs together going toward the press center; the weapons Max had made them aimed in front of them. There was no need to scan the perimeter since the AI transmitted the exact position of every terrorist, but old habits die hard, and each of them was instinctively checking his sector.

The first thing Michael saw when they came to the glass doors of the press center was a deeply disturbing scene developing inside. Two young women and one boy, barely in his teens, were kneeling with their hands tied behind their backs. Behind them was a big black flag with some white writing on it and, in front of them, three terrorists were holding big scimitar swords in their hands.

One of the terrorists was behind a camera tripod filming the horrific scene. The leader was screeching into the lens about the just punishment of the infidels.

"We are out of time," Michael said through the comm link. "This is going down now. Do all of you have your targets in sight?"

Within a second he received the confirmation.

"Tyron, the two with the swords on the left are yours, the

leader and the one on the right are mine; the cameraman is the last, so we can share. As soon as we start the music, Alice, Pete, and Zac—neutralize your targets."

"Okay, on one."

The *Boost* running through his veins made the entire scene so much sharper. The whole team activated *Boost* so they could gain those precious seconds of slowed time and accelerated reflexes. Michael's hand was rock steady as he aimed at the forehead of the first terrorist assigned to him.

"Three..."

Murat al-Rashid was finishing his long rant and was starting to signal his executioners.

"... Two..."

The three men with balaclavas on their heads were raising their swords, positioning themselves behind their intended victims, preparing for the final act of decapitations.

"... One."

Michael's weapon, set on semi-auto, spat three flechettes into the Murat al-Rashid's head. A fraction of a second later, the first terrorist with the sword received the same treatment. He followed his rifle sights to the cameraman; unfortunately, six flechettes didn't do his skull any good as Tyron shot at him at the same instant making the top of his skull fall in a different direction than the rest of the body.

The eight suicide bombers did not fare very well either. In the span of a few seconds, their dead bodies were lying on the ground. Alice and Pete had practiced the exact order in which the marks should be eliminated, so when the time came to act their movements were precise, their aim unwavering.

Zac was pulling the trigger when Michael said *one*, his second target joined the first in the span of a heartbeat. He entered the back of the truck only to see a big yellow barrel with a radiation sign on it. Attached to it was a complex explosive device with a mass of wires he couldn't even dream of disarming. Luckily, he didn't need to; Max's nano-pack melted into it the moment he placed it on top of the device. All the indicator lights on the device dimmed and then turned off. He just shook his head and hurried towards the assembly point.

After taking the remote detonator from the terrorist leader, Michael and Tyron left the three terrified people, who were still not sure what had just happened. Then, followed by Tyron, he quickly ran to the extraction point. Zac joined them on the way, and they used the same ropes to climb back to the roof's underside. The motorized spools were pulling them upwards at considerable speed. They repeated their monkey bars retreat and climbed to the top of the roof. Alice and Pete beat them to the transporter and were already sitting inside.

"Max, take us home," Michael said as the transporter's doors were closing.

The entire operation had taken only a few minutes of active time. It was done without unnecessary delays and procrastination. Most people never realized that these sorts of things were decided in a matter of seconds. It was as different from the movies as could be.

He looked at the four people beside him and was suddenly filled with an overwhelming sense of pride. They had done it; they saved so many souls today. He crossed his fingers hoping all of their missions ended up this easy, but he sincerely doubted it.

The invisible aircraft lifted from the Millennial Arena's roof and silently glided into the dark sky.

CHAPTER 20

Washington, D.C. The White House - Presidential Emergency Operations Center

President Craig Garner was having one of the worst days of his life; for the man who preferred to have hair-pulling situations under control, today was the day when he felt as if he had none.

He felt so tired. Like everyone around him, he had not slept last night and only the constant supply of coffee kept him alert.

It all started the evening before when he was watching a game on TV and then his Secret Service detail barged into his room. Without so much as *please*, they hastily hauled him to the bunker. He knew that resisting them was futile. When they received an evacuation order they would disregard everybody, even him, until they arrived at a secure location. The only information they gave him was "Terrorist threat."

As soon as he arrived, Martin, an agent in his security detail, informed him about what was happening in the Millennial Sports Arena. For the next hour, his eyes, like billions of others around the world, were glued to the TV screen—watching the unthinkable.

After 9/11, security measures had been tightened to a very high degree all for the reason of preventing exactly this kind of attack. Somehow, all their extensive preparations had failed, and he was forced to listen to the deranged demands of a religious fanatic who was holding twenty-five thousand of his people hostage. He knew not one of those demands could be accepted. When his Chief of Staff started talking about a compromise, he silenced the man with one sharp look. Even if the price was the lives of all those people in the arena the country could not bow to the terrorists. This was his final word on the matter, and he had no other option but to refuse them, even if it cost him his very soul.

The negotiators tried to buy some time, so a rescue plan could be formed, but it was as if the terrorists didn't care if their demands were fulfilled. They could not even stop the live transmission because that would mean certain death to one person for every minute they were off the air.

At one point, the most horrifying thing happened. The terrorists were about to decapitate three young people on live television, blaming *his* procrastination as a cause. One of them was a young boy, barely out of his childhood. While the terrorist leader was spewing some religious drivel about punishing the infidels, the three hostages were trembling and kneeling in front of the three executioners who held big swords in their hands.

He'd already given his consent for the SWAT teams to storm the arena, even knowing that particular order would result in many innocent deaths. There were no other options and he prayed for a miracle but not believing that it would be granted.

Many of those around him, and the majority of the people watching from their homes, averted their eyes; not wanting to see such a disturbing scene. Tears were streaming down their faces, and they held those closest to them for support. But he could not look away; he steeled himself to keep his eyes on the screen. This was his burden to carry, and he needed to keep looking out of respect for the three young lives that he'd sworn to protect when he took this office… but was unable to.

That is why he saw the exact moment when the miracle he was praying for happened.

The three terrorists with the swords and their fanatical leader died in what seemed to him as the same instant. The white letters on the black flag behind them turned red and there was a fine red mist falling on the three bound people.

He held his breath while his mind was frozen in shock. Had the SWAT teams managed to get there in time? But there was no sound of gunfire. He glanced quickly around and saw that no one had an answer; they were all as confused as he was.

While one of the girls and the young boy were sobbing, looking at the floor, the other girl's eyes were staring beside the camera, wide open. The camera was still filming and he could see her lips moving; he took the remote control from the table and pressed the button to increase the sound to the maximum. It was barely enough to hear what she was saying; it was the same word, whispered over and over again.

"Ghosts… ghosts… ghosts…"

* * *

The Missile Silo

Michael was pouring himself a freshly brewed cup of coffee; it was an old morning habit of his, even if his body did not need it anymore to wake up.

Last night's action was intense and, coming right after their mission in Somalia, it was quite exhausting. Oh, their bodies could have endured far more but their minds were beaten. That was the main reason why they'd barely talked on the flight back to the silo.

Elizabeth and Anna were waiting for them when they came back, and so were Natalie and Lee, the two little girls Elizabeth had transported to the silo. Nobody was really in a good mood, but they all put on happy faces for the children.

Mary was with her husband on the AutoDoc level while he was undergoing the regeneration treatments for his missing hand.

It always amazed Michael how much energy children had even after all they had been through, refusing to fall asleep until they had seen the team was home safely.

The reason for the team's low spirits was not remorse for ending the lives of fifteen terrorists which was akin to taking out the trash. But all those security guards who lost their lives were a bitter pill to swallow. The sobering thought was that if they had arrived just a bit later, the whole world would have watched scenes of diabolical murder and destruction.

Soon after arriving back at their missile silo base, each of them went to their separate levels. Michael took a long shower and hit the sack. He heard and felt Elizabeth come in a little while later; she hugged him from behind while he slept. It was so calming that he didn't even have any bad dreams, only a good night's rest.

Every morning TV news show was in a state of frenzy. Every channel in the world was covering the same story. They all had identical footage but a hundred different theories about how the terrorist attack had ended. Dozens of commentators in different languages, and all essentially saying nothing.

The images of security guards lined up in body bags were disheartening. They'd died while doing their jobs, trying to protect the innocents. The terrorists' actions did not end with killing those heroes. They had also damaged all the families they belonged to; the people who were now grieving and would never see their loved ones again.

While part of Michael felt regret for not being able to arrive sooner, deep inside his soul a knot of anger and hate was solidifying, aimed at all those responsible for last night's events. The terrorists who did the deed were punished, but there were others out there, the people who'd financed it all, who'd planned it, and those who had given the order. While Murat al-Rashid had led the attack, he had not been smart enough to organize it all. If he ever found out who the members of this 'High Council' were, his hand would not waver, and he would end them without a second thought.

Be that as it may, now was not the time to deal with that; now his main concern was Alice.

Max had shown him the footage of her interrogation and it was gruesome. She extracted the intel but the lines she had to cross to get it were beyond the pale. She would have never been put in such a situation if it weren't for him.

What made him feel even guiltier inside was that if he had to choose again between her peace of mind and getting the info, he would make the same choice because the stakes had just been too high.

He needed to talk to her right now. The same type of conversation Jack had with him, a long time ago. There are times when necessity asks you to do more than you are prepared for, and afterward, you need someone to tell you it was all right, and for the greater good. Otherwise, self-doubt and insecurity would worm their way inside your soul, and tarnish it.

Half an hour later, Michael and Alice were in a transporter, hovering twenty miles (32 km) above the silo. The surrounding view was mesmerizing, right in the middle of the stratosphere. The curvature of the Earth was surrounded by a blue layer that merged with the black one above. Clouds were slowly passing beneath them, a perfect place to find your center and inner peace of mind.

Only Alice was not looking at that image, her gaze was fixed on her hands. She was rubbing them against each other, trying to scrub off things that weren't there. Michael waited until he thought she was ready, so their silence lasted a long time before she uttered the first word.

"You saw what I did," she said not as a question, but as a statement of fact.

"Yes."

"I've lost count of how many times in the past I needed to extract information from very bad people. But... there was this imaginary line of the things I would never do... the line I've never crossed before. I... have never gone that far... It was horrible. I could see myself doing those things to him as if I was someone else. He cried and begged... but I did not stop... until he broke..."

Michael nodded. "Yes, it was terrible, but it was also necessary; you saved all those people by doing that."

Her head moved from side to side, negating his words.

"Maybe we could have gathered the intelligence some other way. Max would have seen the beginning of the attack— "

"Look at me, Alice!" Michael said using his commanding voice, conditioned with years of training, she snapped her head.

"If you hadn't done what was needed, twenty-five thousand people would be dead, and God knows how many more after that nuclear waste poisoned the area."

"But— "

"I'm not finished," he cut her off sharply. "Max calculated the timing of the events. If we had arrived ten minutes later, there would have been nothing we could have done to stop it. The SWAT teams were about to storm the place and the terrorists would have activated the bombs. The mere fact we made it in time was a miracle you are directly responsible for."

He could see that she wanted to say something again and lifted his hand in a halting motion.

"Without the intel you extracted, today would be the blackest day in our nation's history. All this amazing alien technology we have, all our upgrades, would have been useless to prevent the tragedy. Therefore, if you are looking for someone to join you in this pity party, you are looking in the wrong place. Alice, you have nothing to be sorry for, and we are all so damn proud of you."

She held his fierce gaze, searching for the truth in his eyes. Then, the wall of guilt broke, and she relaxed. It was as if someone had lifted a tremendous burden placed on her shoulders. Tears started streaming down her face while her tense and rigid posture relaxed.

"Thank you... I needed that," Alice whispered while the first tremors were beginning to shake her body.

"I know, little sister," Michael said, calling her by the nickname they'd given her a long time ago. He opened his arms and she fell into them laying her head on his shoulder.

Alice cried for a long time, but it was a good kind of cry, cathartic. One that washed away all the doubts, self-recrimination, and guilt.

They stayed like that for a while, looking at the white clouds beneath them as they passed by in their never-ending journey.

CHAPTER 21

Washington, D.C. The White House - The Situation Room

"Mr. President, we have the preliminary reports on the attack."

President Craig Garner was sitting at the head of the full briefing table. Sitting around him were the most powerful people in the country, from his Chief of Staff and the Vice President to the Joint Chiefs. This was an emergency meeting about answering *the* question everybody in the world wanted to be answered.

All the information that's trickled since the attack has been... sketchy and weird. Oh, most of the things were explained, who the terrorists were and how they'd managed to execute the entire attack. He had already been briefed on everything but the most important thing which was still a mystery—who had stopped it?

When he heard about the truck bomb with radioactive material, a chill had run through his body, as if someone had walked on his grave. At the time, he had to take a shot of whiskey to calm himself. His hands started to shake as he contemplated the magnitude of the disaster if that bomb exploded.

He looked at the intelligence major who was submitting the report.

"So, did you manage to find out who saved our asses?"

The major looked quite uncomfortable. "No, sir, but we do have some clues. The investigation team has come up with a few conclusions."

"Yes, go on…"

The younger man cleared his throat and pointed to his presentation, using a remote control to show various images on a flat-screen TV mounted on the wall.

"As far as the evidence shows, all the terrorists died in a time frame of a couple of seconds, and not only the ones that everybody saw on TV, but all fifteen of them. Every single one was hit with multiple headshots in a highly coordinated attack and it was done using unconventional rounds."

"What do you mean by unconventional rounds?" the President asked.

The major pointed the remote and changed the image on the screen. The picture of a small black dart was shown beside a ruler to put its size into perspective.

"And what's that supposed to be?" the President asked.

"Sir, that is one of the rounds retrieved from the body of a dead terrorist. The analysis done on it tells us that it's made of Wurtzite Boron Nitride, which is the hardest synthetic substance known to man, much harder than a diamond in fact."

"Who makes them?"

"Sir… nobody does. It has completely stumped our weapons experts; they don't know what to make of it."

The President closed his eyes, rubbing his temples.

"Okay then, what else do you have?"

The major looked the President in the eyes. "The bomb experts have come to the conclusion that the explosive devices on the entrances, and the dirty bomb in the basement, were all neutralized by an unknown chemical agent. The leading theory is that an extremely powerful acid was poured on them, which melted their triggers and electronic components, rendering them inoperable. But so far, no trace of any residue has been found on the scene, it baffles our investigators."

A slight headache that the President had been feeling for some time was threatening to turn into a full-blown migraine.

"So, we don't know what, how, or who... do we actually know anything?"

"Well, sir, one of the girls on last night's broadcast said she saw her rescuers after the paramedics gave her a sedative to calm her down. She claims it was *ghosts* who saved them."

"Ghosts... of all the things in the world... ghosts."

President Garner did not know if he should laugh or cry.

The major saw the look on the President's face and hurried up with his presentation. "Sir, there is footage missing from the arena's CCTV systems. We believe that someone hacked into the system and deliberately deleted the files. But at least one of the civilians managed to record something with his cell phone. We're still interviewing people and hope to discover others."

The major pressed play on a prepared video and the image showed an empty corridor. At one point, the picture became a little blurry then it sharpened again.

"That's it?" the President questioned incredulously.

"No, sir, this is the same video, slowed down and enhanced, the edges of the distortion were color shifted for improved contrast."

The slow-motion video was eye-opening. It captured two transparent human figures running down the corridor. The President's eyes, like all others in the room, were wide open looking at the constantly replaying video loop.

"Ghosts..." the President murmured.

"One of the analysts borrowed from The Defense Advanced Research Projects Agency is certain that those are highly sophisticated camouflage suits, which bend visible light. DARPA has been working on a similar project for some time now, but he claims what those people are wearing is decades ahead of the current state of technology they are developing."

After several seconds of silence, the President asked the high-strung major. "Anything else you want to add?"

"No, sir, this is all we have right now, we'll inform you if any new information becomes available."

"Thank you major. Make sure that video is not leaked to the press. Dismissed."

As soon as the major closed the door behind him, the President turned to the members of the military in the group.

"Please tell me that this was done by one of your clandestine black ops teams, the ones you don't even keep on the books."

The gathered generals looked among themselves but, in the end, they all shook their heads.

He closed his eyes, "I didn't think so, but it was worth a shot. So… what do you all think?"

Maybe that wasn't the question he should have asked. For the next forty minutes, almost every single one of them had something to say. Unfortunately, nothing very useful or constructive was offered.

Some of the Joint Chiefs wanted those people found and arrested and some wanted to give them medals. In the end, they finished the meeting without actually making a firm decision.

Only the Vice President and his Chief of Staff remained in the room.

"Whoever they are, they saved countless lives last night, so I am leaning towards rewarding these people if we ever find out who they are."

The Vice President's face looked like he had bitten into something sour.

"You don't agree, Philip?"

"Craig, I get your point, these people truly did do something remarkable, worthy of our praise. Still, I cannot disregard the fact of what they are. What we have here, is essentially a highly sophisticated paramilitary unit, operating within our borders. With game-changing technologies that we cannot even understand, let alone emulate. Think of a scenario in which they decide to eliminate the entire Executive branch of the government; all of our security could do nothing to stop them. I am not saying they would, nonetheless, they do have such capability, and that scares me. I am still grateful for what they have done; even so, we need to find out who they are exactly, and what their intentions are," Vice President Philip Cain said, looking at the President.

His Chief of Staff agreed with what the Vice President said and he could not find a good argument against it.

"All right, we'll see how the situation develops and then we will make a decision. At this moment, we don't have enough information to help us decide one way or the other."

A few minutes later, he found himself alone in the Oval Office. He took out a bottle of whiskey hidden behind a bookshelf and poured himself another shot. He lifted the glass in a salute to the unknown heroes who had answered his prayer and saved so many of his people and then emptied the glass in one gulp.

Now he had to hope his speechwriter could spin this story to their benefit for the upcoming press conference in half an hour, because, for the life of him, he didn't know what to say to them.

President Craig Garner looked at the bottle in his hand and regretfully sighed, then returned the twenty year old bottle of liquid courage to its hiding place.

* * *

The Missile Silo

A few hours after the talk he'd had with Alice, Michael was waiting for his father to arrive while watching the President's address on a holo-screen.

The entire speech was bland, to say the least. There were plenty of positive words but nothing concrete anywhere in the entire speech. The main piece of advice was for people to remain strong in this troubling time. The press didn't like it and weren't afraid to show it.

His father was bringing Doctor Ross to be reunited with his family and the doctor didn't know a thing about it. It was a good thing that they had already transferred some medical nanites into him. While riding in a transporter was exciting, seeing his family safe and sound could be fatal. Max had found out the doctor had a bad heart. His son-in-law was still undergoing treatment in the AutoDoc but it seems that completely regenerating a missing limb isn't an easy thing to do. Unless, as Max had joked, the man wanted to have two left hands.

"They are on final approach," Max informed him.

"Okay, I'll meet them in the hangar."

The hangar was what they called the top level of the missile silo. Since the roof was designed to be open for the missile that'd been here for decades, Max made the top floor into a hangar for the transporters. It was quite convenient since there was an elevator entrance in the hangar connecting to all lower levels.

Michael was exiting the elevator when the roof opened up and the transporter, with its camouflage active, lowered itself to the floor.

His father was the first to exit the aircraft. "Michael, I'm so glad to see you," Robert Freeman said with a smile on his face and gave his son a big hug, patting him on the back. While still holding him in an embrace, he whispered close to his ear. "I saw what happened at the Millennial Arena; you made me the proudest father in the world."

Michael could only nod as he patted his father back in return. A strange elation filled his chest; it was funny that even after all these years, his father's approval still meant so much to him.

The man who exited next was dressed in an embodiment of old, wise scientist fashion. A tweed suit, big glasses, and white hair that had a mind of its own. It was as if he took Einstein in his wildest moment and made him into his fashion ideal. The lines on his face spoke of an immense sadness that was eating him from the inside. For all that, he still had the bearing of a very proud man.

"Michael, may I introduce you to Dr. Benjamin Ross," his father said, pointing at the man who was looking upwards as the hangar roof was closing.

"Dr. Ross, this is my son, Michael."

The old scientist approached him and shook his hand.

"Pleased to meet you, Doctor Ross."

Very few times in Michael's life had he ever been the recipient of such a piercing gaze. The old man was entirely focused on him and he could almost sense the vast intelligence behind those squinting eyes.

"So, you are the leader of this... well, I still don't know what exactly this is. Your father was not very forthcoming with information. Would you care to explain why I needed to travel halfway across the country in this impossible flying craft? Who built it anyway? There is no pilot, so I assume it's remote-controlled, but what powers it? — "

"If I may interrupt you," Michael said, raising his hand. "Everything will be explained to you if you just show a little patience." Maybe it was a bit rude, but he had to cut off what was promising to be an endless line of questions.

"First, I have something to show you, if you will follow me."

He started walking back towards the elevator and, a few paces behind him, his father and the doctor followed.

The elevator was quite spacious with high polished wood paneling and an attached screen for choosing a destination. A digital screen mounted above the door showed that they were going nine levels down to where Mary, the doctor's daughter, currently was. One level above the AutoDoc and close to her husband.

The elevator door opened with a little ping and the sound of children laughing could be heard by those inside.

Anna and Mary were sitting on the floor, playing with Natalie and Lee. Michael couldn't help but smile at the scene of happy children, knowing that until yesterday they had nothing to smile about.

Dr. Ross walked into the vast room and his eyes instantly fixated on his daughter.

"Mary?" His voice was a mix of disbelief and wonder.

Mary saw her father at the same moment. "Daddy!" she screamed and jumped from the floor, running towards him. They met halfway and cried, while holding one another.

Anna was guiding the girls toward the elevator. "Come on, children, let's give them some privacy."

After they were all back in the elevator, Anna pressed the button for her floor. One of the little girls looked up at Michael and asked quietly, "What's going to happen to us now?"

Michael didn't know how to answer so he quickly contacted Max on his CEI. "Do they have any relatives?"

"No. With their parents' deaths, they are all alone."

Michael took a breath and then kneeled so he could be at eye level with the girls.

"I know you miss your parents and you feel scared and alone. But no matter what happens, I will make sure that you have a safe home to live in and you will be well taken care of. You'll never have to go through what you did at the pirates' camp again. And that's a promise."

The girls exchanged a look between themselves, turned back to Michael, and said, "Okay," at the same time.

"Can we visit with Tyron, please?" one of them asked, looking at Anna.

"Yes, we can. Just let me tell him to expect us."

Michael raised an eyebrow. "You like Tyron, don't you?"

"Yes!" They synchronously answered, "He tells the best stories."

"Oh, I'm sure he does... Have fun," Michael said as they were exiting the elevator on Tyron's level.

"Max," he said after he was left alone with his father in the elevator. "Tyron tells stories?"

"Yes, he is quite a talented storyteller, and the children feel safe around him, and highly entertained."

"Right... I didn't know that," Michael said, smiling and thinking about the seven-foot-tall (2.1 m) mountain of a man.

Michael turned to his father. "Dad, there are a couple of beers with our names on them, let's go find them."

For the next hour he talked to his father about how things were coming along. He had to tell the entire story about Somalia and the Millennial Arena. It was quite relaxing, just sitting and talking to his dad; something they didn't do often enough.

After his father left to see how Dr. Ross was doing, Michael went to the lounge. It was one entire level turned into an informal meeting place. There was even a pool table and one giant holographic wall that acted as a TV screen. Elizabeth, Alice, Pete, and Zac were all looking at the dozens of news channels right now.

"So, what is the latest news?" he asked the silent crowd who all had their eyes glued to the screen.

Elizabeth was the first to answer. "At first, there were many wild theories, but nothing definitive. And then fifteen minutes ago, a video of you guys leaked and the whole thing got wild."

"What video? We were camouflaged!" Michael asked while his stomach tightened in anticipation of the answer.

"This one," Elizabeth answered, manipulating the remote control. There was a computer-enhanced, slow-motion video with two transparent figures running along one of the arena corridors.

"Damn, somebody filmed us. What are the reactions?"

"Divided; some people say it's all fake, part of some elaborate hoax. Then there are the alien theories, next-gen military tech, take your pick. Those who believe the video is real are calling you guys 'The Saviors'. And the officials are merely reciting that the whole thing is under investigation and that they have everybody working on it."

He did not like the fact that there was a video of them even after Max had deleted all internal recordings from the arena.

"Michael... the entire arena attack stinks," Elizabeth said after a pause.

"What do you mean?" he asked and turned from the TV to look at her directly.

"It was too organized, or maybe the better word is scripted. The speeches, live television, beheadings, truck bomb. As if they were all acts in a story, every step is building on the previous one. Something is nagging at me about this whole chain of events. As I said, it has the feel of a movie script."

Michael looked at the ceiling and said, *"Never do an enemy a small injury."*

All the others looked strangely at him.

So, he continued, "It's something that Niccolò Machiavelli wrote: *"If an injury is to be inflicted on an enemy, it is to be so severe, that the enemy's retaliation need not be feared"*. Because if you leave an enemy with a small injury, he will get back at you the first chance he gets."

"You think what they were planning would be a *small* injury?!" Elizabeth asked with a raised voice.

"Yes and no. You have to look at the bigger picture, see the entire forest, and not get distracted by the trees. There was always a strange balance between terrorist attacks and natural responses to them. If they are small enough the response is mild, but look at 9/11 and what followed. You are right; this thing makes no sense unless it was a plan to provoke a response, a domino effect. Think for a second, what would have happened if they were successful. The death toll would have been in the tens of thousands, people and children dying from radiation poisoning would prolong the suffering. As monstrous as it would've been, this attack would not have defeated us, in fact—it would have enraged us."

Michael paused with his eyes focused on infinity, trying to grasp the explanation almost within his reach. "This would have provoked a war; the entire Middle East would have gone up in flames. Anybody connected with the attack could have expected the sky to fall on them. And that's why the whole thing was building to the greatest emotional impact."

"Follow the money," Elizabeth said. "That's what my instructors always pointed out, follow the money, and you will find the source."

Michael nodded. "We know that this 'High Council' is in all likelihood behind all this, from the Ariz Rama connection; and from everything we have found out, they are all about power, control, and money. Religion does not influence their decisions; it is only a tool. Every action has its reaction so we need to figure out who would have had the most to gain. When we can answer the question of who would profit the most from this conflict, we will be one step closer to finding their identities and stopping them once and for all."

The atmosphere in the room was sober and thoughtful; that

The Spaceship In The Stone

someone could even contemplate ending so many lives for more profit was monstrous.

His father entered at that moment, "Michael, Dr. Ross needs to speak with you."

As he was leaving, he could hear his father asking the others, "All right then, will someone tell me who rained on your parade?"

* * *

"Dr. Ross, my father said that you wanted to speak to me," Michael said as he entered the day room of the doctor's assigned quarters.

"Ah, Mr. Freeman," The older man responded and stood up from his chair when he heard Michael.

It was such a short time ago, but the man looked changed, as if he'd lost an entire decade of his age.

"Don't stand up on my account, and please call me Michael. When someone calls me Mr. Freeman, I have an urge to turn around and see if my father is standing behind me."

The old man smiled. "All right, Michael, then I'm Ben. All that doctor stuff and nonsense always made me feel like I was putting on airs." Ben's face became serious. "I… I want to thank you for saving and bringing my daughter and son-in-law back to me. Mary told me how it happened, and I will be forever grateful to you."

"I'm sure anyone would have done the same if given the tools we have."

"I doubt that; this world has become a cruel and uncaring place, where everyone is only motivated by self-interest. I tried everything, even begged those whose job was to protect people, but no one would do so much as lift a finger to save them. I think that most of them were offended that I brought my problems to them, as if they couldn't be bothered."

The echo of the pain Michael had noticed when he first saw the doctor, was still in the man's eyes.

"When I talked to Mary, she said that she wants to adopt the girls. They have no one left in this world and I guess they bonded while they were in captivity together," Ben continued.

Michael nodded. "I can understand that but the legal side of that can be quite problematic. If she goes to the authorities… for now, they can't tell them how they escaped from the pirates. Besides, I think your son-in-law will have a say in the whole matter."

"Mary doesn't want to go to the authorities; she feels they let them all down. Maybe it was my influence, but she does not trust them anymore. About the girls, I believe Adam would be in favor of the idea; you see, they cannot have children and were planning to adopt. I am the only family they have left alive. They want to do what is best for the girls."

Michael could understand Mary's misgivings and knew that if ever a situation arose when one of his people was captured, he would move heaven and earth to get them free. And he would exact a heavy price on the perpetrators, to be a lesson for all others who harbored such intent.

"And speaking of my son-in-law, I saw that AutoDoc he was in… you have access to such amazing technologies, I hope you don't mind, but your father has told me some things about your situation, highlights mostly, it is quite an incredible story."

"Yes, incredible, but very true; your son-in-law should be out of the AutoDoc by tonight."

"His hand…"

"Is being regenerated as we speak."

Ben pondered that for a minute.

"My question is why do you need me? Why all this effort for a broken, old man?" Ben asked.

"Aside from the fact that rescuing your family and the girls was the right thing to do, we need you for your expertise. Our ultimate goal is to create a space-based society. That means space stations and habitats, colonies on different worlds, and exploiting the abundance of material floating around in space. I need you to create a step-by-step plan of how to achieve all that, taking into consideration that there will be thousands of people living together, and we are not the most amicable species at the best of times."

Ben's face expressed surprise, elation, and concern. "Alright, I have done some theoretical work in those fields, the majority for NASA. We made a collection of *what-if* scenarios and many of them can be adapted to your needs. But this is an enormous task that will require engineers, psychologists, nutritionists... I can think of another dozen specialists that will be needed."

"And you will have a generous budget to hire whoever you think will contribute. Even so, we are under a time limit, we cannot stand aside and let atrocities happen when we have the power to prevent them. As a consequence, that will inevitably draw attention to us. In addition, you will have Max to assist you."

Ben looked confused. "Max? Who is Max?"

"I see my father didn't tell you everything. You could say that Max is our residential AI," Michael smiled, "Max, say hello to Ben."

A few feet away from their table, a familiar hologram appeared, *"Dr. Ross, it's a pleasure to make your acquaintance."*

Ben was at a loss for words, staring at the apparition with an open mouth until he recovered.

"AI! You have an AI... ah... hello Max."

Michael suppressed a laugh and stood up. "Why don't I leave you two alone, so you can get to know each other a little better? Max, give Ben the full story."

The AI nodded and turned to the older man. "*Dr. Ross, I have read everything you've published. I'm interested in...*"

Michael could hear them continue their excited and quite technical conversation as he was leaving the room. No matter how fascinating a discussion between one of the Earth's top scientists and an AI would be to listen to, he had many things to do.

CHAPTER 22

Washington, D.C. - Hashim Osmani Residence

Hashim Osmani was livid, and the state of his trashed office could attest to that.

All those years of planning, uncounted millions in expenses and bribes... all of it for nothing.

The Millennial Sports Arena attack was supposed to be the crowning achievement of his career, something that would get him the top position of the 'High Council' hierarchy, but now everything was ruined.

It was not the lost money, time, and assets, which troubled him the most. It was the reaction from the 'High Council', the consequences that this failure would inevitably have on him. This was his plan, he was the one that sold them on it, and the amount of money they were about to lose was obscene.

Everything was prepared for the United States' retaliation towards those they would have found guilty; all the fabricated evidence would have been damning.

It was a brilliant plan, utilizing predictable human responses to certain situations. Events after 9/11 were a cheat sheet of how to manipulate the decision-makers in this country. At first, the death of so many civilians would have created considerable fluctuation in the stock market, and that could have been exploited. Inevitable wars would have started, and wars were always profitable. Weapons, medicines, food, supplies… as wars are an expensive endeavor. They could have made a ridiculous amount of wealth, especially by supplying both sides.

Trusting him to get the job done, the 'High Council' had invested dozens of billions, by buying factories, stockpiling weapons, investing in stock markets… the list was extensive. The only situation he never considered happening… was that there would be no war.

Oh, a limited response would happen but nothing like what he was counting on. Those barrels of nuclear waste he acquired, at a considerable price, would have made sure of that.

He was watching it all on live TV with a glass of champagne in his hand, toasting Murat al-Rashid for a job well done. In his head, he was already imagining the ceremony in which the 'High Council' was awarding him with more power and influence. In turn, that would have made possible his final play, for the position of the *Primus*.

Then, in a split second, all his hard work was undone. Hashim saw his carefully chosen patsy collapse the moment he finished his speech. A few small holes appeared in the man's forehead, and Murat's eyes glassed over as if someone had turned off the light behind them.

At first, he could not believe what was happening, to be thwarted so close to triumph was unthinkable. He pulled himself away from the shock and jumped from his chair; champagne glass falling to the floor and breaking into hundreds of pieces. Hashim did not care about a cut crystal glass or the priceless Persian rug that was soaking up the wine; he was moving as fast as he could toward his office desk and the burner phone he kept there.

He'd believed that Murat al-Rashid would not fail him; the man was an insane religious fanatic with a death wish. At the same time, as a precaution, he had ordered one additional trigger to be installed on the truck bomb. A trigger that was programmed to activate when it received a call from this particular phone number. With trembling fingers, he dialed the number and pressed the little green button… and nothing happened. The TV continued to show a live feed with an image of three bound people. There was no explosion, no matter how many times he furiously mashed the button. That was the moment when he realized that for all intents and purposes… he was ruined. About the same time, he started smashing everything he could reach in his office.

When he calmed down, Hashim tried to find out how his plan had come undone and was met with another failure; not one of his sources knew anything. All of his connections, sleepers in various agencies, and high officials he held in his pocket, couldn't provide one iota of information. Taking all that into account, he suspected that whoever was responsible for the attack on Ariz Rama was also responsible for this. The same complete lack of information drew too many similarities to be disregarded. In his mind, only someone from the 'High Council' had that many resources and knowledge of the operation. This was an attack on him directly, someone wanted his position and would go to great lengths to achieve it. He was all alone and nobody could be trusted.

As things stood right now, Hashim knew that he could not go to the next Council meeting. They would never allow him to leave the castle alive. Failure of this magnitude was unacceptable, so he needed to change the situation. To do something so drastic it would put his plan back on track again. And he needed to do that soon because the 'High Council' was bound to organize an emergency meeting as a result of this disaster.

He was fast running out of time.

* * *

Transporter 001 - Destination: Ozark Mountains

A few weeks later, Michael, Tyron, Pete, and Zac, were sitting in a transporter, heading toward his grandfather's cabin. It was the day Michael had waited for a long time. By Max's calculation, the ship would be finally free today from the incredibly tough crystal matrix it had been encased in, and Max would finally be mobile. It was an incredible material; besides being harder than diamond, it was also impervious to radiation, and no signals they tested could pass through it. Max was sure that, in time, he would be able to reproduce it and they could put it to good use.

They'd already said goodbye to Dr. Ross, or Ben, as he insisted everybody call him. He joined the team and was on his way to start a research group under Genesis Corporation. It would be tasked with finding solutions to the problems they would be facing. Problems that were purely theoretical, as far as the rest of the world or even the research group would know. More than anyone else, Ben was in constant communication with Max, exchanging ideas through his CEI, which he'd gotten as soon as he found out about the upgrades. Of course, he did not get the same upgrades as the team, but a civilian version that lacked some bells and whistles he did not really need.

His son-in-law, Adam, came around quite confused. When he'd lost consciousness, he was being held by Somali pirates, missing one hand and feeling all hope was lost. Now he was complete again but in a very strange place. Luckily, Mary calmed him down and explained what they'd been through and how they ended up in a silo. In the end, they both decided to follow Ben and help him establish a research group. Since they were both theoretical physicists, they had a lot to offer.

The twins, Natalie and Lee, went with them. As far as the rest of the world was concerned, they were a legitimate family now. Max had created new identities for all of them, and those could safely pass all the tests. He did mention, in passing, how he hacked all the relevant databases. It was sad, watching them leave; the girls made the silo a happier place. Michael would never say a word about it, but he saw Tyron wipe a few tears from his eyes.

Right now, they were in Austin, Texas. Max rented a research facility for Ben there and bought a big house for them all to live in. They chose that location because of the proximity to the Center for Space Research at the University, fertile ground from which to recruit the types of people they needed.

Pete and Zac were looking at their tablets. While Pete was reading a book about some immortal named Adam who was friend with vampires on his, Zac was playing a video game. By his expression and occasional swearing, he was killing endless hordes of bad guys.

Max's face appeared on the transporter's wall. *"I have detected an anomaly near the cabin."*

"What kind of anomaly?" Michael asked.

"It would appear that someone flew a drone up there and parked it facing the cabin. It's camouflaged to blend with the ground and it's quite hard to see. There's a good chance it has a surveillance camera attached."

"So how come you didn't detect it sooner? Like... when it first arrived there," Pete said, raising his head from the tablet.

"Since the move, the security on the cabin's location has dropped in priority. The area around the ship is still heavily monitored, but the cabin only receives occasional sweeps by satellite surveillance," the AI answered.

"We can assume that someone found it, not that surprising really since that is the reason why we moved," Michael said and smiled. "Gentlemen, if someone went to all that trouble to find us, I would hate to be the one to disappoint them."

"We're willingly walking into a trap," Zac said while pausing his game, "it should be fun to spring it."

"The cabin itself is clean. I placed several sensors inside. But once that surveillance drone transmits your image, there is a good chance that someone will come calling."

Max parked the transporter a mile from the cabin, and the team (dressed only in regular clothes), proceeded toward it. The AI had already done a thorough sweep of the whole area and could only detect the drone. Two satellites were now in stationary orbit above them, observing the area for irregularities.

Acting like a bunch of guys without a care in the world and who were enjoying a weekend trip, Michael and the team arrived at the place he considered his home. They deliberately chose a path that would put them in the field of view of the drone's camera. The only suspicious thing to those watching would be that they didn't arrive by car, but Michael hoped the backpacks they were carrying would make the watchers assume the group had been hiking.

He unlocked and opened the front door then closed it when everybody was inside. After opening a few windows and putting some music on the stereo, they exited the cabin through the back door and ran back to the transporter.

It was a good thing that Elizabeth insisted they bring their full gear, packed in the trunks. Originally, Michael hadn't seen the point in that since they weren't planning to be in action but was now grateful for her foresight. It took no time at all for them to put on the battle-suits and, with active camouflage, return to the woods around the cabin. Now, they could enjoy the old military tradition of 'hurry up and wait'.

It was two hours later when Max informed them, *"There is an SUV coming up the road."*

* * *

Ziad was in a state of considerable emotional turmoil; ecstatically happy and deeply enraged at the same time. Ever since the day he had to run away in disgrace, he could not find a moment of peace, and every once in a while, his hands would start shaking. He finally had to admit to himself that he'd felt fear and that was a blow to his self-image. The only thing he could think of was killing Michael Freeman.

Yes, he'd found his nemesis' name; it had taken some time and a hefty bribe. A corrupt law enforcement officer ran the picture he gave him through facial recognition software and came up with the name… Michael Freeman. Ziad had repeated that name a thousand times, and every night he fell asleep with a different fantasy of killing the man. Nevertheless, deep inside, he knew that they were all fantasies; he'd looked into those eyes and was not planning to give his enemy any time to respond. Quick and dirty, that was the key.

Bringing Michael Freeman's head to Hashim Osmani was not important anymore. He saw how spectacularly the Millennial Arena operation had failed and he did not have much faith in Mr. Osmani's life expectancy anymore. Even someone as powerful as Hashim Osmani answered to those above him and they were not known for being forgiving.

All that was irrelevant now. The surveillance drone he had hidden close to the cabin had shown him that his enemy had finally returned, accompanied by a few friends. Ziad rushed to the cabin in another stolen car, far above speed limits.

He was throwing all caution to the wind with only one thought running through his mind… how he would finally end the source of his fear.

* * *

Ozark Mountains - The Cabin

Michael was standing beneath a big tree some two hundred feet (60 m) away from the cabin. His camouflage was active but he still felt more comfortable behind the cover. Pete, Zac, and Tyron had spread out for the most effective field of fire. The last two hours had been rather boring, but now his heart started beating faster, preparing his body for action.

The SUV parked a long way from the cabin, and he immediately recognized the tall man who exited it. The last time he saw him was on that day when he and Dave were shot at the recycling plant. Michael's grip on his gun tightened and, if his face could've been seen underneath the camouflage and the helmet, the spectator would've stepped back from his angry sneer and the low growl that had started in his throat.

Without waiting for even a second, the man reached back into his car and pulled out an RPG, which he immediately aimed and fired in the direction of the cabin. Flechettes that Michael fired at the man, in an attempt to ruin his aim—arrived a split second too late. The thermobaric warhead had already exited the tube and flew directly into an open cabin window.

It exploded into a fiery inferno while the man responsible for it was falling down with multiple punctures from the flechette rounds.

Michael could only watch as the cabin his grandfather had built, a place of his fondest memories and the only place that felt like home—was destroyed. He started walking towards the man, filled with rage. A few feet away from the fallen assassin he turned off his camouflage.

"Who are you?" Michael asked through clenched teeth.

The man was having trouble breathing, the bloodstain on his chest indicated that one of the rounds must have punctured a lung, yet there was still easily recognizable hate in his eyes.

"Ziad... what kind of *Shaitan* are you?" he answered, breathing heavily.

To the man, Michael looked like a nondescript human figure dressed all in black, so he used a new addition Max had installed on all their helmets, the holographic ability to mimic transparency.

Ziad's eyes opened wide, and the look of rage intensified and mixed with madness. But there was something else in it now; there was a trace of fear.

"You! ... Michael Freeman... Damn you to hell!" Ziad shrieked.

"Ah, I see you know who I am, that doesn't explain why you tried to kill me right now or your attempt before. If you wouldn't mind explaining..." It was a long shot but there was no harm in asking.

"You're supposed to be my ticket to the big league, at least your head was. You killed Ariz Rama and his people; did you think there would be no consequences? You and everyone close to you are marked for death."

Michael looked at the pitiful man, so riddled with hate that he was making threats, even defeated. Then Ziad looked again at Michael and a new realization came into his eyes.

"It was you... that suit makes you invisible... you're responsible for our failure at the Millennial Sports Arena."

"Were they friends of yours? My sincere condolences, but you know what they say, *live by the sword—die by the sword*."

The man coughed and trickles of blood ran from the corner of his lips. Even so, that fanatical look was back in his eyes. "You may have sealed Mr. Osmani's fate but that doesn't matter right now. One way or another—your life is over."

He started laughing even though his lungs were filling up with blood. One hand, which Michael thought was pressing down on his wound, started rising. Michael heard a distinctive sound—the same sound he had heard many times in his life—the click that a grenade makes during its activation.

There, in Ziad's hand was a shape he recognized. Not that he'd seen one in recent years, but some things you never forget. A V40 Mini-Grenade, smaller than a golf ball, but this was a case where size did not matter. He knew that there was a four-second delay before the detonation.

The most sensible thing right now would be to run, but that smile on Ziad's face infuriated him; this man had disturbed his life, shot Dave, and destroyed his home. He had a score to settle, and that grenade was resting there in the palm of the murderer's hand, as an offering. Using a move he had seen once before, Michael grabbed the grenade and utilizing his intense strength shoved it into the man's mouth. He could feel Ziad's teeth breaking around his fist and the jaw dislocating by being stretched beyond its limit. He jammed the grenade into the assassin's throat. It was a similar move to what Tyron had performed on the gang leader, but with a very different result.

There was one last look of disbelief on Ziad's face before Michael jumped over the hood of the car. As his feet touched the earth on the other side, he heard a loud explosion and felt an immense pressure wave pushing on his back.

If he wasn't wearing the helmet, he would literally be eating dirt right now or might even be dead. The suit detected several points of impact, mainly on his upper back and on the back of his head. Nobody ever said that it would be healthy to stand too close to an exploding grenade.

The team was by his side in seconds, helping him up.

"Boss, let's not do that again," Zac advised.

"One moment you were talking to him and the next you're jumping over the car with a red cloud of destruction on your ass," Pete said to him while trying to clean some patches of grass that were stuck on his battle-suit.

"Duly noted," Michael said. "Pity about the cabin… I'm going to miss this place."

"Well, maybe there are things we can salvage from it, the garage looks all right. Why don't you and Tyron look around while Zac and I clean up this mess?"

"Yeah, thanks, guys. Max, see if you can find anything on this Mr. Osmani. That is the only clue we have."

"Okay. But when you finish here, come to the ship. It's almost time."

Michael used the water hose to put out a few remaining fires. Since the explosion was from the inside the pressure had managed to knock out most of the walls and made a big, unholy mess. Despite the damage, there were still things that could be salvaged.

Pete and Zac were standing by the car and looking at the body of the dead assassin, at least the parts that were left.

"We can't ask him any questions but there is one thing we know."

"What's that?"

"He really lost his head," Zac murmured.

"Yep, blew a gasket," Pete retorted.

"Flew off the handle."

"Blew his top."

"Went Ballistic."

"Blew his stack."

"Went to pieces."

"Blew his fuse."

Zac looked at Pete, "I'm not so sure about that last one."

"Well, grenade - fuse, it kind of makes sense."

"We better find a shovel. This is going to be messy."

"Wanna flip for it?"

"Yeah, sure, why not."

CHAPTER 23

The Missile Silo

Considering that she was now officially unemployed, Elizabeth had never worked harder in her entire life. She was not alone in this as every one of them was helping with some project to advance their objectives.

Her sister concentrated on building a positive public face for Genesis Corporation. She was constantly busy writing mission statements for several projects, making websites, and designing promotional materials that were being prepared in advance for some of Max's schemes. Elizabeth often wondered if Anna was keeping herself buried in work so she wouldn't dwell on all the things that had happened to her. In spite of everything, she seemed much happier, more driven than ever, and full of optimism. Max was keeping an eye on her and would tell them if Anna was having any problems.

Jack was still traveling the country, conducting interviews, and judging if people would be good candidates for their future society. He talked with retired and disabled soldiers from every branch of the military and those who never got to call themselves astronauts but were involved with various space programs. He was calling in every day and sending them selfies from some of the more interesting places he visited.

Michael's father was doing something similar. All over the continent, he was establishing think tanks similar to the one Dr. Ross created in Texas. Max was already getting some hard data, which let them hone their plans to some degree. Particularly concerning structural designs, social structure, and demographic makeup of potential habitats.

Even Dave had to travel a lot, with constant complaining, of course. Max's hunger for building material was starting to surpass what could be hauled to Dave's nano-factory. The old man, with the new constitution of a twenty-year-old, was flying around in his own personal transporter and was making deals to buy e-scrap or entire scrapyards, as fast as he could. He'd made Max customize his transporter to include a regular bed, bathroom with a shower, a fridge, microwave, and a cooking plate. *The creature comforts of civilized life,* as Dave called them; he was perfectly satisfied to sleep inside the aircraft at night. It couldn't be said that he was *roughing it*, since he had transformed his transporter into a futuristic version of an RV.

Alice and Elizabeth were doing the work that would normally take dozens, if not hundreds, of people. However, they did have a fully functioning AI, an advantage no government or agency in the world could compete with. In fact, most governments would've even been jealous of the size of their intelligence network and various assets all over the world. Besides, everything was done electronically and, with Max's help, made almost untraceable. Max could have done most of it alone, but he had a problem with subtlety. His approach was a bit blunt since he tended to use a stick much more than a carrot. The fact that they had dirt on so many people was one thing, but you needed to make them do the things you want without crossing the line. Alice was a natural at this; she could blackmail, cajole, and bribe people in the same sentence.

The entire line of tasks was done in preparation for new things to come. As Max said, there were inevitable storms on the way, so it was only prudent to make a bulletproof umbrella.

Today was a special day, the spaceship in which Max was housed was about to come out of its tomb. There was already a parking space made for it inside the silo's hangar, and she personally couldn't wait to see the alien shell which housed Max.

She hoped there would be no more situations like the one in the Millennial Sports Arena. In addition to being dangerous, it could seriously jeopardize their plans if they were discovered prematurely. There was no question that eventually they would need to come out into the open. Too many people were now involved and the magnitude of their undertaking ensured it couldn't remain a secret indefinitely. Despite being a successful mission, the Millennial Sports Arena had also been an operational secrecy failure. Her experience as an FBI intelligence analyst told her that right now there were dozens, if not hundreds of people all around the world, analyzing the entire incident in minute detail. Going through every piece of evidence, every testimony. When so many inquisitive minds were concentrated on a singular event, they were bound to find something even an AI overlooked.

Despite all that, she was proud Michael did not stay on the sidelines. Proud that he did not have it in him to let people be put in harm's way and not intervene. And yes, their plans could change, and new problems might emerge, but the lives of innocents were worth a thousand times more than any hypothetical obstacles. If a similar situation presented itself, ten out of ten times he would react the same way, and damn the consequences.

Only time would tell.

* * *

Ozark Mountains - The Spaceship

An hour after the gruesome death of Ziad, Michael and the team were waiting close to the place where the ship was about to rise from the ground.

Max had created an entire support structure above him to prevent potential cave-ins. He'd even constructed a false roof door, similar to the one that closed the roof on the silo's hangar; with soil and grass on top. There would be no reason to suspect something was buried underneath. They were all standing in silence, except Zac, who was grumbling about never making another wager with Pete again.

"It's time," Max transmitted to his CEI.

The large rectangular patch of ground in front of them lifted half a foot (15 cm), then split in the middle and slid to the sides. This revealed a big black hole underneath. The spaceship slowly ascended into the air and then stopped, hovering above the hole with its bottom level with the surrounding ground. Bright rays from the sun reflected off its pearly iridescent surface for the first time in 12,900 years.

Michael knew its shape from the diagrams Max had shown him; even so, seeing it with his own eyes for the first time was quite a rush. The lines were very organic and flowed from the tip to the end. The ship had been designed by someone with an eye for beauty and attention to detail, resulting in a serviceable spaceship that was also a work of art at the same time. For all the technology it held, the ship was barely thirty feet (9 m) long, with a shape that vaguely reminded him of a white apricot kernel.

"So, Max, how does it feel to be free from the... stone?" Michael asked.

"That sounds like I was the Excalibur, would that make you King Arthur?" Max joked.

"I don't want to burst your bubble, Max, but you are a little extra heavy at the back to be a sword," Zac said, kneeling on the ground to see underneath the spacecraft.

"Hey now, that can hurt my feelings, I think I'm rather easy on the eyes."

"Undoubtedly, with a new paint job, you are going to look like a million bucks," Pete said.

"You mean like this."

The entire ship started to psychedelically change colors, going through dozens of them until it settled on being completely transparent.

"Where do you think I got the idea for the camouflage?" the AI smugly replied.

Michael approached the ship and laid his hand on the invisible surface that after a few seconds returned to its off-white iridescent color.

"Every ship deserves a name and I think you already came up with a perfect one for it," Michael said and after a little pause, continued. "Excalibur… the spaceship in the stone."

Michael's proclamation caused a completely new round of jokes, mainly instigated by Zac, until Max, who was strangely quiet for some time now, interrupted them.

"Some new information has appeared inside my memory banks."

The tone of Max's voice and the seriousness of such information silenced them all.

"What do you mean appeared?" Michael asked.

"It would seem that when the ship reached the surface, a physically disconnected memory module slotted back into place. It was done by design. There is only one thing on it… a map of the world with one location distinctively marked."

Michael could feel his heartbeat reaching a new tempo. "Where?" he asked, holding his breath. This could be it, the answer to the origin of the ship. A topic all of them had discussed numerous times.

"I checked with modern maps to confirm the location, but there is nothing there on the surface. It is in the Western Pacific Ocean, a place commonly known as the Mariana Trench."

"Mariana Trench? The deepest part of the world's oceans. That Mariana Trench?" Michael incredulously questioned, looking at the ship which housed Max's mind.

"Exactly; I guess if you want to hide something, you place it somewhere where nobody can ever find it. No human civilization in the past even dreamed of reaching those depths, and only recently did we manage to construct a few vessels that could withstand such pressure which is why only a few people have dared to make the descent. Unfortunately, almost the entire trench is marked on the map so it's going to take some time to reach it and scan it all."

Michael ran his hand through his hair. "So far, this is the only clue we have of the ship's makers, maybe there we will find the answer to why the spaceship was buried here."

"I already have some basic designs for undersea robotic drones; they would need some redesign due to the immense pressure on the bottom, but it's doable. I will set the entire operation in motion and as soon as they find something, I'll let you know."

"Okay, let's gather all the things we managed to salvage from the cabin and then the rest of you head back to the silo in a transporter. I'm going to take the *Excalibur* for a little test flight," Michael said as he touched the surface of the *Excalibur* one more time with a small smile on his face.

* * *

Spaceship Excalibur - Earth's Orbit

Michael floated within the *Excalibur*. He asked Max to turn off artificial gravity and to project an outside view on the holographic walls. For the first time in his life he was experiencing the same conditions the astronauts did. Floating above Earth, free of its gravity... weightless.

He came here alone because he wanted to get a bit of perspective and to think. What better place than this where the whole planet could be seen just floating there in space. The beauty of it was leaving him speechless.

The ship had climbed into the sky effortlessly while the camouflage made sure no detection systems would see it. Max flew it to the approximate place where the ancient recording of the planet was taken. There were some differences, but all of humanity's endeavors, throughout all of history, hadn't really made much of a mark on such a vast scale. Oh, the night lights that came from the big cities were something new, but if you turned them all off and disregarded all the ice that had melted away from the poles, the planet looked almost the same as it had all those thousands of years ago.

His eyes encompassed this beautiful jewel of a planet that held the entire human race on its surface. He turned towards the Moon and all its countless impact craters; they were testaments to the uncaring nature of the universe. A constant reminder that the Earth was under unceasing bombardment from space. If only one big asteroid hit it, in just the right way... it could bring that eternal night, the end of humankind.

He turned his gaze back to Earth, trying to find the position of the silo by only using his eyes. Everything he cared about, everyone he loved, was on that blue ball in front of him. And an uncountable number of mothers, fathers, and children. All of them trying to make life better for themselves, succeeding and failing in a constant struggle. Maybe he could not change the entire world, but he could change one small part of it, and ensure the species would survive.

He turned around and looked into the vast deep blackness. Only interrupted by the faint glowing light of the far-away stars. The distances were almost unimaginable, but the very existence of this ship proved that life, different from the one evolved on Earth, existed out there as well. It was simultaneously a comforting and frightening thought. They may be friendly… or not.

"Max, do you think we will succeed?" he asked the invisible AI, who out of respect for Michael's private, introspective time, didn't show his hologram.

"If we play our cards right, and with a little luck… we will. I could give you percentages, mathematical equations, and probability predictions, but in the end, the deciding factor is a person's will. That willingness to push on, to see the goal in the distance, and to strive towards it. You get enough people working towards the same objective, and you can do wonders. Besides, it's not a question of if we can do this, it's a question of whether we can afford not to."

Michael floated there for a while longer, enjoying the weightless state and tranquility of space. He realized that no matter how profound this experience was, he was experiencing it alone, and that felt lonely and hollow. There was no need to do that anymore.

"Max, take us home."

CHAPTER 24

Washington, D.C. - Hashim Osmani Residence

They say that a cornered animal is the most dangerous one and Hashim Osmani felt like he was backed into a corner. As he'd predicted, the 'High Council' did organize an emergency meeting, the very one he was currently *not* attending. There was a high probability that he had already been sentenced to death, but he was betting it all on a small chance that he could pull off a miracle. He even sent them a message, ensuring them that he would rectify everything and that the plan would very soon be back on track. For that reason he was doing something he had never done before—he was actively participating in an attack.

Hashim was not comfortable with it, but he could not trust any of his subordinates to not mess everything up. The entire operation needed to go just right for him to survive the wrath of the 'High Council'.

During his career, he had sent countless men to their deaths, it was the easiest thing in the world for him. Yet, exposing his own precious life to these dangers had been the complete opposite. This was all or nothing; if he failed today—he would be dead just the same. That is why he put everything he had on this last roll of the dice, every single man under his command would live or die with him.

Obtaining information on the location of the target had been a stroke of luck. One of his highest-placed informants, who he had some very incriminating files on, had practically offered it. Trying to get in Hashim Osmani's good graces was a sensible thing to do, but he would have paid millions to acquire it. There was barely enough time to get all of his people in position.

Tonight, he would kill the President of the United States.

* * *

USA, West Virginia - George Washington and Jefferson National Forest - President's Lodge

President Craig Garner was sitting in a rich, leather upholstered chair, with a glass of twenty-year-old whiskey in his hand. For the first time in a long while, he felt relaxed. The events of the past few weeks had taken their toll on him. Everyone wanted an explanation, from the press and the public to the foreign powers concerned with the level of advanced technology displayed in the Millennial Sports Arena attack. Absurdly, they demanded information about the invisibility suits and the advanced weaponry that had been used.

Justifying their demands with concern that such imbalance could cause great shifts on the geopolitical stage. Not that he could tell them anything except vague theories. Military Intelligence and alphabet soup agencies were unable to find a single lead. If that video had not leaked out his life would be much easier right now. Due to this unending pressure, he decided to take a little vacation from the constant chaos his office had transformed into. Two days without the constant stress and daily grind of an entirely thankless job. Camp David would have been a logical choice, but he wanted a little more privacy.

It was a pity his wife was on a humanitarian mission in Africa since she loved their little hideaway. It was a timber lodge inside George Washington and Jefferson National Forest. A secret hiding place when the burdens of the office became unbearable. Of course, the secret was a broad term here, since there were forty Secret Service agents with him. It had taken some serious convincing for them to allow him to come here so soon after the recent terrorist attack. Fortunately, additional accommodations had been built around the lodge so there was enough space for them all.

He could not help but look back at how he'd ended up here; his life had taken a few sharp turns over the years. From his days in the Marines to the wide range of jobs he'd held after returning to civilian life. He tried his hand at writing and discovered to his, and everyone else's surprise, that he was quite good at it. In the next few years, he had turned from a wage slave to a respected author with more money in the bank than he had ever thought he would have. He got his law degree late in life just because it was on his bucket list. For some reason, he then turned to politics and in retrospect, that was not the smartest life choice he ever made.

His goal had been to change things, to help people lead better lives. He had watched as those who were supposed to lead the nation to a brighter future—slept on the job. As if each new leader were just a copy of their predecessor, not truly improving things, and simply continuing the same old politics. Looking from this perspective, he was not sure if he could blame them anymore; trying to make a significant change was like swimming upstream in molasses.

People did not realize how many limitations were inherited with his office. The real power was in the hands of old men who liked the *status quo,* and the Senate was full of them. They abhorred change, since they were living rich and comfortable lives, so all progress was looked upon with suspicion. Despite this, or maybe because of it, he couldn't throw in the towel, no matter what. He would still do his best and hopefully leave some kind of legacy for his children to be proud of.

It was getting late and the fatigue from a long day was getting to him; a nice soft bed called him with the promise of a good night's sleep.

That was when he heard the sound of rapid gunfire.

* * *

The Missile Silo

Michael was in his office, reading a report Jack sent him about possible new recruits. A few of the names on that list he knew personally; old Army acquaintances and friends he lost contact with. Unfortunately, a few had failed to pass Max's thorough scrutiny.

"Michael, you need to get to the transporter right now, the team will meet you there!" Max shouted.

He heard the urgency in the AI's voice and, without waiting for an explanation, got out of his office. He had just entered the elevator when he saw Tyron running down the corridor carrying two long cases in his hands.

"Do you know what's going on?" Tyron asked him as the elevator door was closing.

"Not a clue, but whatever it is… it can't be good."

A minute later they were entering the transporter, only to see that Alice, Elizabeth, Pete, and Zac, were already seated with fastened seat belts.

"Grab a seat and buckle up, this is going to be a rougher ride

than usual," Max's voice sounded from the transporter's speakers.

Normal takeoffs in a transporter were smooth and stable, the initial acceleration barely noticeable. This takeoff was anything but smooth; the aircraft shot out of the hangar and into the air like a bullet out of a rifle. The inertial dampeners lessened its great acceleration to an extent, but they could all feel g-forces affecting them. In no time, they had broken the sound barrier and kept accelerating. Michael could see they were on a sub-orbital course and the aircraft's flight smoothed out to somewhat normal levels when they reached the apex of their trajectory.

"Okay, Max, what's this all about?" Michael asked.

"I'll explain everything, but while I'm doing that, you should all start putting on your battle-suits," the AI said in a tone of voice that was more of a command than a request. They looked between themselves and got up, opened the crates, and did what they were told.

"I have searched for anyone bearing the name Osmani, ever since Ziad uttered it. There were several candidates, but one stuck out. Hashim Osmani, the scion of a very wealthy family and at first glance, just one more privileged playboy born with a silver spoon in his mouth. His luxurious lifestyle reflected that fact, but that was all a meticulous cover he'd maintained all of his life. By everything I've dug up, his wealth is quite a bit more than anyone believes, and most of it is off the books. I'd planned to inform you tomorrow about him after I gathered more information, now I think I should have acted sooner," Max said, sounding remorseful.

"There is a good chance that he is one of the 'High Council' members, and as Ziad said, directly responsible for the Millennial Arena attack. The problem was I couldn't find him anywhere since he disappeared off the radar a day after the attack. I tried every trick in the book with no results, so I backtracked, looking for any

The Spaceship In The Stone

connection between Basim, Ziad, Murat al-Rashid, and Hashim Osmani and I struck gold. Several of the contacts that interacted with some of them had their phones activated. The strange thing was that for the past day, all of them were in the middle of the George Washington and Jefferson National Forest."

"What are they doing there… camping?" Zac asked.

"Nothing so benign; I used their phones as listening devices, and I learned that they were hiding there, waiting for someone to arrive. Michael, they somehow discovered information that the President of the United States is there right now. They are planning to kill him."

"How sure are you about this? The President is not so easy to kill. Everywhere he goes, the level of his security is quite extensive," Michael asked.

"It's apparently some sort of retreat he rarely goes to and I don't think the security he has with him will be enough. There are eighty terrorists close to the site, heavily armed. They started jamming all communication frequencies a while ago so the President's detail cannot even call for help."

"Shit! That puts a new spin on things. How long would it take for official help to get there?" Michael asked.

"Fifteen minutes until they notice that something is wrong, twenty more before the nearest reinforcements can arrive at the scene. By that time, it will be too late. We will arrive in five minutes… so what is your call?" the AI asked.

Michael looked at the others and received nods of confirmation from all of them.

"We're going in."

"As I thought. OK, Elizabeth and Alice, there are two flechette sniper rifles for you to use from here in the transporter, you will be the overwatch. They were modified after the arena attack for long-range precision. Close to the edge of the transporter, there are two new openings that are the right size for a sniper; your job

is to take out the terrorists from above. For the rest of you, there is a hatch in the center of the aircraft that you can use to jump out, so we do not even need to land. It is going to be a 30-foot (9 m) drop but your reinforced skeletal systems can handle that with ease."

"Well, ladies and gentlemen, it would seem we are once again called on to save the day," Pete said boastfully while caressing his rifle.

"Your relationship with that weapon disturbs me on a very deep level," Zac commented while shaking his head.

It felt like mere seconds until they were above a big timber lodge in the woods. To their eyes, the terrain below looked like a war had been fought here. Elizabeth came close to Michael and touched his chest for a second before she ran to her sniper position.

Michael took a step out of the hatch and fell through the open air. For a moment a flashback to the time he'd dropped into that entrance shaft flashed in front of his eyes, but it was gone the next instant when his feet touched the ground. The landing was jarring, but nothing that would debilitate him in the coming fight.

His HUD marked enemies with a red halo around them. It was the same effect Max used during their training, although Max had never thrown in so many opponents at once. Red silhouettes were all around them. Wasting no time, he aimed his gun and started taking down targets.

"This is what they call a target-rich environment," Zac said over the comm links while doing the same thing as Michael—turning red human silhouettes into gray ones.

It was a slaughter.

With their enhanced reflexes, HUD overlays to guide them, and the sheer destructive power of the flechette rounds, the terrorists' numbers were falling by the second. From above, Elizabeth and Alice were dealing with all the stragglers, not directly in the

The Spaceship In The Stone

team's line of sight. Their high vantage point gave them a unique and unfair advantage.

Yet, their opponents did not stay still, waiting to be killed. After the initial surprise, they realized someone was killing them and then started panic firing in the approximate direction from where the noise of supersonic rounds came from. The bullets they were firing in the team's general direction actually managed to kill some of their own people, but they did get a few hits on the team; not that it mattered since the battle-suits were designed to withstand bullets from a much higher caliber. Michael and his team did not slow down.

Sooner than anybody expected, it was over; not one terrorist was left alive. Unfortunately, the numerous bodies of Secret Service agents told the story of how they'd held their ground, giving their lives to protect the man who led their country.

Max's voice cut through the silence, *"There are still some terrorists inside the lodge, run!"*

* * *

USA, West Virginia - George Washington and Jefferson National Forest - President's Lodge

President Craig Garner was seething in anger, looking at a monitor as the brave Secret Service agents did their best to stop the horde of mindless terrorists… and failed.

As the first shots were fired, two of his bodyguards rushed into the room and carried him down to his basement and into a secure panic room. This was the second time he was undergoing such an *extraction* in the last month, and he felt it was an omen of darker times on the horizon.

On one wall of the tight space, several monitors were showing the images from outside, so he was able to see how his entire

Secret Service detail was murdered; all but the two agents who were with him. They did not sell their lives cheaply, dozens of terrorists were killed in the assault, but the bad guys had the element of surprise on their side and were using grenades and RPGs. He had no illusions about what his fate would be, and was thinking about how his wife and children would cope with his death. A part of him was glad that the order of succession was so well established, there would be no ruling vacuum at the top their enemies could exploit; the country would endure.

In an instant, exactly as it happened with the Millennial Arena attack... everything changed. The normal sounds of gunfire were muffled with a new sound. It was as if several sources were merged into one loud explosive noise. The effect on the terrorists was devastating. They started dying in great numbers and very quickly.

He had a suspicion of *who* was killing those terrorists, but he was not sure even they could help him now. For the last few minutes, five terrorists had been connecting blocks of what seemed to be plastic explosives onto the panic room's door.

* * *

Hashim was not pleased with how things had turned out. Too many of his people had been sacrificed to enable him to reach inside the lodge. He was aware that there was a half an hour window in which the operation needed to be finished and he was already running behind schedule.

His biggest problem now was that the President had escaped to an armored room. Fortunately, he'd planned for that eventuality and fifty pounds (22 kg) of C4 were being connected to the metal door; more than enough to finish the job. It still wasn't as good as capturing the man and filming his death, to be put on the air for the entire world to see, but it would have to do. The detonator was

The Spaceship In The Stone

set and one of his men volunteered to press the trigger. Remote detonation had failed him once, so he was not taking any chances. Since the man was in an advanced stage of cancer, he had nothing to lose.

As they were preparing to leave, sounds of continuous gunfire could be heard from outside, and it was not the same sound the guns he'd equipped his fighters with made... these were much louder. Secret Service reinforcements could not have arrived so soon as he'd made sure that all external communications were jammed.

Hashim ordered the four men with him to go and see what was happening while he stayed near the explosives. If this interruption to his plan was what he suspected... well, it was a good thing he came prepared.

* * *

Michael, followed by his team, ran through the ruined lodge door and then they split up. Pete and Zac went upstairs, while he and Tyron went down to the basement level. Max had already sent them schematics for the building, but he couldn't access security cameras since they were in a closed system.

The sounds their boots made on the wooden floor must have given them away. A sudden hail of bullets intercepted their path. Not even slowing down, Michael gunned down two targets and saw Tyron finishing the remaining two. They proceeded to the back of the basement, where, if the plans were correct, the safe room was located. They both slowed down considerably, pointing their weapons in front of them, watching for potential enemies.

Michael was the first to enter the narrow corridor leading to the safe room. He saw a man sitting in front of the large metal door with a hell of a lot of explosives attached to it. The thing that immediately drew his intention was the detonator in the man's hand connected to the explosives. He was thinking of ways to disable him while walking slowly inside when something cracked beneath his feet.

"Stop right there or I will activate the explosives! I know you are invisible!" The man yelled.

From the pictures Max had shown them, Michael recognized Hashim Osmani. In those photos the man had been well-dressed, smiling, and confident. The creature in front of him, dressed in military fatigues, had the wild look of a madman.

Michael looked at the floor in front of him and saw that there were hundreds of hollow glass beads tossed all over.

"Show yourself or we will all die!" Hashim shrieked.

He didn't need a lie detector to see the madman was telling the truth, so he deactivated his camouflage and appeared in front of the terrorist.

"Hashim Osmani, I presume... Ziad sends his regards," he said to the sitting man.

Hashim's eyes were wide open, as he looked at the apparition before him, then his face turned into a scowl the moment he heard the name of his assassin.

"Ziad... so you made him talk... I will kill him for that."

"There is no need to exert yourself; he had an unfortunate accident with a grenade exploding in his mouth," Michael replied.

Hashim held up the detonator, showing it to Michael, his finger was touching the big red button.

"Drop your weapon and take off that helmet, I want to see your face."

Max spoke through his implant, *"With such a large amount of explosives in an enclosed space, even your battle-suit may not be able to keep you alive. Use your judgment, but know that Hashim is not a fanatic per se. Judging from his psychological profile, he very much wants to get out of there alive."*

The Spaceship In The Stone

Michael lowered his gun on the floor and took off his helmet. "I'm curious, why the glass beads?" he asked.

"I saw the video so I brought them with me. Never in my life would I have thought I'd need to watch out for an invisible man."

"Oh... that's very smart. Tell me, Hashim, why would a member of the 'High Council' go through all this trouble? What is the reason behind it all?"

Hashim's face paled. "You... you are not connected to the 'High Council'... I was wrong..." he murmured, and then his face turned into a mask of rage. "You do not understand what you have done. This was supposed to go according to my plans, and we would have earned hundreds of billions; until you interfered... damn you!"

Michael looked at the furious man, "Aw, shucks... I'm sorry?"

The look that Hashim gave him could have melted iron.

"What are you going to do now, Hashim? I don't think you planned this through."

"Now the President will come out," he pointed with his head at the camera above the metal door, "or I will activate this C4 and he will die anyway. Then the two of us are going to walk out of here and you will do nothing to stop us."

Hashim had the look of a man who had found a life vest while drowning in the sea. This crazy plan, which he probably just thought up, was his way out, and he was holding onto it. Michael was waiting for one thing... the right moment.

"You really think— "

The lock on the security doors clicked and Hashim looked in that direction.

This was the moment Michael was waiting for.

One of the things Max had recently made, in his never-ending crusade for new improvements, was a very special knife. Made to look like a standard Ka-Bar, it had one distinctive feature... It was very sharp. Maybe *sharp* was too mild a word for its monomolecular edge since it could cut through almost anything. Its edge was maintained by the nanites whose job was to keep it always in perfect condition.

The moment Hashim turned his head away, drawn by the door's lock, Michael grabbed the knife strapped behind his neck and sent it in Hashim's direction. He'd carefully calculated the force of the throw, the spin, and the position of his target—so the knife hit exactly where he wanted. Right into the wrist of the hand holding the detonator.

The hand separated from his body and Michael, using all of his enhanced speed, managed to catch it before it hit the floor. It felt creepy prying open a still warm severed hand, but that detonator had to be secured.

Hashim was looking in shock at his bleeding stump as if he could not believe that his hand was missing. That didn't stop Michael from banging his head against the wall and knocking him out. He kneeled before the plastic explosive and started pulling out detonator caps.

Two Secret Service agents exited the room with their guns aimed at Michael yelling at the top of their lungs. "Put your hands in the air!" "Lay down on the ground!"

Michael didn't turn around, he just continued what he was doing. "Gentlemen, if you would be so kind as to *not* distract me while I'm disarming enough plastic explosive to send us all to kingdom come, I would be much obliged. Besides, putting my hands in the air while trying to lay on the ground sounds quite physically challenging; you need to sort out between yourselves what you want."

The two agents shared a confused look, still aiming their guns at the kneeling Michael.

"Stand down!" The voice of President Garner hollered through the small space.

The Spaceship In The Stone

The agents looked at the President, not changing their stance.

"I said stand down! If he meant us harm, he'd have done it by now. He could have stood aside and done nothing and we'd be dead. Now lower your weapons—that is an order."

As Michael was standing up after finishing his task, he could see that this time the two agents had done as ordered. He looked at the President of the United States and had to stop himself from saluting. After so many years in the service, standing in front of the commander-in-chief almost activated that gut reflex.

He nodded his head and said, "Mr. President." Then, looking at the two agents, he continued, "If you have any intention to interrogate Mr. Osmani here," he pointed with his chin at the unconscious man. "I would suggest you tie that stump. I don't think he has much blood left to spare."

"Do it," the President ordered his agents.

One of the agents approached Osmani's body and used a zip tie to stop the blood flow.

The President suspiciously looked at Michael. "How did you know that they would attack here?"

"We were searching for Hashim Osmani there," he pointed at the terrorist. "Tracking the phones of his people led us here."

"Well, I have to thank you for saving my life. What's your name?" the President asked.

Michael considered for a moment, and then realized that the cat was already out of the bag, so he simply answered, "Michael."

The President offered his hand and Michael shook it.

"Thank you, Michael. Additionally, thank you for saving so many lives in the arena, the whole nation owes you. Why don't you step into the open? You could make a real difference to this country; they desperately need a hero."

Michael shook his head, "I don't care for the accolades Mr. President; they have no meaning to me. My goals lie in a different direction; thank you… but no."

A small frown appeared on the present face, "If you don't care, why do you involve yourself at all, at the Millennial Sports Arena, and here?"

"Because I can't ignore the bad things that happen to innocent people, not when there is something I can do to stop it."

"So join me, this country is hurt and needs to heal, so many people already consider you their guardian angel, you can help it heal."

A shadow of sadness crossed Michael's face, "I don't think it's just hurt… I think it is broken. Once it had the dream and funnily enough, everybody called it *the American dream*. But little by little that dream turned into a nightmare. Now everything revolves around money and power, big industry, and the accumulation of wealth. It's not only this country either; the same thing is happening all over the world. As if the whole of humanity is infected with some sort of disease and I don't know if there is a cure."

Michael paused, then shook his head, "I think you are an honorable man but that puts you in a minority among your colleagues. I hope you can fix the cracks in the foundation holding this nation together but I am not sure if those who oppose you would ever allow it. How many politicians, those who are responsible for leading the people—are honorable? How many would do the right thing without first looking out for their own self-interest?"

The President kept silent, knowing that the answers to those questions were the reason for his many sleepless nights.

Michael pointed at Hashim. "That same hunger for money and power was the cause of everything this sorry excuse of a human being has done. The arena, this attack on you, and many more crimes were committed by him on behalf of an organization that calls itself the 'High Council'. They are hidden power players on the world stage, causing an unbelievable amount of death and

The Spaceship In The Stone

suffering; provoking wars and disputes between nations, and they're not doing it for some religious belief or a higher purpose. They are doing it solely for money and power."

The President listened to him with a thoughtful expression on his face. "That's one more reason for you to help us bring their crimes into the open."

Michael closed his eyes, "I will try to stop them myself without coming out into the spotlight. They have people everywhere and my anonymity protects me from their reprisal." He took a deep breath and realized what he needed to say. "You said that you and this nation owes me a debt, then repay it by not interfering with me. I and those who follow me have a dream; we want to start over, to learn from the mistakes of the past and do better. We will not interfere with you, or this country in any way. We will even help you as much as we can, but our ultimate goal is to find new frontiers... like our forefathers did before us."

The president looked somewhat confused and a bit disappointed but he nodded acceptingly. "I can't say that I understand what you're planning, but I see that you are set on your path, so I will do everything in my power to, as you say, not interfere with you. Michael, you must understand that even as the President of the United States I don't make all the decisions, sometimes all I can do is minimize the damage."

"I'll settle for that," Michael said with a smile.

The crunch of the glass beads indicated that someone else had entered the room, the two agents started to raise their weapons, but a wave from the President stopped them. They all watched as a barely perceptible apparition got a hold on the knife embedded in the metal security door and pulled it out; a second later the knife itself disappeared. The apparition picked up Michael's gun and helmet and then handed them to him.

A deep, rumbling voice said close to them, "Michael, we need to leave."

"He is right, the Secret Service reinforcements are closing in on your location, you need to get out of there ASAP," Max added through his implants.

While the agents and the President could not see Tyron, they could almost instinctively feel his massive presence.

"Mr. President," Michael said with a nod of his head, and then he put the helmet on his head, activating its camouflage. In the next instant, he too disappeared from their sight.

Only the sounds of their footsteps gave any indication to the President and the two agents that Michael and Tyron were walking away; their eyes told them that they were staring… at ghosts.

CHAPTER 25

The Missile Silo - A Day Later

The operations room was packed full with every seat occupied. Michael looked around the table and saw the entire inner circle, plus the people who were most important in the organization they'd created. Tyron, Pete, Zac, Alice, Elizabeth, Max, and Anna were full-time residents of the missile silo, but for this occasion, the others have flown in after getting the summons. His father, Jack, Ben, and Dave completed the circle.

"I called you all here to get your opinion on recent events and to discuss the next phase of our plan for the future," Michael said.

"Most of the world has seen those recent events," Jack said, shaking his head. "I remember you saying something about flying under the radar. Recently, almost every move you make gets a prime spot on the evening news."

"It couldn't be helped," Michael replied, "we couldn't let such atrocities happen, no matter how much it messes up our plans."

"I understand that, and support it, but Michael... you shouldn't have let them see your face."

He nodded, "Yes... that is going to change things. I didn't

have any choice; it was either that or allow Hashim Osmani to detonate that C4. I saw it in his eyes, as much as he wanted to live, he was not bluffing. CCTV cameras captured my image, and even if Max used his digital wizardry to erase the recordings, there was still the President and two agents. We could not erase their memories. With a good sketch artist, identifying me would be easy."

"They will be searching for you, no doubt about it. What's more, all the alphabet soup agencies will not let you be, no matter what the President says; they play by their own rules. And don't disregard the fact that they leak information like a sieve, so it won't be long before the foreign agencies smell blood in the water and they have even fewer scruples," Jack replied.

Michael had a sobering expression. "I know. And once they start digging, they are going to find connections to most of you. Elizabeth, Anna, Ben, and Dave are the ones they will have the most trouble tracing. Max will try to muddy the digital waters for the rest. How long that will hold… we cannot be sure."

Even Zac did not feel it was an appropriate time to make fun of something when everyone around the table was showing grim expressions.

But Michael was not finished, "That's why Max and I came up with a plan. Max, would you explain."

The AI's hologram stood up from his chair.

"Once we found out that the clue about the shipbuilders is at the bottom of the Mariana Trench, I realized that we would need to have a base close to it. At first, I was planning to build a small outpost, but our situation has changed since then, so I decided to greatly expand on that plan. To cut a long story short, I managed to acquire an island."

"You bought an island?" Dr. Ross said incredulously.

"No, I didn't buy an island, but I managed to lease one. Its name is Pagan Island and is a part of the Mariana Islands

archipelago. The most advantageous thing about the island is the fact that it's currently uninhabited, so there are no nosy neighbors."

"Wait a minute, isn't that an island with an active volcano?" Michael's father said in a concerned voice. "I remember reading something about it, years ago, when it erupted."

Max waved his hand and dismissed it as irrelevant data. *"Technically, there is an active volcano on it, but it has been dormant for a while now. By my calculations, it will remain inactive for a decade or two. Anyway, the lease is for two years and by that time it will no longer be of concern to us."*

"People are going to have a problem with that, whenever anybody tries to do something on those uninhabited islands, there are all those preservationist groups ready to protest about it. And how did you even get permission to lease it?" Anna asked.

"Let's just say that certain politicians have a vast interest in keeping some things away from the public eye. Furthermore, all those who would have something to say about it have been taken care of. Their sudden financial windfalls will ensure we have peace and quiet for the time we're on the island. With the stipulation that when we leave, all traces of our occupation must be removed."

"So, you basically used blackmail and bribery to get what you wanted?" Dave questioned.

"I wouldn't put it so crudely, but you are right, in general principles."

"What are your plans for the island? Do you want us to move there?" Jack asked.

"For a period of time... yes. The distance and somewhat isolated location will help greatly with our security concerns. Yet, only relocating again is not a solution, it's not the final goal. This was always in the plans, but the circumstances are forcing our hand to move the schedule at a faster pace. I have already begun

the construction of preliminary infrastructure. In essence, it will be one single structure that can be easily removed when we decide to leave. Here is the diagram."

A hologram of a strangely shaped island appeared above the table, with the digital representation of Max's finished structure.

"Max, why do I find that shape so strangely familiar? Tell me you're building a giant Frisbee," Zac half-jokingly quipped.

"Is that what I think it is?" Dr. Ross questioned.

"Well, for one, it's not a Frisbee Zac, and Ben, while I don't know what you're referring to, I can safely surmise that you're on the right track. After all, you gave me the original idea for it." The smile on Max's face had a large dose of mischief in it.

"It's a spaceship!" Anna voiced what everyone was thinking.

"And Miss Miles gets the golden star. Correct, it's going to be a spaceship," the AI cheerfully proclaimed.

"I cannot guess the dimensions, but that thing seems huge," Dr. Ross murmured, leaning forward in his chair to get a better look at the diagram.

Max gazed at the image like a proud father would look at his favorite child. *"It is bigger than any craft humanity has ever built before. One mile in diameter (1.6 km) with a circumference of a little more than three miles (5 km) and with multiple levels."*

It took a few moments for the people in the room to process the dimensions of the spaceship.

"Jesus Christ, that's insane! Can that thing even lift off the ground, let alone reach space?!" Robert Freeman exclaimed.

"With enough Gravity-drives working simultaneously, it can. I'm not saying that it will be easy to build this spacecraft. There will be plenty of setbacks I can foresee even now. Our demand for materials will go up by many orders of magnitude, especially for rare metals. Even so, with well-thought-out logistics, it can be finished sooner than you think."

"What is your obsession with flying saucers? Transporters

could be explained as a quirk, this one represents a pattern," Elizabeth said with a smile.

"Max, there is no way that thing will go unnoticed," Robert Freeman interrupted before Max could answer.

"Oh, it will be noticed all right; I could digitally change all satellite imagery, but passing ships and surveillance airplanes will undoubtedly get a look at it. We will not even try to hide it; Genesis Corporation may even make a documentary about it."

"Say what now? I don't get it," Pete said.

"As far as the world is concerned, we're building an experimental inflatable biodome; that also answers your question, Elizabeth. it's the case where 'need must when the devil drives'. To make the whole ruse more believable, it's essential for it to be built in the shape of a dome, or of a discus, if you could see all of it. Genesis Corporation will outwardly use the biodome for the research into closed ecosystems. At first, it will be an inflatable shell, with the holographic layer showing a fake movie of busy scientists working on benign research. Of course, underneath it, the ship will be constructed. The inflatable shell will be ready in a week. The first thing after that is building residential facilities so we can start moving people there."

"And that's how we will foil their plans in locating us," Michael said. "Once we start gathering acceptable candidates, our exposure will be far greater with an increased number of people. You all know that those who will oppose us are going to go after our family members as soon as they catch any scent of the operation. Therefore, the plan is to move them to the island before then. We can even transport pre-made temporary housing for those who are most critical, after that, as new space becomes available more people can be transported." He looked at Jack. "How many of the people you recruited would be willing to move there?"

Jack contemplated for a moment before answering, "If you include the families... more than five hundred that I am sure of, so we need to think about schools for their children and basic facilities. At least a thousand more are on the fence, but they will probably agree to come if they know what the ultimate goal is. Besides, a chance to live in a tropical paradise is not something they'll pass up."

"Dad, Ben, what about the scientists?"

His father was the one to answer, "Most of them don't really care *where* they work since they live in their heads most of the time. If you can provide adequate living conditions and a reliable Internet connection, we can have around one hundred and fifty ready to arrive in a few months."

Dr. Ross agreed by nodding his head.

Michael turned to the AI, "Max, did you manage to find out anything more about the 'High Council' or any of Hashim Osmani's associates?"

"It seems that any leads or connections they had with him were swiftly eliminated. I have a bunch of dead ends, but I will not stop searching for them. I did manage to clean out most of Mr. Osmani's accounts, and his generous contribution will greatly help with our endeavors," the AI said smugly.

Michael shook his head and said, "All right, there are some more details to be ironed out, but if everyone is in agreement, we'll start this next phase of our plan." After he got confirmation from every person around the table, he continued, "Now, Elizabeth and Anna were gracious enough to make us a home-cooked feast in the kitchen, and if I heard correctly, there was some mention of a three-layered chocolate cake. Let's go eat."

What followed could not really be described as a *stampede* but there were some elbows involved.

The last one to leave the room was Zac. He paused at the door and took one last look at the holographic projection of the Pacific island.

"Pagan Island... this will be fun."

With that, his hunger took precedence, and he followed the direction of the enticing scents his nose was detecting.

* * *

Sleep did not come easy to Michael that night. He laid on the bed, listening to Elizabeth breathing, and watched the shadows on the ceiling above him. They were being thrown by the pale moonlight from the completely realistic holographic window mounted on their room's wall.

So many things had happened which changed his life in ways he wouldn't have even dreamt of before.

The *Michael Freeman* who fell down the entrance shaft was a different person than he was now. Tired, crippled, washed-up, and a bit depressed. With no job and with a disheartening string of broken relationships making him wonder if something was seriously wrong with him. Now, he was living a life that was totally opposite of all that. Sure, it was far more dangerous, with God knows how many people wanting to kill him. There was a freaking international criminal organization that was right now burning him in effigy, even if they were not sure who he was. They will undoubtedly cause more trouble in the future. Not to mention all the official government agencies that would soon be after him too.

At the same time, his life was graced with so many blessings he could hardly believe. This woman sleeping beside him was more than he could have ever hoped for, and for some strange reason, it seemed she loved him; there was no doubt in his mind that he was feeling the same towards Elizabeth Miles.

He had a real, honest-to-God spaceship, and so many more people who had become integral parts of his life. They were all willing to follow him in this crazy dream of his, to reach for space with both hands and carve out a piece of a more promising future for themselves. Far more than they could ever achieve on Earth. The team was back together and he was grateful for their support, as well as all the hard work they did on his behalf. This improved body with an extended lifespan was nothing to frown on, either.

However, a new feeling was growing within him, one of rage and anger.

Here he was, trying to do something good, to make a new future for humanity, while those that were on the darker side were trying to stop him, knowingly or not. So many people who chose to do the wrong thing, to selfishly better themselves at the expense of countless others, and by doing so proclaim themselves his enemies. Terrorists, slavers, drug dealers, killers and rapists, corrupt politicians... there was no end to those who embraced evil.

He will continue to do everything he could to protect the innocents; it was not within him to cower in fear or to allow that evil to prosper when he could do something about it. It would probably bring more trouble on their heads and wasn't the smartest thing to do. However, the memories of Anna after her attack and rape, Elizabeth in that cage, Natalie and Lee, the two ten-year-old girls that the pirate was going to sell to a whorehouse... made his face into a fierce grimace.

He now had the means to strike at the heart of those who thought themselves untouchable and a group of people who would follow him to the very gates of hell, and beyond.

The gloves were off now, and no mercy would be shown for those lowlifes who thought they could spread pain and misery with impunity. He would use all these advantages the alien spaceship gave him to reach out and touch them, whoever they were. It would not be a pleasant experience for those people, even if they managed to survive it.

If that made him the judge, jury, and executioner—so be it.

EPILOGUE

Washington, D.C. - Number One Observatory Circle - (Official Residence of the Vice President of the United States)

Vice President Philip Cain was not in a good mood. But, looking at him, it was hard to tell. One of the things he always took great pride in was his complete control over his emotions and facial expressions. That control was a deciding factor in why he never lost a game of poker, except when it suited him.

Even when alone, he always presented a carefully cultivated persona; an image of composure, sophistication, and culture. It was one of the secrets of his success, but there were other secrets, those no one knew about.

Even his rise to this exalted position of the Vice President of the USA was planned by him from the start. He could have easily run for and won the Presidential election. But a step away from the ultimate spotlight suited him more. From here, he could influence decisions and stay away from the direct, piercing gaze of the media. The office of the Vice President granted him a certain amount of power, but that power was minuscule in comparison to what he wielded as *Primus* of the 'High Council'.

The position he inherited from his father, who in turn inherited it from his. Philip Cain was bred and conditioned from birth to rule the undeserving masses, to be first among all men. That was the belief his father had ingrained into his very soul, that he was better than anyone else, and that his ultimate destiny was to control and direct the path of all humanity.

Then, that idiot, Hashim Osmani, almost messed up his plans. The Millennial Sports Arena attack was an extraordinary failure, but he'd never had any high hopes for its success. The money invested had been from those beneath him so he hadn't lost a single dime. He would find a way to exploit their failure, making his hold on the entire Council much stronger. Also, the atmosphere of widespread and heightened fear could be exploited for his personal gains.

Still, Hashim Osmani's senseless attack on the President without asking permission was… unforgivable. Not that it mattered, but the crazy fool should have done the right thing and fallen on his sword. It was a moot point now anyway; Mr. Osmani had died from a heart attack while recuperating in his highly secured room at the hospital. He smiled, thinking of one of the quotes his father often said; it was by Joseph Stalin. *"Death is the solution to all problems. No man—no problem."*

Nevertheless, there was a new *problem* he needed to deal with, a new player that had to be taken off the board. Just an insignificant upstart who thought he could change his fate; it would not be the first, and certainly not the last idealist he had put beneath the ground.

He had listened to that idiot babble some utopian nonsense on the confidential CCTV video from the President's attack and realized he could potentially become an obstacle for his future plans.

As Mr. Stalin had said, problems of such nature have an easy solution. First and foremost, Philip Cain was born to rule.

The Vice President took one last look at the file he had been reading, before exiting the room. It was a thick Military Intelligence file, with an oversized *TOP SECRET* stripe across it.

The name scribbled on top of it with a big black permanent marker was… **MICHAEL FREEMAN**

The End of Book 1

Thank you for reading the first book of The Space Legacy series.

For updates about new releases, and the next books in the series, follow me on my Amazon author page or visit:
www.IgorBooks.com

The adventures of Michael, Max, and the people they've gathered around them—are just beginning.

AUTHOR'S NOTES:

I hope you've enjoyed the first book in The Space Legacy series. As I mentioned above, leaving a review (or a star rating) on Amazon would really mean a lot—a few words about a book will go a long way. They help to reach new readers and in turn, help me to continue writing more books. (It's the circle of life thing.) And if you really, really enjoyed it, then please help get the word out!

* * *

I started writing this book in late 2017. I didn't rush it because I enjoyed the creation of the story. It was like watching a movie playing inside my mind while trying to record all the best parts on paper (I didn't actually use paper, but you know what I mean). So, during 2018 and 2019 I finished the first one and wrote a few more books, but I didn't publish a single one. Why? Well, despite what some people may think, publishing a book can be a bit pricey. That is, if you want to do it right with the quality standards close to those of traditionally published ones.

From editors to cover designers, formatting, and more than a few additional costs that I didn't even know existed. One thing was for sure—I didn't have that kind of money. (It's like that old one where it is better to sell razor blades than to make razors.)

Therefore, in 2019, I decided to start posting the story online as a free web novel. Two chapters each week and I offered additional chapters on Patreon for a few bucks. It was slow, but I saved every cent from it and in the next two years I managed to save up enough to finally publish on Amazon. Oh, yeah, and I kept writing more books in The Space Legacy series during that time. Also, I started an entirely new series called Adam Novus Chronicles. That one is an urban fantasy, another genre I like to read. In a way, Michael and Adam are reflections of one another. They have somewhat similar mindsets and backgrounds, except that one lives in a world very much like our own with an advanced alien technology added to it, and the other is in a world where magic is a thing.

In the end, I write because I love to read and I write stories I would like to read myself. If you're game, buckle up and join me on a few wild rides of imagination.

Thank you for reading.
Igor Nikolic (January 2022)

P.S. If you spot an error, feel free to report it at www.IgorBooks.com/beta. Ten thousand eyes are better than two and five thousand brains are better than one. I want this book to be as good as it can possibly be. Thanks.

- amazon.com/author/igornikolic
- goodreads.com/igorbooks
- facebook.com/IgorBooks
- patreon.com/Igi
- twitter.com/IgorBooks
- instagram.com/AuthorIgorNikolic

ABBREVIATIONS AND GLOSSARY

AI - Artificial intelligence.
AI-Core - A solid cube of alien processors and memory. Capable of storing and running a copied sapient mind.
ASAP - As soon as possible.
AutoDoc - A healing machine utilizing nanites. Equipped with diagnostic scanners and rudimentary intelligence.
Battle-suit - An advanced form of flexible armor created by Max. Enabling the wearer survivability in extreme situations. Combined with the helmet it creates a closed system that can be utilized underwater or in toxic environments.
Balaclava - a close-fitting garment covering the whole head and neck except for parts of the face, typically made of wool.
Boost - A technique that uses CEI's ability to manipulate the endocrine system. By infusing the body with a cocktail of organically produced chemicals, it can enhance the user's physical and cognitive functions for a short period of time.
C4 - A common variety of the plastic explosive family known as Composition C.
Catheter - A thin tube made from medical grade materials serving a broad range of functions. Catheters are medical devices

Abbreviations and Glossary

that can be inserted in the body to treat diseases or perform a surgical procedure.
CCTV - Closed-circuit television.
CEI - Cerebral Enhancer Implant. A supercomputer that is implanted under the user's occipital bone. One of the main functions is the control of medical nanites within the body.
Circumference - The linear distance around a circle.
Darwin Awards - A fictional award which is given out to people who commit acts of utter stupidity that often involve their own injury or even death. It is given in recognition of the individuals who have contributed to human evolution by selecting themselves out of the gene pool via death or sterilization by their own actions.
Delta flyer - From the *Star Trek* universe. A specially designed Starfleet shuttlecraft constructed by the crew of the *USS Voyager*.
Delta Force - An elite special mission unit of the United States Army. The unit is tasked with specialized missions primarily involving hostage rescue and counterterrorism, as well as direct action and special reconnaissance against high-value targets.
Diameter - A diameter of a circle is any straight line segment that passes through the center of the circle and whose endpoints lie on the circle.
Dodo bird - An extinct flightless bird that was endemic to the island of Mauritius, east of Madagascar in the Indian Ocean.
Endocrine system - A series of glands that produce and secrete hormones that the body uses for a wide range of functions.
ESA - European Space Agency.
FAA - The Federal Aviation Administration of the United States is a national authority with powers to regulate all aspects of civil aviation.
FBI - Federal Bureau of Investigation. The domestic intelligence and security service of the United States, and its principal federal law enforcement agency.

Abbreviations and Glossary

Flechette - A pointed steel projectile with a vaned tail for stable flight.
FPS - First-person shooter (Game genre)
FN P90 - A compact personal submachine defense weapon designed and manufactured by FN Herstal in Belgium.
FUBAR - A military acronym that stands for F./Fouled Up Beyond All Recognition/Any Repair/All Reason
Gallium - A chemical element with symbol Ga and atomic number 31.
Gestalt - Used to describe the sum of the entire mind. Including all memories and thought processes.
Ghillie suit - A ghillie suit is a type of camouflage clothing designed to resemble the background environment such as foliage, snow or sand.
Gordian knot - A knot tied by Gordius, king of Phrygia, held to be capable of being untied only by the future ruler of Asia, and cut by Alexander the Great with his sword. A problem solvable only by bold action.
GPS - Global Positioning System.
Graphene - A semi-metal. Crystalline allotrope of carbon, atoms arranged in a hexagonal lattice. Strongest material ever tested. Melting point at least 5000 K. (8540.33°F /4726.85°C)
Gravity-drive - A gravity manipulation engine. Utilizing available celestial gravity sources to provide motion.
Hal 9000 - A fictional AI and the main antagonist in *Arthur C. Clarke's* Space Odyssey series.
HUD - Heads-Up Display
Humpty Dumpty - A character in an English nursery rhyme. Typically portrayed as a personified egg.
IRS - Internal Revenue Service
ISP - Internet service provider
Joseph Stalin - *Ioseb Besarionis dze Jughashvili* (1878 – 1953) was a Soviet revolutionary and politician of Georgian ethnicity.

Abbreviations and Glossary

He ruled the Soviet Union from the mid-1920s until his death in 1953.

Ka-Bar - A popular name for the combat knife first adopted by the United States Marine Corps in November 1942.

Lutetium - A chemical element with symbol Lu and atomic number 71.

Main Asteroid Belt - A circumstellar disc in the Solar System made by millions of asteroids. Located roughly between the orbits of the planets Mars and Jupiter.

Mariana Trench - The deepest part of the world's oceans. It is located in the western Pacific Ocean.

MI - Machine intelligence.

Millennium - A period of a thousand years. (Plural: millennia)

Monomolecular - One molecule thick layer. In this case, the edge of a blade.

Nanites - Electromechanical machines whose dimensions are measured in nanometers. Used in construction and medicine. First found on the Excalibur as one of the essential systems, and later upgraded by Max.

Nano-factory - A construction facility that uses nanites for its operation. Its size can vary depending on available space. Needs an MI to control the nanites.

NASA - The National Aeronautics and Space Administration. An independent agency of the executive branch of the Federal government of the United States responsible for the civilian space program, as well as aeronautics and aerospace research.

Neodymium - A chemical element with symbol Nd and atomic number 60.

NSA - The National Security Agency. A national-level intelligence agency of the United States Department of Defense.

Oxymoron - A figure of speech in which apparently contradictory terms appear in conjunction.

Abbreviations and Glossary

Play-Doh - A modeling compound used by young children for arts and crafts projects.
PR - Public relations is the practice of managing the spread of information between an individual or an organization and the public.
Prowler - A multi-role trans-atmospheric Starfighter used by the Peacekeepers in an Australian-American science fiction television series *Farscape*.
PTSD - Posttraumatic stress disorder. A mental disorder that can develop after a person is exposed to a traumatic event.
Puddle jumper - A small spacecraft used in a Canadian-American adventure and military science fiction television series *Stargate Atlantis*.
R&D - Research and development.
R&R - Rest and recuperation.
RPG - A shoulder-launched anti-tank grenade launcher.
Runabout - A class of small, multi-purpose starships in the *Star Trek* science-fiction franchise.
Ruthenium - A chemical element with symbol Ru and atomic number 44. It is a rare transition metal belonging to the platinum group of the periodic table.
Saw - A 2004 American horror film. It is the first installment in the Saw franchise.
Shaitan - A malevolent creature in Islamic theology and mythology.
Shuttlecraft - A fictional vehicles in the *Star Trek* science fiction franchise built for short trips in space.
Skynet - A fictional AI and the main antagonist in the Terminator franchise.
SNAFU - Status Nominal: All F. Up.
Status Quo - A Latin phrase meaning the existing state of affairs. To maintain the status quo is to keep the things the way they presently are.

Abbreviations and Glossary

Stratosphere - The second major layer of Earth's atmosphere. It starts from around 10 km (6.2 miles or about 33,000 feet) above the ground at middle latitudes. The top of the stratosphere occurs at an altitude of 50 km (31 miles). The height of the bottom of the stratosphere varies with latitude and with the seasons.

SWAT - Special Weapons And Tactics. A law enforcement unit that uses specialized or military equipment and tactics.

Tantalum - A chemical element with symbol Ta and atomic number 73. Used in the electronics industry for capacitors and high-power resistors.

The 'High Council' - An international criminal organization that controls a large percentage of the world's criminal activity. Funding terrorist groups, inciting wars, manipulating the markets.

Thermobaric - A type of explosive that uses oxygen from the surrounding air to generate a high-temperature explosion.

Think tank - A group of experts brought together to develop ideas, make suggestions and give advice on a particular subject.

UFO - An unidentified flying object

Uncle Sam - A common national personification of the American government or the United States in general.

UV - Ultraviolet is electromagnetic radiation with a wavelength from 10 nm to 400 nm, shorter than that of visible light but longer than X-rays.

Wurtzite Boron Nitride - Extremely strong material, having a strength 18% stronger than that of a diamond.

X-wing - A Starfighter from the fictional Star Wars universe.

ALSO BY IGOR NIKOLIC

The Space Legacy Series:
1. **The Spaceship In The Stone** (Book 1) Amazon & Audible
2. **Max's Logs Vol. 1** (Book 1.5) Amazon & Audible
3. **Orbital Ascension** (Book 2) Amazon & Audible
4. **Max's Logs Vol. 2** (Book 2.5) Amazon
5. *Ancient Enemies* (Book 3) Amazon
6. Max's Logs Vol. 3 (Book 3.5) - **TBP**
7. Solar Incursion (Book 4) - **TBP**
8. Max's Logs Vol. 4 (Book 4.5) - **TBP**

Adam Novus Chronicles Series:
1. The Death Curse (Book 1) - **TBP**
2. Tales Of The Hidden 1 (Book 1.5) - **TBP**
3. To Rule In Hell (Book 2) - **TBP**

***TBP** - **T**o **B**e Published

Printed in Great Britain
by Amazon